First there was
A MAN TO DIE FOR
winner of the 1992 Rita Award

"A wicked prescription guaranteed to give you sleepless nights."

—Nora Roberts

"Dreyer . . . levels a roguish sense of humor at the medical establishment in this entertaining romantic thriller."

—*Publishers Weekly*

"Eileen Dreyer creates the sort of skin-crawling suspense that will leave her readers looking with a wild and wary eye upon anyone at the other end of a stethoscope."

—Elizabeth George,
author of *A Great Deliverance*

"Hold on to your hats and get ready for the scare of your life as Eileen Dreyer makes a courageous emergency room nurse the target of a fiendish serial killer. . . . In a triumph of superb writing, Ms. Dreyer keeps us in a turmoil of agonizing suspense. . . . All things considered, you just might want to postpone that doctor's appointment for a while."

—*Romantic Times*

"A great psycho thriller . . . a suspenseful, chilling contest between battered ~~j~~ ~~ice~~ and pure evil."

~~T~~he Macon Telegraph

Then came
IF LOOKS COULD KILL

Also by Eileen Dreyer

A Man to Die For
If Looks Could Kill

Available from HarperPaperbacks

✦ *Nothing Personal* ✦

EILEEN DREYER

HarperPaperbacks
A Division of HarperCollinsPublishers

HarperPaperbacks   *A Division of* HarperCollins*Publishers*
10 East 53rd Street, New York, N.Y. 10022

Cover photograph by Herman Estevez

First printing: March 1994

Printed in the United States of America

HarperPaperbacks and colophon are trademarks of
HarperCollins*Publishers*

❖ 10 9 8 7 6 5 4 3 2

ACKNOWLEDGMENTS

To the usual list of culprits, as ever, my thanks. You put up with a lot this year. My special thanks to everyone at the St. Louis County Medical Examiner's office, with special thanks to Dr. Mary Case and to Mary Fran Ernst, investigator extraordinaire, for teaching more than I ever wanted to know about death investigation. I hope you can excuse the dramatic license. Thanks to the lovely folks at McGurk's, where the research was always fun; and, of course, to Paddy, Martin, and Pat for letting me share their music. If I could play like you guys, I wouldn't waste my time writing books. And finally, to the real Pig Nurses from Hell. All the Pig Nurses. You know who you are.

One more thing. In response to everyone who will inevitably ask, no, St. Simon's is not a real hospital. It is not based on a real hospital in St. Louis or anyplace else. I swear I made it all up. The other landmarks, however, are real.

Every normal man must be tempted
at times to spit on his hands,
hoist the black flag, and begin slitting throats.
　　　　　　　　　—H. L. Mencken

✦ Prologue ✦

ON FEBRUARY 20, Kate Manion had the chance to see her hospital from the other side. It was an opportunity she hoped never to have again.

Kate was a critical-care nurse, one of those purposeful, talented people always dressed in scrubs and lab coat, a stethoscope slung around her neck and pockets filled with penlights, scissors, and trauma-scale charts, who walked through an emergency department with the purpose of MacArthur stepping out of the water at Leyte. Which Kate did. At least until she ended up on her head in a ditch alongside Highway 44 with an ambulance and a candy-apple-red Firebird wrapped around her.

If it had been her Mustang, somebody might have blamed Kate. After all, she did drive it fast—often a little too fast. But that was what Mustangs were for. Besides, Kate was a good driver. She knew all the quirks and eccentricities of her car better than her ex-husband had known hers. Kate would never have let her car land in a ditch.

1

But Kate wasn't driving either vehicle. The guy driving the Firebird would have been arrested on the spot for driving under the influence and vehicular manslaughter, if he'd lived long enough for the cops to get handcuffs on him. By the time that determination was made, though, Kate was already on her way to the medical center in critical condition with chest and head injuries.

Within an hour, Kate was in surgery to repair the small laceration she'd suffered to her aorta and the clots she'd collected on her brain from the depressed skull fracture. She had tubes stuck into her chest to reexpand her collapsed lungs, a tube in her trachea to help her breathe, one in her stomach to drain away any digestive juices that could compromise her breathing ability, and another in her bladder to make sure her urine was clear and neatly collected. She had three large-bore IVs in her, one in each arm and one in her subclavian vein, to replace fluids and electrolytes; an arterial line; an intracranial pressure sensor to measure the potential threat to her brain; a Swan Ganz pump to measure her blood volume and cardiac output, and a blood pump to reinfuse her with the red cells she was losing through those chest tubes. And with all that in, she still managed to make hospital history. On February 24, Kate Manion became the only intensive-care patient in medical center memory ever to successfully kill her nurse.

✦ Chapter 1 ✦

SHE DIDN'T MEAN to do it. After all, Kate knew better than most people how badly nurses are needed. Even bad nurses. And her nurse was certainly a bad nurse. But by the time the woman met her fate, Kate wasn't in any shape to think clearly at all. In fact, by then Kate was so bruised and battered, not just by the accident but by her stay in intensive care, that she wasn't sure she wasn't already dead. She wasn't sure of anything except that she wanted out.

She didn't exactly wake up in the unit. She became aware, in a series of fits and starts, as if the breakers were being thrown on each of her senses and the janitor in charge couldn't figure out how to get them all going again at once.

First there was pain, waves of it, bathing her like one of those hot lights at McDonald's, so that if her body had been a hamburger she would have been a meat briquette. Pain: her head, her chest, her legs; pounding, swirling; sometimes constant, sometimes a red tide that broke over her and then receded.

3

It rode in and out on sounds. Familiar sounds, noises she knew somehow and hated. Noises that made her want to scream more than the pain.

"Her ICP's up again, Fran," she heard somebody snap. "Don't you think you'd better call the Bagel Man?"

Bagels? Did she want bagels? Kate couldn't remember. She couldn't remember anything but how badly she hurt, how she wanted to get away. How she couldn't move, except she seemed to be doing it against her own volition, turning one way and then another, her joints screaming in protest, the noises following her wherever she went.

"Almost finished," another voice answered, a voice that tapped some instinctive button in Kate. Something unpleasant. She hated that voice. She wanted it to go away and let her sleep. Somewhere deep in the ooze she'd once called a brain, she wondered why she knew this and nothing more.

Then it came to her that suddenly she could see. And she knew her ICP was going to hit the roof, because she realized what everything else meant.

Acoustic tile. The spidery arms of machinery, IV tubing snaking down from half a dozen plump clear bags and one smaller red one. Labels and tubes and a television turned to *Wheel of Fortune*. Banks of monitors and stock carts piled to the brim. White-coated figures scurrying around in a kind of weird, aimless dance choreographed to the tune of endless ventilator alarms.

She was in the hospital. Her hospital. She was

a nurse, she remembered, this was the ICU, and she hated this place. She hated working here. She hated all the damned beeping noises, the same ones that followed her to sleep, even on a good day. Phones and monitors and ventilators and pagers. Endless, annoying, insistent, just like now. She hated the smell, that cloud of unwashed body, unbrushed teeth, and disinfectant.

She was paralyzed. She couldn't move, couldn't talk, couldn't breathe. Somehow, she was awake, her eyes open, and even without her help she was breathing through a tube hooked up to a machine.

That wasn't possible.

She must be dreaming. That was it. Nobody would have done this to her. You can't just intubate a conscious person and put her on a ventilator. And yet she felt tape stretching the skin of her face. She felt the plastic tube against her teeth. She felt the air rush in as the square beast squatting by the bed clicked and whirred.

Why? Was she being punished? Had she mouthed off to the wrong person and been caught by a new disciplinary policy she hadn't heard about? Or was it worse? Could she have died somehow and was being made to pay for her sins?

For the way you've talked about my gomers, Kate Manion, I sentence you to an eternity on a ventilator.

No, no, no! She'd never meant it. It wasn't as if she'd hurt anybody. But a person could take care of only so many gomers and not go crazy. Patients never getting better, never really going home, human factories of bodily waste. Endless care, minimal brain power, usually no chance of survival. A syndrome the critical-care vets called P cubed—Piss-Poor Protoplasm—the bane of nurses everywhere, bodies that never seemed to work any better than the brains fueling them.

All right, so she'd done her share of gomer jokes. So on occasion, she'd called a comatose patient Gomer Toes. Maybe she'd even called the step-down unit Beach-Blanket Gomer. But she had never once bad-mouthed a patient to his face. She shouldn't have to pay like this, for eternity. Hooked up to machines, forced to listen to the endless echoes of even more machinery through the white and surgery-green rooms of the ICU, smelling like a five-day-old fish and annoying every hospital employee in the afterlife.

She wanted to cry. She wanted to run. She wanted to be wrong. Then she saw who her nurse was, and she knew for sure. She was in hell and she was being taken care of by Mr. Spock.

"I'm telling you, Fran," somebody called out at the edge of her vision. "She needs some kind of pain control."

"What she needs," Mr. Spock answered, pointy ears quivering almost as much as his three chins, "is another shot of Tubarine."

Not Mr. Spock, Kate realized sometime later. Worse. Much worse. At least Mr. Spock could work machinery. She was being cared for by Attila the Buns.

It just proved she was in hell, hurting, terrified, confused, swimming in a sea of technology like a giant man-of-war, no substance, all mass, and she was in the very unstable hands of Attila the Buns.

So-called because of the size of her set and the set of her attitude, Attila had been the only ICU nurse to flunk critical-care training four times. She had bad breath, worse manners, and no skills. And yet, because she never complained about what Administration did, because she could keep a clean station, she would work forever.

Forever. Kate had been right. She had to remember what she'd done to deserve this. She was in hell, and she had to repent.

The question was, was Attila in hell too or in heaven? After all, every time she took the eye patches off Kate to check pupils, she was smiling.

Would God let Attila take her Trekkie ears into heaven? Kate wasn't sure. But then, she wasn't sure why she was sharing hell with a whole covey of nuns, either.

Did nuns come in a covey? she wondered giddily. Maybe a gaggle. A nine. A nine of nuns. That was it.

Kate saw them—every time she could see, that is—for those moments Attila let down the patches that were meant to protect her eyes, since with a load of Tubarine on board she couldn't so much as blink. Fancy name for curare, that time-honored poison for South American spear tips. Used for people going under anesthesia to facilitate the placing of the endotracheal tube. Extended use for people needing to tolerate artifi-

cial ventilation or for head-injury patients who
needed complete body rest, to keep their intracranial pressure down.

Beep. Correct answer. You, Kate Manion, go
on to Final Jeopardy. With the nuns. The nine of
nuns that was even now swinging into formation
out in the work lane. The antibiotic ointment that
went with the patches smeared Kate's focus, but
she saw them: white on black, some of them; others in expensive brown polyester, as if God
demanded you not only give up worldly ways but
taste as well, even if you were out of the habit.

They seemed to float at the edge of her comprehension; she thought they were chanting.

Maybe she was in purgatory, and they were
there to speed her way north. Kind of like celes-
tial cheerleaders.

"Intercede for her now, Holy Mother and
Blessed Octavia, and give her health."

Kate really appreciated that. Maybe the nuns
could talk God into taking away some of the pain.
Or maybe they could have a word with Attila,
who had elevated patient assessment to the
Marquis de Sade Invitational.

She'd be good. Get the nuns over here so she
could tell them. Get God down here. But then He
was probably sitting up there laughing with all
those whiny people Kate had chastised at one
time or another.

As if in answer, a man appeared right over
her, blocking out the nuns. Short, squat, with hair
sticking out his nose and a big mole on his chin.
Not God; the wicked witch. The Bagel Man.

"If that intracranial pressure would just ease up," he was saying to someone else as he flashed a penlight in Kate's eyes and blinded her even more, "I'd pull the tubocurarine right now. But until I'm sure she's clear, I'd rather leave her be. Has Martinson evaluated the ARDS?"

Begelman. Neurosurgeon. How could he be in her hell? Kate wondered. He was Jewish. Jews don't believe in hell. Maybe a cameo appearance to increase the terror. Worse than gomers. She was going to be a vegetable. All matter, no brain. She didn't want to be a vegetable. She did not want to have gomer toes.

ARDS. She knew that from somewhere too. Maybe he was spelling something so she wouldn't understand. Speaking Latin. She knew she should have taken it in high school.

He never noticed that anybody was home and replaced the patches without once addressing her.

She hurt. She was scared. She was in the dark, and the nuns were at it again.

And on the other side, some rail banger was whining "Nurse, nurse, nurse" without stop. No doubt about it. She was doing the big time.

Somewhere along the way, Kate must have gained a fuzzy comprehension of what was going on. She did her best to behave so the monitors would stop beeping, so her chest would stop screaming. She did her best to float into a kind of nothingness, dipping into unconsciousness when things got too hot topside.

She knew somewhere back in her swollen, sore mass of brain tissue that she'd been injured badly and was being therapeutically paralyzed to control the needs of her body so it could heal without her interference. She remembered that ARDS was Adult Respiratory Distress Syndrome, a potentially fatal complication of trauma that demanded prolonged use of the machines. She knew other nurses came and went, things got better and worse, and Begelman was followed by Martinson, whom she liked and tried to talk to, although he couldn't hear her either.

She knew co-workers drifted in and out, familiar faces she tried to smile for. Some were friends who laughed as if nothing was wrong even while their eyes lied. A few showed up, she thought, just to make sure she was helpless. She didn't try to smile for them.

B.J. was there, off and on like the nuns, except that he kept holding her hand and scowling at her as he drank his Dr Pepper. And of course Tim came, everpresent in unusually rumpled scrubs, his forehead tight with a fear that wasn't just show.

But it was hard to hold on to sense in the unit. Kate never really slept. There was never silence or darkness or peace. There was never quite a respite from the pain, although the Bagel Man evidently agreed with the unseen voice about pain control and her ICP and put Kate on a morphine drip, which did blur the edges. It also provoked a few unexpected visitors that only Kate—and maybe the nuns— seemed to see. Kate was, after all, a cheap date.

The nuns never did talk to her. At least she didn't think they did. They were too busy praying over a little girl in the next bed, the daughter of a local leader whose devout Catholicism was matched only by his ardent social climbing. The nuns, members of the Order of the Sweet Savior, were looking for a miracle for their founder, Blessed Octavia Van Peebles, that might nudge the church into considering her for sainthood. The little girl, the nurses whispered angrily, had died of Reye's syndrome six days ago. Only the machines kept her alive—the machines and those damn nuns, who had imposed on a grief-stricken family so they could claim fame for a grim-faced ex-duchess who had devoted her life to training rich little girls to be rich social doyennes.

But then, maybe the nurses had it wrong. Because one night when the patches were down Kate could have sworn she saw old Octavia herself wandering through.

She tried to say hi, but evidently dead blesseds can't hear damned souls either. So Kate watched the nun, smaller than she'd imagined, wander through the unit, stop to check something out at the charting table, and then pause by the little girl's bed.

"Dedicate yourself," she said in sonorous tones that echoed in Kate's head.

"Okay," Kate agreed, figuring it was the thing to do, although she was sure that happened in her head, too.

The nun just nodded solemnly and left.

But then, maybe the nun hadn't been there at

all, because only a little while later Kate found herself conversing with her grandmother, and her grandmother had died when she was ten. Come to think of it, her grandmother wasn't any more fun now than she had been then. Next, her mother made an appearance, and Kate decided morphine wasn't all the fun it was cracked up to be.

She gave up and invented patterns in the ceiling tile, whether she could see it or not.

And then Attila was back. Without the ears, this time. Somebody must have noticed and suggested she ditch them while handling heavy equipment. Attila was a Trekkie, Kate remembered. Devoted enough to use the *Star Trek* theme as the bride's dance at her wedding to the supervisor down in processing. Must have been a real visit to Vulcan. Kate thought she might have been there last night as well.

"Good morning," Attila chirped, her cheer as determined as her actions. She already had a cup of coffee handy as she pulled down the patches and checked the monitors. Attila drank coffee like the rest of the world breathed, a brew so strong you could lose spoons in it.

Kate stared. She felt herself already starting to sweat; she didn't know why. Maybe because she knew it was time for turning and torture. She hated Attila. She wanted out. She thought maybe, if she could just move, she could get past her and out the door into heaven. At least plead her case.

Whatever her case was.

She couldn't think very well. She tried to brace for the pain. She didn't think she'd ever be free of it again. I promise, she thought fervently, seeing the grim enthusiasm on Attila's face. I will never ignore a patient's story about pain again. I will never in my life say the words, "This is going to be a little uncomfortable now. . . ."

"This is going to be a little uncomfortable now," Attila announced, and Kate saw she was sweating too. Probably couldn't wait to get on with the torture *du jour.*

The nurse reached down with ring-ladened fingers and ripped the tape that held the tube in place from around Kate's face. Kate screamed. No one heard. She fought the paralysis, the morphine, the dim voices that sounded a lot like machines at the back of her mind. She couldn't do this again. She couldn't let Attila touch her.

Attila ripped new tape and lifted Kate's head to rewrap the tape all the way around her throat. Kate screamed again. She was sure Attila was just going to unscrew her at the neck and walk off with the pertinent parts. Attila never so much as blinked. She was looking pale, though. Maybe she did hear Kate. Maybe she was in hell too, having to take care of a vegetable for eternity. It'd serve her right.

Except the vegetable was Kate, and she had no intention of hanging around.

Attila bent to jiggle the chest tube where it entered the left side of Kate's chest, just to make sure it was stable. It set off a firestorm all the way to Kate's toes. Kate fed on air from the machine. She braced herself. She lunged.

She caught Attila right around the throat.

Attila squeaked.

Kate tried very hard to ask her to stop, to just take it a little easier. She just wanted Attila to listen. She didn't. Attila dropped dead right across Kate's chest, taking the chest tube with her.

✦ Chapter 2 ✦

WAKING UP THE second time was something of a good news/bad news joke. The good news was that after the incident with Attila, the Bagel Man decided the only way to control Kate was not just to paralyze her but completely snow her. And digging back out from under that kind of avalanche was a slow and dreamy process.

By the time she was really coherent, the tube was back out, one of the chest tubes had followed permanently, and the ICP monitor had been removed. Kate knew her name, knew the name of everyone who took care of her, and could pronounce them all without so much as a stutter. She realized how badly she'd been trashed when just that feat alone brought tears to the eyes of Hetty Everson, who'd taken over her care. The last time Hetty had cried had been the day Administration instituted an open visitation policy in the units.

The bad news was that what Kate woke up to was John McWilliams. Sergeant John McWilliams, the tallest, broadest, blackest African American in the city of St. Louis and its surrounding communities.

15

Detective Sergeant John McWilliams of the St. Louis County Police Detectives division of Crimes Against Persons.

It wasn't that Kate didn't like John. She really did. He was one of the most accommodating police officers on the county force, happy to use his impressive height and even more impressive scowl to help keep the wealthier drunks and more violent crazies under control if needed.

But Kate suspected that John wasn't here to keep her quiet.

"You got some trouble, little girl," he said simply.

John was also a native of Jamaica, with the loveliest accent and deepest voice in Kate's experience. Kate had often said that when she finally gave in to auditory hallucinations she'd demand John's voice.

It still amazed her that the very clannish county police had accepted John. Not because he was black. Because he wasn't from St. Louis. In St. Louis, a person was defined by what high school he or she attended, and John had attended none of them. Worse, John didn't even know where any of them were.

Word was he had secured his position through a cousin on the force and the highest scores ever recorded in the sergeant's exam. Kate could never understand why he'd taken all the trouble in the first place. After all, given the choice, who would choose winter in St. Louis over winter in Jamaica?

"Aren't you gonna tell me how good I look?" Kate asked, her voice raspy and low from the tube.

John laughed in delight. "Girl, why would I tell you somet'in' like dat? You look like bloody hell."

Kate managed a grimace without moving too many sore body parts. "Thanks, John. I knew I could count on you."

"Dey took your hair, you know dat?"

She hadn't known dat. For the sixth or seventh time just since she'd tried to move in bed, Kate wanted to curse. Her beautiful hair, the only decent thing heredity had thought to bestow on her, thick and black and curly from her Irish daddy, and some yutz had buzzed it so the Bagel Man could get at her brain. Didn't it just figure? On soap operas they could do complete lobotomies and not even bend a strand.

"Where's the Little Dick?" she asked, stalling. Wanting another smile from John before they got down to business.

Little Dick Trainor, John's penance for his audacity. His partner. Where John gained ground through persistence and knack, the Little Dick managed through political savvy. A short, surly redneck who was more bigoted than his partner was delightful, he had won his nickname the old-fashioned way.

"You know Dickie don' like hospitals," John said evenly.

Kate managed a grin of her own. Waiting for Dick to hit the floor in the ER had become quite a spectator sport.

"So other than complimenting me on my looks, what's shakin'?"

"Not Frances Crawford." When Kate didn't answer fast enough, he leaned in a bit. "I t'ink you call her Attila. Not a very polite thing to do, little girl."

"You never worked with her."

"Won' get a chance to, now."

Which was when just what had happened the last time Kate had really had her eyes open well and truly sank in. Her heart sank.

"Oh, God . . . it wasn't a hallucination."

"Don' I wish it were, chil'. Dat girl's as dead as a big fish, and dey foun' her wit' your hands roun' her t'roat."

Kate wondered whether John would understand that she wanted to laugh. Not because it was all so absurd—although God knows it was—but because it was so damn pathetic. No matter how much Kate had hated Attila, she couldn't ever imagine killing her. Attila had problems enough of her own without Kate's adding to them. Husband problems, co-dependency problems, children problems. Problems the big, slow, infuriating woman would never have a chance to clear up now. And so Kate wanted to laugh to clear that hard knot of tears from her throat.

"They're sure."

"Sure she dead? Lord, I hope so. She been boxed in a wall since yesterday."

Kate glared, not in the least amused. "That it was . . . you know, me."

"You wanna see pictures? Security managed to get some real nice ones wit' a Polaroid before you two got unglued."

Wonderful. It would probably end up in the Pig Nurses from Hell newsletter Kate helped edit. Just what she needed. Nobody would believe she never really meant it, because Kate had threatened Attila with bodily harm the last time Attila left one of her transfers unattended.

"Actually," John was saying as he rocked back on his feet, "I do 'preciate you posin' for dat picture. If you hadn't killed her for sure, I t'ink I have to suspect ev'ry one of de crazy people in dis hospital. Nobody real sad to see her go."

Like Kate had said, Attila would never have walked away with Miss Congeniality.

"Is this where I call my lawyer, John?" she asked. " 'Cause it might take a minute. Right now I can't even remember my lawyer's name."

John let loose one of his rolling laughs that made the monitor tech look up and smile. "My, my, you do try an' look at de wors' side of life, don' you?"

"I try."

"Well, try dis. I am informin' you of your Miranda rights, jus' because I be askin' you a few questions. You wan' your lawyer, I'm jus' as happy to wait. But de smart money says da mos' we could get you on is reckless use of surprise."

"What do you mean?"

"You scared her to deat', girl."

Should that have made her feel better? Kate wasn't sure. She did know it was time to dial in her morphine again. Her head was pounding like a boom box on rap, her chest felt held together with barbed wire, and she was beginning to realize that the big lump propped on those pillows was her left leg, which hurt even worse. Above and beyond that, she much preferred dosed unreality to this stuff.

"So what do we do now?" she asked.

John smiled, all teeth, like a big old alligator. "Well, I don' know about me, but you have the right to remain silent. . . ."

Kate was tired. She knew every procedure the staff performed on her. Blood samples and chest X rays and Swan readings and percussion and breathing treatments and catheter lavaging. Vital signs and turning and coughing and endless assessing. She'd done it long years ago in training, and once when she'd been bumped to ICU for an ignominious six months late in her career. She'd hated doing it to other people. Now she knew she hadn't hated it nearly enough. No patient deserved this kind of abuse.

And then, to make it worse, the next person to wake her up was Martin Weiss. Chief surgical resident, by turns infuriating, difficult, and terrifying. As patronizing as they came, expecting people to excuse his behavior because of his talent. Darkly handsome enough to get laid, not kind enough to have friends. Getting more unpredictable by the minute until there were whispers that he was sampling some of the product himself.

"You're lucky to be alive," he announced, pulling his stethoscope from his pocket.

Kate didn't bother exchanging platitudes with

him. She didn't like Martin. She liked him less when he yanked back the sheet to reveal Kate's unshaved legs and the catheter drainage tube taped to her thigh beneath the scant cover of the patient gown. When Weiss threw up the gown to examine her, she saw the livid scar that bisected her chest with obscene staples, and she was ashamed of her own body. She was ashamed that someone she didn't like could expose it for anyone to see. She was ashamed that what she might have thought private and special was no more than the same meat she had turned and prodded and listened to each time she'd checked a patient.

So she didn't answer. Instead she squeezed her eyes shut, her hands fluttering toward the sheet, toward a modesty she'd never realized she needed.

"Neat trick with Attila," he said, slapping a cold stethoscope against her breast and making her flinch. Making her swear that she'd never let him get away with it on one of her patients again. "Wish I'd thought of it."

"I'd be happy to trade places any time," she offered.

He laughed. She wasn't trying to be funny.

Then she gasped. He hadn't even had the courtesy to lie and say it was going to be a little uncomfortable. He'd just leaned against the broken ribs so he could get a better listen to her lungs. Kate opened her eyes and grabbed his stethoscope to get his attention.

"Shit, Martin," she snapped, with what breath she had left. "Your diet low in torture today or what?"

He straightened like a shot, pulling hard to retrieve his equipment. "What's the matter with you?"

"At least beg my pardon. That hurt!"

Martin's expression grew a little more dangerous than usual. He was fondling the damn thing as if she'd yanked something much more personal than a stethoscope. "Don't ever do that again."

"What," Kate asked, "get hurt or let you touch me?"

He didn't even answer. Making sure he checked her drains and chest tube one more time, he simply walked out without covering her back up. It was Edna Reabers, the unit head nurse, who saw Kate struggling to get the sheet up and came in to rectify things.

Kate didn't say anything about Weiss's behavior. Edna, a vague middle-aged woman whose talent was anal retention and whose only remarkable feature was her perfectly pristine white uniform, was from the old school that forbade such luxuries. But she took an extra few minutes to tuck Kate back in and give her a few conciliatory pats, and that was enough to get her on Kate's Christmas cookie list for the rest of her life.

Then, as the light dimmed imperceptibly against the wall so that Kate thought maybe the sun was beginning to set, she opened her eyes to find yet another white coat staring at her monitors. Yet more pockets filled with penlights and clamps and tourniquets. Yet another name tag.

"Slut puppy," Kate rasped in greeting.

Jules looked down from her great height. "Whore dog."

And they both smiled, the kind of teary, longtime-friend smile that said what Kate didn't have the strength to anyway.

"You're a fuckin' mess, girl."

Kate sighed, shifted in bed a little, and waited for the protests from every limb and corner to die before answering. "That's what I keep hearing."

Juliette Pfeiffer was a big woman, red of face, red of hair, red of temper. She was the Jeff to Kate's Mutt, and few people knew how gentle the heart was at the core of a woman who carried around a coffee mug that proclaimed, EXCUSE ME. YOU'VE OBVIOUSLY MISTAKEN ME FOR SOMEBODY WHO GIVES A SHIT.

"Tim finally went home."

Kate was glad. "He was holding my hand, wasn't he?"

"All the time. He was so cute. Actually got the powers that be to let him off call for three nights so he could harass the help. I think that's a first for surgical residents here."

Sweet Tim. Steady, reassuring Tim. Tim with his passions, his demons, his secret loyalties. Tim was everything Martin Weiss wasn't, and just the thought of him waiting with her through that nightmare made Kate smile.

"Has he asked you to marry him yet?" Jules asked.

"I just moved in with him six months ago."

Jules wasn't in the least put off. "I figured a quick stint in the unit would convince any man you were too good to lose. I guess it must work better for some people than others."

"Probably somebody who hasn't had her head shaved and every orifice introduced to a plastic hose of some kind."

"I'm sure that's what made him cry."

Sly Jules. Smiling Jules. Kate wished Jules knew the truth.

"Don't feel compelled to comfort him," she teased anyway.

Jules grinned. "He wants me, I can tell. He's just achin' to sneak in and see what I hide in my truck."

Kate didn't want to laugh. She almost did. The idea of the meticulous, elegant Dr. Timothy Ransom Peterson III mixing it up with Jules in her old pickup truck was enough to send Kate's imagination straight into overload. Jules, one of the best trauma nurses Kate had ever met, who had her masters degree in social service, spent her leisure time handcrafting brightly beaded leather moccasins and collecting road kill for the pelts in a battered pickup that sported a bumper sticker reading BECAUSE I'M THE MOTHER, THAT'S WHY. She'd been one of the few people to get back at Weiss by leaving one of her trophies in his call bed after he'd questioned her judgment, sanity, and parentage in that order in front of a patient.

"Hard as it may be to believe," Jules said, "you look better."

Kate could deal with almost anything but this. "Oh, man, Jules," she said, sighing. "This sucks."

"Yeah, kid. I know."

No, Kate thought, you don't. Kate hadn't. Not until now. Not until she'd been tied naked to a bed and made to give strangers control of her body. Not until she'd lain in her own sweat and been unable to escape. There was nothing Kate hated worse than feeling helpless like this. Nothing.

"I guess my car's totaled," she said, wanting to talk about anything else but this.

It didn't take a rocket scientist to understand the stiff silence that met her statement.

"What?" Kate demanded.

Jules looked up at the monitor again. She looked down. Something flickered and retreated in the bright blue eyes.

"A mess," was all she said.

Kate immediately feared the worst. "Oh, God, I didn't take somebody else out with me?" She heard the steady beeping of her monitor stutter a little. She felt it in her chest with a rush of fear. "Tell me it wasn't my fault, Jules."

"It wasn't your fault," her friend said without hesitation. "You don't remember?"

Kate relaxed a little. "Nothing. Just . . . eating Sunday dinner in the lounge with Tim. I remember how beat I was. What day is this?"

"Saturday."

Saturday. Good God, she'd been here almost a week! Almost seven days completely lost to the mists and the theater of the absurd.

"Do you know? What happened, I mean."

"Telephone pole bit you."

Now Kate was amazed. "I fell asleep? I never fall asleep."

"Listen, kid. They're making faces at me. You get some sleep."

Sleep. Seems she'd done that. She'd wrapped her beautiful, shiny, vintage, midnight-blue Mustang around a telephone pole. And then she'd killed the nurse who'd taken care of her.

It was B.J. who told her the truth. Right after he had the lady from Patient Accounting for lunch.

Kate had actually been managing some sleep. Uninterrupted, dream-free, restful sleep. She should have known it couldn't last.

"Excuse me, Ms. Manion," a high-pitched voice interrupted.

Somebody was bumping against the bed. Didn't they realize that hurt?

"Stop it."

"Your nurse said you were awake."

Kate didn't even bother to open her eyes. "She lied. They're all liars. Didn't anybody tell you that?"

"It's important that you talk to me. You've amassed quite a bill here, and we can't locate any family to guarantee payment."

"No," she said, still not bothering to face the woman. "No family."

None who would answer. None who would want to be found anymore. But that wasn't anyone's business but hers.

Kate recognized the voice now, clipped and precise, like an algebra teacher. Mrs. Warner. Patient Accounting. Kate had personally kicked the woman out of more than one intensive-care room when she'd marched in to inform the patient that since he'd failed to take his acute inferior myocardial infarction to the hospital covered by his HMO, he wasn't going to be covered and what did he wish to do about it? As if that was going to help a guy with a big old heart attack feel better. Oh, well, they said paybacks were hell.

"I'm not paying, Mrs. Warner," Kate assured her. "Not a penny. I plan to suck off the hospital as long as I can and then sue for not reading the surgical release forms to me in Spanish. Got any problems with that?"

This time Kate got her eyes open. Mrs. Warner must have been impressed, because she took a full step backward.

"Don't think I don't know who you are," the sharp-faced little woman accused, levering a pencil at Kate like a lance.

"Well, good. That's one of us."

"I'm still trying to clean up the mess from when you erased the Breedlove file from the computer."

That actually made Kate smile. "Didn't you read the new directive? You're only allowed to harass people for payment for six months after their insurance company pays you. It's a law. I was just trying to help."

"That problem would have been resolved soon."

"Their little girl died. I didn't think they needed to be tortured by you too."

"You have no right blaming me. It wasn't my fault."

"That's right. It's never anybody's fault anymore. You're all just doing your jobs."

"Well, I'm sorry if you have a problem with that. My job right now is to discuss your insurance. It isn't going to cover all this."

Kate just sighed. "Of course it isn't."

"Not only that but there's the question of how you were injured. The incident report can't be completed until you talk to the hospital lawyer, and until that happens—"

That got Kate's eyes finally and permanently open. Her chest was hurting again. "Lawyer? Incident report? What the hell are you talking about?"

"Well, you were off hospital property. You can't possibly expect workmen's compensation."

"Workmen's . . ."

She tried hard. Dug through the morass of memory, desperately sought out anything that would sound familiar. Anything that would connect her, a telephone pole, and workmen's comp.

"Get out."

The words came from the doorway, quietly, succinctly, and with an authority Mrs. Warner couldn't ignore.

"The nurse told me it was all right," she protested weakly.

Kate turned to take in the vision of Woodstock Past approaching at a martial pace and knew help was at hand.

He obviously wasn't going to waste any energy on the now hapless Mrs. Warner. Taking hold of her by the lapels of her lilac double-knit suit, he heaved her from the room with one more "Get out" and then turned to greet Kate.

"You can't—" could be heard from the work lane before another door slammed.

"Beej?" Kate managed.

"Breathe," he commanded. Kate should have been mad that there was a wry twinkle in those gray eyes.

"What did she . . . mean?"

"Breathe some more. Then we'll talk. The monitor tech is using your rhythm to teach the rhumba out there."

She breathed. Her visitor held on to her bed rails and watched the monitor.

B.J. was there. Good old B.J., with his denim and tie-dyed uniform, his ubiquitous bottle of Dr Pepper, and his perpetual scowl. The only way Kate could tell he was on call was the fact that his hair was tied back. Other than that, Dr. Brian Joseph O'Brien went out of his way to thumb his nose at propriety.

He was also notoriously short of fortifying platitudes.

"What was she talking about?" Kate demanded, feeling the pressure ease, hearing the staccato of her heart slow perceptively.

Pulling a cigarette from the pack in his sleeve, B.J. didn't even bother to put it to his lips. He just stuffed it behind his ear to match the pen on the other side. "Woman's an idiot. You havin' gas yet like a good girl?"

Kate actually wanted to smile. Thank God B.J. was a doctor. He'd make a lousy minister. Come to think of it, she'd written every prescription he'd ordered as an intern because he couldn't spell, either. But that had been a few years ago. Now he was here in her room glowering at her as if she'd just wet the bed.

"As sore as I am, I wouldn't know if I blew up," she informed him, getting a hand up and noticing that IV tubing snaked from its back. That hurt too. What a surprise. Somebody'd managed to get a Cathlon in her hand the size of a garden hose. That'd get them a gold star in the Pig Nurse newsletter. "You never answered my question."

Evidently he wasn't going to, either. "You were dead, ya know."

Kate was well used to his abrupt changes of course. This time, though, he caught her up short.

"But I'm feeling much better now, thanks."

She thought of all those hallucinations, the cast that had peopled her hell, and she wondered.

"Arnstein cracked your skinny little chest right in ER. They said the blood was a foot deep. He rode the cart all the way in with his finger in your aorta. Quite a sight."

It was Kate's turn to scowl. She'd participated in the Rodeo Roundup herself, straddling a dying patient as the trauma team pushed the cart carrying them through the halls toward OR at breakneck pace. It was a hell of a ride, especially if you could feel the life slipping away beneath your fingers. But Kate didn't think she wanted a surgical resident yelling "Yippee-o-ki-yay!" atop her as they made that sharp turn down by the

elevator banks. Especially Arnstein. He'd probably
felt up her lungs while he was in there.

"You're a comfort, B.J.," she assured him
dryly. The funny part was, he was.

He leaned right over the bed rail, his soda forgotten, eyes suddenly avid. "Well?"

"Well what?"

"Tunnel? Voices? Visitors? What was it?"

Kate couldn't think of any better retreat than
just closing her eyes. She should have expected
this. Maybe if she weren't still draining any number
of bodily fluids out through plastic tubes, she
might have. She knew what B.J. wanted. He wanted
verification. He wanted to be able to share something very special with Kate. At any other time,
Kate would have been touched. B.J. didn't hang
around intensive-care units just for the view. B.J.
didn't do live people. B.J. was a medical examiner,
a forensic pathologist whose work was almost as
legendary as his personality. Even for Kate, B.J.
wouldn't have crossed the barrier he'd imposed
on himself almost ten years ago, unless he'd had a
reason. He'd come for answers. And she had
none.

"Can we talk about it later, Beej?" she asked
wearily.

She could hear him trying his best to maintain
control. This was important to B.J. It was kind of
important to Kate, too. She had the feeling that
when she had more energy, she was going to be
really pissed about the answer she'd finally have
for him.

"Jules tells me you don't remember anything."

Kate opened her eyes to see a curious softening in his. It should have forewarned her. "Just who the president is, and who wants to remember that?"

"Well, you're a big girl. . . ."

That was the intro she knew she didn't want. Her chest began to tighten again. Kate imagined it was right where Arnstein's fingers had been. "Spit it out, boy. Who did I kill?"

His eyes flashed like agates. "You didn't kill anybody—not counting Attila anyway."

"Beej—"

He waved a hand at her, as if she had no sense of humor. She bet, when he'd been lying in bed twenty-two years ago earning his own scars, his sense of humor had been a little slim too.

"You were on a transfer. A little kid with total body trauma you took by ambulance because you couldn't get the helicopter. Remember anything now?"

Transfer. Again she fought for images, sounds, anything.

"Nothing," she admitted, with a sigh that belied the fact that the monitors were starting to dance again.

Kate saw Terry Martin, her nurse for the day, detach himself from the desk and lean in the door. "B.J., this isn't funny," he warned, an eye obviously on the same monitors.

B.J. didn't even bother to turn around.

"Yank it off fast," Kate told him. "It ends up hurting less."

B.J. respected that kind of advice. "Ambulance was sideswiped by some asshole playing chicken on the highway. Everybody went tit over tail down the embankment." Kate saw the final tally in those deceptive eyes before he ever told her. "The only one they pulled out alive was you."

"Who was the team?" She asked anyway.

"Pepper and Theresa."

God. Oh, God, no. Not strangers, like many of the transfer teams. Local paramedics, a team she'd helped train and then recommended to the board of the fire district. Fire-eaters with good hearts who must have pulled real big strings to help her get that baby out the door in a hurry. Who were dead now because of her.

Kate didn't cry. She'd forgotten how to do that a long time ago.

"Phyl didn't want me to do it, did she?"

Phyllis McGill—nicknamed by the less charitable as Phyl the Gorilla, after a legendary beast of a much sunnier disposition still stuffed in the St. Louis zoo—Kate's supervisor and not ever to be confused with someone who liked or respected Kate. A classic case of the Peter Principle caught in a middle-management squeeze and rendered totally incompetent.

It must have been a hell of a fight.

"She accused you of grandstanding."

Kate wished she could breathe better. "Oh, I probably was. You know how I love to show off with a bad baby or two . . . the baby was lost?"

"Just God's way of saying it was that kid's day to go. If it makes you feel any better, they found you wrapped around him, like you were trying to protect him from the fall."

It didn't make her feel better at all. "How old?"

"Four."

Kate might not have remembered what happened, but she bet she knew. Patient with no insurance, taken to the very insurance-driven St. Simon's Medical Center, aka St. Serious Money, in the Better Part of Town. Maybe the doc on hadn't believed the little thing was quite as bad as Kate thought. Maybe they just didn't want to spring for the money to transfer him to one of the pediatric neurosurgical units down at the kiddie hospitals in the city. One way or another, Kate had probably spent frantic minutes on the phone trying to convince someone to take him and then find somebody to ship him down. And then someone to approve payment for the helicopter, which cost a fortune, or even a transfer ambulance with full support team, which still cost some bucks. Everything cost bucks in medicine.

If it had been a late shift, Kate never would have had a problem. One of the supervisors would have okayed everything. Being away from all the brass tends to give a person initiative. But Phyl had no initiative. She had a budget. And helicopters and paramedics simply stretched her budget to the point where she might not get her year-end bonus.

And Kate, as usual, had undoubtedly handled the whole thing with grace and dignity. She wondered if she'd called her supervisor a worthless maggot again.

"Here, Kate."

She felt a cold swab against her arm and realized Terry had appeared at her side with a syringe of something.

"Get out of here with that shit," she said, her voice a little thin.

"It's nothin' but a little Valium. You need it right about now."

Kate turned her head so she could glare at him eyeball to eyeball. "And I'm refusing it. Now, go away."

Terry wasn't used to being contradicted by his unit patients. Kate could see his instinctive displeasure, the urge to control. And if B.J. hadn't been there to tip the balance, Terry probably would have ended up winning, because Kate suddenly realized she was just too tired to fight.

But B.J. *was* there.

"Hard to sneak in an injection with a witness standing here," he drawled.

Even here in the unit where B.J. rarely visited in his official capacity, the crew knew his reputation. Terry recapped the syringe and turned away.

Kate turned back to B.J. and the answers she knew he'd give her.

"I really did kill Attila, though, huh?"

"All right," B.J. snapped. "Yes. You killed her. There is dancing in the streets, and several of your cohorts have asked if you do requests."

"I really didn't mean it," she insisted. I just wanted somebody to listen to me."

B.J. shook his head. Somehow he'd gotten a second cigarette over that left ear. "The Bagel Man is still trying to figure out how you managed it on so much Tubarine."

"Determination."

"That's what Administration is probably afraid you'd say."

"How old was she, Beej?"

His eyes clouded briefly, and Kate saw what the rest of the world wouldn't. "Thirty-four."

"I didn't mean it," she said again, her voice even smaller.

B.J. actually patted her hand. "I know it, pogue. I know it."

This time, Kate did cry.

✦ Chapter 3 ✦

"WHAT ARE YOU gonna do," Kate demanded some seven days later, "throw me out?"

They were all there: Kate; Phyl, her supervisor; Mrs. Warner; even the hospital lawyer, an unctuous, well-dressed yuppie whose specialty was real estate. Considering how much land Serious Money had taken over in the last five years, he was probably the most important man on the board. Right now he was raising Kate's blood pressure.

"I'm sure this is distressing for you," he soothed, as if she were a witness he'd just exposed in full view of the jury box.

Kate leaned a little across the big conference table, her eyes rabid. "No," she disagreed gently. "Having a little boy die because this hospital dicked around with a transfer *distresses* me. Knowing that two very good paramedics died because of the way we were forced to transfer that little boy *distresses* me. This *disgusts* me."

He just shrugged, his thousand-dollar suit shimmering slightly in the expensive lighting they saved for the executive offices. "I'm afraid you don't leave us any alternatives here, Kate."

They had lain in wait, letting her gain her strength, murmuring platitudes about taking care of their own, sending their messages of support and comfort through the fifth person at the table, who was at this moment staring at the rather large picture of Sister Maria Goretti Simmons, the founder of the hospital, as if hearing her sonorous tones right through the fifty years since the good sister had died.

Kate wondered what Sister Goretti, who had founded St. Simon's, would think of this. Especially since the woman watching her was the last of their community to grace the hospital grounds, Sister Ann Francis, a vague, sweet, ineffective ex-pharmacologist the staff called Sister Mary Polyester. A hand-patter of the first order with an apple-doll face, the little woman had for the last five years been semiretired into pastoral care and general goodwill, where she wandered the hospital holding hands and dispensing doctrine like Pez.

It was a real hanging jury, if Kate had ever seen one, all gathered to teach her the facts of life about hospital bills, insurance, and workmen's compensation. According to them, Kate so far only qualified for the first.

They'd had a volunteer sweep her from her room in a wheelchair and deposit her in the executive suite so fast Kate shouldn't have been able to bring along any help. Fortunately for her, they'd passed Tim in the hall. He had invited himself along without hesitation.

"Now let me get this straight," Tim said evenly,

his handsome blond features arranged in a professional mask, his Virginia drawl bored, his attention
on the elegant surgeon's hands he'd folded before
him rather than on the people arrayed across the
table. "You're saying Kate isn't qualified for workmen's compensation for her injuries because, a,
there was a question about the transfer and, b, she
was off hospital property at the time she was
injured. And because her injuries left her with retrograde amnesia about the incident, she can't
defend herself or enlighten you. Now since her
hospital insurance policy only covers eighty percent
of costs, she now owes you all in excess of ten
thousand dollars."

"We simply need to clarify matters," the lawyer
said with a sympathetic frown. "The hospital can't
be held liable in the matter, since it was something Ms. Manion took on at her own risk. Surely
you can see that. But I think we're making her a
most generous offer. We'll cover another five percent
of her bill if she signs a release from responsibility
right now."

"And what about her job?" Tim turned to Phyl.

Phyl sputtered, her jowls quivering. "Well . . .
well," she offered in a high, thin voice that sounded
like a bad violin over the intercom. "Kate is enti-
tled to four full weeks of accrued sick leave. But
we can't guarantee her a return to the emergency
department. I can't wait that long to fill her position."

Kate rubbed her head. "If I could look at the
chart," she suggested, even knowing better, "it
might help me remember something pertinent."

The lawyer—what was his name: Furly, Hurly,

Curly?—was already shaking his head before Kate finished. "That's not possible, and you know it. That chart is confidential material."

Kate laughed before she could stop herself. "It is for anybody trying to argue with you."

Stop, she commanded herself. Take a breath. You can get the chart some other way. It was just that they were penalizing her for a giant hole in her memory, so she couldn't fight, couldn't even agree if their action was really called for. She couldn't do anything, and Kate didn't take forced inactivity well.

"Mr. Gunn could have had you fired for jeopardizing the lives of Billy Rashad and the crew of that ambulance," Phyl snapped in her most aggrieved voice. "There wasn't any reason the regular transfer crew couldn't have been used to transport that little boy. Be thankful you still have your job."

Another sympathetic voice heard from. Kate fought the edges of black rage by clamping her hands around the armrests of the wheelchair until her chest hurt. She still couldn't remember what had happened, but she knew one thing. There had to have been a damn good reason for her to coerce the crew from Lindbergh into helping her. Either the transfer ambulance hadn't had a full life-support team or they would have taken too long to show up. That little boy must have been real bad.

"I'll tell you what," she managed to say. "I'm not signing anything. I'm not agreeing to anything until I talk to my lawyer."

Lawyers again. She'd pay somebody just to tell her there was nothing he could do. But she had no choice. She couldn't simply let them win.

There was an uncomfortable silence on the other side of the table. Kate should have stared them all down. But she couldn't do it without opening her mouth, and that would have sealed her fate on the spot. So she held still, willing herself to silence, and stoked herself on the simple support of Tim's hand on her arm.

"I don't think Mr. Gunn will allow me to make this offer again, Kate," the lawyer said, as if instructing a very slow child. "And Mrs. Warner will be more than happy to show you just how fast your bill is mounting up."

That brought Kate's head up and her eyes open. "I'm sure she would." There was nursing care and the long round of IV antibiotics she'd needed to counteract a hospital-acquired strep infection. There were daily chest X rays at a hundred dollars a pop to make sure her lung had remained inflated, physical therapy for her broken leg, and echocardiograms to watch out for any problems from her surgery. There was pain medicine and dressings and lab work and IV fluids. And after today there would undoubtedly be sedatives. She was furious. There was nothing Kate hated more than being trapped, and they had her by the short hairs. Both sets.

Not only that, but the orders had come right from the top. Leo Gunn, the chief administrator, CEO, and camp commandant of St. Serious Money. Gunn's only concern in the matter would have been that keeping-the-blame-from-the-hospital business. Kate could be a pain in the ass, but she wouldn't be as inclined to complain in the millions of dollars as the family of that little boy. Therefore, if they were going to do it, Gunn would rather they do it to Kate.

"I think Kate told you what she wants to do," Tim announced, the scrape of his chair almost lost in the carpet as he got to his feet. "Now I'm going to get her back to her room—unless you plan to transfer her to Regional."

Regional. The city and county hospital where all indigent patients ended up. The gun-and-knife club, the city's AIDS center, where they'd undoubtedly told her to send Billy Rashad in the first place. The temple of desperation.

"Don't be melodramatic, Doctor Peterson," the lawyer said evenly. "Kate's one of our nurses. She stays here, where she belongs." And with that, he also got up.

Everybody else scraped right alongside. Even Sister managed to find her feet, smiling vaguely at everyone.

Tim unlocked the wheelchair and backed Kate away from the table.

"I need a decision by tomorrow," the lawyer said.

Kate ignored him. Tim ignored him. Only Sister moved to hold the door open.

"God bless you, dear," she said with a beatific smile to Kate. "And remember, everything will be taken care of. You do look so much better."

Kate couldn't help smiling back. "Thanks, Sister."

She didn't bother to say good-bye to her supervisor, who stood alongside like a rather lumpish guard dog.

"There has to be something I can do," Tim insisted as they headed down the carpeted hall.

Kate shook her head. "And let them get their claws into you? Forget it. You only have another year to go on your residency. Keep your nose clean."

"But Kate—"

This time she tilted her head back so she could look straight up at those classically chiseled features, the soft, sweet blue eyes. The frustration that twisted it all into familiar agony. God, she loved him. If only things were different. If only she could give back half of what he'd given her.

"But Kate, nothing. You're vulnerable, Tim, and believe me, they wouldn't hesitate a minute to go for the kill if they found out."

So intent were they that neither heard the door open to the other conference room.

"Why, Kate Manion, isn't it?"

Kate swung around even faster than Tim, her heart thudding with the possibility that they'd been overheard. But from the expression on the face of the approaching gentleman, they were safe.

"It is," he said with a big smile, a pile of files in his arms, his posture bent forward just a little to take in Kate in the wheelchair. "Hello there, Doctor Peterson."

Tim nodded. "Mr. Fellows."

Mr. Fellows's attention was already back on

Kate, his pleasantly patrician features folded into concern. "This is wonderful. I didn't think you'd be up and around so soon. Says a lot for the talent around here, doesn't it?"

Kate didn't quite manage a smile for the senior vice president of Serious Money. She didn't know much about him except that he'd personally convinced some very top-notch physicians to join the team in the last few months, and he was rumored to be a closet Barry Manilow fan.

"I was just discussing my health-care benefits," Kate said.

Fellows looked up in time to see the door open down the hall and Mrs. Warner step out.

He gave a funny little shake of his head without looking back to Kate. "They should have waited." Another shake, and his attention was hers again. "Don't worry about it. You just get better. And don't worry about Frances. We all understand perfectly."

Kate would have loved to have felt reassured, but she'd been in the business too long. As the staff was fond of saying, a free pregnancy test should come with every physical.

"Thank you," she said instead, knowing anything else would come out shrill and accusing.

Tim damn near attained warp speed with that wheelchair to get them away from the administrators before anybody else caught up. "You're not going through this alone," he insisted yet again as they swung off the elevator onto the fourth floor: post-op, rehab, and ladies' lingerie.

"How can I?" Kate asked. "None of you will let

me. I'm just not going to have you throw yourself on a grenade to save me. I always manage to float to the surface in these things."

They didn't stop, didn't even slow, as the world of the hospital went on around them on the surgical floor. Central-supply techs restocked Nurseservers, and nurses bent over charts. Secretaries fondled phones, and patients trailing IV lines and pushing poles tried to remember how to walk and breathe at the same time.

Kate and Tim, so long inured to the sights, didn't even notice, like background music in a movie. Their focus was on each other. Anyone who saw them might have thought they were sharing the silent communication of people in love.

"I'll call Steve," Tim said with a quick nod, as if punctuating the end of the discussion. "You can't say no to that."

Steve Peterson, lawyer to movers and shakers, schmoozer with the elite. Hot, hungry, and carnivorous. Tim's brother and the only other holder of Tim's secrets.

"Thank you." Kate acknowledged his help with a big grin and was relieved when Tim smiled back. "That would be defense enough. Now put me to bed and get back down to the unit where you belong."

Kate turned to find the door of her room open and groaned. There was an ambulance cart inside. That could only mean one thing: she had company. Damn. She didn't want to be social, especially with somebody she didn't know. She wanted to curl into fetal position and curse. Steadily. Fluently. And she didn't feel like doing it in front of people.

"Where the hell have you been?"

It wasn't people. It was Jules. Jules and Sticks and Parker from the emergency room, all in scrubs and wearing big silly grins. And right behind them were McMillan and Kramer from the Lindbergh Fire District, decked out in full uniform, as if they'd just swept in with a new victim. Only there was no one else in the room.

Kate took another look around as Tim brought her to a halt just inside. McMillan, a balding, skinny black guy with a taste for English Leather, promptly closed the door behind them as if this were a clandestine meeting of a new fraternity.

"Didn't I get the invitation?" Kate asked dryly.

Jules just kept grinning from her great height, like Buddha in scrubs. "Word is out that you were just downstairs being taught the difference between a valued employee and a pain in the ass."

"Wanna see the rack marks?"

"Well, then, that explains why you forgot what today was."

Kate took another look around, saw more silly grins. "I'm sure you'll remind me."

Jules just shook her head sadly. "Short-term memory still screwed up, huh? Well, that's what happens when you do spin-the-wheel in the back of an ambulance."

"Jules . . ."

Jules assumed an air of solemnity Kate hadn't seen since the day the big woman had pronounced the Lindbergh mayor's mother's favorite parakeet dead after these same paramedics had brought the poor thing in with breathing problems. The breathing hadn't been the problem by then; the broken neck had, from where the men, in an effort to reassure the distraught old woman, had applied pressurized oxygen to the pet and proceeded to shoot it across the room into the far wall. Four times.

"It is," Jules intoned, hand over heart, "the highest holy day, and this heathen forgets. Well, we're just going to have to do something about it."

The highest . . . ? Kate dug around in the pile of memory chips that had been dislodged and sought some kind of calendar. It was early spring outside. She could see the faint blush of green as the afternoon sun caught it outside her window. It was . . .

"Oh, my God!"

A general nod met her astonishment.

"Precisely," Jules agreed. "Saint Patrick's Day. And where do we go on Saint Patrick's Day?"

Kate looked around, the initial surprise melting into something far more dangerous. She wanted to cry again, damn it, and every one of them knew it.

"McGurk's," she admitted, finally seeing the whole plan. "But you can't do that."

"Can't do that," Jules scoffed in her worst Irish accent. "Did you hear that, lads? Can't. Up the rebels!"

"Up the rebels!" everyone answered as McMillan rolled the cart up to the chair.

"Do you want to go along?" Jules asked Tim.

Tim's smile was strained. "I'd rather have my toenails pulled out."

"Tim doesn't like Irish music," Kate admitted as Sticks helped her out of the chair and over to the cart. "It's our only constant source of conflict."

Tim shrugged good-naturedly. "She has no taste."

"Which explains why she's living with you," Jules countered happily.

Tim bent to give Kate a kiss good-bye. "Be home before eight. You're grand rounds tomorrow."

"In that case, I'm never coming back."

They processed out of the room, Tim in the lead to intercept nosy staff and Jules bringing up the rear like the bishop on Holy Thursday.

"Where are you going?" Peggy Turner asked predictably as she rounded the desk, her hands full of two o'clock meds.

"Therapy," Tim announced easily. "She won't be needing her pain med this afternoon."

"Maybe never again," Kate admitted as she rolled by like an Egyptian queen on her barge, the sheet neatly up to her chin to hide the kelly green scrubs she'd absconded with, a paramedic on each end.

Peggy wasn't impressed. "I think I'd better check on this."

"Call O'Sullivan," Jules suggested. "He'll okay it."

O'Sullivan was the orthopedist who'd put Kate's tibia back together. Besides the fact that it would take Peggy until tomorrow morning to find

him, they all knew he had a healthy respect for
the high holy days himself.

So away they went, in procession, right down
the staff elevator to the back hall and the emergency exit, where a retired Lindbergh fire ambulance waited. And this time Kate remembered
every mile of the lights and siren as they swept
east toward the city and Soulard, where St. Louis's
most famous Irish pub was located.

"Up the rebels!"

Kate lifted her glass but couldn't quite focus on
it anymore. The room was packed to bursting, the
noise deafening, and the immediate company
wonderful. Fifteen of them, all told, both medical
center personnel and Lindbergh staff, squeezed
into about four square feet of space at the front of
the bare brick and plank pub to give Kate the kind
of support they knew she'd need. There were
enough dead soldiers on the high scarred tables to
start several bowling teams, and the air was thick
with smoke and hops. There were green bowler
hats, green ears, green pins with obscene sayings,
green clothing of all kinds. The crowd was boister-
ous and friendly, and the band was one of the
best, the music at once exhilarating and sad. Reels
and jigs and hornpipes played in minor keys on
pipes and fiddles and squeeze boxes and bohrans.
Kate couldn't have been happier.

"I believe I've discovered a breakthrough in
medical research," Parker said, leaning forward a
little to toss his green plastic lei over the top of

Kate's outstretched toes. Several other leis hung drunkenly over her cast, and she had at least four green baseball caps on her head to cover the lack of hair.

Kate looked up from her wheelchair and tried to focus on her friends. Some were on the high stools that were McGurk's hallmark. Others had given up and plopped down on the floor right in front of the stage, snarling at anybody in the over-crowded room who tried to object.

Parker had claimed a chair just over Kate's right shoulder and perched there like a large gnome. A paramedic/RN who had come to the ER directly from the city fire department, Parker had the build of an elf on steroids, the mind of a bookie, and the hands of a violinist. Scuttlebutt said he was dating one of the residents, a veritable flagship of a woman named Lisa Beller. Kate would have loved to have seen it, especially since Parker needed a stepstool to do CPR and stuttered whenever he saw a naked woman.

"A breakthrough?"

He nodded, his button-black eyes a bit fuzzy. "Medicine will thank me. I've discovered a troubling association."

Kate looked around to see what Parker was focusing on, and then realized he couldn't focus on anything. "What's that?"

He frowned importantly, which made him look like a frog. "Polyester and emphysema. I think there's a link."

Kate laughed.

"I'm serious." He giggled. "Just how many

gomers have you seen come in wearing natural fibers?"

"Eyes right!" Sticks barked in her best British-field-officer voice.

Every female staff member turned right. Catching sight of the intended target, a healthy young male with great buns and an obvious sense of rhythm, Kate removed one of the hats and held it over her heart.

"Wonder if we could up his rebel." She sighed with delight.

"You have no right to drool," somebody accused with a soft punch in the shoulder. "You have Tim waiting at home."

"Tim doesn't care," Kate assured her, utterly fascinated by the view. "He says I can look at the menu all I want as long as I come home for dinner." Except she hadn't had dinner since she'd moved in. She hadn't had dinner in a very long time. Made looking at the roast across the room all the more tantalizing.

"Bend over!" Jules yelled to the young man, who was decked out in soccer shorts and little else.

"You're all disgusting," McMillan snarled as he watched for any kind of female equivalent.

"Amen," the women intoned reverently.

Kate replaced her hat. "What's she doing here?" she demanded, pointing past the multitudes between her and the front door, where Edna Reabers, the supervisor from SICU, was standing.

Several heads turned. Jules lifted a hand in greeting. "She works for us now."

Kate almost dislocated her neck trying to look all the way up to Jules's face. "Wrong-Way Reabers? You're crazy. She spent all last week sponging the dust off my respirator in the unit."

"She's been demoted. Working nights in the ER from now on."

"But that's cruel and unusual punishment!"

Jules nodded. "For her too."

"But why?"

"You kidding? She's only two years from retirement."

And, if Administration had its way, she would end up quitting in disgust and distress sometime short of the date when retirement benefits actually had to be paid out. Nothing was more expensive or more quickly gotten rid of than a loyal employee. The groan of distress from the ER crew sounded suspiciously like someone clearing the bellows on a bagpipe.

"Well, we'll have the cleanest goddamn crash carts in the city," somebody said.

"Code drugs arranged by size and color."

"Names sewn into the collars of every lab coat down there."

"And you guys haven't even heard about her past lives," Kate informed them. She had also worked with Edna Reabers.

"It could be worse," Jules offered, draining her beer just as the waitress swung by with the next round.

"Yeah? How?"

"They could have transferred us all to the unit."

Nobody could really argue the point. Especially Kate.

"Prepare to smile and be friendly," Jules commanded.

Smiles were applied.

"Hi, everybody." Edna greeted them as if she were the last white missionary in Africa.

"Hi, Edna," they all chirped, like a dutiful class.

The band was beginning to straggle onto the stage. Kate was having trouble getting her head off the back of her wheelchair. She didn't particularly care.

"Could you lose me on the way home?" she asked no one in particular, her gaze on the faint design of the stamped tin ceiling past all the smoke.

"Well, that's why we brought you down," Jules assured her. From where she was perched on one of the high stools, her puffy face seemed to hover in the air like the Wizard of Oz. "Gunn wants us to just drop you at Barnes, see if you're any nicer to them."

Kate snorted. "I'm nice. I even let one of those crazy nuns give me a rosary."

"Nuns?"

"The ones in the unit praying over the Winkler kid. I don't suppose we got a miracle."

It was up to Edna to shake her head as she set her purse down and picked up a drink. "She died last night."

" 'Bout damn time," Parker intoned. "I was tired of curtsying every time I saw a mink comin' around the corner."

"Pretty little girl," Kate mused, by now adept at seeing past the tubes and wires.

"Smart little girl," Jules retorted dryly. "Went out on her own terms."

"Damn," Kate offered with a dry smile. "I'm sure glad I came out to have you guys cheer me up."

"Wanna hear a good one?" Sticks asked, leaning over.

Sticks was another of the staff anomalies. A pockmarked, whey-faced kid with a mouth like a sewer, the young tech had what Kate called Appalachian blond hair, interchangeable bead-and-feather-earrings, and a butterfly tattoo on her butt from when she'd played drums with a rock band in LA; hence the moniker. Sticks was the ER root system for the grapevine, a natural gossip diviner.

"Yes," Kate assured her, "I want to hear a good one."

"Attila's husband and boyfriend both attended her funeral."

Kate had to admit it was good.

"Oh, my God," somebody yelped right by Kate's left ear. "What's *he* doing here?"

All eyes turned. It took Kate a minute longer than the rest to find out what the new ruckus was about, probably because she was about at waist level with most of the crowd. It made visibility a little tough—unless she could talk another of those soccer players her way.

"What the hell's he got under his arm?" one of the newer members of the group demanded before Kate could answer the first question.

Kate was already grinning. "His pipes."

B.J. wouldn't be happy. He hated being unmasked like this.

"He plays this stuff?"

"Quite well. It got him kicked out of his room more than once in his halcyon days as a resident. Some people just have no ear for music."

It was B.J. who had introduced Kate to Irish music in the first place. Bent over the odd contraption called the uileann pipes, he produced notes that could have scared a banshee. Intense, fierce, as if he were personally strangling every one of those notes from the ethereal plane, betraying a passion he'd firmly deny if anybody caught him. Which they just had.

"How do you know him so well?" Sticks asked, puffing on an unfiltered Marlboro.

"We did time together down at Saint Louis U when he was a house staff and I was a puppy nurse."

Two driven people wary of involvement who'd recognized each other instantly and kept in contact no matter where they were.

"Is he good in bed?"

Kate laughed. "Beats me. I've never known him to let anybody close enough to find out."

Sticks nodded to herself, two fingers wrapped around a lock of hair as if curling it on the spot. "I bet he's *real* good in bed."

Kate didn't bother to answer. She bet he was too. It wasn't that she'd never considered it. B.J. had the fierce dark looks Kate preferred, and Kate always felt he would handle a woman just about the way he did those pipes, as if he could lose his soul in her. In fact, there had been a couple of times when they'd come close, usually after imbibing more than was intelligent. But in the end, it seemed the stakes were too high for mistakes. Kate needed B.J.'s sense more than his pheromones.

"Don't let him know you're here," she advised the group.

"Hey, B.J.!" Jules immediately yelled in her best truck-stop voice. "Can you play 'Hunka Burnin' Love' on that thing?"

B.J.'s frown was mighty, but his surprise didn't match Jules's when he did just that. It was one of the most unique sounds Kate had ever heard. Then he spotted Kate and scowled all over again.

"Do you have a note from your mother?" he demanded of her, leaning over the railing that had been erected just for the holiday to keep the rowdier celebrants from toppling into the band.

Kate figured her grin was pretty silly by now. "Occupational therapy," she informed him, lifting her glass. "See? I can care for myself."

She was probably the only one who saw the humor way back in those deep-set eyes. "Tim should put you on a leash."

"He does," she assured him with a wicked grin. "But only when I ask."

B.J. just shook his head. "I can't leave town for a minute."

"Six years in Philadelphia is not a minute, you asshole," Kate retorted equably. "How's your mother? I keep forgetting to ask."

His mother, whom he'd ostensibly come home

from the big city to keep an eye on after her third heart attack. "That's okay, pogue. You keep forgetting *your* name. She's fine." Giving Kate a sudden squint, he tucked his pipes under his arm as the rest of the band tuned up behind him. "You didn't tell me."

"I know I didn't," she answered, knowing perfectly well they weren't talking about B.J.'s mother anymore.

"You will."

Kate would have felt a lot better if he'd smiled about it. Or if he were still safely separated by the thousand or so miles to Philadelphia. B.J. was much too insightful to have nearby if you wanted to keep secrets, and Kate was a person who gave away her secrets with the greatest reluctance. She'd actually been relieved when he'd informed her of his decision to accept a job on the East Coast as an assistant medical examiner. It had meant they could still stay close, but as neatly separate as they'd always been.

And now he wasn't just back, he was right in her face, which made Kate truly appreciate the term *ambivalent*. Especially at this moment, since she did not want to discuss tunnels or lights or feelings of warmth of any kind with B.J., who was only a little more obsessed by near-death experiences than he was by his pipes.

"She was buried in full uniform, ya know," Sticks proclaimed, sending Kate's and B.J.'s heads around in some confusion.

"Who?" B.J. made the mistake of asking.

"Attila."

"Her nursing uniform?"

"Don't be silly. Her Star Fleet uniform. Wish I could have seen it." Sticks gave way to a wistful smile. "Her husband came as Kirk, and the boyfriend came as Picard. Says something about changing times, ya know?"

Kate snorted. "And they were both screwing Spock."

Jules gave her head a mournful shake: "The old battle bridge just isn't what it used to be."

"I have to go," B.J. offered with some bemusement.

Jules flashed him a four-point smile. "Play 'Misty' for me?"

B.J. did all his commenting with one eyebrow and turned.

"What the hell does *pogue* mean?" Sticks demanded. "You two are always calling each other that."

Kate's grin was private. "It's kind of an Irish endearment."

"I was an Irish soldier on the field at Drogheda, you know," Edna mused, watching B.J. settle back in. "I was slaughtered by Cromwell himself. It's why the pipes make me cry. And I can't take care of people with sword injuries. Too personal."

For just a moment, every other person—at least in the hospital party—stared at the nondescript woman in her still perfectly pressed uniform. Then they turned on Kate, who simply shrugged.

It was Parker who recovered first. "So," he

said, leaning over Kate so she couldn't miss him. "Now that you've taken care of Attila for us, who's next?"

Kate waved her beer at him in objection. "My career's over, thanks."

"Oh, fine," Jules retorted. "Get our hopes up and then back out. I mean, just think of the possibilities."

Kate ignored her. "Up the rebels!" she yelled, loudly enough to make her chest hurt.

"Up the rebels!" the room answered in thunderous ovation.

The band members lifted their beers in salute and bent back to coax magic from their instruments. A waitress paused over Kate's head and pointed at her Guinness. Kate just nodded. She'd been right about not needing pain medicine. Probably wouldn't hurt sometime soon to get some food in her, too. The memory of it might help her survive the steam-and-fry cuisine back at the hospital.

"Hypothetically." Parker nudged Kate on.

"Hypothetically, hell," Jules shot back. "Our wages just got frozen for the third time."

Kate looked up, amazed. "You're kidding."

The group answered in one low snarl.

"Oh, that's right," Jules said. "You haven't seen the notice. We're having budget problems. Hiring and wage freezes for the foreseeable future, at least in the critical-care areas. Although I think the new CVICU is getting more money."

Well, that took care of that. Kate drained the beer in her glass and began her wish list. "I say we go for Phyl first."

"Don't waste your time on middle management," Edna intoned seriously. "Go right to the top."

It took a minute for anybody to get past the shock to answer.

"All right," Kate managed, an eye still on the placid features of the former unit supervisor. "How 'bout Salvatore? I heard he was the asshole who refused the helicopter transfer on my baby."

This time it was Jules who shook her head. "He never got the chance."

Kate spent a moment focusing on her. "What do you mean? He was the pediatrician on duty that night."

"But he wasn't the trauma doc on that night. I take it you still don't remember?"

"Less and less as the night goes on. Who was trauma?"

Jules's smile was not a pretty sight. "Sam the Sham himself."

Well, at least it was an answer that made sense. Dr. Samuel Fleischer, M.D., F.A.C.S., chief of surgery. A much, much bigger fish to protect than one pain-in-the-ass ER nurse. The kind of surgeon who did his best to diagnose and treat over the phone, which in a surgeon is an unpopular trait.

"The man with no hemorrhoids," she retorted blackly.

"The perfect asshole," the rest of them chanted in unison.

"Well, then, it's settled. He's next."

"Not good enough," Edna insisted, already to the bottom of her beer and turning to the second half of her boilermaker.

"What?" Kate demanded. "You wanna just take a squad in there and level the whole place?"

"Not the whole place. Merely the head of our happy little family."

With the alcohol sloshing around, it took everyone a moment to come up with a common name. It was up to Sticks to blurt it out.

"Gunn?"

Edna shrugged her bony shoulders and slammed down a shot of twelve-year-old Hennessy's. "And why not? Can you think of anybody more deserving?"

"You want it alphabetically?" Jules asked and then bent to Kate's ear. "Good thing we've got the ambulance. I think she's a Saint Patrick's virgin."

"Not anymore," Kate assured her sincerely.

"It's perfect," Edna insisted, her eyes glazing with disconcerting speed. "It's toward the beginning of the alphabet, he's the biggest asshole, and he told me to my face I was too old to look good in a white uniform."

"Well, hell, let's kill him three times," Sticks drawled.

Jules lifted a glass. "May he sleep with the fishes."

Another glass rose. "Swim with the cement."

It was beginning to look like a beer forest. "Suck wind with the gomers."

"You sure we can't try one of the fire board members first?" McMillan whined.

"All in good time, my son," Jules assured him with a pat. "All in good time. These thing must be done . . . delicately. Up the rebels!"

"Up the rebels!"

"Death to the enemy!"

"Death to the enemy!"

"Say your prayers, Gunn, because Kate's comin' back to get you."

Actually, Gunn wasn't the next one to die. It was Mrs. Warner.

Three days later, just as the day shift was ending and the staff was clotting up elevators, one of Mrs. Warner's subordinates found it necessary to enter the inner sanctum. Under normal circumstances, no one was encouraged to breach Mrs. Warner's door. She didn't really see a need to socialize, and the people who knew her agreed enthusiastically. But Tina Parkway was too new to appreciate the barrier. So when she knocked on the closed door before she went home for the day, she didn't think anything of opening it right up, just as she would have any other office in the hospital.

It was then she realized that she'd been hearing Mrs. Warner's printer stuttering away without stop for the last hour or so, the kind of subliminal sound that doesn't break through until it doesn't accomplish anything except create a round or two of "If only . . ."

If only Tina had paid closer attention, she might have actually seen Mrs. Warner die instead of just found her slumped sideways off her chair, completely covered in computer paper as it rose off the machine and folded over her like a perforated shroud.

Tina wouldn't have stepped farther in to find that only one line of type appeared on the computer screen, that being: I GUESS PAPERWORK ISN'T AS IMPORTANT AS I THOUGHT.

Tina would have screamed anyway. Even working in a hospital, she hadn't seen that many dead people, especially ones who had just made her work through her lunch for the fourth day in a row. Which meant Tina wasn't sure whether she screamed because she was startled, frightened, or ashamed that she was so relieved. It didn't matter. In the end it accomplished the same thing: another round of Harass Kate, who happened to have been witnessed arguing with the decedent not too long before her death.

✦ *Chapter 4* ✦

THIS TIME IT was the Little Dick doing the questioning. Kate mostly just sat there and held her head, which was still sore from the beating it had taken three nights ago.

"You didn't like her."

Kate laughed. Then she winced. "Let me count the ways."

"You threatened her when you were in the ICU."

"Actually, B.J. threatened her."

"He's being questioned too."

That got Kate's head up. She laughed all over again, which made the waterfall of silver bells on her earrings tinkle in response. "He's doing the autopsy on her."

That didn't please Dick at all. "How do you know?"

"He told me, right after he told me she became one of her own statistics. I made him a bet that her chest cavity was empty."

Dick's brow darkened noticeably. They were sitting in Kate's half of the room, the other bed temporarily empty and surgically made since her newest roomie was down in the OR for a bowel resection. The room faced west and the afternoon sun, which flooded in to brighten the ubiquitous tan wallpaper that graced all the patient rooms except down in OB, where flowers ran riot over the walls. A couple of straggly plants sat on the windowsill, and a walker waited unused by the bed. Kate was stretched out in the easy chair, her casted leg propped on the ottoman.

She'd graciously given Little Dick the hard-back chair, where he now sat as if impaled on a post, notebook in lap, his mud-brown polyester detective sports jacket with its county emblem as limp as his brown-and-white check shirt and brown tie. Dick was a full head shorter than Kate, even sitting down. His hair was lacquered, his mustache full, his eyes glittering. He did everything but go on point.

"You want to make this easy, or you want to make this tough?" he asked in his just-too-high voice. "You're already under investigation for one suspicious death in this hospital."

Kate knew she should have been paying closer attention. But her head hurt. Her chest hurt from trying to get used to using elbow crutches. Beset by an increasing claustrophobia, she was waiting for Tim to show up to escort her away from this hall of moaning, muttering people. For some reason, this made Dick seem just a little sillier than usual.

All Kate could think of was that polyester-emphysema corollary of Parker's. Dick had a real fondness for double knits and tobacco, two definite danger signs. Maybe she should warn him.

"What were you doing between noon and three yesterday afternoon?" Dick asked, eyes on his notebook.

Kate didn't even have to think. She moved her head a little again, just to hear her earrings. "I was napping. I do that a lot lately."

"Did anyone see you doing this?"

Dickie was not good for Kate's health. He kept making her want to laugh, and that hurt too. "Well, if I'd been awake while I was doing it, I'm sure I might have noticed."

Dickie just glared.

"I was asleep, Dick. And the door isn't locked. Check the notes on my chart. Tracy might have peeked in around change of shift."

He wasn't appeased or amused. "When was the last time you saw her?"

"Who, Tracy? She was just in ten minutes ago."

Dickie wasn't in the mood. "Mrs. Warner."

"Oh, her. Saint Patrick's Day, around four in the afternoon. We had a charming little chat about the debt I owe the hospital."

"A situation that still hasn't been resolved, from what I hear."

"My lawyer's looking into it."

"Have you ever heard anyone threaten any member of the staff here?"

Kate thought of the other evening at McGurk's and smiled. "No. I don't suppose we can hope she was just called to her maker in a timely fashion?"

✦   ✦   ✦

They couldn't. B.J. knew it perfectly well. But he looked anyway, sure he'd find something else that could possibly excuse Mrs. Walker's ungainly nosedive into her data base. This was a task he was performing in the postmortem room at the George Gantner Memorial Building, where the county medical examiner's office was located. His hair pulled back and his jeans traded for gown and surgical gloves, he was bent over the heart everybody swore Mrs. Walker didn't have, inspecting its arteries as Jimi Hendrix echoed around the room like a chain saw on high speed.

"Nada," he muttered impatiently, tapping a forceps against the countertop so the sound echoed in the empty tile room. "Come on, old woman. There had to be something wrong with you. I don't have all day."

The majority of the old woman he was addressing lay behind him on one of two metal tables, naked and staring and gutted, her organs long since sacrificed to the gods of forensics. B.J. had checked her lungs, her heart, her digestive tract, her blood. He'd looked for any kind of tissue beneath her fingernails, defense injuries on her hands and arms, suspicious contusions or breaking of the hyoid bone. Needle marks. Anything. He'd found nothing to explain the fact that Mrs. Walker had probably had a hell of a near-death experience, right before she had the real thing.

The only option left was to peel back her scalp and lay open her brain, on the chance he'd find evidence of a catastrophe, one which would have been enough of a surprise that she would only have had enough time to type that enigmatic little message on her computer before her own system crashed. But from what he'd found so far, he didn't have much hope.

The rest of her had been as clean as a baby's conscience. Well kept, astringent almost, as if she'd purged herself regularly to flush away the residue accumulated from her work. No signs of abuse, but no signs of celebration either. Her insides had been as tight and unpleasant as her face, which didn't help B.J. in the least. He had a bad feeling about this.

Focused on purple haze and unblocked arteries, it took a minute for him to realize the door behind him had hissed open.

"Yeah?"

"I've missed you too, sweetheart," came the rather acerbic voice.

B.J. didn't exactly smile as he finally looked up from his work to find a sprite with a punk haircut and spotless lab coat perched in his doorway. "Spit it out, Mandy."

The laugh was purely feminine. "What makes you think I have something?"

"That superior tone of voice. And the fact that I haven't found anything but the healthiest dead woman I've seen. Now, what is it?"

"Weird," she said, easing in to lean against a counter, her head bobbing instinctively to the music, her fingers littered with rings. "Where's the Little Dick?"

"Where do you think?"

"Amazing how convenient those calls are he

gets. Right about the time you start digging deep, isn't it?"

B.J. did his best to keep his temper. "What's weird?" he asked, as gently as he could, considering the fact that he had no answers, no help from the detective of record, and no aspirin to take care of the hangover he'd collected at McGurk's over the weekend. "There was quite a bit to choose from."

"The coffee. We've run it three times, and we sure came up with something, but we're damned if we can figure out how it could kill somebody."

"What?" he damn near shouted.

"Carbamazepine."

B.J. found himself staring down at the shiny red organ in his hand: silent, still for the first time in over forty years. Possibly felled by a felon—a felon with imagination.

Carbamazepine. A very effective little drug used for seizure disorders. Of which Mrs. Walker had no history. Which would logically mean she would have no reason to put it in her coffee or anyplace else. On the other hand, it shouldn't have killed her all by itself.

It was time to open up that brain and see if her secrets lay there.

"She's not on any prescription medicines," Mandy offered, obviously having peeked at the investigator's notes.

B.J. balanced the heart in his hand as if weighing the problem. "Yeah, I know. There wasn't anything else in the coffee? Nothing that maybe wouldn't mix with the carbamazepine?"

Mandy shook her head. "Cream and fake sugar. I found neither on a contraindicated list."

"You got the blood and vitreous started?"

"Spinning down now."

B.J. nodded. If there was anything to be found, Mandy would find it. One of four toxicologists on staff at the ME's office, she held a Ph.D. and had the street sense of a Crip. She also had one of the best tox labs in the state no more than twenty feet down the hallway in which to work her magic.

"Well," B.J. allowed, his attention returning to the organ in his hand and the victim to whom it belonged, "something killed her. Let's find out what."

"And then call the Little Dick," Mandy suggested. "I heard him say something about going over to grill Kate Manion."

"Good for him," B.J. said. "It'll put hair on his chest."

B.J. turned back to his work, thinking he'd just wander over to check on Kate later anyway. There were very few people left in this world B.J. counted on. Kate was one of them, and he'd damn near lost her a couple of weeks back. He'd actually visualized her there on his table, open and staring like Mrs. Warner, all her sass and sense lost to his shiny knives, and it hadn't pleased him at all. His mother would have said he was getting sentimental in his old age. He just knew he'd already lost too many friends to suit him, so the ones that were left meant more.

Besides, he wanted to know what she'd seen

as Arnstein had pumped her heart into action with his bare hand. He wanted to know why she wouldn't tell him.

"Because nothing happened!"

Kate saw the astonishment in B.J.'s eyes. "What do you mean nothing?" he demanded.

"Nothing," she repeated. "Zip. Zero. Blackness, void, and then the circus in the unit. I had neither tunnels nor lights nor otherworldly visitors— except for a few dead relatives I was chatting with in the unit, but I put that down to the morphine. Besides, they certainly wouldn't have been there to guide me to a better place."

B.J. shoved his hands deep in his jeans pockets and stared out the window. "I was counting on you."

Kate snorted a bit unkindly. "I did my best," she assured him. "But I guess if I'm not going to get anything inspirational after a fifteen-minute cardiac arrest, then I must not be on the near-death-experience tour list."

She could see frustration bunch up his shoulders. Kate knew she was the closest thing B.J. had to a friend in this town. She was certainly one of only a handful anywhere in the world who knew what had happened to him in 'Nam. In fact, she might be the only person alive who knew that Brian Joseph O'Brien had more than a passing acquaintance with a near-death experience himself.

He'd told her about it almost eight years ago, one night in December in the St. Louis University

Hospital ER, when the two of them had been hip deep in the flotsam of holiday parties and ice storms. B.J. had been pulling his ER rotation, and Kate, fresh from school, had been working one of her first nights in charge.

They'd had a really bad one, teens who'd been tossed out of a sports car and under a truck. Trauma was trauma, but when the faces are too young to die, they have to be purged. B.J. had offered his story of transformation and under-standing in a small bemused voice, as if he could somehow infuse the restless souls of those children with his own certainty.

Scrubs bloody and rumpled, hair still matted with sweat, obligatory can of Dr Pepper in one hand and cigarette in the other, he'd spoken of how he'd lost his fear of death at the ripe old age of seventeen in an evac helicopter over Da Nang in 1972 when his heart had stopped beating seven minutes shy of the evac hospital where they were rushing him. He'd floated, he said, lifting away beyond the chopper to watch the medics frantically pounding on his chest, squeezing fluids into him, screaming at him to hang on. He'd been drawn into the tunnel, seen the light, heard the soft sounds of comfort. He'd barely made it back from what he'd once half facetiously called the sea of love.

In B.J.'s words, the experience had screwed with his priorities in life. After all, once you've been seriously dead, the little shit just doesn't carry the same weight anymore.

It was the reason, finally, that B.J. had found

his way to forensic pathology. B.J. had simply reached the point where he couldn't converse with people who wasted their lives having anxiety attacks over parking spaces and the price of toilet paper. That kind of interchange was never a question with his patients, who had no problems left with priorities. The fact that his work could still make a difference to the few living souls he could tolerate, like Kate, had been the bonus.

Absurdly, Kate felt as if she'd finally let him down. "Hey, pal," she accused. "Imagine how disappointed I am. I've been getting this hard sell on what a strange and wonderful trip it is, and I didn't even get to go."

B.J.'s answering smile was just as irreverent as Kate had hoped. "And here I thought I'd be able to teach you the secret handshake."

"Knock, knock."

They both turned to see Tim standing in the doorway, his blond hair framing his chiseled face like a halo. Angels would have wept to look that good. Raphael would have grabbed a paintbrush. Kate thought about the waste and smiled anyway. She'd deliberately broken her alarm clock right after moving in with Tim, just for the pleasure of having him wake her every morning.

"Hey, big boy," she said with a grin. "Wanna go get some Guinness?"

Tim stepped in, hands, as ever, in the pockets of yet another pristine lab coat, the perfect foil to B.J.'s rumpled comfort. "I hear you've been given an honorary chair down there after the other night."

"The one in the bathroom," B.J. retorted dryly.

Tim and B.J. did that little male shuffle of acknowledgment as Kate went about getting in another set of earrings—sparkly moons and diamonds this time—and reached for her newest best friends, the metal elbow crutches that were still making her ribs grate. At least they gave her mobility. She did her best not to vocalize any of the chorus of displeasure her body set up as she stood and swayed with the dizziness that always surprised her with movement, another pleasant reminder of her mortality. Her luck: she got all the grief and none of the glory.

"Where are we going?" she demanded. "Tony's? Kemoll's? Dominic's?"

It was Tim's turn to shuffle. "The cafeteria. Security has been warned not to let you past the front door. Said it's bad for hospital PR."

She shook her head. "No sense of humor. Would you mind swinging by the ER? I wanna say hi."

"You wanna harass Phyl, and you know it."

Kate flashed him a big grin. "I know it."

Tim shook his head like a patient father. Kate could see he understood, though. It was what had gotten her through that first day upright: the promise of getting down to where the real heart of the hospital was for her. She'd been sitting in that damn chair all afternoon like a kid waiting for her mom to get home to take her to the park. Well, it was time to get her shoes on and go. Back home where the trauma code roamed. Noise, lights, action. It was just too damn quiet up here, where sick people thought silence would heal.

By the time Kate managed to straighten all the way back up into walking position, B.J. was at the door on his way out. B.J. was not the park and field-trip type. "Well, if you remember anything interesting, let me know."

"Interesting?" Tim echoed, instinctively moving closer to help Kate along. "You talking about Warner?"

That brought Kate to a full stop. "God, I forgot. What did you find out?"

B.J. shot her quite a look. "Give away clues to the prime suspect? Don't be absurd."

"Thank you, Hercule Poirot. What did you find?"

"Carbamazepine in her coffee and a big bleed in her head."

"Subarachnoid?"

He nodded. "She blew like a bad boiler on the *Titanic*."

Kate had her crutches fitted. She was itching to visit her friends. She didn't move. "From carbamazepine?"

B.J. shrugged. "From something. Maybe you just pissed her off one too many times."

Kate offered a particularly charming grimace as Tim passed over Kate's official Pig Nurse's cap to cover the buzz. "Why not? I already have Attila on my head. I probably killed Warner too. While you're at it, check and see if I was in Dallas in 1963." She settled the cap so the pink snout pointed forward and the white nursing cap pointed backward, right between the pink pointy ears. It's the small details that make a difference.

"So it wasn't murder?" Tim asked, forehead puckered, hand at Kate's elbow.

B.J. shook his head. "I didn't say that, either."

And that was that. Kate could see it in the set of his features.

Murder. Kate tried rolling the sound of that one on her tongue and found she didn't like the taste at all. Even with Little Dick's histrionics, she hadn't really believed Mrs. Warner had been murdered. After all, everybody in the place talked about revenge. It was the favorite topic of conversation, after sex and bad shifts. But nobody would ever seriously think of doing it. Murder went against everything they'd been trained for, had dedicated themselves to.

Did she really believe that, though?

"Who'd do it?" she demanded, suddenly feeling a little more tired.

"Little Dick Trainor thinks *you* did," B.J. said.

"He doesn't count. Who'd really do it?"

For a moment there was silence as the three of them considered implications. The hospital went on around them, voices drifting in from the halls, the elevators dinging softly, an IVAC beeping on somebody's IV. Familiar, comforting sounds to Kate, who had burrowed into hospitals like a mole uncomfortable in the light outside. But B.J.'s announcement took Kate's sense of balance with it.

"Ridiculous," she said, straightening, as if that would carry her conviction. "Check her insurance policies. I bet one of her family offed her to get money. Murder's always committed by next of kin."

B.J. just lifted an eyebrow.

"Well, all you have to do is watch *America's Most Wanted*," she protested lamely.

"Code blue, Medical ICU, room five. Code blue, Medical ICU, room five," the intercom announced.

"Oh, shit!" Tim snapped by way of saying good-bye, and whirled out the door.

Kate slumped a little. "I'm hungry."

B.J. grimaced. "So now I'm supposed to take you?"

Kate leveled quite a smile at him. "Well, Tim's gonna be busy for a while. That was Mr. LaPlante that just went."

Mr. LaPlante, who had had one too many cigarette-and-leisure-suit combinations, was a gomer of epic proportions whose family refused to give up, even though the only healthy thing about the man was his hospital bill. Kate felt for Tim. He'd be up there for an hour, stabilizing the poor bloated oblivious thing, and then end up having to do it all over again in no more than four hours. Maintenance had been known to set time clocks by Mr. LaPlante.

"If you'll tell me one thing," B.J. said, leaning back against the wall.

"Anything. I'm starved."

She should have seen the bemusement in his expression sooner. "How long have you been living with Tim?"

"About six months. Why?"

"You two getting married?"

Kate hated lying to B.J.; she didn't do it well. She tried anyway. "We've talked about it."

"Kate." B.J. looked disappointed. "Don't insult my intelligence."

Kate knew she was still short a good supply of blood, because when it drained from her face she almost passed out. B.J. had no idea what he was doing.

"How did you know?" Kate asked.

"That he's gay?" B.J. shrugged. "Unlike most of the medical staff around here, I pay attention."

"Don't . . . you wouldn't . . . you haven't. . . ."

"Said anything? Don't be stupid. I'm not going to do anything to jeopardize the career of one of the only two surgeons I consider any good in this place. Tim's business is his business. I'm wondering about you."

Kate actually had to sit down in the chair for that one. Her ears were ringing. "Jesus, don't scare me like that. Anybody found out . . . well, you know what this neck of the woods is like."

"As enlightened as the Inquisition." B.J. gave a crisp nod. "Especially when it comes to surgeons. But what's in it for you? Last I heard, you hadn't taken a vow of celibacy."

Kate thought of life with Tim and smiled. Her version of safe sex, she guessed. Tim slept in gym shorts and made it a point to keep himself in top physical shape. He and Kate were comfortable together, friends without interfering agendas who could criticize and compliment with impunity. Tim didn't mind that Kate found him distressingly beautiful, and Kate didn't mind so very much that Tim didn't want to get too close.

Besides, Tim was gentle and supportive and

caring and creative. He coordinated her wardrobe better than she did. Every time he'd come to visit her in the hospital, he'd brought new earrings to wear with very short hair. He was a brilliant doctor who was old-fashioned enough to be passionate about his work. A girl could live with a worse person. Kate had most certainly lived with worse.

"I guess he's my beard, too," she finally admitted. "He's a good friend who doesn't demand too much. And after Michael the Perfect, just what I need to keep any more real involvements at bay."

"I told you that asshole was wrong for you."

Kate glared at him. "You told me when your blood alcohol was four-hundredths of a percent away from dead. You think I'm going to take you seriously then?"

"I dispense some of my sagest advice at moments like that."

"You also told me Elvis was alive and working in radiology."

His grin was grudging and cute. "He was. He just slipped out before I could prove it. Now, let's eat."

They ate. In fact, they were fêted. It didn't take a giant leap of logic to figure out that word had gotten around that Little Dick had been in to interview Kate, or that it was about the demise of Evelyn Warner, personal favorite for more than one lounge dart board. There wasn't exactly any applause when Kate hobbled into the cafeteria. There was, however, a general raising of coffee cups and more than one offer of compensation.

"Somewhere there's a murderer who's pissed you're getting all his attention," B.J. informed her dryly.

Kate took a small bow and maneuvered a crutch around so she could get her tray. "How do you know I didn't do it after all?"

B.J. actually snorted. "Because you'd never have the patience to set her up. You'd just beat her to a pulp."

Oddly enough, the rank humor and objectionable insinuations offered by a definite percentage of the staff members made Kate feel comforted. No one had ever stood up for her before. No one had ever thrown insults like bouquets of bright flowers. Kate smiled and kept on smiling until she reached the emergency room, all the while dreading the moment when they would turn against her. Because throughout her life, whenever there was a moment like this, there was a moment like that.

By the time she finally made it down to the ER, Kate was really getting tired. Not tired enough to give in to a wheelchair, as Parker suggested in less than moderate tones; a girl still had her pride. But her gait was decidedly slow and faltering, and her fondest thoughts focused on how the dizziness would fade once she was horizontal again. First things first. Kate had to soak herself in the ER for a while before giving in.

It was the first time she'd set foot in the place since the accident. She'd thought about it a lot as she lay in her bed, listening to the hall noises, smelling the hall smells, anxious with the collected anxieties of every person who waited there for relief, for answers, for death. Even with other people around, people she knew, she felt afraid and restless in a place that sparkled but didn't feel clean.

The emergency room was fresher. Crisper. The smells weren't waste but flux: disinfectants, floor wax, exhaust from the ambulances; popcorn and coffee, the staples of a place where meals were at a premium. The outside air washed through every time a door sighed open so that no smell or sound permeated, and patients rotated through too quickly to mark the corners with their scents.

Kate was refreshed every time she smelled the place, basked in the babble of the radio, the distant moan of a siren, the beeping and trilling and clatter of the machinery that lived there. Like the first whiff of smoke to an old fire horse, the smell of alcohol and Betadine sent Kate's adrenaline spilling, and she readied for the charge. It was a high like no other in life.

She came to a halt at the head of the ER hallway so she could watch the constant motion, staff bouncing in and out of rooms like random electrons in a charged ion. She listened to the voices, a chorus of dissonant distress, punctuated by bursts of laughter or tears. She slowly inhaled and sated herself on the fresh aroma of movement. She waited for the hit of adrenaline.

She waited.

And she only felt tired.

"Hey, killer, nice to see you."

Kate hadn't even realized Jules was working. The big woman ambled over from the central desk, stethoscope dangling, pockets bulging, lab coat already stained with the day's detritus. For a minute Kate couldn't answer. She was trying to get over a perfectly irrational hiccup of terror.

Nothing excited her like walking onto the hall of an ER. Better than sex, better than chocolate. Action in the fast lane.

But it wasn't there. That clutch of anticipation, that brightening, that sudden shift into gear. She'd depended on it.

Suddenly she wondered just how long it had been since she had last felt it. Like the time she'd faced Michael and realized he had broken her faith one too many times.

"Kate?"

This time Jules was looking a little worried. Kate did her best to smile, wondering whether she could will the infatuation back. Wondering what she could possibly do if she couldn't, since this was the only place in the world she belonged.

"I'm disappointed," Kate managed, shifting a little so her ribs would stop protesting. For the first time since leaving the floor, she wondered when her next pain med was due. "The place hasn't fallen around your heads without me."

"Sure it has," Jules assured her blithely, patting her on top of her pig-snout cap like a puppy. "We just can't let it look that way."

"Sure you could. Just till I get back upstairs."

"When you comin' back?" one of the secretaries asked, only her head visible behind the desk.

"She doesn't want to come back here," Parker said on his way by.

"Sure she does," Jules argued. "Kate loves disasters, don't you, Kate?"

"I love disasters," Kate parroted instinctively.

"Then when do you think they'll let you back?"

"I don't know," was all she could say. Because for the first time since she was twelve years old, suddenly she didn't want to.

✦ Chapter 5 ✦

"YOU KNOW HOW you can tell a hospital in Saint Louis?" a surgeon had once asked Kate. "By the emergency sign in front and the crane in the back."

Truer words, Kate thought, had never been spoken. St. Louis, for its size and population, had an abundance of hospitals. Even after growing up in the city and succumbing to the lure of the only growth industry in the area besides beer, Kate had never had a great desire to study the history of the system. She was, however, well acquainted with its present, having worked in two of the metropolitan area's largest hospitals and knowing people who worked in several others.

All in all, there were over sixty-five hospitals, clinics, outpatient surgical centers, and various and sundry psychiatric and detox units. It was a booming business that tended to clump around the major arteries of the metropolitan area like bad cholesterol. A calling administered to by the charitable of several faiths until recently, when the religious rosters had dwindled and the money-

making possibilities had soared. Where once
Sisters of Mercy, St. Joseph, and Charity had swept
through hallways, men in three-piece suits now
reigned. Where each unit had stood in splendid
isolation, buyouts had followed the same trend as
everywhere else in the eighties until there was
Barnes West and Deaconess West and St. John's in
Washington, also lovingly known as St. John
Boy's, all satellites of the older, larger, more estab-
lished institution of the same name closer to the
city center.

As for Serious Money, it had begun life under
the auspices of the farseeing Little Sisters of Good
Grace for the care and treatment of indigent tuber-
culosis patients. Taking advantage of low land
prices the nuns had situated themselves far from
the teeming city so their patients could indulge in
healthy country air. For a time, St. Simon's had
been nicknamed St. Send Us Anyone, and they'd
lived up to the name.

Progress being what it was, the population
caught up with the hospital not long after tubercu-
losis, in that incarnation, went the way of the
leech. The nuns expanded their facility into a
teaching institution with ties to Missouri University
and fought off the inevitable drain of vocations to
the convent until they could no longer deny the
fact that they, like every other order in the neighborhood, would have to rely on lay help.

That was when Leo Gunn took over. That was
when staffing dropped and profits rose. That was
when, as Mr. Gunn liked to put it, charity was introduced to reality. Kate preferred to refer to it as the

GM revolution in hospital administration, when TLC went from Tender Loving Care to Totally Low Cost, when black ink and bottom line became the only acceptable goals.

Kate had fought the tide longer than most. She was, after all, an incurable optimist. Somewhere she'd gotten stuck back there where patient care meant just that and not client relations. Where one worked with a patient to restore health rather than negotiate with a consumer to protect the hospital from litigious problems.

Kate was a dinosaur, and damn proud of it.

But as she sat in her room with the dusk gathering outside and the chatter of the hospital much too distant and low to soothe her, Kate found herself wondering if this particular dinosaur had just met her meteorite.

She'd managed to get back upstairs from the emergency department under her own power. Then she'd refused her pain med. Not out of displaced heroism but out of misery. If she was going to feel bad, she might as well make an evening of it.

She'd stood down in the ER for a good hour, laughing at the dismal jokes, asking about the patients, sucking in the exhaust fumes like her last cigarette, fighting off the panic.

She felt like a woman who woke one morning to realize she no longer loved her husband. Who wondered just how long it had been since she had loved him. She still saw everything that had attracted her to him, endeared him to her. But what had once been exciting now inspired nothing but weariness. Weariness and fear for a suddenly uncertain future.

What the hell was she supposed to do now? That passion had been all she'd had. It had been the only thing strong enough to offset the disillusionment, the frustration, the dismay of modern medicine.

Without it, what was worth fighting for?

She was a nurse, Kate thought, her chest burning, her head throbbing, her sea legs suddenly missing. There were thousands of different jobs for a nurse. She could do them all. She just had to find the right one, the one that made her feel as if she belonged.

"Oh my dear, don't you look well!"

Startled, Kate looked up. She hadn't heard anyone enter. When the light flipped on, she realized why. It was Mary Polyester, clipboard in hand, smile on face, comprehension noticeably absent. Kate was not in the mood for platitudes and vague comfort.

"Hi, Sister." Ungraciously, she didn't move.

The little nun seemed not to notice. She just bobbed her head and checked her list. Kate wondered offhandedly whether it showed if a patient had been naughty or nice. Maybe the answer to her own question was on that list somewhere.

"Is there anything I can get for you, dear? A rosary, perhaps? It says here you're Catholic."

"No thanks, Sister. The sisters who were up in the unit gave me one." She kept it under her pillow like a talisman. Not so much because she believed in its magic anymore as because she still held out hope that she was wrong.

Sister smiled and nodded. "Oh, yes. Yes. They

were here for a miracle, weren't they? Not here, though. The good Blessed Octavia will have to find her power somewhere else, I imagine."

Kate couldn't figure a better answer than "Yes, Sister."

The little woman kept nodding, her rheumy blue eyes directed to the darkened window, her free hand at her chest, as if keeping herself on the earthly plain by force. "A sweet child, Kate. A poor innocent. It shouldn't have happened."

For just a wild moment, Kate let herself wonder which shouldn't have happened. The illness? The prayers? The determination for a miracle? Or all of it taking place under the roof of St. Simon's? Once again, though, she reverted to training.

"Yes, Sister."

For some reason, that brought the little woman back to earth. She smiled, her tiny features exploding into a web of wrinkles beneath the white habit. "But you," she said with satisfaction. "You're doing fine, aren't you? Just fine. I knew you would. I knew it would make a difference."

"Yes. Thank you."

A nod, as brisk as a spring stroll. "And I think the baseball caps and earrings are quite charming. You tell them that, all right?"

Tell who?

"Oh, and here, I almost forgot." Reaching into her habit pocket, she pulled out a little clear plastic pouch and plopped it into Kate's hand. Inside, nestled like a sleeping snake, was one of those mass-market plastic brown rosaries that nuns the world over give good schoolchildren and worried patients. Kate figured it wouldn't hurt to double her mojo. She just shut up and accepted it.

"Thank you, Sister."

But Polyester had already turned to leave. Kate ended up shaking her head, which made her latest set of earrings, dangly red rhinestones, dance against her neck.

"Yes, Sister."

She closed her eyes and tipped her head back against the big chair. . . .

"Kate?"

The voice was hesitant. Even so, Kate heard an edge of incipient panic that brought her upright and her eyes open.

The evening nurse was perched halfway in the door, body poised for flight.

"What's wrong, Tracy?"

"Uh, I know this is . . . well, are you up to a little IV?"

"I have one, thanks." Kate was already reaching for her crutches. She recognized that tone of voice. She imagined the announcer on the *Titanic* had sounded just as timorous when he first mentioned the little problem they were having with the ice.

"It's Mr. Peabody in four-fifteen," Tracy apologized, already moving aside to let Kate by. "His IV came out and we can't get it restarted. I only have agency nurses on, the supervisor's busy, and ER just got in an accident and can't send anybody."

"And?"

Tracy took a deep breath, which upped the ante. "And he's been having chest pains."

They headed down the hall, where remnants of families migrated toward the elevators at the end of visiting hours.

"What's he here for?"

"Gallbladder. Fourth day post-op. He was doing fine. We're trying to get Weiss now."

Kate just grunted. Her buddy Weiss. No wonder Tracy was panicky. If Weiss was the resident on the case, God only knew what disaster was brewing—assuming that Weiss showed up in time to orchestrate it.

"Did you call EKG and X ray?"

Tracy looked positively aghast. "Without a doctor's order?"

They'd reached the door to room 415. Kate only had to take one look inside to hear the shark music in her head. There was no mistaking that particular color of pasty gray. Mr. Peabody didn't just need a new IV. He was getting ready for that big bus ride to the pearly gates, and there was no one on hand but Tracy and Kate and the agency nurse, who was already hovering at the bed to cancel his ticket.

"I'll tell you what," Kate suggested, her voice instinctively settling into that lilting, calming tone she used for very serious situations and mad animals. "I'll do the calling. Get me an eighteen Cathlon and try and find the medical resident. I think Lisa Beller's on, isn't she? And call the unit. You're gonna need a bed."

"But Kate," Tracy insisted, dead serious, "you can't do this."

Kate grinned. "What are they gonna do, shave my head and break my leg? Who's the primary?"

"Doctor Fleischer. We've been trying to find him all afternoon."

Kate fought a groan. The music amplified in her head. Oh, well, nothing she could do but jump in the water. Tracy couldn't take the initiative, especially with Fleischer. He'd flay a floor nurse alive for acting like an adult behind his back. And it was a cinch no rent-a-nurse was going to rock the boat. One of the few perks of the ER was that you could get away with some major shit if you just shucked and jived in the right order. The difference between living in a land where disaster was a surprise and where it was the rule.

It took out the option of floor work in the future, though. Kate could only survive so many broken legs.

"I'm not in any shape to do CPR," she told Tracy in that same tone, as she turned to head into the room. "Let's get going."

The other nurse, a handsome graduate named Paul Cantor, had his eye on the administrative suite. Right now he looked only fractionally more frantic than Mr. Peabody as he stood with one hand on the older man's wrist and the other clutching his stethoscope as if it were an umbilical cord. Kate wasn't at all sure who was having more trouble breathing. She didn't blame either of them in the least. All Mr. Peabody needed to do was tell her he was going to die to complete the picture, because that was exactly what he was trying to do.

"Vitals?" Kate asked, smiling down at the sweaty, panting little man.

"Eighty over forty," Paul answered, his voice a squeak. "Pulse one-ten and irregular."

Kate nodded. "Hi, Mr. Peabody. Hear you're not feeling well. Paul, get the cart."

"Who are you?" Mr. Peabody demanded as Kate carefully reached up to rip the oxygen cannula from the wall where it was always kept at the outlet.

"I'm a nurse," she acknowledged, seeing his attention on the earrings and the Malcolm X ball cap she'd been given by Parker down in the ER to go with the scrubs she'd adopted. "On light duty. Is the pain worse when you breathe in?"

"No . . . no, it's just . . . heavy. I don't . . ."

She didn't let him finish that thought. It would just head in directions she didn't want to take. Well, at least he wasn't throwing an embolism. Heart attacks she could manage, at least until the cavalry arrived. "Are you allergic to anything?"

The little man shook his head as Kate fitted the oxygen under his nose and dialed it up.

"Paul, get me some MS too," she said, as he headed out the door. If Kate was lucky, Tracy would find a medical resident quickly enough so they could give the morphine sulfate right away, or at least cover Kate's butt when she did it. It was the only thing that was going to help. Kate spent valuable seconds getting rid of the crutches and testing her balance without them. Then, retying the tourniquet Tracy had just loosened around Mr. Peabody's slick, pale arm, she began looking for a vein.

Kate heard Paul running down the hall as she palpated with one hand and phoned with the other. Overhead the intercom paged Dr. Weiss and Dr. Beller stat to four west. Kate bent to the IV, praying that Beller would beat Weiss in the door.

"EKG to room four-fifteen stat. Respiratory therapy to room four-fifteen stat," the intercom announced.

"That for me?" Mr. Peabody asked, his face tightening up.

Kate slapped at his forearm with impatient fingers, trying to bully a vein into existence for her use. "So we can get rid of that pain," she said. "That okay with you?"

"I'm dying, aren't I?"

Now he'd done it.

"And have me be the last thing you see?" she demanded with a grin even as Tracy slid back into the room with the new IV cannula and the crash cart. "I'd never be that cruel."

"What the fuck do you think you're doing?"

Kate would have recognized those dulcet tones anywhere. Weiss was definitely in full cry. Kate didn't bother to look up from Mr. Peabody's wrist. The IV was more important than Weiss's attitude, although something about it made Kate wish for some protection at her back. She did her best to pretend he was addressing Tracy, who had begun to shake like a wet poodle.

Weiss didn't buy it. "I asked you a question. You got bored, did you, and decided you'd be a hot dog on somebody else's division? Is that it, Manion?"

"Mr. Peabody has crushing substernal chest pain," Kate announced calmly. "It does not increase on inspiration. His rate is irregularly irregular and his pressure's eighty over forty. He's four days post-op. Wanna listen to his chest, Martin? Tracy asked me to try and restart the IV for them."

At least he couldn't argue that much. If Kate had been in Tracy's shoes, she would have done the same thing.

To Kate's left, Tracy was reaching over to try and get electrodes to stick to that slippery chest, and behind her the EKG tech clattered into the room.

"Did I order any of this?" Weiss demanded, not moving.

Kate did her best to focus on the hairy wrist, the feel of the catheter slipping through interstitial tissue, seeking out the elusive vessel and at least a semblance of stability. "Lisa Beller said to get started until she got here," she lied, praying Tracy wouldn't give her away. "I'm getting started."

"Well, stop. I'll reevaluate the patient. If that's all right with you, that is."

"Soon as I'm finished with this," she said, shutting her eyes, letting the feel guide her. Zen nursing. Feel the vein. Coax it close. Convince it to give itself up for the betterment of the patient.

The vein didn't give a shit about karma. It slithered away twice as Weiss chewed Tracy out for calling Kate instead of him. As he accused Kate of trying to sabotage his place on the staff. As he stood rooted behind Kate, his stethoscope swinging from his hands with a curious swishing sound, forgetting completely that he had a patient lying there listening to the diatribe.

"IV's in," Kate announced, her eyes popping open again. Thick, dark red swelled into the catheter. Snapping the tourniquet loose, Kate replaced the needle with the IV line. Tracy gave her a gentle nudge toward the monitor, which was showing multifocal PVCs, damn near on top of the T wave. The arrhythmia from hell. Better and better.

"Doctor Weiss, Doctor Fleischer's on the phone," Paul intoned from the door, his voice trembling a little.

Kate turned just in time to see the whites of Weiss's eyes. "You think I can just fuckin' fly up here? You think I can fuckin' guess what's wrong with a patient? I'll tell you what, I'll take his goddamn pulse and *you* talk to his goddamn doctor."

Oh, shit. They weren't just in trouble. They were in Trouble. Weiss was quivering like a dog on scent. His hands shook. His skin was as pasty as his patient's. His eyes were wide and glittery, never quite resting as he took in everybody in the room. This wasn't a typical Weiss tantrum. This was the stuff of nasty rumors. The resident's usually handsome features were curiously slack and stupid looking, even for the volume of his attack on the staff, and there was spittle in his beard.

"Well, what do you think?" he snarled at Kate. "Want my job? Want my fuckin' name tag? Might as well. You do just what you want. Just like with that little kid. Serves you goddamn right. You had no right . . . *no right*. . . ."

Kate thought fast. God knows, Tracy and Paul

weren't going to help. They were both staring at
Martin as if his head were spinning. And poor Mr.
Peabody was getting grayer by the minute.

"Martin," Kate suggested, trying her best to
ignore the part about Billy Rashad. "Since Doctor
Beller told me to go ahead and use ACLS protocol
till she got here, why don't you talk to Doctor
Fleischer? Tell him we're going to have to get Mr.
Peabody back upstairs. Okay?"

He darkened noticeably. "Okay? *Okay?* Is
there anything else I can do for you? Wipe your
ass, maybe?"

It was Kate's turn to feel frantic. She could
hear the soft beeps of the monitor, syncopated
and deadly. She could smell death like a sneaky
fart, just waiting to settle in over Mr. Peabody
while Martin Weiss ranted on about how everybody in the goddamn hospital was out to sabotage him and his career and his love life and his
dick that every man was jealous of.

God, Kate hoped Mr. Peabody wouldn't
remember any of this—if he lived.

"Tracy," she said evenly, giving her own
nudge. "Pull me out a hundred of lidocaine. Get
me a bag hung for a drip. And call Doctor Beller
at the top of your lungs. Okay?"

Tracy looked over at Weiss with eyes like a
cocker spaniel waiting to be kicked and nodded
her head.

The cavalry this time didn't have a bugle. It
had a perfectly pressed lab coat and devastating
blue eyes. "Am I missing the party?" Tim asked.

The collective sigh of relief should have

blown over the flowers on the windowsill. Weiss turned on Tim and started all over again.

"Can you find Beller for me?" Kate asked. "She's medical on."

Tim just nodded and guided Weiss back out the door as if it were regular rounds.

"Tim!" Kate called. "I'm—"

"Go right ahead."

"Jee-sus Christ." Tracy exhaled, her usually placid middle-aged features stricken.

"That boy," Mr. Peabody managed, his face pinched and small, "is one taco shy of a combination plate."

And then he went into cardiac arrest.

Kate didn't get to participate in this particular roundup. As the cart carrying Mr. Peabody trundled down the hall with the IVACs bumping the wall and the respiratory therapist trying to run backward as he bagged the still-unconscious man, Kate watched from where she was holding up the wall opposite the little man's room.

Lisa Beller had walked in just in time to do the honors. Kate thought that had been about an hour ago. She wasn't sure. She was so exhausted and sore she couldn't move, much less think. And she still had to get all the way down the hall to her own room, which was at least three doors away. Some mountains simply seemed too large to climb.

Still stuffing her Merck's back into her pocket, Lisa stopped on her way by to bestow a wry smile. "What, you get the bends if you can't participate in a disaster every few days?"

Kate managed a small grin in response. "Life should never be dull."

"You never said why Weiss was tied up."

"Tim just said he was busy."

Tim, at that minute, was rejoining the scene from the direction of the call rooms. Kate did her best not to drag him into it too soon.

Lisa nodded, the explanation sufficient for the tall, raw-boned young woman. "Well, I signed off on all the stuff you guys did. Good thing *you* were here, Kate. I never could have pacified Fleischer if one of those floor nurses had pulled that shit. Although he wasn't much happier to hear your name. What did you do to him, call him after hours or something?"

"Or something," Kate admitted. "Evidently."

Lisa sighed and rubbed weary eyes. "Okay, then, I'm off to visit the great white massa himself. He said he'd meet us in the unit. I'll let you know if we screwed up too bad. But don't worry. My best subject at Johns Hopkins was sucking up to my superiors."

Kate wished she had the energy to thank Lisa better. "At least the right resident showed up for the code," she said.

Lisa understood perfectly. Reaching over to tweak Kate's cap, she swung on down the hall, whistling some vague tune and waving to Tim so her lab coat flapped like a sail in high wind. If the rumors were true, Parker had great taste.

"I think there's some morphine left in there,"

Tim suggested diffidently as he reached Kate.

Kate turned to find him smiling. That made her even more depressed. It meant she had to move. It meant she had to deal with Weiss. It meant no matter how much she would have liked it, Tim would never take her to bed to make her feel better.

"Tim, do I have any hobbies?" she asked.

That brought him to a dead stop. "You mean, besides annoying senior surgical residents? I'd think that would take up most of your time. Especially since you do it so well."

"No, I mean it. Have you ever seen me cross-stitch or plant flowers or make Elvis pictures out of bottle caps?"

Tim joined her against the wall, hands in pockets, attitude easy. Kate could imagine the frown lines that had taken up residence between his eyes. "Is this one of those meaning-of-life questions?" he asked. "Because if it is, I still haven't come up with an answer myself."

Kate kept her attention on the room they'd just vacated. Equipment and sterile wrappings and yards of monitor strips littered the floor. On the wall, gaudy crayon drawings from grandchildren fluttered listlessly on a cork bulletin board. Flowers and Betadine, the images Kate would always carry of Mr. Peabody. Kate had the Betadine. She didn't have the flowers.

She shook her head, unable to explain her distress. She'd fought the good fight in there. Not with death; that was a fight she was mostly sanguine about. With Weiss. A bigger battle, a bigger victory, a bigger enemy. One she would have savored like a good meal only a few weeks ago. All she tasted this time was acid in her throat. And there was no way she could think of to explain it to Tim. So she lurched into motion and headed for her room.

"Where is Weiss?" she asked as Tim followed alongside.

"He's taking a nap."

Kate nodded. "I should report his ass."

"Right after he reports yours. He's not one of your biggest fans, you know."

"Well, thank God for that. I was afraid the feeling wasn't mutual. The word in the food line is that he's been putting more up his nose than Neo-Synephrine."

"He's under a lot of pressure."

Kate actually had to stop so she could laugh. "Goddamn you, Tim. Can't you be bitchy once in your life?"

His eyes sparkled with mischief. "And perpet-uate the stereotype? Never."

It wasn't until Kate was safely tucked in bed, her cap added to the collection that was growing from the orthopedic frame, that she worked up the nerve to ask the really important stuff.

"Was Weiss in the ER the night I transferred that little boy?"

Tim had been all set to head back out the door. Instead, he settled down on the edge of her bed, his forehead folded into a frown. Kate loved that frown.

"You're not still beating yourself up about that, are you?" he asked, taking hold of her hand.

"I just can't remember."

He rubbed at her hands with his thumbs. "It wasn't your fault."

"Weiss seemed to think so."

"Weiss is an asshole."

Kate grinned. "Well, finally. An honest opinion from Saint Timothy the Younger."

Tim actually blushed. "If you repeat it, I'll deny everything. You know how tough a time he has with anybody challenging his authority. Cut him a little slack for a while, Kate. Okay?"

Kate closed her eyes, wishing she could explain to Tim why it was so important to know whether she'd pushed for that baby's transfer out of altruism or obstinacy. It wasn't something Tim would understand, though. So she nodded and pretended to be mollified.

"Okay. Thanks for pulling my butt out of the fire tonight, Tim."

Only Kate and maybe Tim's brother could ever see the shadow beneath that gleaming, sweet smile. "My pleasure. But try and stay out of trouble till I'm back on again. Weiss'll come through, Kate, I promise. I'm working on him."

If anybody else had said that, Kate would have laughed. But Saint Timothy the Younger could, indeed, work miracles.

Nestled back on pillows that smelled like bacteriocidal disinfectant, Kate still felt as warm and comforted as she ever had. She kissed Tim good night, thinking that she was really a lucky girl. All she had to do was figure out what to do with her life. How to avoid the hospital's clutches and reawaken her joy in her job and last another thirty years or so until she could retire and decide just what to do with herself. Until then, though, she was looking forward to getting a little sleep.

Which was, of course, why she had the nightmare.

✦ Chapter 6 ✦

IT WAS AUTUMN. She knew because the leaves had fallen across the sidewalk, leaving the yard cluttered and dingy. There were clouds in the sky, a sheet of dirty gray that took all the light out of the world. Kate saw the yard, saw the bare trees, saw the house that always needed paint and fixing. She saw her hesitant approach as if watching from a third eye.

Quiet. The neighborhood usually ricocheted with the play of kids, the revving of teen engines, the arguments of middle-aged parents.

But this time there was a kind of sullen silence over the street. A pall, her teacher would have called it. All Kate knew was it made her heart beat faster. Louder. Louder than the scrape of her old saddle shoes across the concrete walk. Louder than the rasp of the screen door that seemed to shift in the wind, even though Kate couldn't hear the wind, couldn't see the trees moving.

Only Kate moved, even though she didn't want to, dressed in her green plaid uniform, the white blouse a little grimy, the sweater already a size too small, the shoes ugly and chafing.

The door was open, gaping like a missing tooth into the darkness. Into the living room. Into the place she always tried everything she could think of to avoid.

Open. Silent. And Kate was afraid.

The front steps were uneven, listing off the old wooden porch. A dog should have barked. Kate should have heard the TV on in the living room. She heard nothing. She didn't see anything but a shadow.

A shadow, moving.

She screamed.

And bolted upright in bed to have John McWilliams grab her.

"You better now, little girl?"

Kate was still shaking. It made her so mad. She hadn't had the nightmare in so long. At least a year, when she'd finally told Michael to take the big hike. Always the same dream, the same afternoon, the same slow walk up to the porch, the same frustrating end.

Nothing. No pictures, no sound, no answers why she would dream it and why she wouldn't dream all of it.

"I'm okay," she assured the frowning policeman, knowing she wasn't. "It's just a stress dream I get. It doesn't mean anything."

"Took five years off my young life when I hear you screamin' like dat."

It was morning. Kate could hear the rush-hour traffic outside, the rumble of breakfast carts down the hallway. She still felt tired and sore and shaky. Her heart rate didn't seem to want to climb back down from the stratosphere. And John was bringing her more trouble. She could see it in his nonchalant manner.

"Got a few minutes?" he asked, his soft brown eyes wary.

Kate just snorted. "I guess this means I'll have to cancel that bike trip I'd planned along the Katy Trail. What's up?"

"Thought we'd have a little coffee."

John shared certain inalienable rights with B.J. One was that he refused to socialize when he didn't have to. This was not small talk.

Kate grabbed the cap with the pink flamingo sticking out in front and plopped it on her head. "Good. That means we can blow this pop stand."

John's smile brightened carefully. "You gettin' tired of de accommodations?"

Kate was busy swinging her legs over the side. "My butt has a permanent dent from this damn bed."

"Jus' a second," he demurred, not moving.

The caution in his voice brought Kate to a halt. "Do I need to be Mirandized again?"

The second shrug said it all.

All she could see was the panic in little Mr. Peabody's eyes as he'd caught sight of a bald woman with hooker's earrings come to save him. "Damn. I was hoping we'd pulled it off."

"What?"

"Who's blaming me, Weiss? Fleischer, who

couldn't be bothered to answer the goddamn phone when his patient infarcted?"

"Girl," John retorted evenly, "what the hell you talkin' 'bout?"

Kate realized that at least her priorities hadn't eroded any. John hadn't come about Mr. Peabody, at all, which meant the relief Kate felt at knowing the little man was still okay was quickly tempered by new unease.

"I got into another . . . disagreement over policy yesterday," she explained. "I just figured no good deed would go unpunished."

"It wouldn't be 'bout somet'in' called an MAO inhibitor, would it?"

It was Kate's turn to look confused. "John, what the hell are *you* talking about?"

"Why I'm here, girl. Mrs. Warner. Don't tell me you forgot all 'bout dat poor ol' lady now, did you?"

Actually, she almost had. Cardiac arrests had a way of doing that to her, even if they weren't her own. "Of course not. But what does she have to do with MAO inhibitors?"

"You know what dey are?"

"Sure. Antidepressants. Testy little devils that require very strict dietary and medicinal restrictions. . . ." The light dawned. "Oh, shit. Oh, shit, John, of course. I should have remembered. They got her with the carbamazepine, didn't they?"

John was looking less pleased by the minute. "I gotta talk to B.J. 'bout sharin' information wid' you, don' I?"

Kate didn't pay any attention. "So she really

was murdered. I should have figured it out the minute B.J. mentioned the carbamazepine. Nobody with two working brain cells would give a patient on MAO inhibitors carbamazepine unless they were looking to reconstruct Mount Saint Helens. There are warnings about mixing those two in everything but *The New York Times*."

"What do you mean you should have figured it out?"

Her back protesting almost as much as her backside, Kate retrieved her crutches and the earrings with the big rhinestone palm trees to go with the pink flamingo on her head. "I didn't kill Mrs. Warner. Now can we walk around, John?"

"Only if you promise to 'splain 'bout dis figured-out stuff, and maybe 'bout why I should Mirandize you for somet'in' I didn' even know you did."

The floor nurse caught them coming around the corner.

"Where are you going?" she demanded over her half glasses.

Kate never slowed down. "Anywhere."

"You have PT at ten, Martinson wants another tidal volume on you, and the lawyer wants to see you again."

Kate was doing all right until that last part.

"The lawyer?" she countered, slowing to a halt right in front of the elevator banks.

The nurse, one of the vets who made floor work look easy, just smiled, charts clutched to ample middle-aged chest like schoolbooks. "I got the message from one of the Administration secretaries. He needs to see you this morning. Something about Mr. Peabody."

Kate's stomach plummeted. The chickens had come home to roost after all. "I'll go quietly, officer," she all but begged of John. "Just take me quickly."

John's gaze was measured. "You a bad girl again, huh?"

"She's always a bad girl," the nurse assured him brightly. "It's what makes her our hero."

Kate just snorted. "Never again. In fact, I'm thinking of going back for a degree in hospital administration and making everybody else's lives miserable for a change."

The elevators dinged, doors slid open, and a couple of lab techs stepped off, their hands full of equipment to draw blood. Before they had a chance to realize it was Kate they were after, she stepped on and punched the button for second sublevel: emergency, surgery, X ray, and all points between. Kate headed for it like a rabbit going to ground.

"Come on, John," she urged. "You're the one who wanted to talk."

John just made it on board before the doors closed.

The doors opened again to the cool echo of tiled hallway, the purposeful shuffle of feet, and the steady whine of wheels. The bracing aromas of disinfectant and fresh wax, real hospital smells, were barricaded behind doors decorated in diagnostic jargon. Kate didn't even wait for John as she turned for the back door to the ER.

Morning was usually a quiet time here: cleaning and stocking and organization, long breakfasts and in-service training sessions. Most people didn't really begin noticing their discomforts until they were up and moving around. Even with the notoriously short-staffed shifts at St. Simon's, day shift eased into the chaos. Evenings jumped in up to their armpits the minute they stepped through the automatic doors.

For some reason, this morning the night shift had never stopped. Debris littered the floors and laundry carts spilled over. Lights blinked, alarms buzzed, and radios stuttered and squawked. The nurses working the day shift, so used to being able to stoke their fires before needing them, sputtered about like bumper cars, their orders just a little harsher, their faces tight.

Within a minute of stepping in the back door, Kate spotted the signs of a multivehicle accident with injuries, two asthmatics, a croup, and a possible stroke. And that simply by the equipment she saw in the halls, the ancillary personnel popping unexpectedly from rooms, the sounds and smells and orders.

Just a week ago, she would have instinctively made for one of the rooms, if only to check what was going on, to be a part of it. This morning she turned purposefully for the lounge.

"What was it you remembered?" John asked as he preceded her.

But Kate was still distracted by what was going on out in the hallway.

"What do you mean, you don't have a bed?" Parker was asking, evidently on the phone.

"Where do you want me to put this little girl, the cafeteria?"

"No, ma'am," somebody else was saying farther down the hall. "We don't take reservations. That would be in violation of medical statute number seven-twenty-four B."

"Katie?" John nudged.

She looked up, startled and a little chagrined to find that for a minute there she'd gotten lost.

"Somebody killed dat poor woman," John said quietly. "I need some answers."

It took Kate a moment to shift gears, her cogs a little sticky. She wanted to be out in the lane. Instead, she walked on over and poured herself a cup of coffee.

"That poor woman was a tyrant," Kate retorted evenly. "She hassled staff and harassed patients. She had the heart of a stone and the sense of a chicken."

Folding his oversized frame into a chair, John observed her quietly. "And?"

Kate sighed and stood where she was, still too unsettled to sit. "And you won't hear a lot of wailing and gnashing of teeth. . . . She really was murdered?"

"She really was murdered."

Kate shook her head, sipped her coffee, and did her best to dredge up an emotion that didn't want to come. She should at least have pitied the woman. After all, she'd worked with her for almost four years. They'd crossed paths, shared auras. Once Mrs. Warner had even gotten Security for Kate when she'd locked her keys in her car.

It didn't seem to matter. All Kate could feel was the frustration that welled up every time she thought of the pencil pushers who seemed to confine her life lately.

Mrs. Warner had just been doing her job. She'd been making her numbers match. She'd conveniently forgotten that each number corresponded with a person. It had been up to people like Kate to deal with the consequences.

Edna Reabers scuttled by the lounge door trailing paperwork. She looked like a woman tired of treading water who'd just spotted a dorsal fin. Kate didn't want to work with Edna. She didn't need the additional hassle of handling an anal-retentive ex-supervisor with minimal trauma skills. But Kate felt for Edna. She hurt for this poor thin woman who was struggling so desperately to stay afloat without getting chewed alive. Who cared in her own way. Kate did not feel for Mrs. Warner.

"What do you want me to tell you, John?" Kate finally asked. "That she didn't have an enemy in the world? That only a monster would do something this horrible?"

"I want you to tell me who could do it."

Kate swung on him, her mouth open, her brain stalled. She couldn't even come up with a good *What?*

"What the hell are you doing standing up? Sit down. Better yet, lie down."

Desperately glad for the interruption, Kate turned to find a hairy oversized troll standing in the doorway in rumpled scrubs and OR cap.

Looking as if he'd be much more comfortable forging magic gold deep in a mountain than storming the halls of a hospital, Dr. Stan Begelman was nonetheless one of the best neurosurgeons in town, as testified to by Kate's condition.

"Hey there." She greeted him with a big grin that belied the turmoil John had just incited. "Been picking somebody's brain again?"

Begelman just shook his head as he walked in. "I should have hit that vocal shutoff switch while I was in there, shouldn't I?"

"Too late now. I'm not planning on giving you another chance."

Another sad shake, as if Kate were simply more than he could take. All the while his eyes were twinkling beneath the gray and black hedge he referred to as eyebrows. It would be so easy to get ugly in his business. A lot of neuro guys did, God complexes with no patience and less personality. After all, the best you usually got was damaged goods, even after all the hard work. But Begelman had defied the odds. Kate was glad she'd been lucky enough to get him.

"Sit down, damn it," he insisted. "You make me nervous. I keep seeing you toppling over on those damn things and ruining all my hard work." She made a face at him, but she sat. He nodded. "And, by the way, you still don't have full hand strength back on the left. Don't miss your PT."

"Yes, Mom."

This time she got a classic wave-off as he headed for the always-brewing coffeepot. He didn't even get the pot lifted when contestant number two checked in.

"Doctor Begelman. . . . Hey, Kate. Nice hat."

"Thanks, Jules. What are you doing on days?"

"Waiting to get a chance to go home from nights."

"You getting overtime?"

"Don't be silly. I'm finishing paperwork. That doesn't rate money, and you know it."

Kate shook her head, all too familiar with the tune and lyrics. "Tell 'em to get screwed."

Jules shook her head back. "Before or after my kid's surgery?"

There was nothing more to say and they both knew it, so Jules turned on her original target.

"Suzie Walsh has your lady in MRI, okay?"

Begelman did everything but spit out his coffee. "Suzie? That idiot? How the hell did she end up taking care of my patient?"

A fair enough question. An even better question would have been how Suzie had ended up with *anybody*'s patient. A sharp-tongued, brittle young brunette with a fondness for gold and nicotine and less sense than compassion, she had won the KEFNAR Award from the Pig Nurses two years running, KEFNAR being the acronym for Kept Employed For No Apparent Reason.

It would have at least made sense if she'd been one of Phyllis's cronies. They all had great job security, no matter how bad the staffing got. But Phyllis didn't seem any more enamored of this employee than anybody else.

"She obviously didn't run fast enough the

other way," Jules said. Suzie was also notorious for managing to be nowhere in sight when anything really serious or unpleasant came in.

Begelman sighed. "Well, there's not much harm she can do in MRI. I'll check on her in a second."

That taken care of, Jules turned to the really fun stuff. "So, Kate, I hear you have a command performance this morning."

"What did you do now?" Begelman asked instinctively. "I thought you'd managed to put yourself out of action."

"Not me," Kate admitted. "Don't forget, I'm the one who can get herself in trouble while paralyzed and on a ventilator."

"Remember?" he demanded with an outraged huff. "It took me two days to get your ICP down after that little stunt."

"How'd you hear already?" Kate asked her friend.

"You kiddin'?" Jules demanded. "You haven't heard Weiss ranting and raving down here?"

Kate sighed. "Fine. Another voice of paranoia heard from. I imagine his version is that I personally sucked the life out of his patient before he had the chance to pull me off him."

"We talking about the same Weiss? He's planning on storming the meeting and personally holding Fleischer from your lily-white throat, girl. According to him, if it hadn't been for you keeping your finger in the dike till he took over, there wouldn't have been a patient."

For a minute all Kate could do was sit there, staring like a landed fish. Maybe she should try some of that stuff Weiss was doing. It certainly seemed to improve reality. And God knew Kate's reality could stand some improvement.

"Are you telling me you didn't dramatically save a life yesterday?" Jules asked with a deadpan face.

Kate opened her mouth a little wider, poised for something to say. When she realized she really didn't have anything worth saying, she just closed it again.

Jules laughed. "That's what I thought."

"What's what you t'ought?" John asked.

It didn't bear repeating. Kate took the offensive with her eyes wide open. "Guess what, Jules? John here says that Mrs. Warner was murdered."

That brought the conversation to a neat halt. Kate knew she was being a jerk. She had no business pulling this kind of stuff. She kept her attention fully on Jules so she could ignore the strangled little noises John was making alongside her.

"Sneaky little bastard, too. Mixed her a cocktail of MAO inhibitors and carbamapezine."

If John had expected outrage or amazement, he must have been disappointed. All Jules did was wave off Kate's statement with much the same gesture Begelman was so fond of using.

"Well, shit, that just means it could be anybody on seven floors. Everybody knew she was on the stuff."

"Ever'body but ever'body we talked to," John countered softly.

Jules gave him a big grin. "Didn't talk to the right people, now, did you?"

"Dat why I'm talkin' to Katie here."

Jules just laughed. "Hell, she's not the right people either."

John remained suspiciously quiet until the room once again emptied. Kate waited, unsure how he'd react, unsure how she wanted him to. No matter what her reasons were, she knew better than to compromise a cop. Especially one who had taken such good care of the people in her ER over the years. With Little Dick it would have been a matter of pride. With John it was cowardice, pure and simple.

He made her wait as he calmly sipped his coffee dry. He was letting Kate sweat.

"So," he eventually said. "I guess dis means you don' wanna help us."

Kate closed her eyes and listened just a little more to the sounds of the ER. The voices of her friends, the people who did their best with what they had, who fought the good fight without a net. Who depended on each other to be there, to stand by them. To stave off the Mrs. Warners of the world.

Kate knew them. She respected them. She needed them.

"No," she said simply. "I don't want to help you."

Not because she was afraid to face a killer. Because she was afraid she'd know the face of the killer.

Which meant, she supposed, that it was only poetic justice that when she finally made it back to her room half an hour later she found the note on her pillow.

It wasn't much of a note, as notes went: plain white paper, folded in half with the kind of crease that would have won an award from the Anal Retention Society of America. Innocuous. Unremarkable. For some reason, just the sight of it gave Kate the shivers.

She didn't open it right away. Instead, she checked the room, from radiator to bathroom. She even took a quick look into the hallway. No one lurked beneath beds or crouched in showers. John had left Kate down in the ER when she'd demurred about having to at least comb her hair and change her cap before facing off yet again with the brass. She'd stumped back to her room all alone. She was still alone; her roommate, Mrs. Fitzwilliam, was off for one test or another.

Alone except for the paper on her pillow and a new case of the shakes.

She checked the room again, checked the hall, and spent a long few minutes in the bathroom just running hot water over her wrists the way she always did when she needed to settle down fast.

Finally, there was nothing left but to find out what it was. With Kate's luck, it was a threat from Fleischer to settle the matter of Mr. Peabody out in the parking lot at dawn. Maybe a request from the lawyer to submit to drug testing to secure her insurance.

It wasn't. She gingerly opened the paper to see meticulously cut-out letters from a magazine that formed a short, succinct note. It didn't surprise her. Maybe she'd known all along.

KATE. I DO WHAT I CAN. I KNOW IT ISN'T ENOUGH. UP THE REBELS.

"Shit oh shit oh shit," Kate muttered.

She stared at the note and knew she'd been dragged into something she wanted no part of. No part at all.

But then, she hadn't wanted any part of much of what she'd ended up doing in her life. Not really. She'd just wanted to get by, to get through. To survive. And now that she'd died, it looked like for the first time in her life she might not make it.

✦ Chapter 7 ✦

KATE KNEW BETTER. Even so, it was B.J.
she called first.

She heard the faint plaintive wail of the
vileann pipes the minute the secretary picked up
the phone over at the Medical Examiner's office.
"Where is he?" Kate asked.

The secretary, a crisp, knowledgeable mother
of four, just snorted. "The contamination room.
Like we can't hear him in there or somethin'. I'm
surprised those ol' bodies in the freezer don't just
get up and walk out."

"Aw, they're used to it by now. Sounds like
he's into 'The Galway Bay Reel,' Frenetta. Have
him call me when he gets through."

"Gets through? He been in there for two hours
already, girl. That racket don't stop, I'm just shutting the ventilation down in there till he passes
out from lack of oxygen."

"Two hours? What the hell happened?"

"Did a post on a suicide this morning.
Fourteen-year-old who blew his brains out."

Kate heard the faint notes accelerate as B.J.

119

worked his way through the complicated keying of the old reel. Faster and faster, as if he could scare off the restless souls of the saddest of his cases. The oldest of Irish tributes, music in a minor key, played at a breakneck pace as if it could chase away the sorrow.

If he'd already been at it for two hours, he'd be in a hell of a mood by the time he got out. Kate felt sorry for the rest of the staff over there.

"But he was on yesterday," Kate objected, as if that would make a difference.

"The boss is in Kentucky in court. He's covering for her."

See? She was right. No good deed went unpunished. Kate wished there was something she could do besides complicate his life even more.

"I need him to stop by, Frenetta. Would you mind stuffing a note under the door?"

"I would." There was a pause, a sigh. "He drove out to that boy's house himself to talk to the mama. You got any better news for him?"

Kate smiled in spite of herself. For his reputation, B.J. had a lot of women mothering him. With good cause, though. Few people carried their caseloads the way Dr. O'Brien did.

"No," she admitted. "I'm afraid I don't. But it's important."

B.J. was just swinging into "Cat in the Corn" when Kate hung up the phone. She filled up her free time by pulling a pair of disposable rubber gloves from her Nurseserver. She slipped them on, carefully picked up the note she'd received, and dropped it into one of the paper bags stocked in the Nurseserver so it would be safe until B.J. came to claim it. Then she got ready to go down and run the gauntlet all over again.

Kate probably would have been in a better frame of mind to meet the suits if she hadn't happened to see Dr. Fleischer himself in the elevator on the way down.

"I was hoping I'd run into you," he said, with all the heavy threat he could pack into his voice, as Kate stepped on board. It worked well enough that three nurses and a med tech got off on the next floor rather than ride all the way down with the two of them in the same elevator.

"I'm kinda easy to find," Kate couldn't help but counter, intrigued by the bare animosity in the older man's eyes.

At one time, it was intimated by those who knew, Fleischer had been a fairly good surgeon. Not great, mind you, but competent. Then three things had happened almost simultaneously. He'd divorced his first wife, discovered the lure of power and greed with the second one, and lost his only son in a drowning accident on the boy's fourth birthday. From that moment on, Fleischer had given himself up to politics and good living, leaving the messier side of medicine to those who still had a desire to look a grieving parent in the eyes.

Since Kate had been on duty the night his son had been brought in, she couldn't hate him. Since she'd been on more than one other night when he'd come in too drunk to accomplish any more than sexually harass the nurses, she couldn't really respect him either. Which was why when he glared at her like that she didn't really tremble. Knowing Fleischer, it was more than enough to get her on his shit list for the length of her career.

"I've spoken to Administration about you," he said, his faux Dr. Welby looks darkening considerably and his fingers tightening to a sickening white around the handle of the caduceus-decorated mug he kept polished to a gleam and drank from every day, as if reminding the peons just who he was.

"I know," Kate answered as agreeably as she could, when all she could think of was the fact that so far Fleischer had forgotten to put anything in his cup to drink. "That's where I'm going now. How's Mr. Peabody?"

"That's not the point! You do not now nor did you ever in your life hold a medical degree. Am I right?"

Nothing to do but take it. The door opened again to her left, but the crowd waiting for transportation to lunch dissipated when they saw who was already occupying the elevator.

"You are."

"Then the equation is simple. You, the nurse, carry out the doctor's orders. End of sentence."

"There wasn't a doctor there."

"There is never a doctor in the whole hospital?"

You weren't there, you asshole, she wanted to say. You're never there. She wondered again what it was she'd done to this man that could have stirred such heat. This wasn't usual stuff. It was more like a Weiss rage.

"I'm not going to apologize, if that's what you want. I probably won't do it again either, though, after Administration gets through with me."

The doors finally opened onto the carpets and Fleischer held them open in a kind of twisted show of chivalry. "You're damn right you won't. If I had my way you wouldn't be working here at all anymore."

Which meant she still had a job. She wondered why. She wished she felt more relieved.

And then Fleischer leaned very close to her so she could smell the malt he was trying to hide beneath all those breath mints and coffee. "What I really want to know is this," he said, and Kate thought she'd never seen such rage in one person's eyes in her life. "Are you screwing both Weiss and Peterson? Is that why they both defended you?"

Kate had been ready to get off the elevator. At his words she faltered to a halt, dumbfounded, silent, only the tiny bells in her earrings answering as she backed away from him.

His smile was not pretty. "Remember this, miss. A medical license is a hell of a lot more precious than easy pussy. And I hold their licenses."

After that, a session with Fellows and the lawyer was almost an anticlimax.

"All this just for me," Kate muttered, setting her crutches down on the plush carpet of the boardroom.

"All this just for you," Mr. Fellows answered with a deprecating smile from where he sat. He didn't seem to notice that Kate had some trouble negotiating her chair. It was just Fellows and the lawyer this time, with Sister Mary Polyester for choral backup and general support. "We're sorry to bring you back, Kate, but there's something new we have to talk about."

"I think I just had that conversation in the elevator with Doctor Fleischer," Kate admitted, hoping the admission would shorten things. It didn't.

The lawyer looked to Fellows, who looked to Kate.

"Ah, well, that. Yes, we need to discuss that. But we have another problem."

Kate refrained from giving her opinion on the point. She just held on to the arms of her chair, as before.

"Yes?" she answered noncommittally, forcing herself to look at Fellows.

"In fact, it was Sergeant McWilliams who suggested this in the first place."

The light dawned and Kate's stomach sank. "Oh."

"Oh?" Fellows echoed. "You've talked already?"

"Just a little. He wanted me to help in his investigation."

Expressions brightened all around the room. "Exactly," the lawyer concurred, leaning forward so that his paisley power tie rested against the table. "It would be most helpful to the hospital. And you have the time right now. . . ."

"And nothing to do," Kate prompted dryly.

"Kate, we've had a murder here," Fellows said, as if Kate weren't fully aware of the situation. "One of your own co-workers. We've pledged our complete cooperation."

"You mean you've pledged mine?"

Fellows shook his head. The lawyer ran a hand through a very expensive haircut. Kate couldn't help thinking that except for Fleischer's gray hair, the three men were physically interchangeable. Manicured good looks, feral eyes, and power suits. Faceless players in the big game of hospital politics. A trio from the old boy network at the Missouri Athletic Club who effectively ran and ruled the St. Louis community. It didn't noticeably increase her desire to help them out of their jam.

Then Fellows leaned forward, and his paisley tie rested right alongside the lawyer's, like a display at Brooks Brothers. "This can't go out of the room," he said, folding his hands over an unopened file of some kind.

Completely against her better judgment, Kate was intrigued. "What can't?"

This time Fellows sighed. "It seems . . . well, the police are having a difficult time eliciting help from the staff."

"Uh huh."

Fellows leaned forward again. "Kate, you know so many of the staff. They confide in you. All we're asking is that you help the police by sharing any . . . suspicious information you hear. Any—oh, I don't know—feelings you have one way or the other."

Kate stared at him. "Feelings."

"It would be perfectly confidential. To stop the killer, of course."

She'd actually been wavering just a little since getting that note. She'd been thinking of maybe just sitting down with John, just for a few minutes: talk about the hospital, share a few anecdotes. She'd been considering it.

She looked for something from these faces that might tell her she wouldn't be hurting her friends more than she'd be helping them. She couldn't see anything at all. And then the lawyer upped the ante.

"Do you know what publicity of this kind can do to the hospital?" he demanded, pulling his tie away from the table. "There are already television stations calling for information."

Kate sat very still. She waited for one of them to redeem himself. She waited for a reason to help. She waited until the two men twitched in their seats with discomfort.

"Kate," Mr. Fellows suggested gently, his attention on a folder he'd opened in front of him. "I know you don't need any coercion to do the right thing, but you might consider the fact that you broke any number of hospital regulations yesterday. If Doctor Fleischer exercised his right to fire you or revoke your license, you wouldn't even have the health insurance to cover your hospital stay. And to be perfectly frank, it would be much easier for us to get another nurse than for you to get another job."

Extortion now. The famous "You need us

more than we need you." The way the grapevine worked in this hospital, the two of them knew perfectly well that whatever savings Kate had amassed had been wiped out in securing her divorce. They didn't know a debt the size of Texas still hung over her head. A debt she was supposed to have made a big payment on ten days ago.

That did it. Kate saw red. She clutched the arms of her upholstered chair to keep herself in place. She reminded herself to breathe. There were some things that made Kate angry. Some that made her furious. One or two that shattered her control like a wineglass at the sound of a high C, and Mr. Fellows had just hit the winner dead center. He was manipulating her, and Kate wanted to hurt him.

Mr. Fellows tried to twist the knife in a little deeper. He painted the manipulation in guilt.

"I don't think you fully understand, Kate," he said quietly. "After we talk to you, we have to meet with the police again. They've asked the medical examiner to do more testing on the case on Frances Crawford. They think there's a good chance she was really murdered as well."

And B.J. hadn't bothered to tell her? When had they decided? Or did they suspect her in both cases after all?

"Mary Kathleen?"

It was the good sister, papery fingers wrapped around Kate's arm. Kate battled for control. She knew if she reacted now, she'd at least scare the hell out of the little nun. And look what kind of trouble it had gotten her into before.

"Don't call me that," she snapped instinctively. "Ever."

Polyester shrank a little, injured. Kate squeezed her eyes shut rather than deal with the hurt in the little nun's eyes. Kate didn't think twice about facing off with people who needed it, but she'd never been accused of beating up innocents before.

And here these people were punishing her for it. For trying to protect the victims.

Finally all Kate could think to do was run. "I really . . . don't feel well," she lied. "Could we talk later?"

Craven cowardice. She should tell them what they could do with their squeeze play. She should tell them what they could do with any one of their orifices. If she did, she'd be out of a job almost as fast as she'd be out of a bed. Her mother had always told her to pray the Hail Mary for patience. Kate spun through it six times without a pause and still couldn't see past the anger.

"That would be fine," Mr. Fellows acknowledged with an uncomfortable smile. "I'll just leave it to Sergeant McWilliams to follow up, all right?"

Kate couldn't manage much more than a nod. Then she saw Fellows and the lawyer exchange a meaningful look and realized the show wasn't completely over.

"Um, Kate, there is one other thing," Fellows admitted, already on his feet for a quick getaway. "Doctor Fleischer did have a legitimate complaint. You acted completely without doctor's orders yesterday. Mr. Gunn has decided that a verbal warning will be recorded on your file. All right?"

All right? No, not really. The rage flared again.
Kate wanted somebody to at least acknowledge
that she'd only done what she should have done.
But she knew better. So she closed her eyes and
quieted the firestorm in her chest and gathered
her crutches for the long walk back to her room.

Halfway down the hall, she saw Mr. Gunn
coming her way. Another suit, almost interchangeable with the crew she'd just left, but with a little
more self indulgence visible in his florid features.
Dark hair, dark eyes, a man who fondled his tie
when he spoke as if enjoying a little vicarious
transference. The kind of hospital CEO who'd had
a private dining room installed next to his office
so he never had to break bread with his staff.

Kate nodded as she passed. He never saw her,
which was interesting considering the fact that
there couldn't have been too many bald women
in scrubs, crutches, and Seattle Mariner caps roam-
ing Administration. Any other time, Kate might
have forced the issue. Instead, she just kept on
walking. She'd had enough for one day.

By the time Kate made it back upstairs, her
head was throbbing and the room was spinning.
She probably should have crawled into bed and
pulled the covers over her head, but she couldn't
seem to gather the energy to do even that.

She just dropped into the wheelchair that had
been scooted over by her bed and faced the blank
wall by her headboard and listened to the sounds
of the hospital as the evening shift took hold.

She expected B.J. to be the one to find her
there. He didn't. Jules did, flipping on the light

and catching Kate as she sat staring at a perfectly empty brown wall.

"I hate this fuckin' place," Kate said, not caring who it was who answered at this point.

Jules plopped herself down on the bed and pushed the controls to raise the head. "Figuratively, generally, or specifically?" she asked, as the bed whirred and the intercom announced interfaith services in the chapel.

"All three. If I had a half a brain, I'd just quit."

Jules plumped the pillows and stretched out on Kate's bed so she was facing the opposite wall where game shows ruled on the television. "You used to have half a brain," she said evenly. "I think the Bagel Man sold it to one of the South Side restaurants for sandwiches."

Kate lifted her hands in listless agreement. "I knew there was a reason I kept accepting those invitations to be a carpet tester."

A hospital term for visiting Administration, the only hallway with the good plush stuff. The wags said it was because it saved wear and tear on the knees.

Jules didn't move. "Again? Shit, girl, what'd they do, offer you a job?"

At least Kate could still laugh. "Oh, yeah. They want me to take over that hospitality position. You know, the one that teaches all the good little nurses how to be sensitive to their clients. Said I was a natural."

"I'll believe that about the time I believe Gunn takes the vow of poverty."

Kate grinned. "Or Weiss takes the vow of chastity."

"Or you take the vow of obedience."

"Up the rebels."

"Up the rebels."

For a minute the two of them simply rested where they were, Kate with an unblocked view of her oxygen and suction outlet, and Jules watching the tinny excitement as a construction worker from Peoria spun the wheel. Kate imagined people were jumping up and down on the screen.

"What did they want this time?"

Kate sighed. Her first instinct was to unload. Any other time, Jules would have been the first to hear of Kate's latest foray into the land of the plush rugs. Kate knew her friend would be good for a little commiseration, a little outrage on Kate's behalf. But then it sank in what they'd just said. What it could mean. What that little visit downstairs had really been about.

Up the rebels.

Kate looked over at her friend to find Jules transfixed by the action on television.

"Buy a vowel, you jerk," the big woman offered laconically, not even noticing how silent Kate was.

Kate opened her mouth and then closed it again. She wondered just what to say. She wondered, for the very first time, who really could have killed Mrs. Warner.

Jules had been the one to say it: Damn near any person on seven floors could have killed the supervisor. The word about those MAO inhibitors had been on the grapevine ever since Evelyn had bitched to the people in the cafeteria that she had a tough time eating there because the cheeses they insisted on using were strictly against her new diet regimen. The diet regimen that was enforced because of her medication. It hadn't been too tough to come up with the corresponding chemical group.

All somebody would have had to do was check the *Physician's Desk Reference* kept at each and every nursing station in the hospital to see what else Evelyn couldn't mix with her medicine. The list was long enough and the contraindicated medications unrestricted enough that anybody with a modicum of initiative could have gotten his or her hands on them and mixed the lethal cocktail.

It wasn't that Mrs. Warner was dead that finally upset Kate. It wasn't really that she had been murdered. It was that any of Kate's friends could have been the culprit.

Any of them.

Jules looked over finally, a small frown marring her high forehead. "Kate?"

What did she say? God, what did she say, knowing the note was hidden in her nightstand drawer waiting for B.J.? Knowing whoever had written it had given it to Kate as a gift. Knowing there were a limited number of people in this hospital who would give Kate a gift of any kind.

"They want me to help them catch whoever offed Mrs. Warner," she said, hating herself because she watched Jules for her reaction.

Jules didn't disappoint her. She did probably the most classic double take recorded west of Burbank.

"You?" she demanded. "Good God, why?"

"I don't know." Maybe because they think I know the murderer. Maybe to prevent me from protecting him. Or her. "I think they just want John to keep an eye on me."

Jules's grin was purely salacious. "He could keep an eye on me, that's for damn sure."

"And what about those eight kids he has?"

"I'd make each of them cute little moccasins with skunk fur. They'd be the hit of their class."

Kate turned her attention to the closed drawer in front of her. "Who do you think it was?" she asked.

Jules didn't even bother to lift her head from Kate's pillow. "You mean who might have been pissed enough at Warner to box and bag her? You want the list alphabetically or chronologically?"

Kate simply settled her aching head onto her hand. "Yeah," she admitted. "That was kind of my reaction."

"They really think it was one of us?"

Up the rebels. Kate's favorite term. One many of the crowd in ICU and ER had picked up. A message within a message.

"You got any better ideas?"

"What about her husband? Her mother, her sister, her brother? Didn't anybody have any insurance on her or anything? I heard the reason for the antidepressants was that her husband walked out on her. Maybe this was his way of getting a good divorce settlement."

Once again, Kate tested herself for reaction to Mrs. Warner's death. Nothing but a growing dis-

tress that she was going to know who the murderer
was. That she was going to like the murderer better
than the victim. "Unless her husband is a drug
salesman with samples falling out of his pockets, I
don't think he had opportunity."

Jules went back to Vanna White. "Good point.
Well, I feel sorry for John. He's gonna have to wade
through about eight hundred staff members if he
wants somebody with an itch against Warner."

"What about Attila?"

That got brand-new attention. "What about
Attila? *You* killed *her*."

"Maybe not."

"You mean we bribed Security for a copy of
those Polaroids for nothing? Three people on day
shift were going to erect a shrine to you."

For some reason, this was the moment Kate
first really became afraid.

"Knock it off, Jules. Attila didn't deserve that."

"Of course she did," Jules retorted briskly.
"You didn't see the way she bounced you around
when you were up there. She had all the compassion of a pit bull and half the brains."

"And that's a reason for murder?"

Jules didn't answer right away. The action
must have been intense on the television, because
the light flickered across her eyes like heat lightning. "All I know is that a lot of people out there
have been feeling vindicated in the last couple of
days. I've even heard the term Robin Hood
bandied about."

"Robin Hood stole money. He didn't commit
murder."

Jules shrugged, her eyes serious. "I'm not going to say I'm sorry. The preachers in my church have a great line in holy vengeance, and I think those two bats deserved a little."

It wasn't the time for B.J. to show up. He did anyway.

"Shout a little louder," he suggested dryly, strolling in with Chinese food. "The crowd in radiology probably missed that last part."

Jules wasn't in the least perturbed by the interruption. "Do you think I should feel guilty for not being upset that Warner's dead?" she demanded.

"Fuck guilt," B.J. said simply. He set the food down and pulled over another chair. His hair was down tonight, which meant he was off call. It made him look like a pirate, especially since he'd evidently decided not to shave. He was wearing old boots, older jeans, and a fairly new Grateful Dead T-shirt. Kate passed a moment considering the fact that as a psychologist he made a great steamroller.

"See?" Jules demanded of Kate with a wave in B.J.'s direction. "What'd I tell you? And this is a man who deals with murder and mayhem for a living."

"I hear from my sources that you have been approached to play Nancy Drew," B.J. said. "What did you tell them?"

Kate did her best to smile. "To fuck off."

"Really? That's not the way it sounded just now."

"So tell me," she said. "Should I feel guilty because I'd rather protect my friends than find a murderer?"

"You're not going to do it?"

She closed her eyes. She shook her head. "Nope."

She heard B.J. dig into the bag of food. Then he offered his best couch-side manner. "Fuck guilt." This time it wasn't enough.

"You can't mean to drink that shit with Chinese food," Jules objected.

Kate didn't even have to look to know what she was talking about.

"I drink it with everything but whiskey," B.J. answered equably.

Jules shook her head. "That's disgusting."

"It's an acquired taste. Like fine wine."

"Flat Doctor Pepper?"

He popped the screwtop on the plastic two-liter bottle. The hiss of escaping carbonation was conspicuously absent. "Shaking out the bubbles is a great stress reducer."

He'd gotten addicted to it in 'Nam. Flat, warm Dr Pepper, his taste of home, because nobody else in the world drank it, and that was the only way he could get it over there. He'd told Kate one night when he'd been three or four sheets to the wind. Since she understood the need for security perfectly well, she'd been the only one never really to harass him about it.

B.J. made the mistake of thinking he could dig into his Szechuan chicken without interference.

"Code blue, physicians' lounge, first floor. Code blue, physicians' lounge, first floor."

All three of them looked up at the ceiling at once, as if waiting for explanation.

"The doctors' lounge?" Kate demanded. "What the hell's going on?"

Codes happened in the ER, surgery, or the units. A code in the invitation-only world of the private doctors' lounge meant just one thing.

"Doctor O'Brien, please call extension one-four-four-five stat. Doctor O'Brien, call extension one-four-four-five stat, please."

"I'm off!" B.J. snapped, as if that would settle it. Even so, he reached around Kate and picked up the phone.

"That's the doctors' lounge number," Kate advised tersely, her palms suddenly sweating.

"I hope it's somebody worthwhile," Jules muttered, her attention finally pulled from the game show.

"John?" B.J. barked into the receiver. "You know damn well I'm not on. You already called the investigator. Just pretend you didn't see me in the hall." He was frowning. The frown deepened as he listened. Then he sighed. Kate could hear the dissonance of disaster even through the earpiece. "Oh, all right. I'll be down."

"What?" Jules demanded as he hung up. "What?"

But it was Kate whom B.J. faced with the news, his expression bemused. "You know a Doctor Fleischer?"

Kate did her best to breathe past the sudden anxiety. "Sure, we're old friends. Why?"

"He just had a cardiac arrest while talking to John McWilliams about a certain nurse who can't seem to get it into her head not to buck the system.

John figured, since I'd handled the other two staff deaths, I should probably just make it a hat trick."

Kate realized she had placed her hand on her chest, much as Sister Mary Polyester was so fond of doing. She didn't even think to ask why they'd been talking about her.

"He thinks somebody tried to murder Fleischer?"

"Wouldn't you?"

"I'd think his drinking finally caught up with him. . . . No, I'd guess I'd hope it had. Is he . . . ?"

B.J. shrugged. "Every chief of service in the hospital is down there working on him."

It was left to Jules to state the obvious. "Then he doesn't stand a chance in hell."

✦ Chapter 8 ✦

JULES WAS RIGHT. She and Kate followed B.J. downstairs in time to see Parker screaming that he was only going to take orders from one doctor at a time, he didn't care how many initials they had behind their names. Considering the fact that the heads of neurology, urology, psychiatry, and pediatrics were all trying to give orders as fast as the code team and chief of medicine, Parker had his work cut out for him.

Kate had witnessed a few disasters in her time. This was an out-and-out cluster fuck. She could see well-shined tassel loafers sprawled out next to the coffee table. The rest of the patient was camouflaged by one of the techs doing CPR, three nurses from ER trying to squeeze the red crash cart into a fifteen-by-fifteen room with all the milling degrees and half the administrative staff, who stood in a kind of desperate tableau, as if just the collective cost of their suits could somehow provide critical mass and get the heart started.

There was more shouting than in the bleachers at a Cardinals game, and certainly worse language.

At one side, Tim was valiantly trying to convince
the honchos to move the patient to ER for the rest
of the code. Across the room, the chief of urology
was screaming for a catheter, and Parker was
ignoring him as he rifled through the crash cart for
drugs. The only one seeming not to get much
attention, except from the poor tech who was by
now perspiring onto his patient, was the body
attached to the loafers.

John McWilliams met them in the doorway,
looking more irritated than upset. "You believe
dis, doc?"

B.J. didn't bother to go in and add his two
cents' worth to the rest of the useless advice that
ricocheted around the carpet-and-leather-decorated
room. Instead, he took out a cigarette and put it in
his mouth without lighting it.

"What happened?"

"We was discussin' a question 'bout a certain
employee, who should *not* be here to complicate
t'ings, Kate Manion."

Kate didn't bother to take her eyes off the
action, using a crutch to hold her place against
two guys from housekeeping who were trying to
get a peek. "Nice to see you too, John."

Gunn had just showed up. Trailed by several
of his nervous minions, he parted the crowd
before the door like Moses hitting the edge of the
Red Sea, his sole reaction to the disaster an impatient frown.

"This had damn well better be an accident,"
he warned blackly, as if it would make a difference. "I already have three reporters in my office

about the last one. . . . Does that nurse have on
knee socks?"

"And what?" B.J. prodded John, not even
noticing as the retinue swept past.

"Dis Fleischer, he offer me a cup of coffee in
here. Says he has to meet somebody else here
anyway, and he hasn't had a chance to fill his
own mug yet today. So we're talkin' 'bout five
minutes, an' he suddenly starts wheezin'. Pulls at
his tie. Gets all bug-eyed and goes down twitchin'
like a landed carp, you know what I mean. Den
ever'body in the room yells, "'Oh, shit—'"

Kate nodded. "That's medicalese for 'I think
he's in trouble. Somebody call a code.'"

B.J. was still watching. "Nothing suspicious?"

"He scowled at his coffee, like it was too strong."

"You have any?"

"Yeah. Was fine." John held up the paper bag
he'd been carrying. "I got his mug stashed before
all dese nice people show up."

"Suspicious little puppy, aren't you?" Jules
asked, without looking away from where the
chiefs of cardiology and medicine were arguing
over recommended doses of steroids.

John's smile would have made Kate nervous if
she didn't know he hated the sight of dead animals.
"It's why I be de best, little girl."

"Wheezing," B.J. mused.

"Anaphylactic reaction?" Kate asked.

"Anybody know if he was allergic to anything?" B.J. asked.

"Sure. Everything. He ended up in the ER after
dosing himself for the clap once."

B.J. seemed to slump. "Great. Just great."

Kate shook her head in wonder. "If this is our killer again, it's definitely an inside job. And he's better than we thought."

Everybody turned to her on that one. Kate turned to Jules.

"If you wanted to make sure a doctor died, where would you have him drop over?"

Jules's grin was damn near malicious. "Doctors' lounge. He'd be dead before they could agree who goes first."

Which was precisely what happened to Dr. Fleischer. By the time they had a clear-cut chain of command, he was in irreversible shock. It took them another full hour to pronounce Fleischer dead, simply because every physician in the room saw himself or herself lying there. By that time, Kate was long since back up in her room considering the vagaries of fate and justice.

"What do you think?" she asked in a very small voice, some ninety minutes later.

B.J. didn't bother to look up from the paper that swung gently from the forceps he'd swiped. He shook his head.

"Aren't you a lucky girl? Seems like everybody has something to say to you."

Kate rubbed a hand over her face. She'd waited for the dust to settle downstairs before paging B.J. back upstairs to where his dinner still waited for him. In point of fact, she'd half hoped she'd waited long enough for John to have decamped along with the medical examiner's van. One step at a time. One fight at a time.

She'd spent the last two hours trying her best to envision any of the people she knew as a cold-blooded killer, somebody careful and quiet and determined. She couldn't. The people she knew who could be frustrated enough even to consider something this drastic all had good hearts. They simply weren't the kind of people to destroy.

But then she'd looked at it from the other side. Which of the people she knew could have been driven to something like this? Who could be so angry, so burned out, so disillusioned that he or she would think the only way to change the status quo would be with poison?

When she did that, she realized almost any of them qualified, herself included.

She was certainly no stranger to the cold rage that bubbled so close to the surface most days it only needed one very small catalyst to simply explode. She'd certainly plotted her share of revenge against the interchangeable herd of MBAs who seemed to have collectively ruined the practice of modern medicine. She knew, even though she would never tell John, that she'd probably made the same threats on the night when that little boy had lain dying in her ER—and had meant every word.

She wanted to hide the note, to protect a person she might know too well. She did the next best thing. She made sure it was B.J. who saw it first.

He was the one sitting in the wheelchair now,

his feet propped on the end table, his Szechuan chicken in his lap, the evidence dangling dangerously close to the hot sauce.

"Tell me it's nothing," Kate begged.

"It's nothing," he lied obligingly. "You didn't tell John about it yet, did you?"

Kate concentrated a moment on the Pig Nurses cap she held in her hand. "No. I wanted to talk to you first. And then Fleischer got nailed."

B.J. actually looked over. "I do bodies, Kate, not this shit. What did you think I was going to say to you?"

"That it was a sick joke or something, I guess. That it isn't somebody I know doing this."

He went back to chewing and studying. "Not this time. The 'up the rebels' part is a dead giveaway."

Kate shut her eyes. "That's what I was afraid of."

She thought of the pandemonium at McGurk's, glasses lifted, eyes bleary, voices raspy and off-key. She was furious that one of them might have betrayed them all by turning their personal battle cry against them.

"Any ideas?"

She shook her head. "Not one. I don't suppose somebody could think I was the one really doing this and just want to comment, could they?"

"Possible. According to John, the only real message he's gotten so far from this is that no matter who's suspected there will be plenty of help making bail."

"You didn't tell me you were reopening

Attila's file. Do you really think there could be some relationship?"

B.J. went about dropping the note back into the bag and gingerly setting it on the nightstand. "Maybe not. Wouldn't we look stupid if there was and we missed it, though? Especially now that we have a third suspicious death at the hospital to investigate." He went back to his dinner, as if his next question weren't that important. "Why won't you help the investigation?"

"Because I don't have a mother I can go home to who'll make me feel better," she said quietly. "I only have you guys."

B.J. considered her as he pulled out a cigarette and rolled it around between thumb and index finger. "And what if one of us is a murderer?" he asked.

She couldn't help it. Faces flashed in her mind. Jules and Tim. Sticks and Parker and Edna. Suzie. Hetty. Weiss and Beller and a hundred others. People she thought she knew, people she liked or didn't like, trusted or resented or respected. People she'd come to need in her own way, kept carefully at arm's length with humor and challenge so they couldn't be disappointed and turn her away. Friends where she needed family and had none. She simply could not allow one of them to be a criminal.

"I'm not sure I care."

He just nodded. "I think for your own sake you should probably think about it, but if you can't, you can't."

"Why?" she asked immediately. "Why for my sake?"

Little flakes of tobacco drifted down to B.J.'s lap as he gave up molding the cigarette and slid it over his ear. "Because whether you like it or not, your name is still at the top of the file for both Attila and Warner. Because you were seen altercating with Fleischer, whose dying words happened to be a hope that he could yank your license. It just might not hurt for you to keep abreast of things."

She couldn't tell the truth, even to B.J. No one but Kate Manion knew how tenuous her foothold was on the future right now. No one would understand why. She was so afraid of so many things. Of losing the drive to do her job. Of losing the only place she considered home because of it. Of losing the friends she relied on by betraying them. Of being coerced against her will toward any decision, good or bad.

"No."

"Then no it is."

Kate knew that wasn't the end of it. B.J. knew it too. He turned his full concentration on his dinner. "Aren't you due to pay obeisance to the wicked witch about now?"

"I should have been there last week." The loan was due, a five-thousand-dollar payment on freedom meted out to her paternal aunt, whom, if Kate had her way, she'd only see at gunpoint.

"What did she say when you told her why you weren't there?"

"I haven't told her. I never talk to her if I don't have to."

"She hasn't called my mother. Has she called you at Tim's?"

"She doesn't know about Tim." She knew as much about Kate's current life as Kate's current friends knew about her aunt: nothing. Only B.J. knew, from a time when Kate had briefly stayed with his mother. Kate's marriage had been breaking up and B.J. had still been in Philadelphia. His mother, a sweet, intense air force pilot's widow, had needed company, and Kate was delighted to provide it. In return, Sarah O'Brien had somehow found out about Kate's aunt. The aunt Kate never saw, except to make payments on the loan. The aunt who had finished raising Kate after her mother died, who during those long and barren years had cemented Kate's self-image.

"Need a ride?" B.J. asked.

Kate sighed. She hated the idea of taking advantage of him like this. She hated depending on someone else.

"I guess the Bagel Man won't let me near my Mustang for a while, huh?"

"I think they already had Tim hide the distributor cap."

It was a joke. Even so, Kate's temper flared without warning. How dare they? It was her car, her freedom, waiting any time she needed it. Her escape.

This time Kate recognized her shortening fuse. She did her best to hide the flash of rage and fear beneath a methodical pressing of the ball-cap bill between her hands. Careful. Controlled. It seemed suddenly as if it was getting more difficult to regain equilibrium.

"Kate?"

"They say the emotions can be labile after a head injury," she said, with a deprecating wave of her hand. "I found there for a minute I wanted to rip out your lungs."

"Feeling a little cornered?"

She laughed. "Feeling treed like a possum with two legs chewed off."

"You're getting out tomorrow. Won't that help?"

She concentrated on her hat again, on the white edge to her knuckles as she thought of what it was going to be like once she had nothing but the four walls of Tim's apartment to look at, no one but herself to listen to. Help? It was the worst fate she could think of.

"Kate?" His voice was soft, a friendly nudge. Kate wondered if even B.J., who never allowed another living soul into his house, would understand. She looked up to realize that he at least empathized.

"Tell me again," she said. "Tell me it was worth coming back."

For a minute B.J. didn't answer. He just sat there, as still as Kate had ever seen him, his eyes shadowed and distant. "Sometimes," he finally said, never once pulling his gaze away, "the only thing that got me through was that flash when I was dead and it all made sense. Sometimes I think if I hadn't had that I wouldn't have stuck around for the rest."

He had never once referred to the rest, no matter that everyone who'd ever come into contact with him had known there had to have been a hell of a lot of it. Kate held her breath against what he was exposing.

He shrugged, as if his pain was no worse than anyone else's. "At seventeen, most boys are getting laid and getting drunk, not necessarily in that order. I was stuck out in the bush for seven months with a squad of marines, almost without relief. I saw what people were capable of doing to each other. I participated. It's not something that digests well, no matter how old you are. It's especially tough when you're seventeen and you're stupid enough to think you can handle anything anybody throws at you."

Or you insist on being idealistic enough to think that whatever you do can change it, Kate thought. No wonder she and B.J. had kept managing to find each other over the years. She saw her own history in his eyes, only hers had happened before her fifteenth birthday.

"What about this 'fuck guilt' attitude?" It was almost a demand.

B.J.'s smile was dark as he reclaimed the cigarette over his ear and set to mangling it again. "I don't feel guilty about it. That doesn't mean I can forget it."

Kate would gladly settle for that much. "It's time to call John, isn't it?"

B.J. stuck the unlit cigarette in his mouth and chewed. "It's time to call John."

By the time B.J. did track down John, it was from the phone at the medical examiner's office.

He wouldn't have admitted it to Kate, but he ended up heading back to work in the hope he could find something from any of the murders that would absolve her of the need to get involved. Besides, B.J. wasn't much more enamored of going home than Kate was.

"You got what?" the big cop demanded on the other end of the line.

"A note from the killer. Aren't you proud of me?"

"I suppose he jus' walked up and handed it to you, eh, man?"

"Nope. He walked up and slipped it onto Kate's bed while she was talking to you."

John hated surprises. "She had all day to tell me."

"She wanted to tell me first."

"Okay, so she had all day to tell *you*."

"I was tied up with a kid who decided today'd be a good day to ventilate the back of his head. Then I got busy with you, remember?"

Another pause, as John got over his pique and got down to business. "You gonna do de doctor too?"

B.J. rubbed at a set of very grainy eyes. "Yeah. I figured since I had the other two, I might as well. I've made the calls."

"You be aroun' tomorrow when I talk to Kate?"

"Why?"

"To hol' her hand, seem to me."

"I can't think of anybody who needs to have her hand held less than Kate Manion."

"Might change your mind after you hear de news."

"What's that supposed to mean?"

"Means I been asked if Kate Manion is my main suspect."

B.J. sat up straight for the first time in ten hours. "What? Who'd think that?"

"Little Dick, but you knew dat. Also somebody named Inside Source at de hospital, who t'ink de news media be just dyin' to know. How you like dat now?"

B.J. thought of the deceptively tough young woman he'd left an hour or so before. He thought of how brittle those blue eyes were getting beneath all those baseball caps, and he cursed.

"Now you wanna be dere?" John asked.

"What about you, John? You think she's responsible?"

Just the fact that John had to think about it boded badly for Kate. For the first time B.J. questioned his own objectivity, because he wanted to argue with the cop before he'd even answered.

"Dat ol' Doc Fleischer, he had a theory," John informed him. "Wanna hear it?" He didn't wait for an answer. "He decided when Katie kill dat first poor girl, she give herself a great idea how to minimize her problems. After all, who'd suspect a poor sick girl wid no hair?"

B.J. waited. He looked at the poster of Slea Head he'd hung on the wall right next to the gray pinstriped suit he kept for public appearances. Wind and surf, saturated greens and silence. For centuries madmen and monks had inhabited the lonely cliffs at the edge of Ireland. B.J. had spent a month there once, just cleansing himself of humanity, the Irish version of a sweat lodge. Suddenly he wanted to be back there with a fierceness that astonished him.

Because John was right. Who'd suspect a poor nurse who'd just survived the trauma of her life and awakened to find out that on top of being killed she'd been screwed. Who'd suspect her, except everybody in the metropolitan area, once that news report hit the air?

"You maybe want to be dere, if you're Katie's frien'," John suggested. "I got to tell her we gonna investigate her too. And de way Little Dick wanna do it, we gonna scrape up ever' cockroach ever walked across dat little girl's path."

Kate wouldn't have seen it if she hadn't had the nightmare again. Same day, same place, same ending, waking her with the sweats and the shakes. Maybe it had been the news that precipitated it. Maybe she'd heard the beginning of the story even in her sleep. She woke at the end of the piece to see the investigative reporter for KSTL standing in Serious Money's driveway with the emergency sign visible over his left shoulder.

" . . . Officials of the hospital refuse to comment on the allegations of an angel of death stalking the halls of this hospital. One inside source told us, however, that police are centering their investigation on a nurse named Mary Kathleen Manion, who might have made threats to at least one of the victims. . . ."

For the first time in almost a week, Kate asked

for something more than a Tylenol to help settle her down. When the night nurse arrived, though, instead of just Halcion, she slipped Kate a ten-dollar bill.

"Here," she said with a big smile, as if she were placing a sure bet on the derby. "The first contribution to your defense fund."

Kate refused the money. She refused the Halcion. It wouldn't have made any difference anyway. She was never going to get to sleep when she couldn't even breathe. Two hours later her roommate called to complain about the crazy woman who was just standing in the bathroom running water over her hands and cursing.

◆ *Chapter 9* ◆

KATE WAS IN such a bad mood by the time Tim picked her up the next morning she barely spoke to him. She was so preoccupied by the bedpan full of crumpled bills and checks she carried out in her lap that she didn't think to wonder why she was being dismissed via the morgue door rather than any of the more traditional exits.

She did wonder what was going on when, rather than simply pull around the campus to staff housing, Tim drove them out of the grounds altogether. She began to smell a rat when they pulled into a Denny's and exchanged cars for an Oldsmobile station wagon before heading back. She should have realized it belonged to John.

"You'd better not be driving my Mustang around while I've been stuck in that tank of yours," she warned him as Tim held the front door of the apartment open for her so she could stump through.

John unfolded himself from the white leather couch and smiled a careful greeting. "Only long enough to lose de cameras, little girl. How you feelin'?"

"Like warmed-over spit," she admitted, then scowled. "Cameras?"

"All de news crews, dey been waitin' at your hospital to talk to you. We figured you didn' feel like talkin' to dem. Okay?"

She didn't know whether to be grateful or wary. But then, she'd been through so many different emotions that morning already, she wasn't sure she had the energy left for either.

"Thank you," she said, almost grudgingly. "That was thoughtful."

Tim carried her bags back into the bedroom as Carver, Tim's seal-point Siamese, stalked up to sniff at Kate's cast. Kate spent a moment right where she was so the cat could get reacquainted. So Kate could get acclimated.

"Ahhh, home," she said sighing, surprised by the sense of relief at being here. She took a long, lazy breath and came away without so much as a whiff of antiseptic. The living room was clean and crisp and quiet. Shaking her head so her earrings tinkled, Kate stumped on in. "That hospital is a mess, ya know. After my brief sojourn there, I can almost understand why Edna is so anal retentive."

The apartment consisted of the basic square of rooms: living, kitchen-dinette, two bedrooms, less comfortable or notable than functional for a building that had to contain six units and accommodate any variation of family groupings that might come with the house staff.

Tim's apartment was spare, his decorating running toward minimalism just the way Kate liked it, in whites, grays, and blacks, with touches of primary colors in the prints that hung on the walls. He reserved his whimsy for his bedroom, which was thick with hanging plants, and his prejudice for the stereo, which bled Mozart from thousand-dollar speakers.

It wasn't that Tim couldn't afford to live off campus. Most of his prints were signed, and his wine rack held only the best. But for Tim, living on campus was the equivalent of committing to a monastery. The more he could confine his lifestyle here, the less chance he had toward indiscretion. On paper, homosexuality was no crime. In this corner of the world, the people who controlled his residency were far less enlightened, so while Tim depended on the hospital for his training, he abstained, at least while he was on the grounds. And the more he was on the grounds, the more he abstained.

For Kate, this place had become her refuge, and she hadn't really realized it until coming back.

"You been collectin' souvenirs again, little girl?" John asked diffidently.

Kate didn't bother to answer until she'd eased herself down onto the tulip chair by the window, laid down the crutches, and pulled off her newest cap, a lovely chartreuse number with RN across the front in purple, which Tracy had given her after the code on Mr. Peabody.

"Souvenirs?" she echoed. "What happened, somebody call you and tell you I stole the towels?"

John just shook his head and pointed at the bedpan.

"Oh, that." Kate's tone wasn't nearly as light as

she'd intended. "I decided to defray the bills by dancing nude on the countertops last night. That okay with you?"

She'd almost managed to get comfortable. She'd almost managed to delude herself that all she had to worry about was John. Then the doorbell rang and she felt her stomach slide right down to her knees.

"Oh, good." John headed for the door. "Ever'body made it okay."

Kate had just gotten her leg up onto the ottoman. "Everybody?" she demanded.

Tim reached the living room as John opened the door to reveal the next set of players: Little Dick; Tim's brother Steve, the lawyer, who was manfully ignoring the impolite grunts coming from the much shorter and homelier police detective; and a woman who looked like Pussy Galore in a business suit.

"Nobody's asked any questions, have they?" Steve demanded, bearing right in with his briefcase in hand. As near a carbon copy of his brother as was allowed without monozygomatic advantage, Steve was older, less buttoned-down, and avowedly heterosexual, with a wife and three kids on his tally. He belonged, however, to the Gucci-and-BMW School of consumerism. Considering what he was protecting her from over at the hospital, Kate forgave him.

"We've barely said hello," Tim retorted.

Steve grinned. "Hello, Kate."

Kate did her best to smile past that damn panic. It was her cornered animal mode, so old she could actually smell Johnson's No More Tears shampoo when it hit.

"Kate." John spoke before Little Dick had the chance to finish scowling at the decor of Tim's apartment. "Like you to meet de newes' kid on de block."

The vision stepped in, as brisk as her suit, hand outstretched, every male eye on her as she offered a well-worn smile.

"Mary Cherry," she said. "No cracks about the name, please. There isn't one I haven't heard. I'm from the FBI." An ID materialized in the other hand, as if she were used to having to prove her claim.

Kate actually had her hand out for a hand-shake. She damn near pulled it right back in. "Jesus," she breathed, almost oblivious of the cal-luses on the elegant hand she briefly held. "Most people get flowers when they get home from the hospital. I get two homicide detectives, a lawyer, and an FBI agent."

"And your good frien' B.J.," John added evenly. "Right after he be finished wid de good Doctor Fleischer."

Everybody settled in on the furniture without so much as a by-your-leave from Kate. It was all she could do to stay in the room, much less on her chair.

"I don't suppose you all came over to inquire after my health," she challenged. Carver, ever per-ceptive to nuance, climbed right into her lap to keep her pinned in place.

"Did you inquire after Doctor Fleischer's health yesterday, Kate?" Little Dick demanded.

"That's a question," Steve interjected. "I haven't heard any rights here."

"I haven't heard why anybody's here," Kate snapped, and was encouraged to see everyone turn to her in some surprise. Without a word, Tim appeared with a full cup of coffee for her. Then, as if he had truly been her fiancé instead of just her friend, he settled himself onto the arm of her chair and slid a supporting arm around her shoulder.

"John wanted to be able to talk someplace you'd be comfortable," he explained, the apology all in his eyes. "Someplace away from the station. You knew he'd want to talk to you."

Kate spent a minute silently admonishing her friend. "You know about the note?"

"He had to convince me I'd want to help."

Kate cradled the mug of coffee in her hands and settled her head back against Tim's arm. John she could be mad at. Administration, all of them. Even the staff who had filtered into her room throughout the night alone or in untidy clumps to add to the defense fund in the bedpan, their offering carrying an implicit demand. But how the hell could she be mad at Tim? He just wanted to help, as always.

She took a good slug of coffee and almost choked on the brandy he'd added. That, finally, brought a half smile to her face.

"Okay," she said. "Mary, you're the mystery guest. Why don't you sign in and tell us who you are?"

Mary of the exotic eyes and drop-dead figure, beneath all that gray serge, was the behavioral sciences liaison for the St. Louis office of the FBI. In a nutshell, Mary studied up on serial killers. If there was a possible problem within the jurisdiction, she had the training and access to Quantico to expedite information and the talent to command the respect of her peers. John's boss had called her in when they'd gotten the call on Dr. Fleischer.

"You score a point for bein' right, by de way, little girl," John offered Kate by way of explanation. "Results are in. De good doctor had enough penicillin in his coffee to cure de whole county of plague. We foun' it in the nondairy creamer in de doctor's lounge, jus' like you said."

"Pretty good instincts, ya ask me," Little Dick ventured, his eyes never making it higher than Mary's shapely calves. If Kate had been feeling a little more frisky, she might have despaired. Nothing to make a girl feel more feminine than facing off with Miss November when the only thing on your head is a ball cap and your best coloring comes from old bruising. Fortunately for Ms. Cherry, Kate had other things on her mind.

"Why are we talking serial killers?" she asked, absently scratching Carver's dark ears as he kneaded his front paws against her knee. "Isn't that more your slash-and-stash situation?"

Mary actually grinned, which made her look human. And damn if Kate didn't like her. "The papers have called it right. Angel of Death. We get a fair number of those, medical people looking for power, notoriety, heroism. The Munchausen by Proxy variation."

Kate nodded. "Inject a patient with potassium so you can be the first one on the scene to answer the code. I worked with somebody like that once."

Little Dick snapped right to attention. "You never told us that."

Kate smiled benignly, the brandy at least warming her stomach if not her hands. "You never asked."

"Questions again," Steve warned, leaning forward. "Quit dickin' around and decide what we're doing here."

"We're askin' Kate some questions 'bout dat note," John assured him. "Mary wanted to sit in since she's now on de case. Dat okay?"

"Do you want to answer, Kate?"

Kate's laugh was not polite by any means. To Mary's credit, she smiled again.

"I want to take a nap and eat a real steak dinner, John. I want to go back to work like this had never happened. I want to find out who gave my name to that asshole at KSTL so I can personally return the favor to both of them." She wanted to go back in time so she could still save that baby and avoid everything that had happened since, but she didn't tell them that. "I'd be happy to answer any questions John has."

"Will you help us wid de hospital staff?" he asked, all levity missing from those wonderful eyes.

Kate never flinched. "I thought I was the prime suspect."

His smile flashed, big enough to expose a

gold tooth way at the back, so he looked like a pirate. "You are. But don' you t'ink it would be great fun if we snuck in like little fishes and nabbed de real killer while ever'body t'ink we mad at you?"

"No," she said. "I don't."

"Why not?" Dickie demanded.

"Because what you want from me is rumor and innuendo. And I won't have another person have her name splashed on the news like mine, just because I heard she didn't like Fleischer. Shit, if I did, half the women in Saint Louis County would be suspects."

"Women," Mary echoed quietly. "Why do you assume it's a woman?"

"Percentages. Frustration levels. Method of attack. The guys I know fantasize about calibers and garrotes, not poison in the coffee."

Yet another smile. Mary was relaxing pretty quickly here. Next she was going to be unbuttoning that androgynous suitcoat of hers. "Want a job with the FBI? That's exactly the initial profile we're working with."

"That the killer's a woman."

She nodded. "Unless it's a crime of passion or defense, women tend to be much less confrontational in murder. It's societal. Of course, a lot of the pseudo-heroism situations have been male, but I'm not so sure this comes under that umbrella."

Kate went ahead and finished off the coffee, much more comfortable with this line of discussion than the "let's burn our friends" direction. Then she turned on John, who was already pulling out his notebook and pen. "If you're still asking for my help, you don't really think I'm guilty. Why not?"

Kate knew Dick's answer would have been completely different. John, however, settled the notebook in his lap and considered Kate seriously. "I'm not sure of anything, little girl. But I got instincts, and dey say poor Frances was gonna be dead before you got your hands roun' her t'roat. So unless you a miracle worker, you couldn' kill her, now, could you?"

"Not without making medical history. Are you saying you think Attila was definitely part of this pattern?" she asked.

It was Mary who answered this one. "I think so. There still isn't any proof, but that's what Doctor O'Brien is working on."

"What about the note?" Kate asked. "Did you get anything off it?"

"Nothing other than your fingerprints and the fact that the sender is a very careful person. Probably straightens pictures on a wall. Those letters were perfectly aligned. From what John told me and what I see in that letter, I'd say there's a good chance our killer is trying to win your approval. That's why we thought it would be important to include you in the investigation."

"Win my approval?" Kate demanded. "For God's sake, what for?"

"Maybe because she thinks you understand. That you approve."

That made her head hurt even worse. "Wonderful. Just what I wanted to hear."

"Can you think of anyone who might have expressed a sentiment like that?" Mary asked, all business.

Kate couldn't even manage an answer. Tim did it for her.

"So far, anonymous members of the staff have left Kate almost three hundred dollars for her defense fund. That tell you anything?"

Mary's elegant eyebrow lifted. "That tells me a lot. As for the other people at the hospital, we'll get into that later. Right now, with your lawyer's permission, we'd like to go over the night Frances died, if you don't mind."

Kate didn't mind. Steve didn't mind. They ended up talking for another two hours, during which time Little Dick never took his eyes from Mary's legs, Mary never took notice, and B.J. never showed up.

Kate lasted at the apartment for four entire days. For the first two she just slept with both the TV and stereo on and navigated her way to the bathroom, which seemed suddenly half a block away. Carver shadowed her every step, as if he were going to call 911 for her if she toppled over. Tim left the answering machine on so she never had to answer the phone, which was always reporters anyway, and the house was completely stocked, which meant she didn't have to go outside, and that was all right because the story in the news had picked up steam.

The Angel of Death murders, everybody was

calling them. A killer stalking the halls of the hospital. Most of the newspeople were kind enough simply to refer to the prime suspect as a nurse employed by the hospital. But KSTL had blown the lid off the cookie jar with Kate's name. Donations poured in to the defense fund and cranks called to ask if she knew a way to dispose of interfering mothers-in-law. Satellite trucks seemed to patrol the grounds of the hospital like sharks sniffing for blood, and the Administration had put a gag order on anyone but qualified sources talking to the media.

By the third day, Jules had found her way over. By the fourth, Parker and Sticks and Edna had followed, each more frustrated than the last, each brimming with news, gossip, and innuendo. Just what John would have wanted. What Little Dick would have fed on like chum. Nothing concrete, just whispers around the hospital about people who'd had the biggest axes to grind against any of the decedents: a nurse from recovery room who'd had a sexual harassment suit in the works against Fleischer at the time of his unfortunate demise; Hetty Everson from surgical ICU, overheard having one knock-down-drag-out fight with Attila and Mrs. Warner at the very same time about a patient transfer; Weiss getting sudden religion since Fleischer's death, now claiming to be Kate's personal champion.

At least Kate had finally learned the reason behind his sudden conversion. Between Kate and Tim, they'd kept Weiss away from Fleischer and his patient long enough to save Weiss's tenuous position on the house staff roster. Mr. Peabody, upon awakening in the unit, had spoken of a rather odd doctor storming into the room, but without Kate's corroboration nothing had been done about it.

By the fifth day, against the advice of her doctor, her roommate, and her immediate supervisor, Kate spent her dinner hour in the nurses' lounge of the ER. She felt a little stronger. Her hair was finally getting a little curl so she looked less like a cue-ball and more like Leslie Caron in an early Gene Kelly movie. And most important of all, she couldn't stand another moment locked in a room with only Kate Manion to share her company.

Her little secret from the world. Her legacy from that circus she called childhood, which had left her with the nagging suspicion that no matter what she did it would be wrong, it would be insufficient, it would be stupid. Cleverly hidden all these years with bravado, tucked away beneath all the clatter and action of a career amid lights and sirens, damn near bricked in completely behind a solid wall of denial and sublimation. Set free again by a head injury and a madwoman with a grudge. By the sudden realization that if she really was as burned out as she feared, she would no longer have all the noise she needed to drown out the past. By the ruthless manipulation of people with more power than she so suddenly she felt again like that little girl cowering in a corner with nothing to protect her but inattention. Finally, by the need of people who depended on her to protect them when she knew she couldn't.

And on top of it all, she still had to visit Aunt Mamie, who'd be more than happy to reacquaint her with it all personally.

Waiting only long enough to make sure that the latest camera truck was trolling the other end of the parking lot, Kate snuck out the door and hobbled over to the ER in search of noise and action and company to offset the quickly gestating anxiety that never seemed to ease from beneath her sternum anymore.

She got all three. She still didn't get relief.

She watched as Sticks helped a little old man in a flapping patient gown from the bathroom and listened to O'Sullivan yelling at somebody who wasn't holding a leg properly as he reduced a fracture. She saw the multitrauma patient being finished in room one and inhaled the peculiarly musky smell of human destruction. Not just blood but tissue, the kind of smell that made you wrinkle your nose and shy away unless you battled it for a living, a smell she hadn't really recognized as such before. The signature of trauma.

Had she missed it? She'd sucked it in every day for ten years. Addicted to it, to the rush of exhilaration that dancing right on the edge provided, to the intense camaraderie of the people who played there, with their horrible humors, their sharp desperations, their heady triumphs.

But had she missed it? Did any tragedy move her anymore, or was she too dead to feel even that?

"Anybody know where Suzie is?" Parker asked, sticking his head out of a door. "Oh, hi, Kate. Back to work already?"

"Yeah," she said. "I can do anything but walk, lift, and push. Where do you want me?"

"You seen Suzie?" he asked, his expression saying it all. "She was supposed to be back from lunch forty-five minutes ago."

"That sounds about right. What's the matter, you getting soft in your old age? You want as much of a break as she has?"

"I just want the job security she has. The only thing she's done today is talk to her ex on the phone and yell at Sticks for throwing out her coffee. I don't suppose she could be the murderer, could she?"

Kate shook her head. "Takes too much energy."

Suzie was, of course, in the lounge. On the phone. Right in Jules's way as she waited through the news for her visit with Vanna.

"Parker's looking for you," Kate told Suzie, to be met by a complete blank. Nothing new here.

Kate pulled up the couch and collapsed onto it.

"Couldn't stay away?" Jules asked, scooting her chair over a little closer to Suzie's at the table, not so much to see better as to invade Suzie's space.

Kate propped her left leg on the rest of the couch so Suzie wouldn't have a retreat and sighed. "I'm bored."

"Read a book."

"I read a book. I didn't like it."

Suzie scooted over a little farther and kept whining into the receiver. Not a particularly pretty woman, she left one with the impression of a small irritable dog. Kate felt sorry for her kids, who never seemed to get over their runny noses.

Jules never took her eyes off the set as she made another strategic move. Kate hadn't noticed what the anchors were saying up there until she saw the distinctive oak paneling of the administration suite.

"Hey, I recognize that place," she announced. "I was once personally reprimanded there."

"I'll call you back later," Suzie snapped and slammed the receiver down with enough force to shake the table. Neither Jules nor Kate paid notice as she stomped out of the room.

"Has anyone ever figured out why she's still working here?" Jules asked absently as the reporter questioned the hospital's public relations director about the cause of the murders.

"Another one of those unsolved mysteries," Kate acknowledged, by now just as attentive to the TV as her friend.

" . . . The entire staff is cooperating with the police," the PR queen was saying in her most sincere manner. "Saint Simon's has a long history of caring and commitment to this community. It would be tragic to let one single act of mindless violence overshadow that."

"But there's a possibility that up to three murders have already been committed," the reporter retorted. "Is the public in any danger?"

"No, no, not at all. Whoever this disturbed individual is seems to be targeting only very select staff members, certainly not any of the patients, and I don't believe the police think that will change. Besides, with every person in the hospital working overtime to help us apprehend the suspect, we're certain the situation will be over very soon. After all, we're family here. Everyone is pulling together to see that this nightmare is over soon."

Timing is everything, Kate's old drama teacher had once said. So Kate shouldn't have been surprised that John chose this moment to storm into the lounge, fire in his eyes and a doctor's order sheet fluttering from his hand.

"Yeah, I t'ought you'd be here," he accused, waving his prize at Kate as if damning her with it. "I been lookin' all over for you."

"John?" she asked, straightening with surprise at the energy he was expending. "What's wrong?"

"You wanna see what I foun' on de bulletin board in the coronary care unit?" he demanded. "Right dere for anybody to see?"

Kate made a couple of stabs at the paper before catching hold. "Yes," she admitted. "I'd like to."

John let go and Kate finally saw what had him so flushed.

She couldn't help it. It was like getting that perfectly inappropriate impulse to giggle at a funeral. She took one look at what was in her hands and broke out laughing. Then she handed the paper to Jules, who laughed too.

"What's so funny 'bout dat?" John demanded.

What was so funny was the fact that he didn't understand.

It was a note. A very modest note, neatly typed, probably on one of the myriad hospital typewriters on some of the endless supply of paper forms for the hospital's ubiquitous paper-work.

Simply stated, it read, DEAR SERIAL KILLER. FOR YOUR CONSIDERATION:

And then, below the salutation, was a list of names. The first six or seven were typed. After that, another thirty or so had been added in every color and handwriting style imaginable. Several rated comments, and most ratings on a scale of one to ten.

One vote had been cast for Roseanne Arnold, one for Rush Limbaugh, and two for Madonna. Other than that, every name on the list was one Kate would have put there if she'd had enough to drink. Administrators, chiefs of service, a couple of those mindless paper push-ers who interfered with every nursing decision made at the hospital, several workers who man-aged to avoid work at any expense. People more interested in protecting their position than their patients. Suzie had the honor of holding down position number eight, with a bonus of four exclamation points.

"It's a pretty long list," Kate acknowledged.

"Especially for a hospital family that's working together to see the end of this nightmare," Jules agreed. "I don't guess you got anybody to admit to putting it up."

"You're not helpin'," John accused, waving a hand at the thing as if it had come to life and bit him. "You're not helpin' a bit."

Nobody saw Edna step into the room until she pulled the list from Kate's hand. When she saw

that Gunn's name was at the very top, she simply
nodded and handed it back. Then she smiled over
at John.

"One should always prioritize," she said simply
and walked out.

John damn near went ballistic. "What is it wid
you people?" he demanded. "You got murder
victims here, ya know?"

"We know," Kate admitted. "But when the
slaves get to revoltin', John, they don't always
remember to leave the good massas alone."

John was notoriously short of humor. "What
de hell you talkin' about, girl?"

"Control, John. Power. You at least have the
illusion of it. You carry a gun, and whether or not
you're ever going to use it, you can at least pretend it gives you power over something. After all,
how can you lose an argument with a nine mil-
limeter on your side? We have squat. Shit, the way
things are, most days we don't even know who to
go after if we're mad." She shrugged. "We've been
mad a long time now."

Kate wasn't sure John really understood. Jules
did.

"My," she mused with a cat-in-the-cream
smile. "That was quite a speech for you."

Kate just nodded. "Thank you."

"I still don' see it helpin' any, little girl," John
insisted. "I'm standin' here wid maybe three murders and not one decent goddamn clue."

"You have an idea of just what might have set
this off," Kate retorted evenly. "Take it to Mary
Cherry and see what she thinks."

"Mary *who*?" Jules retorted.

But by then John had walked out.

Kate held off as long as she could. Finally, though, it was go home or stay for night shift. She realized it would be a while before she could swing down those halls with impunity, since just sitting in the lounge totally wasted her. It didn't really matter, though. She couldn't go back to work yet anyway. Not till she felt something. Anything.

Hell, she thought, struggling across the drive-way on her crutches, the halogen lights staining the faint green of the lawns and hedges a sick orange in the darkness and turning the soft white of the hospital into a fortress. I can't even feel anything about dead co-workers. How can I feel something about work?

Time, she promised. Let all the traumas heal and it'll come back. She'd wake up one day and cry for Fleischer and Warner and then positively yearn to walk back on the lane. Until then, she should be patient.

Until then, she had only herself to keep company.

Well, she thought, as she slowly maneuvered into the dim apartment, at least I have mail. It was stuffed in the mail slot, slid under the door. Kudos and complaints. Money and ministrations. Kate decided she'd pour herself a little of the old malt and sit down to go through it. First, she played the answering machine. Tim had called twice from his rotation down at Children's. Four or five reporters wanted her exclusive story, including one television magazine who would pay her big bucks to reenact her crimes on film. They kept calling, she'd have crimes to reenact.

And then, the sere, stern voice that still haunted her after all these years.

"You can't escape your responsibilities, Mary Kathleen. I had to contact your workplace to get your number." Kate would personally kill whoever had given it out. "I expect to see you this week, as planned. After all, young lady, you were the one who asked for this arrangement." *Click.*

Kate didn't bother to listen to the rest of the messages. She just walked in and poured that drink, a big one sure to make the dizziness return. Then she slugged a good third down as she listened to some secretary calling on behalf of the lawyer—Curly, wasn't it? Oh, hell, what did it matter anyway?—saying something about liability and insurance. Same old stuff. Kate just sat herself down at the kitchen table with the pile of envelopes she'd collected and stared at them.

Suddenly she didn't have the energy to face what was inside. Struggling to her feet, she shoved the pile away, grabbed her drink and her crutches, and clumped into her bedroom, where Carver was already waiting.

The decor that greeted her was simple to the point of being sterile, with nothing more on the walls than an old yellowed print of Yosemite Falls and a newly hung mug holder with her ball-cap collection on it. There was a radio, and she turned it on. A portable television. She turned that on too, the soft counterpoint of voices a comforting companion. And then, working slowly so she didn't head over on her nose, she undressed for bed, leaving the letters and the murders and the media attention outside.

It took her two more days to gather up the courage to go through her mail. Two days in which she spent her waking hours sitting in the ER lounge and her sleeping moments with the radio on to fend off the silence. And all the while, her second note waited on the kitchen table and she didn't even know it.

✦ *Chapter 10* ✦

KATE, THE NOTE read in perfectly cut-out letters that marched across the page with a precision that would have made a field marshal cry. HE WHO IS NOT FOR US IS AGAINST US. DON'T BE AGAINST US. YOU ARE THE LAST PERSON I WANT TO HURT.

Kate didn't come right across it. She'd been giving grudging attention to the pile as she and Tim discussed a possible weekend trip once she got her walking cast. Tim was all for heading up to Chicago and catching *Phantom of the Opera*. Kate wanted to go to Memphis and see Graceland.

"I would never have let you in this apartment if I thought you were serious," Tim protested with a particularly pained expression as he cut up vegetables for a western omelet.

Kate delighted in tormenting Tim. It was the only thing that felt good these days. She opened another envelope to find just two ten-dollar bills. No note, no name. "But Tim," she protested with every ounce of sincerity she had. "I almost died once without getting to pay my homage to the king. Would you ask me to do it again?"

"You should have said hello while you had the chance."

"I couldn't," she retorted, without much humor. "The only guide I got on my travels was Arnstein, and he led me around with his hand in my chest. Besides, Elvis is still on that spaceship with Princess Grace."

"Arnstein's a pig."

Kate nodded absently. "No argument from me."

"If we go to Chicago, I know some really great places."

"If we go to Chicago, I do not want to spend all weekend in gay bars."

His smile was deprecating. "Spoilsport."

She wouldn't have minded so much if he just hit the fun places with drag queens doing show tunes. But when Tim made his regular pilgrimages out of town, he didn't enjoy gay bars, he checked into S and M clubs for a bout of sexual penance.

"You've got a couple of days off comin' up," she said. "Get all that mingling out of your system, and then we can do the museums and stuff when we go together." She ripped open another envelope. "Besides . . ."

"Besides what?"

But Kate didn't hear him. She'd just unfolded that innocuous little piece of paper, the one that looked as if it had just been stuffed in the envelope at the last minute. The one with the perfectly placed letters.

"Kate?"

Damn him for being sensitive. The knife

slowed midair and Tim's attention was all on Kate. Suddenly she didn't want him to know. She didn't even know why.

So she smiled up at him. "Do I have to do this now, Mom? Couldn't I finish it later after *The Jetsons* is over?"

But Tim wasn't easily fooled. "What's wrong?"

Kate sighed. Tim had to go on shift in exactly an hour and a half, and she wasn't going to let him carry this nonsense with him. She'd just wait and call B.J.

"What's wrong is that the only thing I can think of I'd hate worse than doing this would be getting a transfer to orthopedics. That's what's wrong. Now, chop. I'm going to go through this and piss and moan until I'm finished. Fair enough?"

She wanted him to smile. He didn't. Not quite. "We're gonna get through this," was all he said.

Kate couldn't think of a comeback, snappy or otherwise. So she shut up, smiled, and went back to work.

"I shouldn't have to come over here to talk to you."

Not even ten o'clock and already the day was shaping up to be straight from hell. Kate had left a message for B.J., who was supposed to get back to her. Instead of him, though, she ended up answering the door in her Cardinals sweats and bare feet to find Phyl the Gorilla herself.

"I'd be happy to go over there," Kate told her

supervisor as she let her in, "but you didn't like that much either."

Phyl didn't so much as look around before claiming a corner of the couch and beginning the panty hose ritual. When Phyl was upset, she picked runs into her hose. She already had three this morning.

"You've been asked to call Mr. Wurly's office," she said, again without preamble. "Why haven't you?"

Wurly. That was it. Not very impressive. Kate held on to her temper with sour humor. "I guess this means he doesn't make house calls, huh?"

Phyl just glared. "You might pay better attention, Kate. There's been a lawsuit filed."

Kate found it took a second to even answer. "A lawsuit?" she asked stupidly, finally folding into one of the chairs rather than stand through what had all the earmarks of a fresh disaster.

"From the incident with the Rashad boy. Evidently some ambulance chaser talked the family into trying to take the hospital for everything it can get."

From the little Kate knew about the whole thing, probably the most logical course of events. "And?"

Phyl couldn't even seem to look at her. "And it was thought you should probably have time to contact your insurance company to secure representation before you were served."

"Secure . . . but the hospital covers me."

"Not under these circumstances. You acted completely on your own. You know you did."

"I don't know anything," Kate insisted, rubbing a hand through her new hair as if she could wear away the sudden tension. Well, at least she finally understood why she'd gotten two group appointments with honchos she'd never even been introduced to before. Prophylactic damage control. They'd known this was coming all along. "You mean the hospital is just cutting me loose on this?"

"We have to think of what's best for everyone involved."

It was Kate's turn to glare. "We."

Phyl's complexion mottled with discomfort. "The hospital is going through some delicate negotiations right now," she said. "We can't be mired down in something this complex. It would probably be best if you considered settling."

"No offer to get me a lawyer if I help the police?"

Another definite color change. "You haven't let me finish."

"What is Mr. Gunn more worried about," Kate demanded, "his staff or his negotiations?"

"I'd watch my attitude if I were you."

"What are *you* more interested in, Phyllis?" Kate countered. "Your job or the ongoing loss of life at that hospital?"

That brought Phyllis to her feet. Kate had seen her mad, she'd seen her upset. She'd never seen her frothing.

"You really don't get it, do you?" Phyl demanded. "Who the hell do you think has been the only thing between you and the front door, Kate?"

It was too early in the morning. Too early. All Kate wanted to do was turn on the TV, turn on the stereo, and lose herself in noise. She didn't want to hear this.

"Phyl, I'm sorry."

"No, you're not, damn it. You just don't have any idea what goes on in the world beyond your little niche. You don't know what it's like to have the Administration pushing on one side and you sharks pushing on the other. I'm doing the best I can, Kate. Isn't that enough for you?"

Now Kate knew she didn't want to hear this. It had been so comfortable blaming Phyl. After all, Phyl was the most visible target every time something went wrong. Kate didn't want to think what life must be like in the middle. It was tough enough being on the bottom of the pile without thinking about the pressures the layer above you had to suffer.

All Kate could do, in the end, was climb to her feet as well. "If I weren't driven, I wouldn't be any fun at all." She didn't want to ask, because it would change everything. She did anyway. "You really went to bat for me?"

Phyl actually sighed. "So many times I have splinters. You may be a pain in the ass, Kate, but you're *my* pain in the ass. Now, can't you do me a favor in return and lay off for a while?"

That was when Kate understood just how burned out she'd become, because she realized it had been a long time since she'd really taken a look at her supervisor. Mid-forties, with doughy features and permanent worry lines, making less than the evening nurses did in return for putting up with all that hassle, her talents much better utilized in some kind of account review situation. Kate still didn't think Phyl was doing a good job, but then Kate wouldn't set foot near that kind of position if it came with its own cook and chauffeur. At least at the bottom of the pile, you always knew just where you stood.

"How 'bout some coffee?" she asked with a hard-won smile. "We can work out the terms of the truce."

Phyl didn't bother to move. "Only if those terms include working with the police to weed out the killer."

Kate sat right back down with a groan.

It was up to B.J. when he arrived an hour or so later to pull the two women away from each other's throats.

He'd been having such a good morning. He'd finally come up with the cause of death for Attila, although the mechanism was still a question. He'd finally gotten the keying right on one of the new reels he'd been teaching himself, and his court date had been postponed on the Northside Homeboys case, something he wasn't looking forward to anyway. It would just figure that he'd show up at Kate's door to find himself mired in yet more problems.

"It definitely wasn't you, and it definitely was murder," he announced the minute she pulled open the door.

Kate just stood there. "What?"

"Not what, who. Attila. She's a definite add to the list."

Which was when Kate's supervisor stepped out of the kitchen at the far end of the apartment. B.J. knew simply by the looks on both faces that he'd just added fuel to some fire. His first instinct was to back slowly out the door so he couldn't be incinerated and then run like hell. He considered himself a hero for not doing just that.

Kate stepped back a little from the door. "Come on in," she invited, although the sound of it suggested that she'd just offered room and board to the grand inquisitor.

"Doctor O'Brien." Phyl greeted him with a deferential nod of the head.

B.J. hated that kind of attitude. Beat me, whip me, give me patient orders. "Nice to see you, Phyl. You're looking—" apoplectic. She was looking apoplectic "—well."

Phyl didn't react to his platitude. She simply set down the coffee mug she'd been carrying and grabbed her coat. "Tell her she's not the only person to consider here, please. Tell her that by doing what she's doing, she's helping a serial killer get away with murder."

And with that, she swept into the hallway and out the front door. Kate never so much as moved until the door closed. Then she didn't just move, she slammed. Hard. B.J. winced.

"Another fruitful conference with Administration?" he asked.

Kate didn't even bother to answer. She just stalked over to the stereo and hit the ON button. Then she headed for the kitchen.

B.J. followed, first turning down the volume on Queen so the napping kids in the building wouldn't have nightmares. By the time he hit the closet-sized kitchen, it was to find Kate standing there in her bare feet, mixing brandy into her coffee.

"Oh," he amended with a knowing nod. "A very fruitful conference."

"Shut up."

He didn't bother to ask before pulling a mug off the rack and pouring his own unadulterated portion. "Why won't you help?"

"Because they're assholes."

B.J. just nodded again and thought how a patient was supposed to display increasing good health upon discharge from the hospital. Kate had circles under her eyes and an unhealthy pallor that belied her energy. She wasn't dealing with this enforced rest thing very well.

"I know there's a good reason for this," was all B.J. said.

She glared at him. "There is. I hate being manipulated. Got a problem with that?"

Then she just stalked past and turned up the volume until Freddie Mercury's voice sounded like an approaching siren. B.J. followed right behind and turned it back down.

"This isn't much like you, pogue."

Kate came to a halt and sighed.

"The son of a bitch sent me another letter," she admitted, not bothering to look away from the

Matisse print over the couch. "Only this time I got threatened."

B.J. took a moment to contain his anger. Just what Kate needed right now. "And that's why you won't help?"

He wondered if Kate realized how predictable she was. She spun around on his quiet accusation as if he'd just questioned her parentage. "Don't be a jerk," she snapped. "Of course not."

"Then why?"

"Because . . . because . . ." A myriad of emotions skimmed her features: anger, frustration, confusion, guilt. Oddly enough, he thought, grief. She spun around and communed with Matisse again.

"Why can't the police just build a case on evidence, like they're supposed to?" she demanded.

"Because they don't have any. You want to know how Attila died?"

"No."

"Potassium. It took me awhile to figure it out, because potassium levels are always elevated in old blood samples. But hers were just a little too high."

"How high?"

"Eleven point eight."

The norms were 3.5 to 5.0 mEq/L, and even a little one way or the other could incite possibly lethal arrhythmias; 11.8 mEq/L would produce a dead stock-still heart that no amount of juicing and coercion could change.

B.J. could see Kate's shoulders slump. "How?" she asked. "You can't just sneak potassium in somebody, not if she's awake. It tastes like shit. And Attila was definitely awake."

"It would have had to be hidden. I think she'd been ingesting it without knowing it for a couple of days. Your little surprise just escalated the scenario a bit."

B.J. waited, ever patient when he knew he could expect results.

"Coffee," Kate said abruptly, turning on him.

B.J. waited a little longer.

"Attila spent most of the shift disappearing for a cigarette and coffee. She kept her own pot, because nobody made it strong enough for her. You could have put creosote in that stuff and she wouldn't have noticed."

B.J. found himself nodding. "A lot of people knew about this?"

"Anybody who worked with her. Especially anybody stuck doing her work while she disappeared. Sure."

"Anybody like Edna Reabers?"

Kate stiffened like a bowstring. "Why?"

B.J. did his best to look noncommittal. "She would have known all three victims."

"Don't do this to me," Kate commanded. "What's going on?"

Now Freddie Mercury was singing about champions. B.J. wondered if the tenants upstairs ever complained about the thumping bass in here.

"B.J.," Kate warned, looking more desperate than threatening.

B.J. knew Kate had no respect for a flanking maneuver, so he hit her with it right down the middle. "She knew all three people, she's recently had a pretty big setback, and she's just the kind of careful, quiet person the FBI profile is looking for," he said.

"Says who?"

"Little Dick, for one."

"Little Dick's the biggest asshole of them all."

"What about Martin Weiss?"

Now Kate looked as if B.J. had just pulled an active skunk from his pocket. "Martin Weiss is having trouble enough with his own reality. I wouldn't trust his acquaintance with Edna's."

"There's a murderer out there, Kate. Someone with access to the units and the executive suite and the doctors' lounge. How many people have that?"

"Anybody in the hospital. You know that."

"The doctors' lounge?"

"Oh, B.J., you know better. Where do you think Sticks gets all her soda? She sure doesn't pay for it. And Parker and Lisa Beller have been sneaking off there on nights for almost four months now for a little suckface."

B.J. was finally surprised. "Parker?"

He at least got something of a laugh out of her. "Parker may not be cute, but he definitely possesses every other qualification. They usually go there because they don't want to get caught. After all, it's one thing for a doctor to screw a nurse, but it's entirely different if a nurse is screwing a doctor."

"In the doctors' lounge?"

She scowled at him. "It's the emptiest place in

the world at two in the morning. Just ask Weiss.
It's his favorite place to back nurses against the
wall when he's on call. And when you get down
to it, why does it have to be a nurse doing this?
All you need is a face and uniform everybody's
used to seeing around the hospital to get where
you want to go. That means it could just as easily
be a doctor."

Even though he knew he was doing it, B.J. hit
right below the belt.

"You mean like maybe a gay doctor who
could fool the forensic psychiatrists into thinking
he was a woman?"

That brought her to a dead shuddering halt,
her eyes as cold and furious as B.J. had ever seen.
"Don't," she threatened very quietly. "I'll swear
that you did it before I let anybody offer up Tim."

"Well, they're offering up Edna sometime this
week. She's being brought in for questioning."

Kate slumped, pushed a hand through what
hair she had. "Aw, shit, B.J., they can't do that. It'd
kill her. Administration's just doing this so they
have another mark against her at evaluation time.
'Demoted to ER, questioned in a murder.' Makes it
easier to make her quit."

"I thought you didn't like Edna."

"I don't want to work with her. There's a big
difference. When are they bringing her in?"

B.J. was amazed that he suddenly wanted to
know just what was making Kate twitch so badly.
Why she felt so caught by this investigation. B.J.
never wanted to know about other people. It was
just a sneaky way to make him dependent on

them, so when they died or disappeared or lost their sanity, he had to pay as big a price as they did. He had to be left behind alone.

"Nobody said."

Kate took a solid breath and rested the coffee cup against one hip. Then she faced B.J. eyeball to eyeball.

"Why are you playing for the opposition on this one, O'Brien?"

"I didn't know stopping a murderer put me on the opposition team."

She waved him off as if he were a swarming mosquito. "It's one thing to investigate. It's another to reopen the McCarthy hearings, and that's where this is headed."

B.J. had never heard such illogic from her since the very first day they'd met over a bus accident in the old SLU ER. "You really think so?" he asked quietly.

But she couldn't seem to muster an answer for him. She took off like a bird in flight, downing that coffee as if it were a boilermaker and then hesitating just long enough for B.J. to know she was a hairsbreadth away from pitching her coffee cup at that pristine white wall.

"There's never anything out of place here," she mused, almost to herself. "It's so comforting never to be surprised. To know just what to expect. I think it's one reason I like living here."

Then off she headed again.

B.J. stood his ground and waited to catch her on the next circuit. She made it in record time, skidding to an abrupt halt right in front of him.

"You don't understand," she accused him in a curiously small, little-girl voice.

He nodded. "I know."

She dipped her head. "So what you and John and the Little Dick have decided is that since the evidence is going to be too tough, you're going to try and catch the killer by why-done-it instead of who-done-it. And that's why you want me to play along."

"You know more about what's going on with the staff than damn near anybody else."

"No, I don't. That's Sticks. Talk to her."

"People tend to confide in you." He tried a deprecating smile that brought up all those night shifts they'd shared. "It's a gift."

She didn't buy it. "It's a goddamn curse. And they don't confide in me. They just want me to take responsibility for them so they can sneak by without getting hurt. Besides, I only know the people in the critical-care areas. Not OB or ortho or anything."

"You really think this is the work of an OB nurse?"

"I don't know. You've never met some of the OB nurses. They'd put the SS to shame."

Again he waited. She didn't move this time, just consulted with the tops of her feet in silence, her brow furrowed and her hands clenched, her head moving ever so slightly as she waged some great argument inside that lightning-fast brain of hers, scored by the driving bass and drums of Queen.

She didn't look up at first. "You've never met my aunt."

"Nope." Nobody had.

Kate took a deep breath and faced him, looking suddenly more tremulous even than the time B.J. had walked into the triage desk to find her facing a junkie with a loaded gun. "Would you take me down there?"

They'd known each other damn near eight years. This was quite a first. B.J. was even more surprised to realize that he was going to do it. He wanted to meet this mysterious aunt who had made his own mother wrinkle her nose in distaste. Sarah Brinkley O'Brien did not waste her time dissing other people. She simply . . . wrinkled. And she had definitely wrinkled about Mrs. Mary Anne Henderson.

"Is now good?"

Kate took another breath and straightened as if she'd just been introduced to a firing squad. "Now would be perfect."

B.J. nodded agreeably. "Right after I see that second note."

In 1904, St. Louis hosted one of the greatest world fairs in history in a place called Forest Park at the edge of the city. The world did indeed come to St. Louis and, with it, great notoriety. With the notoriety came money, and with the money came a boom in surrounding real estate. The wealthier families of the city set white flight into motion by building huge mansions in the neighborhoods that surrounded the park, big stone and brick and granite behemoths that had lasted through several cycles of prosperity and neglect with their grace virtually intact.

The area was once again fashionable, the homes renovated and tailored, and the money back, at least in the areas close enough to Highway 40 where crime didn't breach the barri-ered streets.

B.J. had spent his share of time in Forest Park as a kid, skating at Steinberg in the winter and taking dates to the free seats at the Muny Opera in the summer. He'd driven by the great old homes that ringed it without once wondering about them. It would never occur to an ex–air force brat from Brentwood that he'd ever be invited inside one of those old places.

It was where they were headed today.

Kate had said she owed her aunt some money. She failed to mention the fact that the old bat would never need to see it repaid in her life-time. A paternal aunt, from what little Kate said on the way down, Mary Anne "Mamie" Manion Henderson had overcome her Irish Catholic her-itage and married well into the very WASPish upper class of post–World War II St. Louis. She'd moved into her in-laws' house on Westmoreland and never moved out, even after her late husband, Henry Howard Henderson, passed away in the sixties, leaving them without issue or heir.

B.J. had known about Kate's aunt for at least a couple of years. He'd never asked for details. He was sure he shouldn't now. He shouldn't have to know what it was that made Kate leave her gaudy earrings behind on the coffee table or go rigid the minute she climbed into the Jeep. He shouldn't be so curious all of a sudden about a past she'd never wanted to share anyway.

So he drove and he ignored the fact that Kate was holding her Cardinals cap in her hands as if it were a weapon, and he pulled out the bottle of Dr Pepper he hadn't finished yet.

"Want some?"

She never looked away from the traffic ahead. "How long's that been in here?"

B.J. took a second to shake the bottle. When he saw the lack of bubbles, he smiled. "Just long enough."

She couldn't even seem to manage a reaction. If she hadn't been so wired all along, B.J. might have thought she was simply enjoying the weather. The day was warm, the sky high and clear, the sun creating colors where there hadn't been any. But Kate wasn't focused on the sun or the forests of daffodils the highway department had planted. She was grim and stiff and silent, and B.J. retreated to his driving and his Dr Pepper.

He recognized the house immediately when they pulled to a stop in front. He'd seen it every time he'd driven by, a four-story gray-granite mausoleum that squatted at the center of the block without grace or charm. Twenty or thirty rooms with nothing but one old lady and two retainers to take up space. It made B.J. wonder what a childhood spent inside must have been like. But then B.J. had grown up in a series of small base houses and now lived in a four-room house in Brentwood his mother lovingly called the Cave.

He almost made the mistake of helping Kate from the car. She didn't even wait for him to get his own door open before climbing out, cap firmly in place. Even with the crutches and cast, she marched up the walk like Carrie Nation heading for a saloon. B.J. just followed behind, obviously there simply to witness what went on.

"Are you sure you're up to this?" he asked, intrigued against his will.

She sucked in a breath as if it were the last cubic meter of air on earth and knocked. "I'd better be."

The massive oak door swung slowly open to reveal what must have been one of the retainers, a pencil-thin specimen of mummification clad in serviceable gray and silent as death.

"Miss Chambers." Kate greeted her without noticeable inflection.

The woman backed away just enough to let them through. "We've been expecting you," was all she said.

Not exactly B.J.'s idea of a homecoming, considering the fact that his first weekend back from Philly he'd had to wade through about three dozen shouting relatives just to get to the kitchen.

He waited for Kate to make the first move. She did after a moment's hesitation most other people wouldn't have noticed. B.J. did. He wasn't intrigued anymore. He was worried. Even in the sunlight her color wasn't all that good. In the unrelieved gloom of that entryway, she looked cachectic.

To call the house they stepped into dismal would have been a euphemism. B.J. was sure

when the original owners put the thing up
they'd probably trimmed it with all kinds of
gewgaws. The original stained-glass windows
still scattered shards of color across the gray
marble floor. But the rest of the place looked
like a cross between a morgue and an old high
school, with stairs curling every which way and
footsteps echoing endlessly throughout the high-
ceilinged rooms. The cold-storage freezer in the
Philadelphia morgue had been more inviting
than this, and that had been older and not nearly
as well decorated.

Kate didn't give him much more time to rumi-
nate as she turned for the entryway to their left.

"Well, I see you couldn't put it off any longer."

Even B.J. straightened to that voice. He'd
heard it often enough in the person of Sister Mary
Alphonse, his fourth-grade teacher. The sound of
it made him want to pull his hands behind his
back to save them from the ruler. As for Kate, she
lost even more color.

"I came as soon as the doctors let me, Aunt
Mamie," she said.

B.J. couldn't help shooting her a startled look.
In all the time he'd known her, through all the
disasters and challenges, the fights with
Administration and physicians of every ilk, he had
never once been witness to this. She stood so
straight somebody could have hung a sail from
her, head back, chin up, eyes cold as glass. But
her voice didn't match the brittle posture at all. In
fact, it was cowed. Quiet, with just a trace of
shame in it. B.J. was tempted to nudge her in the

ribs and tell her to knock it off until he realized she barely remembered he was there.

"Well, you might as well come in," the voice offered, with just enough self-pity to make it sound as if Kate held the keys to the dungeon. "And who's that with you? Come in here so I can see you better."

The living room itself was straight out of *Citizen Kane,* big enough to bowl in, with an arrangement of couches and chairs dead center, all the color of dust. Perched on one of the chairs like the queen mother with bad hemorrhoids was Aunt Mamie, unsmiling, grim, disapproving. B.J. had the feeling that if Kate had brought Jesus Christ into this room, the old lady would have complained about his beard.

"Aunt Mamie, this is my friend Doctor O'Brien." Kate introduced him as she edged into the living room, the crutches making a curious hissing sound on the floor. "He drove me down."

That got the old bat's attention. She stopped, a tumbler of clear liquid halfway to her lips. "A doctor? Really? This doesn't mean you've finally decided to behave like an adult and stop causing trouble, does it?"

Any other time, B.J. might have laughed. Not Kate, he wanted to say. Kate's expression kept him silent.

He'd spent a career dealing with people in pain. He'd learned to keep his opinions to himself when they would have served no purpose. He'd been in this house no more than three minutes, and already he was having trouble doing just that.

He took another look at Kate, searching for direction. She was already seated, taut and silent and haunted. So he sat down alongside her on one of the brocade couches and faced the inquisitor herself. Small, bright-eyed, with dull gray hair and papery skin. Maybe she'd had beauty of some kind once, but the permanent displeasure on those features had long since robbed her of it.

"Nice to meet you," he said diffidently and noticed that his voice echoed as if he were standing in the middle aisle of St. Mary Magdalen.

The old woman nodded and finished taking that drink, her attention all on Kate, the sparrow hawk spotting small brown feathers. "You owe considerable interest for being late."

"It's there."

A sharp nod. "Well, that's a start at least. Maybe there's actually some hope after all this time, Mary Kathleen. I've despaired so often that you'd ever learn anything, considering the miserable childhood your mother gave you. You can't blame me for it, either, you know. After all, look at the shambles you've made of things so far."

B.J. looked over at Kate, waiting for the fireworks that would have gone off if anyone at the hospital had tried this little act on her. But this play had been rehearsed much too well. Kate's face was as tight as a twelve-hour-dead body as she dug into her sweatshirt pocket for the check she'd already written out. Her hand was trembling. B.J. held on to his silence and his temper with herculean effort.

"Five thousand five hundred twenty-three fifty," she said, handing it over.

It was snapped up without hesitation and examined as if it had been the original Magna Carta. "I do have to give Mary Kathleen that, Doctor O'Brien. She does try to be punctual. It may not be much, but we should be thankful for even small things, don't you think?"

"I think—"

He never finished. Kate shot him one single look that shut him up faster than the back of her hand. Pleading. She was begging him just to watch. To understand without her having to explain. It might have been the toughest thing B.J. had to do since crawling around in elephant grass with an M-16 in his hand, but he did it. Barely.

"After all," Kate's aunt expounded, warming to her subject, not even aware B.J. had spoken. "If you had known her mother, you'd understand. Mary Kathleen is just like her: flighty, undisciplined. High-strung, they used to call it, as if it were an attractive thing. All the girls were. Maybe Mary Kathleen's father could have made a difference with them, we'll never know. He was driven out, driven out of his own house. A bad turn that woman ever came into his life. A bad turn for everyone, isn't that so, Mary Kathleen?"

"She did her best," Kate responded, as if repeating a well-learned line.

Her aunt laughed, and B.J. thought of dead leaves across a road. He was getting sick to his stomach. "Her best. Is that what it was? Well, she drove off her own husband because she wasn't wife enough for him. And she certainly taught you girls well. Good heavens, you divorced and your sisters . . . just what are your sisters doing now, Mary Kathleen? Do you even know, after all the money you spent on them?"

B.J. was sure he'd taken a wrong turn somewhere and ended up in a Tennessee Williams play. This old gal couldn't possibly be real. Kate couldn't be affected by this crap.

But she was. He was appalled to find that she shrank before it, Kate who had stood toe to toe with psychotics and neurosurgeons and never given an inch. She looked suddenly like a very small little girl who wouldn't recognize a word of praise if somebody painted it on her forehead.

And sisters. B.J. had never heard a word about Kate having sisters. God, he wanted out of here now, before it was too late.

"At least I can coerce Mary Kathleen to come see me," the old woman went on, evidently not expecting any answers. "Her sisters, on the other hand . . . well, I can't say I'm surprised. They certainly showed their true colors, didn't they, Mary Kathleen? Even more like your mother than you are."

"Leave them out of this, Aunt Mamie." Kate was looking even more pale, and her fingers were wrapped around her crutch strap as if it were a lifeline—or a weapon. "They turned out fine."

The old woman just huffed, as if Kate were the most callow creature on earth. "How would you know? You haven't heard from them in six years. How would you like sisters like that, Doctor

O'Brien? Did Kate tell you about the loan she took out? To get her sisters as far away from me as possible. Well, she did. She did that. But they won't see her either."

That was it. B.J. didn't care what Kate wanted. There was only so much torture he could witness without intervening.

"I have to get Kate back now, Mrs. Henderson," he spoke up, working hard to keep his voice even. "She's still not recovered from her injuries. You might have noticed—"

Another moue of displeasure. "I noticed. Such a shame. Your one good feature, that lovely Manion hair, and it's all gone. Which reminds me. I refused to wait until it's too late, so I called Marshall to represent you in this . . . unpleasant matter. After all, he knows us. He might minimize—"

Kate was suddenly on her feet. "No. No, Aunt Mamie, I have a lawyer, thank you. No one will bother you over this."

"Well, they already have. My heavens, this morning one of those dreadful tabloid shows called me. If you'd been more responsible, Mary Kathleen, none of this would have happened. But you just don't have a drop of your father in you, I'm afraid."

"I . . . I'll be back in six months," she said simply. "As we agreed."

"No," the little woman contradicted hastily. "As *you* agreed. I was just a convenient source of the cash you needed to get yourself away from your family."

"Yes, ma'am."

B.J. found himself on his feet with a hand on Kate's arm. "Come on," he said, battling the urge to break something. "Let's go."

For a second, Kate hesitated, her eyes on that withered, empty woman on the couch. Waiting, although for what B.J. wasn't sure. Hoping?

In the end, the woman waved them both off as if they were bootboys. "Go on, don't bother about an old woman like me. I'll just wait six months until you decide you can't put off seeing me any longer."

B.J. didn't let Kate hang around for more. He just pushed her right back out the front door.

She didn't even make it to the car before she was on her knees vomiting.

B.J. grabbed hold of her, right out on the side-walk. Pulled out his handkerchief to wipe her face. Tried his best to pretend he didn't notice the tears. He wasn't good at this, damn it. He didn't know what to do. She was shaking and retching, and her cap was on the grass, and he couldn't think of anything to say except he was sorry, which wasn't going to do any damn good.

Finally Kate straightened and accepted the handkerchief with trembling hands, her cheeks mottled with embarrassment.

"This is so stupid," she protested.

B.J. bent to retrieve her hat, never releasing his hold on her. "I was thinking more along the lines of symbolic."

He didn't even get a smile out of her. She just went still, her gaze out to the wide street rather than the house she'd just left. "Aunt Mamie practically raised my father," she said simply, as if that would make all the difference. "I don't think she ever got over the fact that he settled for someone so very much like their parents when he married my mother."

"She's a selfish old bitch."

Thankfully, that finally brought at least a semblance of a smile. "Well, yeah, there's that too."

B.J. settled the Cardinals cap back on her head and steered her for the Jeep as if nothing had happened. She looked abashed and pale, but better by the minute since she'd walked out of that decorated tomb.

"You never told me you had sisters," he said as he settled in.

She didn't bother to look over at him. "Twins, younger than I am. They're . . . they moved away quite a while ago. They're on the West Coast."

"When did your mom die?"

A breath, deep and hungry, as if air were courage. "When I was fourteen. She never got over the fact that my dad left, I guess. After that, Aunt Mamie was in charge."

For a minute B.J. just considered the street before them, wide, elegant, well-manicured. As carefully put together as the decor in Tim's apartment. A proper facade that could hide all kinds of secrets. Then he turned over the engine and headed back through Forest Park toward the highway.

The traffic was heavy through the park on a day as nice as this. The sun glinted on car roofs and the sky sparkled over the soft green trees of early spring. B.J. found he'd lost his enthusiasm for the nice weather.

"Do you know where your dad is now?"

Kate kept her attention on the scenery as they passed the manmade mountains of the zoo. "Nope. Don't care much, either."

"He drank too?"

This time Kate shot him a look that reminded him too much of those moments back in that mausoleum. Dread. He wanted to go back and hit that old woman for doing this to her. Then he wanted to find her father and hit him too. Hard. Just like the old man had probably hit Kate.

"Unless I've wasted all these years playing down at McGurk's," he said instead, "that old lady in there was throwing back straight vodka."

Kate faced front again and twisted her hands in her lap. Made a curious shrugging motion.

At that moment B.J. knew everything he needed to about Kate Manion. Even so, he found himself pushing farther.

"Why don't you tell her to just get screwed?"

"Because I still owe her five thousand dollars," she said, eyes out to the street. "Because she's right. Except for my nursing, I *have* made a shambles of everything in my life."

B.J. didn't insult her by telling her she was an idiot. She already knew that. At least the adult Kate did. But it wasn't the adult who was forced to walk back into that house. It was the child Kate, abused and frightened and unsure, who had learned her sense of worth from dysfunctional adults. B.J.

thought of how he'd spent so much of his own teen years trying to hurt his father for being so protective and strong. He was glad the old man had lived long enough for him to apologize.

Kate finally turned to him, and what he saw was a Kate no one else had ever seen. "Do you understand?"

Kate, the oldest child of an alcoholic. Kate the caregiver, Kate the protector. Kate, who was still paying for siblings who had in the end deserted her. Kate, who was even now being squeezed between the demands of her job, her friends, and her very acute sense of justice.

B.J. did understand. He understood that she knew perfectly well she was being unreasonable. He understood that in the end she couldn't be any different. He understood he had been sent to manipulate her into betraying her friends anyway.

Goddamn it, dead people were so simple. They didn't have Aunt Mamies to screw things up anymore. They didn't have to worry about divided loyalties.

"Yeah," he said simply, his attention out to the street. "I understand. But it's not going to help."

Kate just sighed. "I know."

After that, B.J. simply kept silent. Not because he was troubled by the admissions Kate had made, but by the understanding that no matter what she'd said, or what it was going to cost her, he was going to have to go back and make her do exactly what she didn't want to do. He was going to have to make her betray her friends, a woman who was still trying to protect two absent sisters from the spider who'd raised them all.

He was going to have to play for the opposition, and it didn't make him proud of himself at all.

✦ Chapter 11 ✦

SHE WAS GOING to have to do it. Kate had known it all along. She just hadn't wanted to admit it.

Somebody was killing people. That she could almost live with. After all, the victims weren't people she'd ever cared for. They wouldn't create any kind of hole in her life. Their deaths had yet to instill any sense of urgency in her.

Even the notes had failed to incite any kind of response. They were too impersonally polite to be anything but annoying. *Thanks for paying attention to my acting out, but don't interfere before I'm finished. Have a nice day.* How can you possibly take something like that seriously?

But Kate knew just how surgical the Administration's strikes tended to be. At one time there had been too much unrest in the ER, so instead of addressing the problems, or even listening to the complaints, the Administration had just broken up the staff and transferred them elsewhere. It had taken two years and a lot of bad press to get another good team together, mostly by transferring remaining members of the original team back where they belonged. Kate knew damn well that every person she liked or loved or even respected would be indiscriminately raked over the coals, which might just net the police a killer but would definitely break the spirit of the rest of the staff in the process.

Just like Sticks's little forays into the lounge for soda. Big deal. The doctors had a separate dining area, free refreshments, compensated trips to the Caribbean for seminars. The rest of the staff got free use of the parking lot and the chapel. But Sticks was poaching on the physicians' estate, and Administration was tough on poachers.

And Parker. What would they do to him once they realized he was seriously satisfying one of their senior residents? He wouldn't exactly get a reprimand, but the weight would be felt in small ways: scheduling, attention to details, a sudden escalation of anonymous complaints.

And then there was the fact that Edna had often caught movies on the doctors' lounge television. Edna claimed that because of a bad lightning problem in a former life, she couldn't allow any antennas or cables that might attract lightning at home. So if she wanted to see Sylvester Stallone on TV, she did it on the best set in the hospital.

Little secrets. Little indiscretions that by themselves would have gone unnoticed. Which Kate was privy to. Which, combined with the information about the three murders, could easily be damning.

She had to try her best to keep the investigation

from getting out of hand. And she knew the minute she did, she'd pay for it. No matter whether they wanted justice done or not, her friends would never forgive her for turning against them. They'd never understand that she would be doing it to protect their confidences rather than betray them.

And once again, just like six years ago when Mary Ellen and Molly had found out the truth, Kate would be left alone.

She thought about it all through the meal B.J. sprang for at Steak 'n' Shake, and then on the way over to Clayton, where they went to talk to John about the second note. She thought about it as they stood downstairs in the lobby of the detectives' building waiting for the undercover narcotics officers who shared quarters there to get into some kind of hiding before the civilians were buzzed upstairs. She thought about it and fought the sudden rush of claustrophobia.

She'd tell them later. After she'd had a chance to talk to Jules about it. After she'd watched a little on her own. After she'd had a chance to talk to Tim.

Later.

"Well, don' you look de young t'ing." John greeted them at the top of the stairs with one of his big alligator smiles.

"Save the flattery, John," Kate retorted, clumping past him. "I'm not going to do it."

"You wanna talk to your frien' anyway? I bet she'd like to talk to you."

Kate whipped around so fast she almost overbalanced. "What friend?"

His smile dimmed noticeably. Maybe the Little Dick enjoyed harassing the staff, but John didn't. "Dat sweet lady from ICU. Edna? Dat her name?"

"You know perfectly well that's her name." Kate turned her glare on B.J., who managed to look completely stunned, which for B.J. was a first.

"John?" he demanded. "You were going to wait."

John just shrugged, that same kind of shrug that implied interference by the gods in mortal affairs. "We were, till Dickie foun' dat sweet Edna's name on a big order for potassium. At de very wrong time, you know?"

"Oh, bullshit," Kate snapped. "She just happened to be the one ordering that day, that's all. Where is she?"

Where she was was in one of the offices in the back, her face pale, her unremarkable gray eyes wide, her hands trembling in her lap. When she caught sight of Kate, she almost came right off the hard-backed institutional green chair.

"You too?" she asked.

Kate caught her breath. "No. Are you okay, Edna?"

"We haven't broken out de hoses, if dat what you mean," John drawled from behind her.

Kate didn't even bother to answer. "Edna?"

"I . . . you knew I was a prisoner in ancient Egypt, didn't you, Kate? You never get over the feeling."

Kate slid into a free chair at the small Formica table and sighed. "Of course you don't, Edna."

"Hi, Kate. You're looking better."

Kate had not even noticed the other member of the inquisition squad in the corner: Mary Cherry, once again decked out in a surgically tailored suit, her hair pulled back in a bun that would have made Kate look like an Irish washerwoman but only highlighted the FBI agent's spectacular cheekbones and lustrous eyes. And Kate hadn't thought she could feel worse.

She nodded. "Mary."

Edna sniffed and unraveled a Kleenex in her hands. "You know Miss Cherry, Kate?"

"We've met. Do you have a lawyer, Edna?"

"John offered," Edna acknowledged. "But I didn't want to bother anybody."

Kate did her best not to grind her teeth.

"What brings you down here?" Mary asked, somehow managing to look elegant in a crowded room decorated in governmental notices and procedural manuals.

"Another note," B.J. said from the doorway, where he and John had followed Kate in.

John already had it in his hands. Mary came right to her feet, forgetting Edna, forgetting Kate, forgetting the note pad she'd been scribbling on.

"Note?" Edna asked.

Kate settled her head into her hands. She should call Tim. He'd be heading home sometime soon and wonder where she was. She had the feeling it was going to be awhile before she'd get a chance to join him.

"Shit."

Kate got her head up and turned it. She couldn't

imagine what could make Mary Cherry swear. It sounded so unnatural. What she saw was John standing in the doorway, the note carefully held up in a gloved hand so Mary could read it. Mary was bent a little, and she was frowning at the thing as if it had somehow betrayed her.

"Shit what?" Kate asked.

"Do you think this will show up on my record?" Edna said, wiping the table in front of her with the tissue. "I'm not doing very well down in the ER so far, and I'm too old to try and move to another hospital, you know?"

Kate found herself patting the woman's hand. "I know."

No one else seemed to be paying attention. John and B.J. were watching Mary for some further sign, and Mary was still watching the note, all three of them crowded in the doorway as if to prevent people from leaving. Kate wondered if she'd missed something.

"Shit what?" B.J. echoed.

Mary plopped her elegant hands on her hips and sighed. "Shit I don't know," she admitted. "Something's not right."

Both men bent to look closer. Edna rubbed at a spot that had probably been on the table since the Nixon administration. Kate waited.

"It's just like the first one," John prompted, his accent fading as he concentrated.

Mary nodded emphatically. "I know. Same tone, same precision, same everything. But something's wrong."

That was evidently when she realized her

chief suspect for sending said note was sitting not five feet away. Looking over, she actually scowled. Then she turned to Kate, who was watching the whole thing not just with mounting trepidation but with perfectly reprehensible curiosity.

"Can you hang around for a while so I can talk to you?"

"I'll need to call Tim and tell him. And then lie down for a few minutes."

All three looked at one another. "We have holding . . ." John offered.

There was a summary shaking of heads.

Kate sighed again. "Never mind. An office chair will do. After working nights this long, I can sleep damn near anywhere."

She proved just that after leaving a message for Tim on the answering machine, picking up her own messages, and trying very hard to get through to anyone in Administration who had information on the Rashad case.

"I thought you'd want to know," Phyl said bluntly on Kate's machine. "The papers have been served here, just like I said."

That was it. End of message. Unfortunately, when Kate tried to track down somebody for enlightenment on what the lawsuit would specifically mean to her, she came away empty-handed. It seemed that now the hospital had determined she was on her own, they couldn't quite decide who might have the necessary information she needed or the authorization to share it. So nobody gave it to her.

She left her last message with Tim's brother,

Steve, and sat back in her chair to wait for the
news to sink in.

The worst nightmare in a nurse's career: a
lawsuit. A big one, judging by the careful reaction
of the secretaries at St. Simon's. She should have
been panicked. At any other time in her life, the
very idea of forfeiting not only every penny she
had but her career as a whole to the gaping maws
of personal-injury lawyers would have sent her
screaming into the night.

Maybe she'd just been through too much.
Maybe she was just anticipating what else she was
going to have to suffer. Or maybe a person could
only take so much terror and rage at once.
Because it simply didn't sink in. In fact, by the
time Mary finally came back to discuss the note,
Kate was sound asleep in a metal-and-cardboard
chair with her casted leg up on an overturned
trash can.

The nap helped restore everything but her
temper. By the time B.J. drove her home after
another two hours of Twenty Questions, Kate was
stretched too thin even to feign politeness. She
simply wanted to get away from all the pressure.
Just for a little while, she wanted to be left alone.
Which was why she kept her news about cooperating to herself, and her eyes shut all the way
home. There was only so much she could share in
one afternoon.

The grounds of the hospital had once been a
quite parklike place. Unfortunately, that had been

before Interstate 270 was built, medicine boomed, and ancillary care centers became all the rage. Now the campus looked like public housing without the flower beds, stark cubes of white that crouched amid the surrounding office buildings and fast food franchises like an elephant hiding in the bushes. Kate felt the pull of ambivalence the minute she spotted it.

It was home. It was hell. Well, she thought with a sigh as they pulled up the driveway, at least nothing much had changed in her life.

Tim's car was in the apartment lot, and Jules's truck was in the ER parking. Another small indiscretion. Jules hated walking in from the employee lot, so she parked in the free parking out front by the ambulance entrance. An offense punishable by firing. So far Security was more afraid of Jules than of Administration, so she got away with it.

Kate decided that after all the caffeine John had poured in her, she was much better suited to sit in ER than in the pastel pillow of Tim's apartment. Besides, Tim listened to nothing but chamber music. It was enough to make Kate homicidal. She had B.J. drop her off right behind the Maryland Heights ambulance that had just pulled up.

"You're sure?" he asked, looking uncomfortably paternal.

Kate shot him a scowl that would have silenced a psychotic. "I'll talk to you later, okay?"

Even B.J. knew when to back down. He just nodded and headed off. Kate spent a minute stretching out the kinks she'd picked up from sitting in office furniture of the Marquis de Sade school and B.J.'s Jeep with the shot suspension, and then she followed the noise inside.

Maybe she'd been hoping it would be better each time she walked in. It wasn't. The place was packed to the rafters with the latest flu epidemic, a rash of the accidents that always happened in nice weather, and general spring depressions. Within minutes, Kate spotted Parker and Jules and Sticks, all barking at each other and tossing charts with a purpose that could only mean another twist of the rope from the bosses.

Wonderful. And she'd been looking for support.

With a healthy sigh, she resettled her crutches and headed down the hall to get herself some aspirin from the med prep. A few people said hello, but the volume level from the patients was enough to provoke more grimaces than smiles.

Right across from the med prep, Sticks was trying to shave a chunk of some guy's head in room four while he pissed and moaned about some woman sneaking up on him at the wrong time. He had a faceful of blood and, from the sound of it, a gutful of beer. The denizens in their natural habitat. Kate just grabbed her aspirin and some water to flush with.

She had one tablet halfway down her throat when she was interrupted.

"Excuse me."

Kate turned at the polite request and almost aspirated her aspirin. A very nice young man with bright blue eyes and long blond hair stood before her draped in nothing but what looked like his mother's best chintz drapes, curtain rings and all.

But then, Kate thought, she was a nearly bald woman in a cast, a red sweatsuit, and a baseball cap backward on her head. He probably felt right at home.

"Yes?"

He smiled and nodded. "Can you tell me where I might find Persephone?"

"Persephone?"

He nodded, shyly excited. "Yes. I'm Spring, and I need to tell her it's time to come out."

"Oh." Kate nodded. "Of course. Persephone. Hey, Jules, didn't I see Persephone over there with you?"

Jules looked up from the chart she was working on. "Oh, now, Mr. Spring, we've talked about that," she protested, getting to her feet. "Remember? You're going to meet Persephone in the subterranean caves on the fifth floor."

Fifth floor. St. Simon's Land of Enchantment.

"See?" Kate smiled brightly. "I'll bet if you go back to your room, your guide to the netherworld will be waiting for you already."

"You're sure?" he asked Jules. "That other man told me she was in the police car and she wasn't."

Jules was already there, slipping an arm around the young man's shoulder. "Of course she wasn't," she agreed gently, her earlier frustration briefly vanishing as she dealt with her patient. "How can she possibly bring the world back to life staring down the muzzle of a shotgun?"

Kate actually found herself smiling right along with Mr. Spring.

He turned one last time for Kate. "I remember now. I'm sorry to have bothered you."

"My pleasure."

"I'm so sorry about your injury. What happened?"

She couldn't help it. "Achilles heel."

Her little friend trotted off, exposing more humanity than a season should, and Kate went back to her drugs thinking that maybe she could just deal with the Fantasy Brigade. She'd at least gotten a little giggle out of that one.

"My, look at you! I'm so glad to see you looking so well."

Speak of the Fantasy Brigade. Kate hadn't even noticed old Polyester floating down the hallway like a vague apparition. The little nun patted Kate on the arm as if she'd just caught her playing hooky and smiled.

Kate did her best to choke down the second aspirin and smile back. "Hi, Sister. Busy tonight, huh?"

Sister Ann Francis nodded emphatically. "I know I should be up visiting with the pre-op patients, but I feel I can do so much more here."

"Get the fuck outa here!" some drunk screamed at the top of her lungs a couple of doors down. Kate was just sure she'd love a visit from the little nun.

That translucent skin seemed to compress a little at the sound, and then Sister Ann Francis smiled. "We who dedicate ourselves to serving others serve the Lord, Kate. We'll find our reward in his glorious heaven."

Kate nodded instinctively. "Of course we will."

The last time she'd bought that line had been the first time she'd tried to run away from Aunt

Mamie. A short run, after all the effort she'd put into it, all the hope she'd invested in it. All the faith she'd wasted.

The world was what she saw here. Nothing more, nothing less. But there was something to be said for an institution that protected people like Sister Mary Polyester, kept them feeling useful long past when the rest of society would have let them go. Come to think of it, if it weren't for that unfortunate obsession about past lives, Edna probably would have made a great nun. Kate should talk to her about it. Sometime before she had to work with her on the lanes.

Kate was watching as the psych-intake counselor ushered Mr. Spring past the two security guards who were hustling in from the other end to add their weight to the work of convincing the drunk overdose to hang around. She actually thought Mary Polyester had already gone.

"I worry so much for Juliette," the little nun suddenly said.

It took Kate a minute to realize that the little nun was talking about Jules. "Why?"

The minute Kate said it she wanted to take it back.

"She's been so upset lately that she's been using the fax machine to send out threatening notes."

"What?"

The nun gave a little shake of her head. "I thought one of her friends should know. I don't want her to be hurt, you see?"

"Threatening? Who?"

And for just a moment, the fog lifted. "Oh," Polyester said with a soft smile, "the usual culprits. Tell her to stop, Kate. Before she gets caught and fired. She has babies to take care of."

Faxes. Oh, great. Not just the Fax Fairies, from which every unit benefited, those anonymous wags who sent notes through machines and tube systems preaching anarchy and satire. The sayings that ended up on bulletin boards everywhere for at least five minutes before the powers that be ripped them down, since they proclaimed such truths as WORKING HERE IS LIKE WORKING IN A WHOREHOUSE. THE BETTER YOU DO YOUR JOB, THE MORE YOU GET SCREWED. That was frowned upon but expected, something Mary Polyester would never consider out of the ordinary. She was talking serious shit.

And Kate hadn't heard a word about it. Pulling open the drawer marked ASA, she pulled out a third aspirin to follow the others.

Suddenly she wanted to go listen to chamber music and talk to Tim about gender identification. She wanted to ask Mary Polyester more about Jules's indiscretion. But before she had the chance to ask, the cry of "Get Security!" rose from beyond the double doors to the front. Aspirin halfway to her mouth, Kate turned to see the doors to triage slam open. Before anybody could react, a skinny brunette with melting mascara and matching tattoo burst onto the work lane.

"Where is that son of a bitch?" she screeched, brandishing, of all things, a fire poker. "I'll kill him!"

The aspirin hit the floor as Kate struggled to reclaim her crutches. "Oh, Jesus!"

"Get outa my way!" the young woman warned, her hair color matching the mascara that ran down her face and the jeans she wore beneath her lovely Billy Ray Cyrus T-shirt. "I didn't hit him hard enough before, that fornicatin' sack of shit!"

Which was when Kate noticed there was blood on the poker. "Security!" she yelled, instinctively moving to block the woman from the rest of the patient rooms. Then she realized that the rest of her defensive line was a fifty-something year-old nun.

Kate heard a scrabble of feet from the room where Security had been camped. The woman raised the poker, fire in her bloodshot eyes and murder in her heart. She was no more than fifteen feet away.

"Move!" she screamed and lowered her head like a battering ram.

"Oh, my," Mary Polyester muttered. "Move aside, dear."

Kate had just been about to say the same thing. Since she was trying to balance on crutches, she was at a distinct disadvantage. She tried to pull the nun to safety. Instead, the nun pushed her out of the way just as the young woman reached warp speed.

"Oh, shit!" Sticks yelled, skidding into the hall and seeing what was about to happen. "She's gonna kill a nun!"

And then Mary Polyester went down in history by bringing the woman down. Kate saw the nun position herself and figured she was just going to make sure the assailant didn't get to the rooms. Instead, she somehow caught hold of the woman's upraised arm with one hand and simply swung her around in a circle. By the time the young woman figured out she was headed back the way she'd come, Sticks and the security forces intercepted her on the way by. Polyester not only hung on to her quarry, she held on so tightly that the poker ended up hitting the floor with a clang.

The language was blistering. The security guards, two ex-football jocks who spent an inordinate amount of time walking around just to hear the leather on their belts creak, slid to a halt as if the Archangel Michael himself had appeared to grab the woman. As for her, she was howling that the little nun had broken her arm.

Sister Ann Francis just smiled and let go. "It's all in the balance, you see," she said simply. "Our order has a very lovely institution for the insane in Texas. I spent a few years there."

Kate couldn't quite shut her mouth. "I guess so."

Still screeching about the philandering husband cowering in room four, the young woman was strong-armed out the door. Sticks gave Polyester a high five. Polyester straightened her short white veil, as if this were the most normal thing in the world, and bustled on down the hall to the sound of scattered applause. And Kate just stood there trying to get her heart to slow into the countable range.

Just a few weeks ago, this little incident

wouldn't have incited more than a couple of four-letter challenges. Now Kate felt as if she were going to faint. This was not good. Maybe she shouldn't even play with the fairy-dusters.

Jules found her holding herself up against the sink of the med prep.

"Did you hear what they did to Edna?" the nurse demanded without greeting as she dumped a couple of amps of Haldol in the contaminated box. Her earlier gentleness was noticeably absent.

Kate stifled an urge to run before things got worse. Jules was redder than usual, and her posture demanded confrontation.

"Yeah, I saw her in Clayton."

"Clayton?" she demanded, straightening so that she towered over Kate. "What the hell were you doing there?"

"Jules!" one of the other nurses yelled from the other end of the lane. "Your patient in six is escaping!"

"Hold the door open for him and wave good-bye!" she yelled back without turning to look. "Well?"

"I've been getting love notes from our killer," Kate confronted away. "The last one threatened me."

"Threatened you."

"Threatened me, Jules. Said that something bad will happen to me if I help the hospital with the investigation."

Jules gave her head a sharp nod. "Something bad will happen to you if you help this hospital do anything but set fire to Gunn's office."

Kate wasn't sure what she'd been expecting. She hadn't expected this. She didn't think she was going to make it if she didn't at least have Jules to understand. And she sure as hell couldn't discuss it in the middle of the work lane.

"You want this tension to go on?" she demanded.

"Go on? Don't be stupid. If this stops, they'll just find another excuse to screw us."

"Jules!" the security guard called from the drunk's room. "What do you want us to do with her?"

Kate saw Jules struggling to maintain control.

"What's wrong?" Kate asked. "What's got you so crazy?"

"Oh, nothing. Nothing at all. It's just that Parker got called in this afternoon and was told it has come to somebody's attention—although no names were given—that he's been taking advantage of one of the doctors. Taking *advantage,* mind. And that that kind of behavior is disruptive to an effective working relationship in the ER, so if he wishes to continue, he may do so from his new job on rehab. It's beginning, Kate. It's just beginning."

Kate couldn't breathe. She found herself staring at her friend as if she'd just spun her head 360 degrees. It was impossible. A coincidence. A really bad cosmic joke. She'd only told B.J. about it that morning. He couldn't have told anybody here. He wouldn't have.

But they'd found out. And they'd acted. And Jules was right. It was only the beginning.

Kate didn't bother talking to anybody else. She just turned around and headed out the door. She needed to call B.J. She needed to hurt B.J. But first she was going to sit in Tim's quiet, soft rooms and slam down a couple of glasses of cognac and think. She was going to wake Tim up and share everything with him and let him help her decide what to do.

The halogen lights had come on. To the west, the sky glowed in pure hues of crimson and peacock, a perfect spring night. Kate didn't often notice spring nights, because they didn't make her feel any better. She didn't now. She just walked back across the driveway, head down, hands clenched around crutches, sidestepping an ambulance and two cars as they swung into the emergency entrance, horns blaring, lights shuddering across the brick fronts of the apartments before her. She could smell the first barbecue smoke of the season and stepped over Big Wheels and baseball bats on the front lawn. She didn't notice the man approach from the parking lot until it was too late.

"Ms. Mary Kathleen Manion?" he asked.

She stiffened like a terrier with a bad scent. "You ask me for an interview, and I'll show you all the tricks I've learned with crutches."

"No interview, ma'am. You are Mary Kathleen Manion?"

"Why?"

For a ferret-faced, bespectacled weasel, he had a much-too-bright smile. "Here."

She accepted the paper from him before

thinking. The minute he spun away, she knew what it was. She'd been officially served. The son of a bitch had probably been waiting right here the whole time she'd been talking to her friends in the emergency room.

Kate knew she should at least look at the damn thing. After all, it would probably mean the last nail in her professional coffin. A multimillion-dollar lawsuit about which she couldn't testify, because she couldn't remember anything.

Instead, she shoved it in the waistband of her jeans and hobbled on up to the porch and let herself into the building.

She hoped nobody had the bad sense to stop and ask about her health.

The coffee from the station was burning its way back up her throat. Her head pounded and her chest ached. She thought she couldn't feel more frantic, more caught. From a threat on her life to Mamie to Administration to the betrayal of her friends, and then the added treat of a lawsuit. A girl simply couldn't have a better day.

The lights in the apartment were out and the stereo silent. Tim must have had a rough shift down at kiddyland. Carver met Kate at the door, pacing right in between her legs and the crutches, which meant the cat was really pissed. Kate wasn't in the mood for that either.

"Knock it off," she snapped, edging him away with a toe.

He veered back in and then swung off toward the hallway, whining. Kate just shook her head. Everybody had something to say tonight. She ignored the cat and turned for the kitchen, where she intended to further deplete the stock of alcohol.

Carver found her there and resumed his attentions. Kate looked over to find a full food bowl and water dish. She balanced on a crutch as she sipped at the fiery liquid, which should settle some of the other brushfires in her. She glared at the cat, who glared back and meowed again.

"What is it, Lassie?" she asked dryly. "Has Timmy fallen down the mine shaft again?"

The cat didn't think she was particularly funny. He made another run for her crutches and scooted away again, back to the hallway. Kate decided she might as well wake Tim now as later. It was his cat. He could deal with him.

She let one crutch rest so she could walk and drink at the same time. It took a little more maneuvering, but she wasn't interested in aesthetics right now. As she followed the antsy cat into the hallway, she flipped on the light so she didn't trip over him in the dark. That was when she realized Tim's door was open.

Tim never left his door open when he slept. Especially if Kate was in a bad mood and needed to listen to music. Carver reached the threshold and turned on her, waiting. For some reason, Kate faltered to a halt in the middle of the hallway.

Light spilled across the cream carpet and illuminated the militarily precise corners of Tim's bedspread. It was empty.

"Tim?"

Out in the kitchen the refrigerator kicked on. A siren growled and lifted outside, making Kate shiver. It was silent in the apartment. Suddenly too silent.

Bile rose in her throat. She broke out in a sweat.

"Tim?"

She stepped closer. Carver waited. He turned and looked into the darkened room as if he could see something she couldn't. Kate followed, her gait suddenly unsteady, her heart stumbling.

And then she saw it. The shadow by the window. Swaying just a little from where the cat must have brushed up against it.

Swaying.

"Mama?"

She was a trauma nurse, trained to act. To face crisis calmly, efficiently. Experienced enough that she couldn't remember the last time she'd frozen in a crisis. But Kate didn't hear the drip of liquid as the brandy spilled from the glass she forgot. She didn't notice that Carver brushed up against her or that the phone began to ring. She didn't hear the peculiar keening noise in her own throat. The sight of Tim's body hanging from the plant hanger froze her into complete immobility.

✦ Chapter 12 ✦

BY THE TIME B.J. got there, the apartment complex looked like a battle scene. Police cruisers and television trucks clogged the parking lot, and bystanders from all over the campus clotted the grounds in chattering little groups. B.J. shouldered his way through with no more than a nod to the uniforms who held the door for him.

Somebody had done a pretty good job with the scene, moving everybody into the unit across the hall so that only evidence techs and the investigator from his office roamed Tim and Kate's apartment. John stood in the hallway rubbing the back of his neck.

"Where is she?" B.J. asked before even checking the scene itself.

" 'Cross de hall. Wid Jules. She de one who called. Came over to apologize 'bout somet'in', couldn't get Kate to open the door, hear dis funny noise like somet'in' bad wrong, and got Security to let her in. She foun' Katie jus' standin' in de hall like a statue, cryin' for her mama. Dis fucker's stopped bein' funny, B.J. Ya know dat?"

B.J. took his first look at the body and grimaced. "I know that." Then he walked over to the investigator on call and got down to work.

By the time he reached Kate, he found her surrounded by women. They were still crowded in the apartment across the hall, another shoebox decorated in Fisher Price and Early American. B.J. didn't see any kids, just doctors' wives and Jules, every one of them making liberal use of the Kleenex box.

Kate sat on the couch, her hands clenched in her lap, her head down, her eyes the only dry set on the scene. The women tried to press tea and Valium on her. Jules hovered over her shoulder, reduced to ineffective little waves of her hands. Even Mary Cherry had shown up, although it took B.J. a minute to recognize her in plaid shirt, jeans, and muddy cowboy boots. She was crouched down next to the couch with a hand on Kate's arm.

Kate didn't seem to realize that any of them were there. B.J. didn't like it a bit.

"Ladies," John intoned behind him, "we gonna talk to Katie here. Okay if we do it alone?"

There was general murmuring and not a little sniffling as the room almost emptied out. Mary didn't budge, and B.J. knew from the look in Jules's eyes that they'd have as much luck getting her out the door as getting an Administration spokesperson in.

B.J. crouched down right in front of Kate. He could see the careful compression of Mary's features, a subtle message of worry. He didn't need that. Jules's red-faced distress said it all.

"Kate?"

Nothing. Not even a flicker of the eyes. She just kept staring at her hands where they were clenched over her knees. She kept frowning as if she was trying to remember something.

B.J. gently pulled her hands apart and took hold of them. "Come on, Kate. Talk to me."

Kate never lifted her eyes to acknowledge him. She just stared at their hands. "How did she know?"

B.J. did his best not to give away his relief. "Know what, pogue?"

She lifted her gaze then, and B.J. was treated to a wasteland. Old pain, old guilt, grown hard and ugly. Hidden all this time behind a smart mouth and attitude. It was all he could do to stay there and take what she was about to hand him. He was just too damn out of practice.

"I found *her,* too. Came home from school one afternoon and walked right into the living room without thinking that anything was wrong."

"Found who?"

"My mother. She'd threatened me for years. Every time I didn't do what she wanted, every time things got tough. Said she'd kill herself. I guess I stopped paying attention."

He held on tighter. Not just for her sake but for his. He heard Jules's instinctive moan of emotion and ignored it. Fought every urge to run and held on to Kate's hands, Kate's gaze. Kate's pain.

She looked up beyond B.J. He imagined she'd finally realized that John was standing back there. Then she shook her head. "The note threatened *me*. Me. I just thought—"

"Katie, chil'," John said, as gently as B.J. had ever heard him. "I know dis is bad, but we gonna need to talk."

"You took him down, didn't you? Please tell me you took him down."

"He's down," B.J. promised.

Her eyes returned to B.J.'s. "I just stood there, Beej. I couldn't even—"

B.J. didn't give her a chance to get going. "He's probably been dead at least a couple of hours, pogue. There wasn't a damn thing you could have done."

"I'm a trauma nurse. . . ." Still in the dreamy half-awake voice, as if she were only working on half volume. "I'm a . . ."

Finally, the tears welled up and spilled over. Her shoulders began to shudder. Her mouth opened wider, as if the words needed more room to work their way out. But there weren't going to be any more words. In their place came the sobs, and she folded in on herself like a slowly deflating balloon. There was nothing B.J. could do but catch her and hold on.

Kate figured somebody finally spiked her coffee to get her to sleep, because she woke up with a furry tongue and a fuzzy head. One thing remained crystal clear, though. Tim was dead.

The sun was out when she woke, pouring through the blinds in B.J.'s rumpled den like butter to melt against the wall. Even so, all she could see were shadows. Shadows and nightmares, the purple faces and swollen tongues and wide eyes of the strangled.

Tim, her sweet, tormented, protective Tim. The sacrificial lamb in a grisly ritual Kate didn't understand.

Kate fought the nausea, fought the tide of guilt. If she hadn't been involved, he might be alive. If she'd been faster. If she'd listened or believed or taken better care of him. An old litany that didn't seem to get any easier to bear with repetition.

What she didn't fight was the fury. There, deep inside like a well of black fire, threatening to char everything else in her.

"You're awake."

Kate didn't bother to look away from the neatly trimmed lawns out the window. "No thanks to you."

B.J. shuffled a little uncomfortably in the doorway. "You're still not as strong as you think, Kate. You couldn't have taken much more without just imploding."

Kate sighed and rubbed at her swollen eyes with the heels of her hands. "I know. I'm sorry."

"Don't be sorry."

Kate looked up in some surprise to see the shadow of a rueful grin beneath all that strain.

"Steve's coming over a little later," he said, one hand propped on the doorjamb, the other already shredding a cigarette. "He wants to talk to you about the lawsuit."

Kate shook her head. "Screw the lawsuit."

"Give Steve something to do," he suggested.

"Besides, he wants to be there when you're questioned again."

Kate just shrugged. She took a minute to look around the house she'd always thought would be decorated in early dust and fast food bags. It was unkempt in a papers-and-magazines kind of way, but not dirty. More cozy, with what looked like cast-off furniture from his parents and overflowing bookshelves. Kate had spent the night on a brown tweed foldout couch across from a top-of-the-line sound system.

"I've never been here before," she said.

"I don't spend so much time here myself."

Kate knew just what his offer had meant the night before. She would have placed bets he'd never had a woman spend the entire night, no matter what kind of calisthenics they'd been involved in. Now that she was coherent enough, she felt honored.

"Thanks. I didn't really want to go all the way to Jefferson County. Besides, Jules just would have wrapped me in some dead animal and force-fed me orange juice and game shows." She rubbed her head a moment, memories skittering a little from the time after she'd dropped off on the couch the night before. "Did I hear the pipes last night?"

"Yeah."

She nodded. "Just wanted to be sure. I was worried it might have been the banshee."

That actually made B.J. smile a little. "Tim probably would have liked the idea of a banshee."

Kate almost got a grin out as well. "Tasteful

but emotional. Good point." The grief caught her by surprise, sharp as new needles. "Oh, Beej," she whispered. "What am I gonna do?"

B.J. never moved. "You're gonna go on," he said simply. "Just like always."

She faced him with every ounce of determination her fury had borne. "I am going to get her," she said. "I'm going to pay her back for this."

"You're going to help?"

"I was going to help before this happened. I just wanted to do it on my own terms, so I could protect my friends." Tears blurred her vision for a minute. "But I couldn't protect my friends, could I?"

"Hey," he said, his eyes and voice belying the levity of his words, "life sucks. That's one of the rules."

"Yeah," she admitted. "It is, isn't it? And I don't even have any pipes to make me feel better."

"We'll go down to McGurk's when this is all over and have an Irish wake for Tim. How's that sound?"

Kate actually found a grin for that one. "I think he'd rise up and haunt me."

"Up the rebels."

She took a fortifying breath. "Up the rebels."

"You can't come back to work. You're not well yet. You don't even have hair."

Armed with her new walking cast, a determination the color of steel, and the knowledge that she finally had the upper hand, Kate leaned forward a little in the burnt-orange chair that faced the Formica-and-metal desk in Phyl's office and stared her supervisor down.

"You can let me do light duty," she said. "Answer phones, make call-backs. That kind of thing. You did it for Suzie when she had her tubes tied."

"That's different."

Someday Kate would ask why. Not today. She didn't have the patience, the sense of proportion. Tim had been dead three days, and Kate needed to be doing something. She needed to be around people who might know something about how he died. She needed to be away from the thick silence in that apartment.

"Please, Phyl. I'll behave. I need the money. I need to be busy."

Phyl's expression immediately crumbled a little. "I really am sorry, Kate," she admitted, digging her fingernails into the pencil she'd been juggling. "Tim was . . . special."

"Yes," Kate answered. "He was. Please, Phyl. Help me out."

Phyl spent a moment consulting the pencil, as if someone had left a message to her imprinted on it. All Kate saw was NO. 2 SOFT. Finally, she sighed. "There *is* some paperwork you could do. We're trying to pull together numbers for re-accreditation."

"Thank you. You don't know what this means to me."

"Have you thought about Administration's problem?"

Kate nodded. "Give me a little time, Phyl. Let

me see how I do just coming back. I have to take this one step at a time."

Phyl nodded and settled the pencil in among a drawerful of about two dozen identically sharpened mates. "I'll tell Human Resources you'll be back part-time after the funeral. All right?"

Kate thought to protest, but she knew what her energy level was like. She just nodded and levered herself to her feet.

"You *are* looking better," Phyl finally said, a bit stiffly. "I'm glad your accident wasn't worse."

For just a moment, Kate almost snapped something ugly. Something that would have implied that four dead in one crash was quite bad enough for her, that this hospital should have taken its responsibilities more seriously.

But too much had happened since then. Too much. She just smiled and mumbled her thanks and got the hell out of the office.

Jules was waiting in the nurses' lounge. When Kate walked in, her friend looked up from the moccasin she was sewing.

Kate closed the door and leaned on it. "I'm back," was all she said.

Jules smiled. "A celebration is definitely in order."

Kate just wished she agreed. "Up the rebels."

Jules went back to her work. "Up the rebels."

Since things were slow between lunch and the evening shift, Kate and Jules had the lounge to themselves. The old tan Naugahyde couch they'd inherited from the doctors' lounge was littered with nursing journals and romance novels. The refrigerator held warnings about food dating and hepatitis outbreaks. The television, a gift from a long-ago doc, was tuned to the closing credits of a game show. Jules commanded the only decent chair in the place, homespun and dyed yarn spilling over her bag and sections of soft leather taking up the table. Kate chose the couch.

"So," she said, leaning her head back against the wall and thinking she should have stolen some more aspirin before she'd made a stand. "You want to tell me just what sedition you're spreading?"

When Jules looked up, her expression was the soul of innocence. A dead giveaway. "Sedition?"

"The fax machine has your fingerprints all over it, old girl."

Jules set her work down. "So what was the deal? You come back to work and keep an eye on the little people for them?"

If Kate had any room left to feel anything, that would have hurt. And she'd thought focusing on something other than Tim might help.

"Thanks," she retorted. "Your faith in me is overwhelming."

Jules's color changed perceptibly. "Well, just what did you expect me to say?"

"Oh, I don't know. How 'bout, 'Gosh, Kate, you've got your hands full enough right now without me adding to it by playing juvenile games with the hospital communications systems'?"

"Do you know what they've been up to since you've been gone?"

"I know they're just itching to use this investigation as an excuse to clean house, damn it. And if I found out you've been playing Captain Midnight, don't you think they will?"

"They're too stupid to figure out I'm parking in the front lot."

Kate tried to give Jules the glare that statement deserved. She probably just looked afraid. "I'm not going to last without you here, and they're gonna get you. I'll guaran-goddamn-tee it, Jules. The dogs are out."

"Are you one of them?"

Kate didn't even bother to answer. She just closed her eyes and willed the chaos in her to ease back down a notch so she didn't physically hurt someone.

"And now for the news at the top of the hour," the television intoned. "Investigation continues into the latest mystery at Saint Simon's Medical Hospital, the death of senior surgical resident Doctor Timothy Peterson—"

"Oh, turn it off," Kate snapped, without opening her eyes. Jules was already on her feet as the news anchor restated the details yet again.

"Hospital spokesmen state that the death was a suicide. Police refuse to comment—"

By this time Kate's eyes were open and she was halfway to her feet. "Those assholes!" she shrilled at the set.

Jules could do little more than stare.

Kate swung an arm at the offending newsperson, who had already segued into the lovely spring weather forecast for the metro area. "Who told them that? Who the hell told them he committed suicide?"

Jules looked poleaxed. "I don't know, Community Relations? It had to come from the top, didn't it?"

"No," Kate snarled. "It did not. They probably interviewed the goddamn gardener." She started to pace, sounding like Long John Silver as the walking cast made a hollow sound as it hit. "They're not going to do this. They are *not*—"

Before she thought about it, she slammed out the door and down the hall to the elevators. She was headed for the carpeting. She was looking for answers.

"But who told them that?" she demanded of Lucy Silhammer, the public relations assistant who typed news releases and dreamed of the big lights of local weathercasting.

"Well, I don't know." The young airbrushed blonde defended herself, her gaze darting behind Kate as if expecting rescue. "We just answer questions. Decisions like that aren't made here."

"Then where are they made?"

"Oh, well, I'm not sure. It might have come from any of the administrative offices. You know, it *has* been busy here the last few weeks—"

"And you didn't bother to check it out? You just told everybody in the metro area that Tim committed suicide so his parents could hear that kind of thing on the goddamn news?"

The girl paled a little. "He didn't—um, commit suicide?"

Kate leaned way over her desk until Lucy

flinched away. "He did not—um, commit suicide. And I want you to tell the press that."

"Me? Oh, no, that's not my job. You need to talk to somebody else."

"Who? Give me a name."

That obviously put Lucy on overload, because she simply sat there, mouth open, eyes blank as a carp. "Why, I—we get the press releases. That's all I know."

"Well, know this. I'm holding you personally responsible. Find out and straighten it out, or I'll cause you so much trouble you'll wish you were a fish farmer."

Lucy actually had tears in her big blue eyes. "You can't threaten me," she challenged, lifting her little chin in defiance. "I'm only doing my job. It's not my fault—I mean, if it's not true."

Kate sought her answers elsewhere. She tried to get the lawyer on the phone at his Clayton office. She tried to get past secretaries in Administration to Mr. Gunn or Mr. Fellows, or any of the myriad faceless vice presidents who might possibly have been in charge at the moment the word was leaked to the press. No one was home. No one was responsible. Kate had four secretaries explain that to her. Then she had the nursing supervisor warn her that if she didn't vacate the carpeted area pretty damn quickly, she wasn't going to have to worry about her job, much less anybody else's.

B.J. intercepted her at the door to the elevators. Kate was primed and lit. And B.J. stood there, a cigarette over each ear, the ponytail neatly tied back, the Dead Head shirt on, hands in lab coat pockets, looking cool as rock and roll. She damn near let him have the first swing.

"What are you doing here?"

"Me?" he asked gently. "Hell, I live here lately. Didn't you know that?"

Kate snapped to a sudden halt. "Nobody else—"

"No. Nobody else. It's okay. I came here to keep you from dismembering any of the administrative staff. Am I too late?"

Kate stole a look back at the closed door that led into the soft, sibilant world of Administration.

"Trying to get anything out of them is like punching a roomful of balloons," she admitted, her shoulders sagging.

B.J. pulled a hand out of a pocket and put an arm around her shoulders.

"I'm not going to cry," she challenged.

"I didn't say you were. I just want to make sure you can't get back in that door and commit mayhem."

She slumped even more. "Did you hear what they did?"

"Jules told me."

Jules. She'd obviously made the call, right after Kate had called her names. Kate shook her head. "They'd rather hurt Tim and his family than take any responsibility for another murder. That's evil, Beej. It's just—"

"They won't have much choice soon."

"It's finished?"

B.J. just nodded. He'd done the physical

autopsy two days ago as Kate had paced his house, but the tox and evidence work had backed up. Kate had accompanied Steve out to the airport to pick up his parents from Florida and then escaped to the hospital so she wouldn't have to face their stark-eyed grief another minute more than she had to. After all, she was going to spend the next two days in close proximity with it at the funeral home.

B.J. took her arm and turned her away from trouble. "We'll talk about it later. Let's get out of here."

"Where?"

"John and Mary want to talk to you," he said. "But I thought we'd do it someplace different."

"Different how?"

"You'll see."

"All this," Kate said forty minutes later in a suspiciously small voice, "just for me?"

"Just for you," B.J. answered from behind her.

Kate couldn't quite get her breath. The sunlight was hurting her eyes, that and the color. She wasn't used to the color.

B.J. had brought her to the gardens. It was how she thought of them, just the gardens, as if they were personally hers, a few acres in the south city where she could go to rest when things got too noisy or stressful.

"I'd forgotten." She was trying to figure out where the hell all the color had come from while she wasn't looking: reds and pinks, blues and yellows and whites and greens. Especially greens, every hue and shade. Greens so sweet you wanted to take off your shoes and soak your toes in them. Greens that took your breath away.

Kate hadn't realized until now how bound she'd become by the sterile walls of the hospital. She hadn't realized just how much she'd missed all this.

"Forgotten what?" B.J. asked alongside her.

She gave a startled laugh, and thought how stupid she sounded. "Spring."

B.J. just nodded. "I thought so."

Kate felt like walking right over to the velvety grass and lying facedown in it. Behind her the Latzer Fountain shot water twenty feet into the air. The breeze ruffled a thousand trees and showered apple and cherry blossoms onto the lawns. Beneath a canopy of oak and ash, dogwood and redbud bloomed, and along the walks, flower beds exploded into a paint box of tulips and hyacinth and daffodils, pansies and phlox and columbine.

Shaw's Garden was a civilized place. A soft, sedate place where Kate had once known how to restore herself.

She stumped along toward the chimes and waterfalls and arbors of the scented garden on the left of the fountain, her head on a constant rotation, the beauty of the place hurting hard, like a too-bright light against sore eyes. She'd never come here with Tim. Suddenly, she couldn't remember why.

"I have a history with this place," she said, almost reintroducing herself.

Alongside her, B.J. laughed. "I know. I was one of the interns you dragged over here after surviving a bad night, remember?"

Kate wasn't likely to forget the looks she got when, still in scrubs, she'd dragged the scruffy, impatient physician through the doors into the sunlight. "I didn't want to see you commit mayhem. I figured a few hours here in the trees would calm you down a little."

"Saved my life."

She did offer a little private smile then. "It was a tough night."

A brutal night. It had taken B.J. two solid hours beneath the trees and three circuits of the seventy-nine-acre complex with its rolling lawns and sculpted flower beds to overcome his already famous rage at the frivolous carnage they'd waded through that night.

Kate had a picture taken here, too. Not of B.J.; a formal picture, taken by the rose garden, of Michael and her on their wedding day. She'd wanted so much that day. She could still see it in the tentative smile she'd worn, in her Laura Ashley wedding dress and her nasturtium-and-lily bouquet. She'd hoped for escape and comfort. She'd ended up with emptiness.

It hadn't all been Michael's fault, she thought, as she reached the arbors and collapsed on one of the secluded little benches by the reflecting pools. He was a cop who defined himself by his rule books. She was a nurse who was never satisfied unless she was mounting an insurrection. Life had been a hell of a lot more fun with Tim, sex or not.

"Where are John and Mary?" she asked.

"We'll meet them at the restaurant," B.J. told her. He stretched out alongside her, his face up to the sun.

Kate reached over and squeezed his hand. "Thanks, pogue."

His smile was dark and knowing. "That's okay," he said. "I owed you."

Actually, John and Mary were waiting for them in a corner of the restaurant patio.

"I don't suppose we could hijack a tram and have this discussion over by the Japanese garden," Kate suggested, as she eased into her chair. They'd let her have one facing the fountain, so she wasn't quite so upset. She could watch the kids play tag with the water and listen to amateur botanists discuss the plant life hereabouts as the four of them talked death and destruction.

"Tough to keep your paperwork from flyin' away," John said, anchoring his with a glass of iced tea. "How you doin', little girl?"

Kate took a minute with the scenery. "Better, thanks. Did you hear what the hospital said about Tim?"

"It wasn't suicide, you know. B.J. here tell you?"

"Not yet. What do you two have on your minds?"

For the first time since Kate had met her, Mary looked less than composed. Once again outfitted in work clothes, today she didn't seem quite as pressed and orderly. Strands of hair snaked out of her chignon, and she kept fingering her Cross pen like a worry stone.

"You gonna help?" John asked.

Kate glared at him. "Don't insult me, John. How 'bout we just get on with it?"

"Dat why we sittin' here instead of out in de county where we belong. Okay?"

Kate couldn't manage much more than a sigh. "Okay."

"Kate," Mary said without preamble, squinting against the sun, "did you notice anything . . . anything unusual when you went in that night?"

Right from the sublime to the terrible. Kate wanted to watch how the light dappled them all like a Monet painting. Instead she steeled herself to the job at hand.

"Besides the obvious?"

Nobody answered.

"I've been going over it in my mind. You know about the process server—"

"We talked to him already. He never went in. Only watched the front door. Since he was just looking for you, he didn't really notice who belonged to what other white coat."

"I didn't see anybody else. You talked to the tenants? The house staff is in and out of that place at all hours."

"We did. Nobody remembers anybody unusual in the hallways. No unusual noises, although it must have happened at cartoon time. The women said they could have missed something during Ninja Turtles."

Kate forced herself to look back. Examine every detail in search of the one that would indict her for negligence, just like she always had with her mother.

"I didn't notice anything," she mused, not even feeling the sunlight on her face anymore. "The only thing out of place was Carver."

"Carver."

"The cat. He made me go in and look. He was antsy as hell." Images flashed relentlessly, old ones too easily superimposed over new, nightmares and reality dancing too close to separate. Suddenly she looked up, surprised. "There wasn't any struggle." She hadn't even realized she'd held the memory until she gave it away. "His room was absolutely clean. The whole place was."

Mary nodded, consulting her note pad. "That's what we're trying to figure out. There was an overturned stool, but the plant hanger held, which means there wasn't a sudden drop, or the whole thing probably would have pulled away."

"Then how?"

"Dere's more." John now. "Doctor Peterson had a big dose of quick-actin' barbiturate in him."

"How?"

"We're checking. When we arrived, the dishwasher had been run a little while earlier. He might have gotten it in a glass. It was enough to kill him all by itself."

"It doesn't make any sense," Kate insisted.

"You're right," Mary said. "It doesn't. That's

why we need your help. We want you to go over what we found with us."

"Found? You got something else?"

Mary nodded, checked her notes, checked B.J. for clearance. "We actually got some fibers this time. White cotton-polyester blend."

Kate managed an unhappy laugh. "Well, that narrows it down to anybody wearing a lab coat or uniform."

"An' a small brown bead," John added. "From a necklace, maybe. You don' wear dat kin' of t'ing, do you?"

"Jewelry and makeup?" Kate countered dryly. "Whatever for? I don't meet anybody but doctors, and I'd rather date a snake, thanks."

"You were living with one," Mary reminded her gently.

Kate didn't bother to set them straight. Tim's sexual persuasion wasn't an issue here. She just smiled and shrugged, wishing like hell she had a better epitaph. "Tim wasn't really a doctor. He cared too much."

John and Mary both checked B.J. for a reaction, but he was busy fondling a pack of cigarettes and didn't seem to notice.

"So the necklace wouldn't have been yours," Mary said.

Kate shook her head. "Most everybody I know wears gold with their lab coats," she said. "But who knows?"

"What about the note?" Mary asked. "What are your thoughts on that?"

"Note?"

This time all three of them paused. Looked at each other. Kate found herself wishing she had more than iced tea in her glass.

"You didn' see a note?" John asked.

Suddenly Kate didn't want to be here anymore. "Come on, kids. Stop yankin' me around. What note?"

"The note that was pinned to Tim's shirt," B.J. said simply.

✦ *Chapter 13* ✦

KATE CLOSED HER eyes and battled back a surge of nausea. She heard a shuffling sound and knew Mary was about to intervene. She heard the sudden silence and knew B.J. had stopped her.

"No," she said. "I didn't see it. I just saw . . . I saw Tim and couldn't move. What does the note say?"

"Nobody else knows about it," Mary warned. "We'd rather keep it that way."

Kate got her eyes open. It seemed enough to give Mary pause. She nodded as if conceding the point, then opened her notebook again.

"Um, here. 'THE RESPONSIBILITY IS OURS, AS ALWAYS. YOU MUST UNDERSTAND. YOU ARE THE REASON.' "

"I'm the reason?" Kate echoed. "What do you mean, I'm the reason? What the hell is she talking about?"

An older couple at the next table looked over at the sound of Kate's raised voice. She willed herself back into control so they wouldn't have to move this discussion somewhere inside.

Somewhere away from the sun and the trees, where shadows weren't just an illusion of the sun but a message.

It was Mary, in her quiet, too calm voice, who brought Kate back. "That's what we were hoping you could tell us."

"Well, I can't."

"Maybe you can"—the agent nudged gently—"but you just don't know it yet. Maybe if we just talked a little—about the people at work."

"Is this all absolutely confidential?"

"Of course," Mary said.

Kate gave all her attention to B.J. "Just like the other morning when I told you about those little 'indiscretions' the staff had committed?" she demanded.

He didn't even have the grace to look chagrined. "I only talked to John about it."

"Well, somebody talked to Administration, because one of those people has already had his file pulled."

It was John who swore. Fluently. "Dickie," he snapped. "I'll roas' his skinny white butt."

"That's what I've been talking about all along," Kate insisted. "Lately Administration's been using pressure to get people either to submit or quit, especially anybody with time served. The information you're asking for from me is the kind of stuff that makes them happier than a shark in a wading pool of new shavers."

"Jus' us," John promised her. "Unless somet'in' concrete turns up. Please, Katie. B.J.'s no help. He don' remember nuttin' 'bout how hospitals are

run. All he remember is bad food, long hours, an'
stupid nurses."

Kate snorted. "Typical resident." For a moment
she retreated into silence. "What do you want?"
she asked finally, knowing perfectly well that she
sounded more tired than determined.

"A way to focus in," Mary said. "Something
more than the popular refrain we hear over there
of, 'If someone else hadn't done it first, I would
have.'"

Kate managed a wan smile. "Last week I
would have been singing that tune myself."

"It's really that bad?"

"It's really that bad. And it's worse for the few
of us left who give a damn about what we're
doing."

"If you get dat much mail, it can't be jus' a few
of you," John suggested.

Kate shook her head. "We've reached the
point where we're staffed by new grads and agency
nurses, because the good nurses are too expensive or too burned out. The ones who have hung
in there have a price on their heads."

It wasn't getting her anywhere and she knew
it. She tried taking a drink of her tea, but she
didn't taste it. She was really in a corner this time,
and it meant she was going to have to offer somebody up, somebody she cared about; she just
knew it.

"Go through the time cards," she said, not
strong enough to face them. "At least for
Fleischer's murder. He drank out of that cup every
damn day of his life, the minute he finished

rounds in the morning. And don't be surprised if our girl had just clocked out when it happened. A lot of overtime happens at that hospital that isn't compensated, because you get reprimanded for running up your time card."

"Can you focus a little tighter?" John asked.

"Dickie's already pullin' cards, but dere are so many. An' askin' doctors don' help, 'cause half of dem don't even notice which face goes wit' what uniform. Other half say God got Fleischer for his sins."

Kate made a show of thinking about something she'd done nothing but think about for the last week. "It's somebody with access to the surgical intensive-care unit where Attila worked. Don't bother with any of the medical or coronary ICU crew. They wouldn't be caught dead in SICU, and if they did the SICU crowd would run them out with pitchforks and torches."

"Why?"

"No one is more territorial than a critical-care nurse. The ER nurses think they know everything, the medical ICU nurses think the ER nurses are idiots, and the SICU nurses think everybody but them got their nursing degree from the Betty Crocker School of Nursing. ER's up there on admissions all the time, though. So get them and surgery, recovery room, anybody working cases that would have been brought in. And get ancillary care: respirator, lab, central supply, X ray, medical services. Anybody with a right to be in the units. House staff, too."

B.J. looked up. "House staff?"

Kate gave him a wry grin. "Not everyone overcame their idealism before entering medical school like you did."

"What 'bout other staff?" John asked. "You know, floor nurses?"

Kate shook her head. "They'd stand out like a sore thumb, especially if they spent enough time there to doctor Attila's coffee with so much potassium. You might check the pool nurses, but I don't see them wandering through the doctors' lounge with impunity any more than the floor nurses would. And not many of them know me well enough to send love letters. No, B.J. was right. It has to be somebody in the critical-care areas: most judgmental, most intense, most decisive, highest burnout."

"Regular staff nurses," Mary offered. "Like you."

Kate sighed and shook her head. "Not necessarily," she admitted, thinking of her little tête-à-tête with Phyl. "Head nurses and supervisors probably have six times the frustration level we do—at least the ones who still try. Oh, and you might want to talk to the housekeeping staff. I think Wanda and Albert are still the day crew up there. They see everything that goes on, and nobody pays any attention to them."

John looked at his list and sighed. "Great. Dat mean we gotta run times on ever'body on two floors."

"Better than everybody on eight floors. You still think it's a woman?"

Mary looked up as if she'd been overheard plotting sedition. "Why do you ask?"

Kate focused on the glass in her hand. "I just can't see Edna having the upper-body strength to . . . to . . ."

Mary nodded. "If it hadn't been for the notes, I'd be tempted to say Tim's was a different murderer. But they're identical. My best guess is she coaxed him up on the stool."

"She got him to hang himself voluntarily?"

The man at the next table looked over again, his features disapproving. Kate's second outburst must have done it, because the couple picked up their trays and decamped, leaving the corner empty. Kate was relieved. She had the feeling she was going to give way to a little more emotion before this was finished.

"Tim died of anoxia to the brain," B.J. said, "not strangulation. I think he just slumped against the rope and cut off his carotids. He also had a subgaleal hematoma from a hit on the head. A tough combination to beat."

"It still doesn't make sense," Kate protested.

"No, it doesn't," Mary agreed. She picked up her pen again and doodled on the edge of her napkin, neat concentric circles in perfect proportion. "But nothing here makes sense. I have a feeling I'm missing something on this one, but I can't tell what."

"Have you heard back from Quantico yet?" B.J. asked.

She shook her head. "Not yet."

"You're definitely calling this serial murder?"

"We have four murders, each one separated by a degree of time. That's all the definition you're supposed to need."

Still, her expression said, she wasn't satisfied. Neither was Kate. But then, Kate wouldn't be until she invited whoever had killed Tim up onto a step stool where a rope hung from the ceiling.

"Why Tim?" Kate asked again. "Tim was one of the last good guys around."

John scratched the back of his neck. "As a warnin' to you, little girl," he said.

"Yeah, but if this whole thing is about frustration over the condition of medicine today, does it make sense that she'd kill one of the last few pure hearts around, even to threaten me into compliance? She had plenty of more sullied souls to use over there, me among them."

Kate saw the look on Mary's face and instinctively turned to B.J. for confirmation.

B.J. nodded. "The man made Schweitzer look like a hack."

"We're not saying she's completely sane here, Kate," Mary warned, using the pen to tap a kind of counterpoint to her words, as if there were some energy source building in her.

"But crazies are the most logical people around," Kate objected. "What they do has to make perfect sense, or they don't do it. Especially crazy people with a mission."

"Why assume her logic system matches yours?"

Kate almost smiled. "Because more than once in my career I've fantasized about doing what she's doing. I had my list drawn up years ago. Sticks has an imaginary bus on which all the

bureaucrats, every asshole physician, and every
nasty patient with an attitude gets a seat. Then she
shoves the bus in gear and sends it over a cliff
somewhere. But you ask her. She'll tell you. The
last person she'd put on that bus would be Tim.
The very last, no matter what."

"But Sticks didn't know Tim was gay," B.J.
said quietly. "Maybe the killer does."

"That doesn't make any difference!" Kate
instinctively retorted.

"Gay?" John asked, eyes widening.

"That *would* make a difference," Mary admitted.
"Who knew besides you?"

Kate turned on her, anxious. "Nobody knows."

"But if the killer did, she might feel betrayed.
It might be an excuse to use Tim to make a point
with you."

"But why not just go after me?" Kate demanded,
finally voicing what she'd been thinking ever since
seeing Tim there. "Why take it out on him?"

She didn't even notice the change in her own
voice as she used old words, responded to old
instincts. She didn't see Mary's eyes soften in a
very unagentlike way.

"Would hurting you have made any difference?" B.J. asked very quietly.

Kate spun on him, ready to bite. Ready to hurt
him, because he knew. He understood more than
she'd ever told him. With one visit to that house
on Westmoreland, he understood that the hold on
her of that horrible place, of all the horrible places
she'd lived, had not been her own life, her own
pain and loneliness and acceptance. It had been

the twins. It had been Molly and Mary Ellen, cowering behind her in the corner, so terrified they wet themselves, too silent, too small, too vulnerable. The hostages for Kate's presence, the tiny blue-eyed girls who could never leave that house, no matter how far they ran. Who didn't call anymore, because even the sound of Kate's voice dredged up every one of those dingy, small, smelly corners.

"But nobody knows," she objected in a half whisper, the ransom just raised.

B.J. didn't even smile. "Maybe not. But everybody in that hospital knows you have an unfortunate habit of championing unpopular causes. They know you tend to go out on a limb without noticing the chain saw, like the night of the accident. Don't you think they knew that what you did for that little boy meant your job?"

She almost didn't catch it. "My job?" she asked. "What are you talking about?"

He looked at her for a moment, those deep-set eyes enigmatic as usual. Out in the sunlight, the breeze caught the fountain and sent the water soaring. Children caught in its path squealed with delight, and the wind chimes sang. Kate didn't hear any of it anymore.

"You wouldn't have been working after that night, pogue," B.J. said simply. "Your locker was already cleaned out when they wheeled you into trauma one."

For a very long moment, it seemed that only Kate and B.J. inhabited that table. She faced him, trying so hard to remember. Wishing she weren't so angry that he had a piece of her memory she didn't. Wondering why it suddenly seemed so important.

"They were going to fire me for that?" she demanded. "How did you find out?"

He pulled out a new cigarette and rolled it between that long spatulate finger and thumb. "There was a lot of shouting going on about it that night. Next morning, suddenly it never happened. That's all I know."

Kate caught herself fighting for memory again, any memory. Something to clarify the five-hour stretch in her life that evidently defined everything that had happened since. Almost an entire shift, so completely lost she felt as if everyone had made it all up.

"So it's back to that again," she said, rubbing at her eyes.

"Back to what?" Mary asked quietly.

Kate shook her head. "Why I'm doing my Sinead O'Connor impression," she said, without looking up. "The whole incident that got me thrown into the hospital and put Attila in my clutches in the first place."

Mary was tapping again. It was annoying Kate no end. She wanted to go home. No, she didn't. She never wanted to go there again, not while the flicker of Tim's shadow still hovered at the back of her mind. She didn't want to face the once-soothing silences and spaces of that orderly little place. She wanted to find a new home, set of rooms without memories, where she could be safe.

She wanted peace, and no matter how far she ran, she couldn't seem to find it.

"I'm surprised I didn't hear about it," Kate said. "That's the kind of thing the defense fund would have loved."

"I heard 'bout it," John admitted. "From Fleischer. It's what he was beginnin' to tell me when he took de big dive. Dat it was de las' straw, you draggin' him in to look at dat little boy. You really were popular wit' dat man, Katie girl."

So that was it. It was too late to ever apologize, but at least Kate understood why Fleischer had been so virulent about that night. Another little four-year-old boy. She must have been crazed to drag him the last place he wanted to go in this lifetime. She probably said something really smart like, "Damn it, are we going to just sit by and watch this kid die?"

No wonder he'd wanted her fired. She wondered just who else she'd personally insulted on the way to getting Billy Rashad out the door.

"Is there anything else?" B.J. was asking.

John and Mary were both reviewing their notes.

"Prob'ly not," John admitted. "Besides, we can always fin' you, little girl."

He'd meant it to be funny. Kate wasn't in the mood for any of them anymore. Out in the garden, a brace of women wheeled carriages toward the English wooded garden, where the dogwoods would create ivory lace and the ground would be carpeted in columbine and azaleas. A couple holding hands strolled back along the path from the lily garden, their eyes only on each other on this fine spring day. The trees sent up a susurrus chorus as the wind fingered through their young leaves. All Kate could think was how sad the wind sounded.

"Tell you what," she said, her eyes on the sculpted beauty of the gardens. "I'm going to take a tram ride around the gardens now. You want me, you come after me."

And before John or Mary could intervene, she did just that.

Unfortunately, Mary waited to take Kate up on her offer until sometime around one o'clock the next morning. Kate had been lying on B.J.'s living room couch, unable to make even a pretense of sleeping, while she waited for him to return from the scene of a multiple homicide. So she'd turned the TV to the weather station, the radio to rock and roll, and left all the lights on to scare away the shadows. A half-empty wine bottle and a half-full glass sat on the coffee table, from where she'd been fortifying herself for the morning to come. Just another perfect evening at home.

The first time the bell rang, she ignored it. She was not in the mood for company, especially the kind of company that couldn't tell time. But her visitor rang again and then again. Kate didn't want somebody else mistaking her silence and breaking down the door, so she climbed off the couch and yanked the door open.

Mary walked right on through into the living room.

"Tell me about that night," she said, turning back to find Kate still standing with the doorknob in her hand.

"What?"

Mary smiled. "I'm sorry. Kate, may I come in? I think it's important. You should probably close the door now."

Kate at least had the presence of mind to do that. "Do you know what time it is?" she demanded, and thought how stupid she sounded. She was in nothing but her nightshirt, sweatpants, and a set of earrings the shape of bananas. Mary, on the other hand, was still in her working uniform and managed to look neater than she had that afternoon.

"I've been thinking about this," Mary offered, claiming the chair and motioning for Kate to take back the couch, as if it were Mary's house rather than B.J's, "and I think that whatever happened the night of the accident is important."

"Is to me," Kate retorted from where she stood. "I'm being sued over it."

"I think you have more at stake than that. I've been on the phone most of the night with one of my friends at Quantico, and he agrees. We think this might be crucial. Would you mind telling me what happened?"

Kate finally pushed herself away from the door. "Why?"

"Humor me."

Kate wished she were more alert. She wished she'd never answered the door, but that was a regret she'd probably get over. So she reclaimed the couch, reclaimed her drink, and proceded to tell Mary about Billy Rashad. She kept the tale short, succinct, and to the point, and still ended up with an empty glass by the end of it.

Kate noticed Mary had pulled one of those little notebooks from some pocket and was making notes.

"You don't remember any of it?"

"Nope. Why?"

Mary looked up, and for the first time Kate realized the agent could look positively avid. "I'm not sure," she said. "Maybe it's nothing. You got into a fight with your superiors over the little boy, though."

"Evidently. Otherwise, I doubt I would have been fired. They hate to pay unemployment too much to throw me out for nothing."

Mary was nodding, scribbling, a few strands of hair working themselves free. Kate wished all this activity was making her feel better. She was still trying to assimilate the fact that she'd been fired. That she'd deliberately hurt Fleischer with the memory of his own son.

"There is always," Mary said suddenly, dragging Kate's attention back, "a precipitating incident. Something that sends the murderer over the edge. A divorce, a fight, an imagined slight. At least in traditional serial murders. You never received a note before the night of the accident."

Kate knew how to play straight man. "No."

"There hadn't been any suspicious deaths among the staff before that."

"Not unless you count Janet Preston down in

the lab. But then, I'm not sure how suspicious bungee-jumping incidents are."

Mary actually bristled with impatience. "Then it may just be that something happened on the night of the accident to make our murderer think you understand so well. The reason the murders started at all."

Kate shook her head. "That kind of thing goes on all the time."

"Maybe, but serial murder doesn't. Our friend keeps thinking you know something you don't seem to. Maybe it's as simple as retrograde amnesia. Maybe something happened on the night you can't remember that changed this person's life."

"So what do we do?" Kate asked.

"I've already talked to John. He's taking care of interviews. We also got a court order for the Rashad records. What I'd like to do is go over them with you tomorrow, if that's okay."

No. It wasn't okay. Suddenly everything was moving too fast. Because Kate knew that, as much as she'd asked for this all along, the last thing she wanted to know was exactly what had happened that night.

She shook her head. Poured out the last of the wine into her glass, as if that were going to help. "No. Not tomorrow." Tipping the glass, she damn near emptied that one too. "Tomorrow," she said, taking a deep breath to quell the newest surge of nausea, "we have a different kind of appointment altogether."

◆　　◆　　◆

Kate hated funeral homes. It wasn't that she found them as barbaric and useless as some people did. Kate had seen too many sudden deaths in her career. She'd held too many people who simply couldn't find closure because they hadn't had the chance to say good-bye. Maybe someday somebody would find a better way than formaldehyde and flowers, but the tradition of wakes and funerals at least gave the survivors a chance to finish their business.

No, Kate's problem was that she'd spent far too much of her childhood in funeral homes. It was a predictable side effect of coming from a once-large Irish Catholic family. Funerals were just as much social events as reunions and weddings—and, in Kate's family, far more frequently attended. It had been her mother's one acceptable excuse to get out of the house. Kate had always been dragged along as an impartial witness for her mother's defense.

Kate still woke up with the scent of old flowers and thick perfume in her nose. She could hear the thin threnody of the two old harpies who had always seated themselves at the back of the room, the back of the church, to provide sufficient grief for the occasion. Only later had Kate realized that the old girls weren't even related. It was simply their function in the community.

She could still sense the whispers of approval over cosmetics designed to cover the ravages of cancer or cirrhosis, the stifled laughter of the men who clustered together in a kind of protective pack by the men's room, the commiserating hum of women entertained by yet another chapter in the desperate life and times of Mary Margaret Ryan Manion.

Funerals. The only recreation Kate was allowed, since as the oldest she would inherit the duty after her mother was gone. They were the first thing she foreswore after she'd been left in charge, the last thing she wanted to do on a spring day that promised neither sun nor solace.

She'd done her best with Tim's parents, a pair of retired professors who met the entire situation with a kind of bewilderment that made Kate think they expected Tim to appear and laugh at the apparition in the casket. They hadn't ever known about Tim's imminent excursion from the closet. Steve, haggard and distracted, had begged Kate to keep it from them. Since it had never been her family, and since it had been Tim's decision to make all along, she agreed. So she played the bereaved fiancée for everybody and actually found some comfort in the distracted affection of these two bespectacled people who bore absolutely no resemblance to either son.

The press had hounded them from door to door, and the funeral home had been packed all afternoon. It helped and it hurt. Kate didn't get any rest, and she didn't get any relief from the decisions she'd made.

"See anything that might be helpful?" Mary asked in her ear as they stood at the wall farthest from the casket.

Mary stood by Kate because anyone else would be too obvious. B.J. simply did not do funerals. Dickie was too much of a jerk to let loose, and John would have stood out like a bear in a snowbank. No one in the room but Kate knew Mary carried a nine-millimeter automatic beneath her severe gray suitcoat.

"I see a lot of angry, upset people," Kate said, instinctively slipping her hands toward where lab coat pockets would be. Except she too was in a suit. Bright, outrageous aqua and purple, spring colors Tim had once pressed on her in a moment of whimsy, topped by the flamingo earrings that had been his last gift. His mother had smiled. Phyl, perched on one of the stiff, uncomfortable couches like a mound of congealing mashed potatoes, looked as if Kate had arrived wearing a teddy and spiked heels.

"Well, don't go anywhere without me," the agent said yet again. As if Kate would forget. As if Kate *could* forget.

Victims. She didn't see the people here so much as suspects than as potential victims.

Kate held her place against the wall by the guest book as Hetty Everson stalked up, eyes bright with unshed tears she never would have wasted on her own patients in the unit, her gait uncertain in unaccustomed heels.

"Who's this?" Mary asked under her breath.

"Nurse from surgical ICU," Kate said. "Took care of me after the accident."

Opinionated, aggressive, burned out with the best of them.

"The press said he committed suicide," Hetty accused Kate as if no one else had thought to do it. "Did he?"

Kate shook her head, always mindful of where

Tim's parents were. "No. He didn't. Anything else you want to know?"

"It's been going around the hospital that you two had been having your problems."

Kate might have laughed if she'd been anywhere but in a room full of gladioli and straight-backed chairs. "No," was all she said, knowing it wouldn't make any difference. People would assign blame as they saw fit. "We weren't."

When Sticks approached an hour later, she had a completely different spin on the subject. She wasn't any happier about it, though. "You gave in and he paid for it."

"I gave in?"

The kohl-rimmed blue eyes were desolate as the girl twisted lank hair around a finger. "You're collaborating with the enemy, and it cost Tim his life. Isn't that right?"

What kind of answer could she give? Kate spent a minute looking over the crowd for any sign of rescue, anything that might make her laugh or relax or even cry. There was just a press of taut faces, familiar faces with judgments already in place. Tim's parents got handshakes, hugs, tears. Kate got suspicion and reticence.

There was nothing Kate could do but face the girl head on. "Give me some options, Sticks. Give me some help."

Sticks was not amused. "Fuck help. Give yourself a seat on the bus," she said, pulling her hand away so the feathers at her ears trembled like leaves in a gust of wind. "I thought you'd be the last one to crumble."

Sticks, who still demanded protection from the world, still needed absolutes. What was it Dickens had said? Nothing is so finely felt in the small world of children as injustice. He would have recognized Sticks in a minute.

It was, of all people, Martin Weiss who offered a shoulder. "Don't let the assholes get you down," he said when he came up, his fingers tattooing an edgy rhythm on Kate's sleeve. "They're not worth the trouble."

Kate saw the groups beginning to form already, even here, and sighed. "Yes, they are."

Martin surprised her by not just drifting back off into the crowd. "Oh, bullshit," he objected, running a trembly hand through his beard. "You never needed their approval before."

"I never needed *your* approval before," she countered with a slow grin. "There's a difference."

The look she got was far too serious. "No," he said, "you haven't, have you? Everything might be a lot different if you had, just once . . . just once."

Kate found herself squinting at him, as if that would help pull him into better focus. "What do you mean?"

But Martin's eyes were across the room, where the new chief of surgery was greeting Mr. Fellows by Tim's casket. "Three more glorious months," he muttered with a too-bright smile, "and then it's my turn with the portfolio and the takeover bids. I'll make sure that *I* show up at one of my residents' funerals just in time to catch the minicams out front. Although how they managed with their hands halfway up the ass of Central Medical Center, I don't know."

"Martin," Kate said, her hand now on Martin's arm, "this is important. What would be different?"

He turned back to her, but it took him a second to refocus.

"What would be different?" Kate asked. "Are you talking about the night of the accident?"

She could almost hear the gears turn, the cogs slip before they caught and held.

"You were on that night." She nudged him, her hand a little tighter around the slightly disheveled tweed. "Weren't you?"

"Of course I was," he said. "You know that."

Kate shook her head. "I don't. I have complete retrograde amnesia for that whole shift. Martin, tell me, please. What was it I did that set this whole thing off?"

"Set what off?" he demanded. "The lawsuit? That's easy, honey. You personally held up that kid's transfer until it was too late. That's what you did."

✦ Chapter 14 ✦

IT WAS THREE more days before Kate began to get her answers. Three days of fending off voracious reporters, of ignoring the slights and silent accusations of her fellow workers, of bearing the terrible burden as Tim's parents finally began to realize that their gentle, beautiful son wouldn't be coming home again.

Kate didn't sleep and she didn't eat. She worked with Steve to decide how best to take care of Tim's things and walked back into the apartment to offer Mr. and Mrs. Peterson the chance to take the little things they wanted until the big things could be arranged. She accepted the grief of Tim's ex-lover and participated in the careful dance of gay friends he'd gathered in the Central West End as they paid their respects, all too well versed in the masquerade families often demanded of them. She fought to keep Carver, and she dealt with insurance investigators, medical school representatives, and funeral home attendants. And through it all, she kept that conversation with Martin to herself.

Her fault. Billy Rashad had been her fault.

How? Could she have really stepped over her own boundary, so caught up in being right that she sacrificed one of her patients? What she'd told B.J. so long ago had been the truth. She did consider nursing to be the one place in her life she had triumphed. Not perfectly, but always with the most honorable intentions. When she'd had a fight, she'd always had it for the right reasons.

She'd always thought.

What if she'd been wrong about that too? What if she'd gotten too caught up in her personal sense of justice? Wound herself up so tightly in self-righteous indignation that she'd ended up playing a deadly game with a child's life?

There would be nothing else left from which to resurrect herself. Nothing she could count on as she tried to find her place again.

She was a nurse. A good nurse. A nurse who gave a damn.

A nurse who could at least count on the care she gave, no matter what else had gone wrong with her life.

Finally, that too might be a lie.

"I'm going to give you some names," Mary said. "Tell me what you think."

Kate rubbed at Carver's ears and stared at the wall. White on white, elegant, empty.

She'd insisted on trying to move back so B.J. wouldn't have more intrusion in his life. She'd seen just how well he slept when she'd stumbled

by his room on the way to the bathroom. He'd
been up already, but his bedclothes had betrayed
the fact that not all the sounds she heard at night
came from the pipes. The mattress was half pulled
off onto the floor, and the pillows and covers
bunched and wrinkled. She could smell bad
dreams in that room and knew B.J. wouldn't
appreciate her asking the privilege of inclusion.

She'd thought if she went home she could get
on with her life, so she'd snuck out right after B.J.
had left for a two-day trip to testify in Louisville.
But she hadn't even been able to rumple the bed-
sheets. When she closed her eyes, she swore she
could sense violence here, as if Tim's life had
been snatched away so quickly he'd left part of
himself behind. She kept looking for the mementos
his parents had taken and surprising herself with
the empty stillness of the rooms.

"Kate?"

"Why are you so involved in this, Mary?" she
asked suddenly, her eyes still on the mottle of
shadows on the wall. She could make shapes
out of them if she wanted. Unfortunately, they
all turned into a long swaying figure of
inevitability. "I thought the FBI just took a consulting role."

Mary shrugged, her neat linen jacket remaining perfectly unwrinkled. "Research. I'd like to
learn more about this type of murder. And I keep
thinking there's something wrong here. The pieces
just don't add up."

"I don't know anything about you."

Mary looked up from her notes. "Pardon?"

"I don't know anything about you. Tell me something."

"What do you want to know?"

"Anything. Where you live. Where you went to school."

"Oklahoma."

That made Kate look up. "Really? I hadn't expected that."

"One place is pretty much like another."

"You married?"

"I was."

"Me too."

"I know. Have you heard from him through all this?"

"Michael? No. He was never one to like being bothered much. I imagine he's sitting in his living room in Eugene, Oregon, watching baseball or something. You?"

"Oh, he's in New Mexico this week."

"Travels?"

"Rodeo."

For the first time in almost a week, Kate burst out laughing. Then she stopped, appalled. "I'm sorry. I didn't mean that."

Mary smiled back. "It's not what you'd expect. I know. Junior's a good man, just not a monogamous one."

"Junior?" She had no business feeling so delighted. "What does he do, ride broncs or something? I don't know much about rodeo. It's not exactly a Saint Louis sport."

"Calf roping. We're working on our third national title."

That finally got Kate's complete attention. "We?"

This time Mary just lifted one of those elegant eyebrows. "I'm damn good on a horse."

"I'll bet."

"Now, how about these names?"

The time cards. Kate didn't want to know. She didn't want to have to suspect people any more than she already did. The distances were great enough over there. She was going to have to go back in to work tomorrow, take up her place in the lounge, and pretend nothing was different. Except that it was. She looked at everyone as a possible suspect, and they looked at her as a traitor. Life couldn't get much better.

"John's whittled it down to about twenty," Mary was saying, eyeing her list. "It would be nice to have some kind of . . . feedback from you on what we've come up with so far."

Kate got up for some coffee. "I guess that means you didn't find anything in their background checks, huh?"

"Nothing blatant. If we were dealing with a psychopath here, we would have found escalating criminal pattern. But I think our perpetrator is an attention-seeker. They tend to be less blatant. Products of dysfunctional homes, adult children of alcoholics, that kind of thing."

Kate reached for the mug she always used and then realized Tim's mother had taken it. A dumb thing to take, an old university mug with a tiger on it. His mother had cried. Kate reached for a blank white one. "Good luck, then. One study says about eighty-five percent of nurses are adult children of alcoholics. A lot of cops, too, if I'm not mistaken. It's that old caregiver mentality. Make things all neat and tidy and happy."

"You know all about that?"

Kate's smile was grim. "I know all about that."

"So do you want to tell me a little about Phyllis, your supervisor? I understand she sat in on a grievance committee with you and several others, like Hetty Everson and—uh, Juliette Pfieffer."

"Only if you tell me about roping calves."

The first person she saw when she walked in the next day was Parker. Smiling, clapping her on the back, welcoming her with apparent goodwill. Name number twelve on the list.

Parker. Seducer of residents, holder of a black belt, absorbed sufficiently in a woman's profession that Mary would happily throw over her prejudices about the perp being a female to include him.

Parker, who stuttered every time he saw a naked woman. He and Lisa Beller must have some interesting postcoital conversations.

"It's been much too predictable here without you," he assured her. "We haven't mounted a full-blown insurrection in weeks."

Kate just grimaced. "Thanks. I'm sure the mini-cams outside would love to hear that."

She was going to get her car back in a few days. The problem was, she couldn't go far, since good old KSTL had shown the footage of her with

Tim's parents and reaffirmed her place on the suspects' hit list. Even her position as victim's fiancée didn't seem to cut her any slack. Not only that, but word was also out about the pending lawsuit. Kate was the suspect *du jour,* and nothing was tastier. She would have been far more upset if it hadn't meant they'd given up on Edna, at least for now.

"Parker," she said quickly, before anybody else could interrupt them where they stood by the med prep. "I'm sorry. I heard what they did."

They. The enemy. The other side. No more was ever needed, no more said, as if naming them would give them greater power. Or as if they had such great power already they didn't even need a name.

"Fuck 'em if they can't take a joke," Parker said. "I love a challenge."

For the first time Kate realized he had a tic, a little pull to his left eye when he was lying. She also realized just how big his hands were for such a small person. But Parker was the gentlest of men. She'd seen him lift frail little old ladies as if they were the most precious cargo on earth, smiling that little-boy smile of his that had made Lisa Beller look down from her statuesque height to notice the man behind the stutter.

Not Parker, she thought. It cannot be Parker.

"You let me know if you need any of your shifts picked up," she said. "As soon as I get out of this cast, I'm gonna need some overtime."

"Yeah, we heard. They still sticking you with the hospital bill?"

"Until I can remember what happened with Billy Rashad. But then, if I do, I'll probably just have to testify at my own malpractice trial."

He used one of those big hands to give her a pat on the back. "Well, then, my contribution to the fund will be well spent."

Kate smiled. "Thanks." She was about to clomp on down the hall toward the nurses' lounge where she was going to be working when Parker reached out to stop her.

"I really am sorry about Tim," he said.

Kate accepted his smile and his good-bye, and then she didn't move. She watched Parker walk away, a sturdy Popeye character from the back. And she thought maybe it couldn't be Parker, but it had to be someone here. Someone who had walked into that funeral with downcast eyes and heartfelt expressions of sympathy. Someone who had been cold enough to pin a note onto Tim's shirt as he died.

Parker strolled into one of the rooms. Farther down the hall Becky Faith, one of Phyl's favorite nurses, was checking crash carts and complaining to Frank Mendoza, the full-time pediatrician, about the weekend staffing. Edna, still on days for her orientation, was on the phone, her brow pursed in concentration. People came and went: supply techs, housekeeping, doctors and nurses, lab staff. People Kate saw every day. People she took for granted. And for the first time she appreciated the scope of John's task. He had to wade through a thousand frustrated suspects, a thousand alibis and motives and histories. And somewhere in there, he had to find someone so clever she could murder three people right in the busiest building in the county without anybody noticing.

Someone so calculating she could manage to murder Tim in the middle of the only afternoon Kate was sure to be away.

"Kate? You okay?"

Kate started at the sound of Frank's voice. Something was bothering her. Something about the idea of the murderer being calculating. Something that suddenly felt wrong.

"I'm just fine, Frank."

Frank hadn't been a St. Patrick's virgin for a long time. A tall, balding man with a long upper lip and a longer forehead, he was slow and steady: a good man in a pinch, a pain in the neck when he stitched, because he tended to try for the perfect scar on every bucking, screaming kid.

"Just getting used to being back at work."

He nodded and turned to walk on with her. "How's it feel?"

Truly? She wasn't feeling anything at all. She wouldn't. Not until Tim was taken care of. Just as she did with tragedy or trauma, she distanced herself from her feelings. Tucked them carefully away in someone else's locker where they wouldn't bother her.

"Great, as long as nobody expects me to run down to X ray for a code."

"I like the cap. It's the perfect touch."

She might have tried to wear the chartreuse one, but somewhere in the midst of the move home it had disappeared. So she'd settled instead for a white corduroy ball cap with a black stripe across the brim and RN in black letters. On the back, in parentheses, it read, *real nasty*.

"I'm starting a pool on how long it takes Phyl to write me up for it," she admitted.

"You think she'll let you keep it on?"

"Yeah. There's a rule somewhere discouraging the display of recent brain surgery to the public. Tends to sap their confidence."

"Phyl's looking for you," the secretary announced without noticeable warmth.

"Put me in the pool for two hours," Frank offered. "I need the money."

"They cut your time again?"

"There's a brand-spanking-new cardiovascular man they want who looks much better on camera. So they're giving him the gift of a new surgical suite in return."

Kate nodded and stumped on down toward Phyl's office. "Two it is."

"Welcome back, Kate," Frank offered in farewell.

Becky looked up from her work with more than the usual amount of venom in her eyes. Kate never looked away.

"It's good to be back," was all she said as she walked on.

She saw him the first time when she went to the waiting room for a soda. The machines were lined up to the left side, right across from the television, so that visitors tended to clump there, bags of chips in their hands, their eyes glazed as they looked up at fictional mayhem while waiting for the results of their own.

It wasn't that he was particularly noteworthy. Especially in a crowd that almost always included at least a brace of concealed weapons and enough tattoos to redecorate the Sistine Chapel. He was just a nondescript kind of guy sitting along the back wall where he could watch the main halls, a newspaper in his hands, his young brown eyes not paying much attention to the stories before him.

So Kate couldn't say why she noticed, except for the fact that he was the best-dressed guy in here, for a Saturday afternoon. She got her caffeine and clumped off to the nurses' lounge, where she was set up.

She saw him again later when she went to lunch.

"Edna, do you know that guy?" Kate asked as she set her tray down at the table. A couple of other nurses had been heading for it too. When they saw Kate sit down, they sidled away. She decided not to notice.

Edna looked up. "No. Why?"

"Nothing. He was in the waiting room earlier. I thought he might be with one of the patients."

"Maybe he's here to keep an eye on all of us," Edna suggested. "So no one else commits a murder."

Kate just snorted. "I hope he knows what poison looks like."

There hadn't been any cheering this time when Kate walked in. No hero's welcome. At best,

Kate had received polite acknowledgment. How the mighty have fallen, she thought, as she took a stab at the mashed potatoes she didn't want. How the guilty will suffer.

Edna was number eighteen, making a match on two out of the four murders with a close for the third. Edna, who had been raised in the old caregiving atmosphere, who had such trouble with high tech, who wore her white lab coat like a nun's habit.

Edna, who had patted Kate's hand when Weiss was such an ass.

Sticks was on the list too, and Jules and Lisa Beller, all of them conveniently close to the deaths in both proximity and motive. There were some discrepancies about Weiss's times, since he was so fond of disappearing when needed, and Hetty Everson matched on three out of four.

Twenty names in all, and Kate was supposed to get them and others in conversation, in the hope of catching some of them in a lie they might have told the interrogators that might belie the normal, nondescript medical kind of background they all seemed to have.

There was a whole team on the thing now, a lot of overtime being racked up at the county homicide bureau. The good news was they'd relegated Dickie to headquarters, to be replaced by one of the detectives who usually doubled in burglary. The bad news was they were all over the hospital, with a command center set up in the doctors' building to facilitate the investigation. They spent all day doing interviews and checking typewriters and lounge magazines, phone logs and meds orders. The worse news was the interviews were turning up nothing but frustration and silence. It was up to Kate to catch the reaction.

"They want something interesting," someone was saying behind her, not paying attention to the fact that the room echoed, "they should try talking to Sue Williamson on the fourth floor. She got caught going to wage and hour over her paychecks, and now they have her pulling every shit shift they can find. She's got four kids, a husband who hasn't had a job in four years, and no help, and they're threatening to cut her time in half if she doesn't behave. It'd sure piss me off enough to pull out the potassium."

"What about Buck Taylor?"

Kate could almost hear the general nodding of heads. Buck was an internist specializing in critical-care medicine, fondly referred to as Dr. Death for his unfortunate code statistics. Buck was also crazy as a bedbug. The latest Buckism had him appearing on the unit at midnight during a full moon in black cape and extra canines, howling. It had taken Hetty twenty minutes to convince him that werewolves howled, not vampires.

"Then there's Lisa Beller."

Kate's ears picked up. She hated herself but kept on listening, remembering she had a job to do for Tim.

"I hear she has a pretty big secret to keep."

"Secret?" one of the aides retorted with a snort of indignation. "Honey, Parker's no secret. Although, from what I hear, he *is* big."

"Not that. Something else. Something in her past. Have you noticed she never talks about it?"

"They really don't understand, do they?" Edna asked all of a sudden.

Kate did her best to listen to two conversations at once. "Who?" she asked. "The floor nurses?"

But Edna was shaking her head. "The authorities. They don't really care why this is happening, and that's the most important part."

"Lisa wouldn't kill anybody," the aide said definitely. "She'd just give him to Weiss and let him do it."

"No," Kate agreed. "They don't understand."

Edna wasn't finished. "I've dedicated every one of my lives to helping others. Every one. And it's always been the same. You'd think somebody would have figured it out by now. You'd think they'd have some charity for the caregivers."

"Weiss," somebody said. "Now there's a trip down psychosis lane."

"What about B.J.?" Edna suddenly asked. Kate almost snapped her head around in surprise. "What?"

Edna smiled, inclining her head toward the conversation. "What about B.J.? Doctor O'Brien?"

Kate wasn't at all sure she was following. "You think B.J. could be doing this?"

Edna shoveled in some spinach. "Why not? He's around more than any other medical examiner I've ever known, and he's killed people before."

"That was different," Kate admonished.

Edna looked up. "Are you sure?"

Which was when Kate realized she'd tried to

handle this much too early. She couldn't keep Edna straight, much less the people around her. Luckily, though, she didn't have to take her seriously.

Which was why she was so angry four hours later when she saw B.J. again, because suddenly she couldn't help but wonder, even for a moment, if Edna could be right.

She actually heard him before she saw him. She'd just finished a grueling forty-minute stint with two middle-aged parents in what was euphemistically called the quiet room, and her throat hurt almost as much as her head and leg. So she wasn't in the mood for games.

"No, Duke, don't!" she heard through the nurses' lounge door. "Don't open the letter!"

Kate almost didn't open the door at all. *The Sands of Iwo Jima,* B.J.'s favorite movie, although Kate couldn't figure out why. It was playing on one of the local channels on the lounge TV, and it was obviously the moment when John Wayne bit the big banzai bullet. Kate opened the door just as he met his fate.

"Aw, no," B.J., protested, throwing up his hands.

"Not again," Kate moaned with a shake of her head as she trudged on over to the sludge left in the coffeepot. B.J. met her arrival with surprising equanimity, considering the fact that he hated being caught having fun.

"He never listens. You look like hell."

Kate turned to take him in and came to her own surprised halt.

He was in a suit, as neat and pressed as a yuppie lawyer, all gray pinstripes and white monogrammed shirt, his loafered feet on the coffee table. B.J., who had participated in his share of war. B.J., who never once talked about it. It still couldn't be B.J.

"My, my," Kate acknowledged with a shake of the head. "I thought I'd never see the day."

"Not a word," he warned.

She never bothered with his threats. "You're either due in court or trying to buy a condo in Ladue."

She had her coffee, so the only thing left was to get her leg up. She did that in the one comfortable chair in the room, her attention on the first hot sip of primordial goo in her cup.

"Hey, Beej," she said, closing her eyes. "What do you think of the rodeo?"

"The what?"

"The rodeo. Did you know that Mary Cherry is a calf roper? I think it sounds like fun."

"I think it sounds like you might have sustained more brain damage than we'd thought."

"Think of it," she said, her eyes open again, her voice just a little too intense. "Wide open spaces, the smell of honest work and leather in your nostrils, the simple life of the cowpoke."

B.J. just ignored her, which Kate knew was probably a good idea. "Do you have any information?" he asked, pulling out a new cigarette to mutilate.

She slumped. "Three new affairs and a floor secretary who thinks he's Ted Kennedy's illegitimate child. I'm woefully short on murder suspects, though."

"You talked to them?"

"Not all of them. I don't get around as quickly as I used to. And then Phyl keeps sticking me in with upset parents because I'm on light duty. What could be more light than telling a mother her sixteen-year-old should have worn his seat belt?"

"I thought you had pastoral care or something for that."

"After the last round of cutbacks, the only thing pastoral care does is interfaith services in the morning and a visit to the pre-op patients, just in case they want to get something off their chests before the big moment. Mostly what the patients end up getting is Sister Mary Polyester."

"What about the priest?"

"Priest? There hasn't been a priest around here in three years. They couldn't seem to work twenty-four hours a day for minimum wage. We get a rent-a-priest from the local parish for Sundays."

"Any idea what's next?"

Kate shook her head. "After Tim, all bets are off. I thought I knew how this wanker was think-ing. But I'll be damned if I know what's going on now. I don't understand it at all anymore."

"You think it's changed?"

"Don't you? I mean, poisoning is a polite way of killing people. You know, almost shy, as if you don't want to get in your victim's face. Tim did not die a polite death."

"I told you, Kate. He didn't suffer. He just

passed out from lack of blood to the brain. He went to sleep and that was it."

"But he saw who killed him. He talked to her. He knew he was going to die. And then whoever did it took the time to clean everything up before leaving again. That's cold, Beej. It's really cold."

"Who do you think is responsible, Kate?"

Kate pushed herself to her feet and walked over to where Phyl had set up a computer link for her to complete her paperwork. The cursor was blinking over last month's numbers. She exited and shut the system down for the next shift.

"I don't know," she said.

"Who?"

Kate turned to see those eyes on her like lasers. What a stupid time to feel comforted by the fact that B.J. never backed down from anything. "I think," she said, "it's me."

✦ Chapter 15 ✦

"WHAT DO YOU mean you're responsible?"

"I think that every one of those murders is some kind of little message just for me. Some kind of gift or punishment for whatever happened the night of the accident."

"You really think that's what set this off?"

"I don't know. Yes . . . yes, maybe I do. Whoever it is seems real intent on making some point, like I'm the biggest idiot walking not to have figured out how clever she is. And the only big hole in my reasoning powers happens to have occurred that night."

"Then who's next?"

"I don't know. Martin Weiss and I sure got into it, evidently. Should I warn him or make sure he isn't packing arsenic?"

"Who else?"

She downed her coffee in a swallow and tossed the Styrofoam at the trash. "I don't know. *I don't know.*" She shook her head and faced her inquisitor head on. "And I don't think I'm the one who's going to find out."

"Why not?"

They heard the footsteps just in time to shut up before the door opened.

"Shit, fuck, fire, folks, it's the end of the world."

It was Jules, knitting bag in one hand, her jacket in the other. There was blood on her hands, and she hadn't even gotten onto the work lane yet.

"Looks like you struck gold on the highway again," B.J. offered without inflection.

She beamed. "Literally. You'd think by now the possums would at least spread the word to watch for things that make growling noises and emit smoke, especially when I'm late for a five-to-two shift. Good thing it's pretty cold out, or I couldn't have left the little devil in my truck. I've never seen you so dressed up before, Doctor O'Brien. You bein' married or buried?"

"Court. I forgot to change before coming over."

Impossible. B.J. could change clothes faster than a chorus girl in a Broadway musical. Kate had seen him do it in the back seat of his Jeep once or twice. Well, not seen, heard. She'd been trying to drive at the time. It made her wonder who the act was for, especially since it was so well known just how seriously he hated getting suited up.

"No kidding," Jules said as she dropped her stuff and washed her hands. "I always kind of pictured you up there in your Guns 'n Roses T-shirt. I'm bitterly disappointed."

For that, at least, she got the semblance of a

smile. "It's tough to get a jury to take you seriously in your jeans."

Her expression tightened just a little when she looked at Kate. "You two putting your heads together on who to report to Administration today?"

"No," B.J. said evenly. "I'm knocking her head against the wall. I came back from out of town to find she'd decamped to the apartment. I wanted to intercept her before she decided to try it for another night, so I came here right after my court appearance."

"Thanks, Dad," Kate retorted blackly. "I can manage on my own."

Those odd silver eyes glinted at her like burnished metal. "Not right now you can't."

"Get her to talk about it," Jules suggested nonchalantly as she headed for the coffee. "She looks like hell."

"Get off my back," Kate retorted, a little too hotly.

That got raised eyebrows from both of them. Kate glared, took a steadying breath, and grabbed for her bag. "I'm going home now. If anyone wants me, my phone will be off the hook until the press find someone more fun to torment."

B.J. never moved as Kate stalked out of the lounge. By the time she clocked out and made it out the garage door to walk to the apartment, though, he was lounging against the outside wall, cigarette already half unraveled in his hand.

"You'd better have been kidding in there," she warned, limping by.

"What kind of pain meds are you taking?" he asked, following, his collar already unbuttoned and his tie fluttering from his jacket pocket.

"Tylenol with codeine. And as you can see, I'm not operating any heavy equipment."

The news trucks were suspiciously absent for once as the hospital settled in for the evening. Kate noticed that and nothing more as she began what seemed like an endless trek across campus.

"Why don't you think you're going to learn anything?" B.J. asked.

She stopped and wheeled on him, suddenly very tired of this line of questioning. "Because no one wants to talk to me, that's why. That's what tends to happen with traitors. Besides, just what the hell do you think I'm going to hear? You think Parker's going to ask me the digoxin dosage needed to kill off a hundred-and-seventy-pound man? I'm getting frustration and rage and a great deal of anticipation, and that's it."

"Who's odds-on favorite for next victim?"

"As a matter of fact," she said, "Martin Weiss. And me. In that order."

He nodded. "In that case, you shouldn't be staying by yourself."

Kate sighed and started walking again. "Don't protect me," she said. "Protect my friends. Our murderer knows just what yanks my chain."

"Yeah, but the last time she yanked, you popped off in the opposite direction."

"All the more reason to protect the others. It's my modus operandi, after all. Defend the innocents, no matter what."

"What if she decides it'd just be quicker all round to get you out of the way?"

Kate waved him off. "Just her and me, *mano a mano,* huh? Not a bad idea."

B.J. actually spun her around. "Kate, I'm not kidding."

But Kate wasn't playing. She was too tired, too stretched, too afraid to walk into that apartment again. She wanted it over. Better, she wanted it all just to disappear, the entire last few weeks, so she could go back to pretending she was a capable strong adult working in a career she still loved. She wanted her delusions back intact, because now that they were crumbling, so was she.

"Isn't John supposed to be having this conversation with me?" she demanded instead. "It's his case."

"You're my friend," he retorted. "And I wasn't kidding in there. I want you back at the house, at least for now."

She wanted to cry. It was those damn silver eyes, one minute so distant, the next as liquid and deadly as mercury. The only reason Kate had been able to stay so close to B.J. all these years was that he only let the real emotions loose in rare, flashing bursts. She couldn't stand more. She knew he couldn't.

Well, damn it, he was letting them loose now, and just this brief glimpse was enough to make a girl wish for things she knew were off limits. She wanted to comfort and hurt and torment all at once, just as women had wanted for the men in their lives since time immemorial.

So Kate looked away, looked down at the new grass, at the dusting of white violets on the spring lawn, on the slow drift of tobacco as it fell from a shredded cigarette.

"I don't think you get it," he said, in an abrupt way that betrayed the cost of his words. "You were dead, you idiot. And I had to stand there and do nothing."

"I'm all right, Beej."

"Well, I'm not."

That brought her head up. She shouldn't have. She should have left it down where she was safe. She wouldn't be safe with B.J. ever again. That careful wall they'd erected so long ago had suddenly disintegrated, and it scared her more than anything else that had happened since she'd awakened to the sound of a respirator.

"Oh, my God," she whispered, another support disintegrating. "You really did forget to change."

He shoved his hands in his pockets. To keep from throttling her, she thought. "I'm not going to stand here in the middle of the lawn arguing with you."

"Then feel free to come to the apartment. I'm not going back to your house. Especially now."

"Why especially now?"

"Because I think we're on the edge of doing something stupid, that's why."

In the end, all B.J. could seem to do was stand there, his hands jammed in his pants pockets, his eyes locked solidly on the lights of the hospital behind them. "It's one thing to lose people you . . . people who mean something to you when you can't do anything to stop it. It's something else entirely if you can stop it and you don't."

Kate was jangling like a high wire in a windstorm. There was only so much more she could take before snapping loose. She wanted to hole up in silence. She wanted to be held, when no one had really held her in years. She wanted to be able for once to be perfectly, simply selfish. And there was B.J., looking for all the world as if he were even closer to snapping than she, his features tight and his eyes brittle as hell.

Fine, she thought. If that's the way it's going to be.

"Come on, damn it," she said, and grabbed him by the arm.

He almost managed to pull loose before she turned him toward the apartment.

"I am not going to argue about anything this important in front of everybody I work with," she told him, shoving him in the right direction. "Now, let's go."

His reaction was, for B.J., pretty sheepish. "Can I get my jeans out of the Jeep?"

"Holy shit, Beej, where'd that come from?"

B.J. stopped right in the middle of pulling his T-shirt over his head. "What?" he asked in a muffled voice.

Kate just kept staring. "That chest."

Down went the shirt to conceal the pertinent anatomy and reveal not a little irritation. "Don't be an idiot. You've seen my chest before."

"No," she admitted, even more surprised than he. "I haven't. I think I would have remembered."

He was glowering now. "It's just a few scars."

But Kate was shaking her head. "Honey, it wasn't the scars I was looking at." She shook her head again and hid herself back in the day's mail so he couldn't realize that she was even more upset than she was surprised. B.J. was the last person she expected palpitations over. "All this time, and I wasted it."

"Kate . . ."

She was grinning, humor the only way she knew to defuse a situation. "I could have sold you to the highest bidder."

He forgave her by heading out to brew up some coffee. "Where's all your mail?"

"This is all my mail. I'm off the hit parade, didn't you know?"

Electric bill, insurance bill, Visa bill, hospital bill. She wasted time opening that one.

"Oh, wow."

B.J. stuck his head out of the kitchen. "What's the matter?"

Kate didn't even bother to look up. Her chest was tightening again with the thought of all the years she was going to have to work to pay this baby off. And just when she'd finally thought she'd be clear and free for the first time in her life.

She never noticed B.J. approach. "I thought they were going to help you with it."

"I told them to get screwed."

He nodded. "Seems reasonable when you're talking five figures."

She dropped the thick computer printout onto

the dining room table and sighed. "I was kinda hop-ing I could prove it was workmen's comp."

"You seen the chart yet?"

She just shook her head. Then she let her other bills follow the hospital charge, which left her with two envelopes. One from the hospital, which she tossed with the bills, figuring it was just another of the same. And one more, a clean, kind of rumpled envelope that seemed innocuous. Too innocuous. Especially since it didn't have a postal cancellation on it.

"Oh, shit."

B. J. must have had the same reaction. He grabbed it from her hand and held it up to the light. "Call John," he said.

"We don't know—"

"Yes, we do. I can see it through the envelope."

Kate leaned in closer, trying to see, too. "What does it say?"

"Stop. Just that. Stop."

Kate didn't move. She could damn near hear the blood pulsing in her neck. "Do you think if I left a return message in my mailbox she'd get it? You know, one calling her out?"

"Don't be ridiculous."

"Ridiculous?" She waved at the offending enve-lope, and suddenly her hand wasn't that steady. "That threat is personal. To me. RIght to me. The message is to me. And even if we do get this thing figured out, nobody's gonna let me stand up and face whoever's doing this."

"You'd better hope to hell not."

"I'd better hope to hell so. Damn it, Beej, I'm

the one being attacked. I'm the one everybody in this whole goddamn hospital is leaning on, one way or another. And it's gonna be just like work. When they want me, they can find me just fine. But when I need a few answers, I might as well try and get God on the phone. Don't I deserve a little personal satisfaction?"

"Not at the risk of your life."

"My life's already at risk. My sanity's at risk, damn it!"

She ended up at the window, the heels of her hands up against her eyes to rub away the flashes of memory that seemed to accompany this emotional bus ride.

"I never once got the chance to fight," she admitted, seeing herself again and again, just holding off the worst. "I never got to get back at them. They all made decisions without even asking us what was best. They kept ignoring us, and I never once got the chance to do anything about it."

He came close, right up behind her. Too close, so that it set off old alarm bells she hadn't heard in years. She reacted instinctively, spinning away.

"It'll be different this time, pogue."

She didn't even realize she'd picked up the vase. "It will *not* be different this time!" she shrilled and hurled it as hard as she could.

B.J. wondered if Kate was shaking any harder than he was. He was still trying to figure out what happened. How a simple act of frustration could cause such a terrifying reaction.

He was standing outside the locked bathroom door, listening to the strangled rasp of Kate's breathing echoing off the tile. He could almost tell where she was just by the sounds, just by years of doing autopsies on battered children. Curled up on the floor, in the corner next to the toilet where she prayed she'd be safe in the only room in the house that locked.

He'd seen kids do it on occasion, the little ones with the lank hair and carefully quiet eyes. Act out and then run, because they knew what was next. He'd never seen an adult do it. He'd never once anticipated that Kate might do it. But then, he'd never had the guts to find out.

"It's just a television set," he coaxed, his eye on the shattered screen, glass littering the gray rug like glitter. Two of the doctors' wives had knocked on the door to make sure Kate was okay. The sound of that thing going had been impressive. Impressive enough to shatter not only the tube but all the defense Kate had built up to protect the raw spots.

"Kate, open the door."

"Go home, B.J." Her voice was small, careful. He could almost see her in there trying to hold herself together. "I'm okay."

"Bullshit."

"Please, Beej, not now."

"You want me to kick in the door?"

It didn't take the sound of the odd little gasp in there to make him realize how ill-advised that demand was. He could almost hear her father's voice: *Do you want me to kick in the door, young lady? Get out here now and face your punishment, or it's going to be worse*. It had probably been worse no matter what she'd done.

And she'd buried it all so deeply it had taken a serial murderer to bring it back up again.

"Pogue, I'm sorry. I didn't mean to threaten. I'm worried about you."

He heard the scrape of the lock and breathed a sigh of relief—another of dread. He didn't want to see Kate coming apart at the seams. He didn't think he could handle it.

Leave it to Kate to surprise him again. Her face was wet, but her composure was completely in place. A mask of control, as if it had been a shower he'd interrupted instead of a flashback. He had to shove his hands into his pockets to keep from yanking her right into his arms and smothering her.

"I really don't want to talk to John again right now," she said simply. "Would you mind doing that? I mean, after all, you have to report back in to him anyway."

"Kate . . . ?"

She shook her head. Smiled. A rueful, stretched smile, but a smile nonetheless, a symptom of returning sanity. "Please. I'm going to take about three codeines and get some sleep. I think that's what I need."

"Not alone."

Her eyebrow lifted. She was back. "That had better not be a proposition," she warned. "I haven't had sex in so long I might even do it with you."

"Humor me, then," he asked. "Let me stay till you're asleep. Then I'll go find John and report in."

She sighed, took a look over at the closed bedroom door across from her own, shrugged. "What the hell."

It wasn't until later, after he'd forced some decaf down her along with the codeine and just enough brandy to warm her stomach, when he was tucking her into that too-neat, too-plain bed, that B.J. got a real smile out of her.

"You're my best friend, Beej," she said, holding his hand. "I don't know what I'd do without you."

B.J. squeezed back, woefully short of grace. "You'd find some other poor asshole with a set of pipes and bother him."

It still made her smile.

"Oh, boy, this isn't good."

B.J. stopped midsentence in his report to John and looked over. Mary Cherry, still in her muddy jeans and T-shirt, was holding the new note from a pair of tweezers.

"What's the matter with it?" he asked.

She shook her head. "It's a copycat. Whoever this was hasn't even tried to match the precision of the others. I think one of her friends at the hospital may have sent this."

"Nice frien's," John groused.

Mary looked up without noticeable humor. "You still have someone watching her?"

John nodded. "Yeah. We had a man in de

waitin' room all day, and dere should be some-body in front of de house right now."

B.J. looked up, even more surprised. "You didn't tell me that. Who's in front of the house?"

"Miller. You know him, from narcotics."

B.J. frowned, suddenly very unsettled. "Yeah, I know him. But I didn't see him anywhere."

But John waved him off. "Course not. He's on stakeout, man. You t'ink he's gonna sit on de lawn in a cop's uniform?"

"I've seen stakeouts before, John. I'm telling you that I don't think anyone was there."

"All right, Mister Medical Examiner. You wor-ried 'bout dat good woman of yours, we'll find out."

B.J. didn't bother with a threat. John was impervious, and Mary wouldn't have understood.

"So, do you think the note is serious?" he asked as John walked into the other room for a radio. The temporary command center was situated at the back end of the administrative suite where the convent used to be, so there were crucifixes above the flow board and mahogany tables for the telephones.

Mary kicked off one of her cowboy boots. "Probably not. Kate said she was facing some frus-tration over there. I think it's just a little more act-ing out. I would rather she was careful, though."

"Shit de damn day long!"

B.J. swung around, knowing the answer to his question before he even asked. "He's not there?"

"Says he followed her over to de hospital 'bout an hour ago."

"With about ninety milligrams of codeine in her system?" B.J. demanded. "I don't think so."

"Well, he gonna check de halls. You want ta come wid me and we'll check on her?"

She was awake. She couldn't say how or why—or for a minute, where she was.

It was dark, the silence oppressive. It was late. Nothing seemed to move outside.

There was something wrong. Carver was on the bed.

Carver.

That one little thing flipped all the cognitive switches, just like in the unit.

There was something wrong. Something in the apartment.

Tim.

No. No it was too late for that. She hadn't been able to save Tim. There was something else going on here.

And then she heard it, unmistakable: the scrape of the door.

Kate held her breath, tried desperately to will her heart to silence. Someone was in the apartment. Someone who might want to hurt her.

B.J. Had he left already? Was he asleep in the living room? Or was he just trying to sneak out without waking her up?

She looked over at the clock radio to find it was almost midnight. Surely B.J. would have left by now. Besides, Carver liked B.J. He wouldn't hide from him.

She listened, straining through the wash of silence. Praying with all the instinct she'd never lost that she was wrong.

Outside, a car slowed and turned onto the grounds. A tree brushed against her window, sounding like a snare drum on a slow song. Inside, though, there was nothing. Nothing but the refrigerator and the hum of Carver's nervous purr.

Kate simply couldn't wait anymore. Throwing off the bedspread, she looked around for a weapon. A quiet, easy weapon. There was nothing: shoes, a belt, a lamp. Her purse was in the living room with its can of mace, and all the knives she could ever want were in the kitchen.

Feeling even more stupid than terrified, she settled on the lamp. She unplugged it, lifted off the shade and crept to the hallway.

Shadows. Terrible shadows, just like that night, inciting shivers of memory, stealthily stealing her balance so she had to lay a hand against the wall to keep the trembling in her knees from pushing her over onto her nose. She wanted to yell, to scare the bandit into moving. She wanted to flip on a light and dramatically expose her tormentor.

She looked for a sleeping form on the couch. It was empty. She looked for a moving shadow in the dining area. It was still. She took in a deep breath and realized something was there. She could smell it. The smell of trauma, of disaster. Kate put her free hand over her mouth and came to a sick halt and didn't want to look anymore.

She didn't listen to the sounds around her, didn't feel the warm nudge of the cat against her ankles. She didn't bother to look away from her dining room, because she knew what was there, even though she couldn't see it, and it was making her sick and afraid.

That was why she never heard the key in the door.

But then the light flipped on and Kate screamed.

Three people dove like a gymnastics team, two of them pulling guns. The third came right back to his feet and headed for Kate. Then he saw what was on the dining room table and faltered to a halt.

Parts of it had fallen onto the beautiful gray carpet, leaving dark, ugly spatters like a Rorschach test. The fur was matted and greasy, a lump of brown and red on the classic teak table.

"Goddamn it!" BJ snarled.

"What the hell is that?" Mary demanded, regaining her feet, reholstering her weapon.

"Road kill," Kate told her in a perfectly quiet voice. "Someone came in my apartment and left it on my dining room table."

✦ Chapter 16 ✦

"CALL JULES," SHE pleaded, her gaze still on the dead thing on her table.

"Are you all right, pogue?" B.J. asked instead.

"Did you see anyt'ing?" John wanted to know, slipping his gun back into his shoulder holster.

Kate faced all three of them, the terror taking her breath. "Call Jules, please. Make sure she's all right."

"Do you know her number?" Mary asked, circling the table like a priestess discovering sacrilege. "Do you want to call?"

Kate couldn't answer. No, she didn't want to call. She didn't want to hear that Jules wasn't there. She didn't want to know it had all suddenly gotten worse.

"She was working until two," B.J. offered, his arm around Kate's shoulder, his posture stiff. "Try the ER. And can we get that thing in a bag?"

"My God," Mary said. "How'd she do that to your TV without you knowing it?"

"She didn't," Kate said simply. "I did."

"There's still glass there, pogue," B.J. warned,

finally relieving her of the lamp. "Don't walk that way in your bare feet."

It was when Kate realized that she was still bare-legged, clad only in her nightshirt and cast, that the shakes set in.

John called. After pulling out the gloves he seemed to carry everywhere and handing them around, he dialed first the evidence unit and then the ER.

"They say she went off to break 'bout half hour ago," he said. "I'm goin' now to check on her. Don' touch anyt'ing till de van gets here, okay?"

Kate was on the couch by now, useless adrenaline flooding her with urgings to flee. John's news only made it worse. She focused on the Matisse on the wall, consciously closing Jules off until they knew. Shutting all systems down so she could deal with what she had to. Just like she always did. Just like she had since she'd been five years old and first understood what it meant when her father walked in the door with that funny sweet smell on his breath.

She knew the van showed up and the evidence techs swept in and dusted and tweezered and Scotch-taped the place for prints and latent evidence. She knew they scooped up the animal on her table and took it back out the door, and B.J. sat beside her through it all, waiting for her to make the first move. She knew she couldn't make the first move, because it would be right back into the bathroom, and B.J. had suffered enough from that one for one night.

She knew it took John a long time to come back.

"Did you find her?" she asked as he walked in the door. She didn't notice how surprised Mary was at the sound of her voice.

John came right over. "It okay, little girl. She was jus' off havin' some time by herself."

Kate finally had the guts to look him in the face. "She's okay?"

He crouched down right in front of her. "Sassy as hell. I t'ink I caught her dallyin' wid somebody."

That got through. "Jules?"

John's smile was piratical. "Some nice young man wid a lab coat an' not much hair."

Jules had been married to Harve Pfeiffer for twenty years now. Kate knew damn well she wasn't going to leave him, even though Harve was another of those perennial no-working nurse husbands. No matter how useless Harve was, he was still the father of her kids. But a . . . dalliance? Kate hadn't known. Jules hadn't even hinted at it, and Jules told Kate everything. Or she used to.

"Now," John said. "How 'bout you?"

Kate took a careful look around. Came up with Mary sitting on the black tulip chair and John still crouched on the carpet. B.J. waited patiently to her left, his features betraying not a thing.

And she felt stupid. Just like always. Knowing she'd reacted too strongly or too childishly, demanding attention she shouldn't have had.

She did her best to smile past the embarrassment. "I'm furious that I couldn't have put that lamp to good use."

John's expression immediately clouded up. "Little girl—"

"It's no use, John," B.J. offered dryly. "I think I let her watch one too many John Wayne movies. She thinks she's going to take our killer on single-handed."

"She broke into *my* apartment," Kate countered, with all the control she could muster. "I should at least get first crack at her."

At her. At one of her friends. She wondered when she'd really begin to believe it.

"Maybe we should pull you offa dis," John mused.

Kate came right to attention. "No," she answered, much too quickly. The very intrigued glances she got made her back down, at least a little. She couldn't quit now. She could feel them taking control away from her again, all of them, and she couldn't let that happen. "Be kinda silly, wouldn't it, after all the trouble you took to get me in the first place? Besides, I have a personal stake in this."

"But you aren't safe anymore," Mary said.

"I won't be any safer if you shut me out. The whole hospital's already made up its mind I'm involved. Now let's stop dickin' around and *do* something."

In the end, none of them could come up with anything, at least on Kate's late-night visitor. Kate had only been awakened when the intruder left, and by the time the three of them had driven John's car from the far end of the campus, there had been no intruder to see. No footprints in the mud except those from a child's size-three feet. No witnesses, no explanations.

Only the word of Bose Miller, the chagrined narcotics cop who'd been slouched in his '76 green Charger, that he'd seen someone he'd mistaken for Kate leave the apartment building for the hospital at about eleven. No, he said, he couldn't say for sure, since he'd never met Kate before this. But he had seen that baseball cap, the chartreuse one with the big RN on it, that John had told him about. And earrings. And she'd definitely been tall and slim, wearing sweats, short hair, and a limp. So he'd followed and gotten himself a cup of coffee in the ER waiting room.

John questioned the ER triage staff where this person should have shown up, but it had been change of shift, the computers had been on the fritz, and a carload of children with the flu had been decorating the floors. Nobody noticed the woman or the cap.

"So: tall," Mary said over coffee at Tim's coffee table. Kate had scoured the dining room table damn near down to bare wood, but nobody really wanted to sit there anyway.

"And thin," John added. "Leaves out Jules."

"And Parker," Kate offered. "He's built like a very short gorilla."

"We can also count out Hetty Everson, who was up in the unit the whole evening, and Doctor Weiss, who was with her. Screaming, evidently."

Only Mary seemed perplexed by this statement.

"It had to be somebody central enough to dis t'ing to know we put a tail on Kate," John said.

"I didn't know about it," Kate protested.

John didn't bother with apologies. "You didn' need to."

Her temper flared again, surprising her. "Goddamn it, John," she snapped, jumping to her feet, "that's what I mean. Do you know what a Little Dick attitude that is?"

Kate desperately wanted to hit somebody. Instead, she stalked into the bathroom, planted her cast and bare foot on the cool tile, and placated herself with hot water. Cheap tranquilizer, but it had worked ever since she was a little girl.

"Kate?"

Kate opened her eyes, saw just what she looked like in the mirror, and closed them again. No wonder he sounded cautious. Even she could see that banked fire look in her eyes. Incipient zealot, she called it. Sense-of-humor shutdown.

"Door's open," she offered, as calmly as she could.

It took B.J. a second to get up the nerve to take her up on the offer. "Kate?"

She opened her eyes again to find him staring at her wrists.

"Pogue," she admonished, "I wouldn't invite you in here to watch me slash my wrists. I just like the feeling of warm water on my hands when I'm upset."

He took another look at her hands and then shook his head. "I've told you I'm no good at this shit."

Oddly enough, that's what made her smile. "I know," she said, pulling her hands out. "I'm sorry you got dragged in. Hell, I'm sorry *I* got dragged in."

"So you're okay."

She laughed. "Define okay."

He just looked at her a minute, his eyes enigmatic, his hands back in his pockets. "So," he finally said. "If I did something stupid like fall in love with you, just how often would we have to go through this?"

Kate couldn't answer him. She couldn't breathe. She wanted him to tell her he was joking. She knew he wasn't by the look in his eyes. She knew he wouldn't allow her to hide, which made it worse.

She stuck her hands back under the water.

"I don't know," she admitted, her gaze fixed firmly on the water as it splashed across her very active pulse points. "This is the first time it's been this bad since I walked away from the convent."

If she wanted a stunned reaction, she sure as hell got it. "The what?"

That actually got a laugh out of her. "I was only twenty. I thought it would be a great place to hide. It wasn't."

But B.J. was already shaking his head. "I'm *really* no good at this shit."

Kate didn't even bother to turn off the water. She just lifted her wet hands to his shoulders and kissed him. "That's what makes you so lovable, you idiot."

She didn't expect him to respond. She definitely did not expect him to kiss her back, and not like that. Not holding on to her as if she were the only thing holding him up. Not with every ounce of anger and pain and loneliness she'd known had been there inside him all along.

She didn't expect to react to it, either, but she did. She did until they were both breathless and just a little dizzy, standing there in the bathroom with the cool tile against her one bare foot and the water splashing into the empty sink.

"You all 'bout finish in dere?" John called, his voice sounding suspiciously amused.

Kate wasn't sure she had the breath to answer. She was absolutely certain it would take a minute to get her legs moving in the right direction, though. Hormones now. Instincts so rusty she had been sure she'd never recognize them again. As clichéd as it sounded, lightning.

"Get screwed, John," B.J. retorted.

Then John did laugh. "I'm sorry, Katie girl. You right. Mary say I acted like a chauvinist pig. Forgive me?"

Kate wondered if she was supposed to feel better. She didn't. B.J.! Jesus, how stupid could the two of them be? How the hell could she have been so close to him for eight years without knowing he could kiss like that?

Kate was positive she had more blood in her cheeks than she'd had since the accident when she walked back out into the living room. B.J. scowled as if somebody had just stolen his Jeep. John grinned and Mary paid very close attention to the notes she'd been taking. And then Jules entered the fray.

John answered the strident knock. Jules barely saw him.

"Your lights were still on," she all but accused as she stalked into the room, her color even higher than Kate's. Kate figured there must be some kind of redness scale for just who it was you'd spent your time kissing. If at least one partner was married, the hue increased geometrically.

She did her best to appear aloof. "I didn't want any of these people to bump their noses on the door on their way out," she said equably.

That did get a smile out of Mary. She still didn't look up from her work.

"Things a little too quiet over here?" Jules demanded, striding right up to where Kate stood, still in her nightshirt and cast. "You decided to send the bloodhounds over to spy on me?"

"Bloodhoun's?" John protested with noticeable lack of emotion.

"I was worried about you," Kate said.

"I'll bet. I heard you'd been gathering gossip today. I guess you were afraid you'd miss me in the report."

Kate stared at her, disbelieving. "I was afraid you were dead."

"Oh, come on. . . ." It took Jules that long to get past the indignation and fully assimilate the situation. "You're in your nightgown."

Kate looked over at John in disbelief. "Didn't you tell her?"

"Tell me what?" Jules demanded.

"She was distracted," John said. "I hadda get back."

"Tell me what?"

"Missing anything?" B.J. asked quietly.

"Yeah," Jules retorted with disgust. "How'd you know? Some asshole stole my possum. I was gonna . . ." Again she stumbled to a halt. This time her eyes widened and she looked around. Saw the splotch that hadn't come out of the carpet, the graveyard of coffee cups the evidence guys had left in a sink she knew damn well Kate kept better cleaned than an OR suite. Took in the fact that Mary was in her riding attire and B.J. was almost completely through a two-liter bottle of Dr Pepper.

She swung back on Kate. "Oh, shit. Oh, my God, Kate. Not on Tim's good dining room table?"

Kate nodded, eyes deliberately away from where she could still seem to see red goo. "On Tim's good dining room table."

Jules distressed was quite something to see. "You didn't think I'd do something like that, did you?" she demanded, red enough to set off alarms.

"I thought somebody was telling me you were dead too."

Jules never bothered with second thoughts about her actions. She just engulfed Kate in a massive bear hug.

"I'm sorry, I'm really sorry. Oh, shit, I should be shot. I'm such a dumb shit, a real grade-A gold-plated sorry kind of asshole. I'm sorry, Kate."

If she could have breathed, Kate would have forgiven her. As it was, she just patted her friend on the back.

"They walked in on me with Davy Gorman," Jules explained, finally backing away, reddening all over again, looking around as if there might still be anyone in this room who didn't know. "From the lab."

"I know Davy," Kate admitted. She didn't tell Jules that even in her affairs she could do better. Davy was as slick as goose snot. Kate had the feeling he was twice as nasty.

"You won't tell them, will you?"

Just once, Kate wished she had a face that discouraged confidence. What she wanted to tell Jules was that she didn't think Administration cared what she did with Davy. What she told her was she wouldn't say anything, just like she'd told the twins, just like she'd told her mother. She knew the staff who depended on the largesse of the hospital administration for their jobs felt just as trapped by whim as any child of an alcoholic. It might have been why she'd given up all their secrets with such difficulty in the first place. Nothing was more demeaning, more demoralizing, than knowing your livelihood often hung on the balance of a bad mood. Nothing bred frustration better than being trapped in a system that insisted it didn't need you.

"Maybe you can help us," John offered.

Jules brightened noticeably. "You want Kate to stay with me?"

"No," B.J. answered. "She's staying in Brentwood for now."

Jules just nodded. Kate watched in silence, her urge for warm water making a quick rebound.

"No," John said, pulling a sheet of paper from his pocket. "But Katie's gonna need help rememberin' dat night. De accident. You know?"

Which was when Kate figured out just what it was John held in his hand. A fax. A fax with more four-letter words on it than a boys' bathroom wall. Evidently Jules figured out the same because first she blanched, then she reddened all over again, her eyes swinging in an accusing arc toward Kate.

Kate just sank into the chair behind her, too tired to convince anybody of anything.

"Don' be lookin' at her," John warned. "You de one couldn't keep her hands off de equipment. We foun' dese little gems when we were checkin' phones. You know, anybody mighta called Tim de day he died, or maybe, oh, I don' know, threatened one of de victims."

"I stopped!" She defended herself as if referring to smoking or shooting up heroin.

John just nodded. "I know. But I figure Mr. Gunn don' have to know we foun' who been sendin' dese little love notes."

Jules eyed him with greater suspicion than Kate. "So I should just consider this as a magnanimous offer to find out what Florence is doing before anybody else."

"Florence?" Mary asked.

"Florence Fucking Nightingale. The current hospital nickname for the killer."

John inclined his head like a high king granting clemency. "T'ink of it dis way, girl. You be protectin' your poor dead animals."

"My animals, hell. I need to protect Kate. The way she pisses people off when she's not even trying, she needs a bodyguard. After what happened tonight, I'd say she's already pretty much pissed off Florence, so it's a dead cinch she's gonna need some watching at work."

John announced the end of the festivities by gathering together his stuff. "Well, if we all very lucky little chil'ren, we won' have to worry 'bout dat. We'll catch her by good ol' police know-how an' you'll never have to worry 'bout her 'gain."

No, Kate thought. That wouldn't be lucky. That wouldn't be what she needed. What she needed was just what they were all afraid of, a face-off with Florence. She needed to be right there in the middle of it all. To redeem herself, she needed to look right into Florence's eyes and pay her back for what she'd done.

Oddly enough, it was Jules who gave her the idea. *She's already pissed off Florence,* she'd said. It was an idea. It was almost a plan. It was better than sitting in that damn lounge doing nothing. For the first time since all this had started, Kate began to feel a little better.

"Katie girl, you listenin'?"

She looked up. Smiled. Pretended to pay attention. "I'm sorry, John. What?"

"First t'ing in the mornin' you get dese locks changed. I don' want nobody else wanderin' t'rough, no matter where you spend de night."

"I'm spending it here," she said deliberately.

B.J. stiffened and didn't say a word.

"Da's fine wid me," John said, not noticing. "Long as you got company. Den tomorrow, you can start on de chart. We'll have it den. Okay?"

It actually took Kate a second to figure out what he was talking about.

"De chart, girl. You gonna be ready?"

All she could do in the end was nod. The chart. The little boy. The truth. She wanted nothing to do with it, but she knew somehow that Mary had been right. Her answers would begin there. Her campaign to win would begin there.

"I'm gonna be ready."

She'd lied. John delivered the chart at about noon. It took Kate until four even to crack it.

In the meantime, she sincerely hoped she went a long way toward pissing off Florence Fucking Nightingale.

"What are you doing?" Sticks asked, peering over Kate's shoulder as she tapped at the keyboard. Sticks, who could be depended on to carry all information straight to the grapevine without passing GO. Kate called up another screen. "It's just amazing what you can tap into on this thing. Don't tell Phyl, but I'm getting employment records for everyone. I think I know just what's going on in this hospital, and it has nothing to do with altruism."

Sticks leaned in a little closer to try and read the screen, which made the feather in her left ear tickle Kate's neck. "You mean Florence?"

"I mean Florence. I mean I think we're all getting sold a bill of goods. If she's an angel of mercy, I'm the pope."

"What are you talking about?"

Kate called up another file. "Attention, pure

and simple. She wants people to notice how smart she is. Big deal."

"Oh, come on. That's stupid. I heard she sent you some kind of notes about the murders, helping out or something."

"That's just to get me to pay attention. And as for helping out, I don't consider what happened to Tim helping out. Do you?"

Sticks had the good grace to blush uncertainly, her skin darkening to an unhealthy brick.

"If she was so great, why kill him?" Kate demanded. "Nope, what she did just made me madder. I'm gonna nail her if it's the last thing I do."

Piss her off. Get the word around that Kate had something the cops didn't. Keep the attention away from friends and right on Kate.

She repeated the lie to Edna and Weiss and a few of the nurses from day shift. "Not only that," she embellished, when Lisa Beller was sitting there. "I have something she wants."

Lisa looked up from the *Cosmo* she was reading. "What's that?"

"The bead she dropped. The brown one."

Kate had asked John if she could bring up the necklace. She just hadn't said she was going to claim ownership.

Lisa ended up dropping the magazine in her lap. "Why are you going to all this trouble?" she asked.

Kate hid her hands beneath the table. She didn't want to admit just how much this meant to her. "Because I'm tired of being the audience.

We're all being taken advantage of here, and I want it to stop."

"I thought you didn't want to help in the investigation."

"That was before Tim was killed."

Lisa nodded, frowned, her features tight. "Take no prisoners, huh?"

Kate settled back in her chair. "Wanna tell me about it? Maybe I can keep it where it belongs."

"Parker said everybody knows."

"About that they do. I'm talking about whatever it is you don't want the powers-that-be to know about your past. Somebody's gonna find out, Lisa. Somebody who doesn't like you."

The two of them sat there for a while in silence, Kate with her screen blinking in the middle of a list of patients seen in the ER by month, Lisa considering the big-breasted, barely dressed woman on the cover of the magazine.

"Have you ever watched anyone die of ovarian cancer?" Lisa finally asked.

Kate sat up a little straighter. "I'm a nurse, Lisa."

But Lisa smiled, which didn't make Kate feel any better. "You're an ER nurse. Swab 'em and ship 'em. You turf the really sick ones out as fast as you can, so the longest you see somebody is three hours. Not weeks. Not months. Not wasting away, babbling and defecating and screaming for relief."

"Your mom?"

She took a deep breath. "My mom, my aunt, my older sister. It seems to have an affinity for my family."

Kate knew where this conversation was heading. She knew what she wanted to say. She felt herself pulling away even as Lisa spoke.

"I am not—"

But Lisa didn't get any farther, because Weiss blew into the lounge looking for something to munch on. Wiping his nose, scratching, hopping a little as he moved. So close to the edge he should have had windburn. Kate wasn't sure whether to be scared or sorry.

Lisa climbed to her feet and fled, leaving Kate to deal with Weiss's unpredictability.

"You heard the latest?" he demanded, just a little too loudly. "We in the know have heard that by this time next month we're going to be swapping bed linen with Central Medical."

"Central Medical?" Kate asked. "What are you talking about?"

"Saint Simon's is going to be three hospitals, not just one anymore. The papers are going to be signed any day on Central Medical's two, in North County and Saint Charles. Isn't it nice? All those fine young urban warriors in the outreaches will now have Serious Money to save them."

"Well, we were the last to really eat a hospital," Kate demurred. She'd wanted more time with Lisa. She knew she'd have to seek her out soon. Instead, she was stuck here with her numbers and Weiss, so she chose her numbers.

The ER census figures she'd been going through were impressive. Higher than she'd expected, higher than she and the staff had been led to believe. They were seeing more patients with less staff than they had three years ago. What the figures didn't betray, though, was that the patients were coming in sicker. With less insurance, less hospital time, less room to be sick, they waited just long enough to require the really high-tech stuff, which drove up their bills just about as fast as the frustration levels of the caregivers.

But then, Kate imagined that frustration wasn't a quantitative figure to be included in takeover calculations.

"We may be the last," Weiss claimed, "but we'll come out the best. I'm just amazed they're playing ball with somebody as sleazy as Gunn."

"Don't speak ill of the signature on your checks, boy," Kate suggested. "He's made this hospital what it is today."

Weiss opened his arms and bowed with a smile that was just a little too bright. "I rest my case. Central Medical must be hip deep in shit. Especially considering the fact that they're still playing ball with a place that's been re-nicknamed Saint Serial Murder."

Kate wanted to tell him he wouldn't be invited to the party if he didn't straighten up. She wanted to plead for all the brilliant talent being drowned in desperation. She knew better. Kate Manion was the last person Martin Weiss would listen to in this or any other incarnation. So she waited for him to scoop up his calories and bounce back out, and then she sat looking at the door to the hallway wishing someone else would come in. Anyone else. Because she was running out of excuses not to get down to that chart.

No one saved her. The door out to the hallway remained resolutely closed, and Kate remained alone. She had no choice left but to get down to business. With sweating hands and faltering courage, she finally picked up the manilla folder in front of her and opened it.

She'd said she'd wanted this. She'd lied.

6:15 PM. 4 Y/O W/M brought into ER via 256 p being struck by motor vehicle. Pt. C/A, crying, on backboard with full c-collar in place. Pale and diaphoretic. Pupils R/R/@3mm . . .

The handwriting was hers, the notes thorough. Kate skimmed them once, checked the lab results, the X-ray results, the doctor's notes and transport sheet provided by Lindbergh's 256 rig. Pepper and Theresa.

Kate tried her damndest to conjure up pictures from the scrawled medicalese, the dry passionless descriptions of a little boy's pain, his parents' nightmare.

She read again. She felt the sweat begin to break out between her shoulder blades. She couldn't come up with a thing. It was like looking at herself in the mirror and not recognizing her own face. Like seeing pictures of a day she'd spent on a beach and not knowing where she had been. She felt disoriented and frightened.

And then she really read over the notes and saw that even the picture she could see was flawed.

The little boy, Billy, had been awake and crying when he'd come in. Fracture of the left leg, two fractured ribs, lots of abrasions, the kind the crew called "road rash." One big one to the left temporal aspect of his head. Cleaned and debrided and slathered with antibiotic ointment. Fracture stabilized in a traction splint. IVs in, total body films done. Initial evaluation done by Dr. Salvatore, the pediatrician on. Dr. Fleischer, notified as trauma surgeon on call, recommended transfer to Cardinal Glennon Hospital for Children, where, since the child was basically stable, his needs could be met without insurance.

The notes looked perfectly acceptable. Treatments, assessments, phone calls, consultations. Kate knew how to read between the lines, though. Weiss had been right. She'd stalled sending that little boy down.

She'd called their ER, called the pediatrician on, the neurosurgeon on, the orthopedist on. Called Fleischer back twice when he'd refused to come in and see the child for himself and forced him into that room when he'd appeared at the hospital on an unrelated matter. She'd demanded that the pediatrician have Martin check too and then argued with him over his basically negative findings. She'd futzed and fiddled and kept from moving that child to the point where she noted repeated discussions with Mrs. Warner, the administrator on call for the shift.

It didn't make sense. If Billy was okay, why stall so long? If Billy was in such bad shape that she had to convince a fire district team to help her get him to another hospital, why had she waited?

And why didn't anything show up in her notes that suggested a problem?

Was she responsible after all?

No other nurse was involved. No other initials appeared beside the evaluation or treatment notations. Only brief mention of the parents, who had spent the time in the quiet room rather than sit with their child as the taps and IVs and X rays were done.

If she'd thought something was wrong, why hadn't she put it into writing? And if she'd thought it, why hadn't she said it?

Closing the file, Kate hobbled over to where the schedule hung. Put together four months at a time and not subject to last-minute change unless for a noted sick day, it accurately reflected the state of the ER the night of the accident.

They'd all been on: Sticks and Jules and Parker. Her friends. Her cohorts, who for some reason hadn't had anything to say about the accident.

Jules, so certain Kate hadn't hurt anybody. So unwilling to talk about what had happened. Kate fought a clutch of fear. Jules knew something Kate needed. Jules, confronted head on, might be able to give Kate the answer to why that little boy had incited so very much.

As if in answer, the door opened.

"Have you seen Suzie?" Jules asked, her features tight with frustration.

It took Kate a second to answer. "No. She hasn't been in here. Why?"

Jules was tapping a foot against the floor, her gaze flickering toward the door down the hall where Phyl held court. "You wanna tell me again why she's still working here? She just got here an hour ago, and already she's taken off for parts unknown."

"You know perfectly well I don't know why," Kate retorted, trying to see something in her friend she hadn't before. "It's one of the great medical mysteries of our age."

Jules snorted like an overheated horse. "Well, when you find out, let me know."

"Jules—"

"Did you talk to maintenance about changing your lock like John told you?"

Kate shook her head.

Jules glowered. "It'd probably be easier if you'd just go to B.J.'s like he suggested, you know."

"Easier for everyone else," Kate admitted. "Not easier for me." Kate couldn't do this any other way. She needed to at least have some clue. "Jules, I've been going over the Rashad chart."

Jules's face immediately clouded over. Kate felt her last hopes plummet. "What did I do, Jules?" she demanded. "Why won't anybody talk to me about it?"

"You didn't do anything," her friend insisted. "Trust me. We'll talk about it after I get this overdose up to the unit. That's if I can ever find the elusive Ms. Walsh. Now, call maintenance."

And before Kate could ask, Jules was gone.

She stood there a minute, impaled on indecision. Knowing she had to learn more. Knowing all her answers eventually would be picked out of the sterile wording of that chart.

She stood there, alone, in the only quiet room on the floor, listening to the world that clattered and pulsed outside the door. Separated, paralyzed, in the only place she'd ever felt comfortable. Struggling to hold back the certainty that she didn't even belong here anymore, which meant she didn't belong anywhere.

To avoid facing that possibility, Kate turned around and called maintenance—and was promptly told she had no authority to request a new lock on the apartment door, because as of the day before she'd been served notice that she was going to have to move out.

"Did you ever find Suzie?" she asked Jules fifteen minutes later, as they stormed the administrative suite.

"No. When I told Parker where I was going, he said fine."

They were headed for the leasing offices that handled all the different properties on the campus, from house staff residence to doctors' office buildings. In her hand, Kate held the slip she'd ignored the day before, the one that stated in the simplest of computer legalese that Kate had thirty days to vacate the apartment since she no longer had a right to be there and there were other house staff on a waiting list for the space.

Her face was a brighter red than Jules's, and her language had been blistering. She'd talked to the clerk and then the computer programmer and then the secretary. Each one referred back to the

computer, which verified the action. Each was just
doing her job. Each had been struck dumb when
asked for suggestions in how to rectify the situation. Kate went straight from logic to rampage,
and had been rewarded with the sound of slamming phones.

"I'm just going so you don't hurt anybody,"
Jules said.

"Is that why you have that IV pole in your
hand?"

"I forgot to put it back down."

The leasing offices were deep in the heart of
carpet country. It seemed only fitting, since
prospective clients would have to mingle with the
staff. Why rent from someone who smells like disinfectant and old flowers?

Kate fought for sanity. She was losing.

"Phyl just told us that we're redecorating the
waiting room again," Jules said, the IV pole
bouncing up and down in front of her like a lance
in a joust.

"God knows we need that more than staffing."

They were just about even with Mr. Gunn's
office, when the hush of the elegant setting was
shattered by a scream. Jules stopped on a dime,
missing Kate with her IV pole by inches. Both of
them took a look over at the oak door that bore
Mr. Gunn's name on a brass nameplate.

Nothing. The door stayed closed and silence
returned.

Kate and Jules turned to check the reaction of
the secretary who sat at the end of the hall to find
out if this was something she was used to. She

didn't blink. Jules checked with Kate and they both shrugged, at least a little appeased that they were going to have something worthwhile to take back with them to the nether regions.

Figuring they could only stall so long, they set off again. This time they only made it five more feet when a second, higher scream stopped them in their tracks.

Then another, and another: shrill, terrified screams that signaled only one thing. Kate reacted instinctively, whipping around to open the door.

It was locked.

"Kick it," Kate insisted.

"You kick it."

The screaming went on and on. The secretary scurried toward them. Jules eyed the door. She shook her head, then lowered it and dove for the door with her shoulder, pushing it right off the frame.

Which was how they came upon Mr. Gunn in full and terrifying seizure on his chrome-and-slate desk, his mouth open, his eyes bugging, his pants around his ankles, and his organ at full attention. And there, straddling it and wearing nothing but her nursing hose, garter belt, and a bright shiny new nursing cap no one had ever seen her wear in her entire career, was Suzie Walsh, screaming her lungs out.

Kate reacted in a perfectly professional manner. She turned to Jules and threw up her hands.

"Oh," they said in unison, with a big nod of relief. "*That's* why she's still working here."

✦ Chapter 17 ✦

IT IS A VERY difficult thing to run a code when you're laughing.

"He was—you know, jumping around." Suzie was stammering, her cap hanging askew and blue mascara running down her face. "And—and making gurgling noises. But I just figured he was . . . he was . . . I don't know."

"Coming," Parker supplied for her as he taped an IV in place on the still unclad CEO.

Her nod was as jerky as the patient's limbs. "Yeah. That's it. But I guess he was . . ."

"Going," three separate people offered.

"Anybody got a rhythm?" Lisa asked at the other end of the body, her voice suspiciously high.

"Nothing but artifact," Kate acknowledged from where she rode herd on the monitor. "That's a hell of a seizure."

"What the fuck did he take?" somebody demanded as they tried to pump a chest that bounced back up in perfect, terrible rictus. The anesthetist wasn't having any better luck getting an endotracheal tube in. He'd managed to pop at least three crowns with the wood pry without even getting purchase past those clamped teeth.

The room was in chaos, furniture pushed against the far wall to make room for equipment and personnel, the expensive Karastan carpet littered with spent packaging and body fluids, and the code being run on a ten-thousand-dollar desk. Three supervisors were taking notes, and four men in administrative attire were blocking the door from letting in more people.

By dint of the fact that she'd arrived first, Lisa Beller was code captain, which was a good thing, because just about as soon as the *Code Blue administrative suite first floor* announcement had gone up, almost as many chiefs of service had shown up as when Fleischer had dropped dead at their feet. Lisa held them off with bright smiles and determination.

"Just how long did he make these gurgling noises?"

"I don't know," Suzie answered with a sniffle over where the vice president of Human Resources was trying to shield her from the view of the audience with his very own Hart Shaffner & Marx jacket. "Forty minutes or so."

Everybody stopped. "Forty minutes?" Lisa demanded before she really thought about it.

"Well, he only got really noisy toward the end. But it's not that unusual. . . ."

The sound of suppressed laughter rumbled through the room like an overhead train as the administrators glowered by the door.

"I tried to help him," Suzie whined.

"We know," Jules soothed, eyeing target zero for a catheter. "You should have hung around for a few more CPR classes, though, Suze. You would have found out you were blowing into the wrong thing."

"You're not even supposed to blow," Parker said. "It's only an expression anyway."

"Did he take anything before this happened?"

By now only the patient's head and heels were on the table. The rest arched in a perfect rainbow, pointing north with unerring accuracy.

"Just—uh, his regular gin and tonics," Suzie insisted. "He always has three, like a ritual. I didn't. I don't—you know—drink."

"Nobody touch the bottles on the counter," Kate directed. "Anybody seen the police yet?"

"Are you kidding? Nobody can get through that crowd in the hallway. I think there are people from four other hospitals out there who just came to watch."

Kate had to admit that for the purpose of revenge, it was a great show. She was surprised more people didn't try and squeeze in the room just to punch Gunn in the chest a few times. On the other hand, she thought she'd heard the click of at least one camera.

"How long have we been at this, kids?" Lisa asked.

"Half an hour," Kate obliged, rubbing at her own chest as she marked a strip that showed nothing but a few miserable blips.

"Any Valium left on the floor?"

"There isn't any Valium left in the bistate area."

"Oh, my! Oh, dear, no."

Everybody stopped. Then they gaped. Then somebody threw a lab coat over Gunn's body, but it kind of tented in an unfortunate way, which just made it all the funnier.

"Sister, I don't think you should be . . ."

But Polyester wouldn't be dissuaded. She approached the desk, her eyes almost as wide as Suzie's, shaking her head. "Haven't you given him succinylcholine yet?" she asked all the stunned, suddenly uncomfortable faces.

Lisa looked at the by-now-contorted purple face of her patient. "Succinylcholine?" she asked.

Mary Polyester pointed. Gunn pointed back. "My, yes. We have a lovely institution for the insane in Texas, you know. It's where I saw this first."

"Saw what, Sister?" Lisa asked.

Polyester gave her a bemused smile. "He's been eating strychnine, dear," she said, and walked back out, still shaking her head.

They tried succinylcholine. They weren't terribly surprised when it didn't work. After another fifteen minutes or so, the code team filtered from the room, to be replaced by the homicide team. Mr. Gunn remained where they'd left him, in a perfect arch over the black-and-chrome desk he'd fitted into his office by expanding two hospital doors in load-bearing walls. It only seemed appropriate.

Still not able to shake the giggles, Kate took advantage of the chaos in the office and headed farther down the now-roped-off hallway to try and convince one of the underlings in the leasing office that she, Kate Manion, forgave the computer for fouling up, even at this time of personal grief and stress. That she hadn't planned to stay in the apartment past the residents' calendar year in June anyway, so the point was almost moot.

All she took away from the confrontation was another dose of frustration and double-talk. Policy was policy, and the people in the leasing office were just following it. Kate had originally headed for the office prepared to argue, to threaten if necessary. Suddenly the effort seemed too great.

Any lingering high effectively wiped out, Kate trudged back down the hall toward the new clot of people shaking their heads in awe at the door to the CEO's office. She caught B.J. inside, sitting dead center in the room in one of the leather swivels from the conference suite, a lab coat and disposable gloves on, his chin in his hands, his consideration on the table display as the evidence techs combed through the debris on the floor. Kate poked her way through the crowd.

"Why do you make your investigator come all the way out here if you're going to show up anyway?" she demanded without greeting, wiping at the perspiration on her face with shaky hands.

He didn't bother to look over. "I've never seen one of these before." His voice had the same note of awe she'd heard out in the hallway.

"I see they came and got the bottles."

He nodded. "I heard you were the first one here."

"The second one. The first one was a little too upset to perform proper CPR."

He gave a distracted grin. "You didn't do mouth-to-mouth on him, did you?"

"Are you kidding? Not after Suzie'd been in here. God only knows where her mouth had been."

"I think it's pretty obvious."

"Can we move the body now, doc?" the investigator asked. Kate knew him from his time in county detectives, a nondescript white guy with brown hair and mustache and deceptively passive eyes.

"Yeah, Mike. I just wanted a look."

The transport team parted the seas with the cart as B.J. got to his feet and peeled off the gloves.

"I think we've just run out of time," he said conversationally.

John heard him from the doorway where he was briefing his team. "You can sing dat in harmony, my man. We got press on us like maggots on meat. And de county supervisor comin' dis way, too."

"Then it's definitely my turn to decamp," B.J. acknowledged. "Tell the high and mighty that Mr. Gunn here has my first appointment in the morning."

"So," John mused as the transporters struggled to maneuver the body the way they wanted it, "dat is what strychnine look like."

"Probably. I can't think of anything else that leaves a body in that condition."

"Well, we have a real good time frame on dis

one. He brought a new load o' party supplies wid him when he came in, and had appointments all mornin' long. I don't suppose you shot anyt'ing into dat boy's drink, did you, Katie girl?"

Kate just let B.J. walk her by. "I still have my strychnine in my pocket."

"Bingo!" one of the evidence techs sang out.

Kate turned to see him straightening from where he'd been going through a trash can. He was holding up a hand so John could see what was nestled in his palm.

A bead. A small brown bead.

John did his own maneuvering to get into the room. "What you know?" he all but hummed with satisfaction. "Look familiar, little girl?"

Kate looked at the oddly carved little bead and shook her head. Something about the bead was familiar, but she couldn't say what. She tried hard to think of anybody from the code team who might have been sporting something like it. "Is that like the other one you found?"

John bent real close over the bead and nodded. "De very same. I owe you a drink, my man. A very, very big drink."

Kate couldn't help casting an acerbic look around the room, which still looked as if it had hosted a frat party. "How do you know it's not from somebody else?" she demanded instinctively. "We did have one or two people in here this afternoon."

"Not in the paper bag with the liquor receipts, we didn't," the tech informed her, holding up both in the other hand.

"Well," Kate admitted wearily. "If you can find anybody who's surprised that Gunn was on the hit list, sign 'em up for swampland."

B.J. seemed much more surprised by the atmosphere in the hospital than Kate. While mini-cams captured concern from Mr. Fellows, the peasants danced in the streets. The same staff that had wept for Tim now gathered to create mythology with chortling glee.

Phyl met them in the hallway by her office, her posture stiff and threatened. "I don't think it's appropriate to share what you saw in that office," she threatened sotto voce.

Kate wanted to laugh. She'd already heard far more interesting versions of what had happened in that office than what she'd seen, and she hadn't denied any of them. Besides, now that the adrenaline was wearing off as fast as day-old antiperspirant, her legs were shaking. She was exhausted and she was afraid, and she needed to disappear fast before she embarrassed herself.

"I think it's the end of my shift anyway," Kate assured her boss. "Would it be okay if I start working later in the day? Say, eleven to seven? I might be able to give a hand to evenings, since they're short-shifted."

"You aren't ready for that kind of stuff yet," B.J. objected instinctively.

"Just computer and quiet room," she demurred. "That kind of thing."

She didn't want to tell him she needed a lot

more time to sit with the evening crew to ask about the chart. She didn't say to either of them that she needed her own answers even more than they needed theirs.

"Besides," she added, figuring she had nothing else to lose. "I need the mornings to figure a way to keep my apartment till June. The leasing office is throwing me out."

Phyl's reaction was at least promising. B.J.'s was terrible and swift.

"What?" he demanded loudly enough for the entire first lower level to hear him.

Kate repeated herself, just for effect.

The effect got better when B.J. let loose with a string of invectives that damn near cleared out the waiting room fifty feet away. Kate wasn't sure whether it made her feel better or worse.

"I'll go talk to them," he said, the sound making every person in sight flinch.

"I'll take care of it," Phyl promised, eyes wide and hands out as if fending off a wild horse from the mares. "And I promise to get someone over right away to change those locks. The shift change is fine, but I agree with B.J. You're not to do anything physical around here until you get a release from every one of your doctors, you hear?"

Considering what she'd just done up in the administrative suite, the warning came too late. Kate didn't bother to say anything. She just nodded acquiescence.

"Now, Doctor O'Brien," Phyl suggested. "Why don't you take Kate home so she can get some rest?"

He did, spinning Kate for the door so fast the room kept following. One down and all the rest to go. John and Mary and Florence were all going to have to wait until tomorrow. Kate was shot. She had a feeling that if she was lucky she'd make it all the way across the grounds before her knees gave way completely. Her brain was already gone, so pan-fried that even autonomic function seemed like a strain. And then she stepped out the doors and realized why Phyl had been stationed to intercept her in the first place.

Her brain must have been working at least a little, because all she could think of was that this must be what the Romans felt like when they were overrun by the Visigoths.

"Miss Manion! Are the police questioning you in this latest incident?"

"Doctor O'Brien, what do you think Mr. Gunn died of? Was he poisoned like the others?"

B.J. pushed one way and the swarm of reporters pushed another, leaving Kate feeling like a bad swimmer caught in an undertow. She tried pushing too, but this crowd was in better shape. They sucked the air away and replaced it with noise and the smell of expensive perfume and sweat. Lights blinded her. Faces bobbed and grimaced, leaving her with the afterimage of brilliant teeth and pancake makeup, Burberry raincoats and spray-painted hair. The adrenaline she thought she'd used up flooded in again, this time producing sheer terror. Her chest, which had been hurting before from the exertion of getting that code started, felt as if it were closing off completely.

"Miss Manion, what about the reports that you're being sued in the death of a child under your care? Did he die of poisoning too?"

That took the forward momentum right out of her. B.J., pushing just behind her, slammed into her back, almost sending her right into one of the female reporters. Kate opened her mouth. She tried to get the breath to deny the charges, to even acknowledge them. B.J. never let her get the chance.

"Miss Manion is going home. You want to talk to me, do it through my office."

The shoving got worse. B.J. began to curse. Kate fought harder for air as the press of bodies buried her, the questions feral and unrelenting. She couldn't see above heads to find out where they were going. She could hardly hear B.J. next to her anymore.

"Please," she tried, knowing damn well she looked like every guilty mother ever sentenced for smothering her baby. "Please, I can't . . ."

She was gulping now, her heart hammering against her ribs, her chest on fire. Her peripheral vision was beginning to dim. She was in danger of hyperventilating, which made her furious. Kate Manion had never had an anxiety attack in her life, and she wasn't going to have one now.

"Miss Manion, did you in fact set this all up just to kill your fiancé? Doesn't he have a rather large insurance policy?"

"Goddamn it, let her go!" B.J. roared right in her ear.

She couldn't even laugh. She couldn't move.

"Miss Manion, isn't it true that your own mother committed suicide? Aren't you the one who found her, just like you found Doctor Peterson?"

That did it. All systems shut down and Kate missed the rest of the questions.

B.J. was beyond fury. He was battling a white-hot rage. He should have known better. He should have figured the pack was circling outside and taken Kate out another way. But he'd been distracted by the sight of her boss, in perfect rictus not fifteen minutes after the code had been called. He'd wanted to know the last thing that had gone through Gunn's mind as he'd gurgled into oblivion. He'd wondered just what that white light had told him.

And then he'd been blindsided by the additional news about the apartment. No wonder Kate had gone down like a prizefighter after a quick one-two.

"Get that shit off me," he heard through the door.

"Shut up," Jules retorted evenly. "You passed out."

"I did not pass out. I don't faint."

B.J. got the door open to see Kate struggling to sit up on the cart. She already had the oxygen off and was batting Jules's protective hands away from the IV they'd inserted.

"Goddamn it, Jules. What is that?"

"That," Jules informed her, "is the IV I got in and the two hundred cc's of fluid we've infused since you didn't pass out. Now shut up and lie down. You've done enough gymnastics for one day."

"I'm going home," Kate insisted, her voice trembling suspiciously.

B.J. saved them both from going after each other. "It was either this or the press," he stated baldly.

Kate turned on him, her eyes flashing fire even in an ashen face. "I overexerted myself a little," she said through clamped teeth. "They were cutting off my air."

He just nodded. "A handy little lesson, considering you keep forgetting about that hole you had in your chest."

"Shut up, B.J."

Behind him, a blond young thing in too-high heels and a business suit squeezed through the still-open door. "Can we get a statement for the press on how Miss—"

B.J. whipped around on her like retribution. "Get the fuck outa here," he snarled.

She got the fuck outa there. B.J. closed the door so fast he almost broke the hydraulics.

"She can't go back out into that mess," Jules protested, then turned on Kate with a big grin. "You should have seen it. He came charging in here with you in his arms, shaking reporters off like water. Three people swooned, I swear."

"Shut up, Jules," they both snapped in unison.

Kate was pulling at the IV with hands that shook almost as much as the ones B.J. had hidden in his pockets.

"Let her go," he suggested. "By now John and Mary have cleansed the temple and it's safe to go through."

"Are you gonna keep an eye on her?" Jules demanded. "I sure as hell don't have the energy."

"I'm—going—home," Kate said.

B.J. couldn't imagine why he had the urge to smile. None of this was funny, except maybe the sight of Kate facing off with Jules like a six-week-old kitten going after the family mastiff. He couldn't think of anything he'd enjoy less than riding herd on a goddamn out-of-control woman with a death wish. Except that he didn't want to lose that goddamn out-of-control woman. He couldn't go through it again.

Almost on cue, the door into the work lane swung open and the skinny tech with the bad skin and feather earrings popped her head in. "Just got a call from John. He says all's clear." Then she turned to Kate, and B.J. noticed that for once the girl actually had color in her skin. "You guys have to tell me all about it, you hear me? Every detail." When Kate didn't answer right away, the tech huffed a little like a man whose phone sex operator has been cut off at the wrong moment and started playing with her hair. "*Every* detail. Phyl wouldn't let me go stick a pin in him to make sure he was really dead. Okay?"

Kate was the first one to nod. "He went down like a champ, Sticks. Now, everybody let me outa here."

Jules immediately slammed those plump hands on even plumper hips. "You're signing out

AMA," she demanded, "just like every other stupid gump who walks out when they're not supposed to. And then you're getting a Stupid Stunt Star in the Pig Nurses' newsletter."

"I'm fine," Kate snarled one last time as she slid off the cart and almost onto the floor.

She wasn't, of course. They were halfway across the campus when Kate came to a dead stop, her hand to her chest. "The file. Oh, God, Beej, where's my file?"

B.J. stopped for her, just as he had the other three times. "What file?"

"Billy Rashad. The accident. I had it on me when that horde descended. Jesus, I hope they don't get that."

B.J. just lifted the nursing bag he was carrying in the hand that wasn't holding her up. "Let's get you inside before you have a full-fledged psychotic break, okay?"

She glared at him, which would have been a hell of a lot more effective if she hadn't looked like an airline disaster survivor.

"You're going to have a drink," he said.

Her smile was sheepish. "I'm going to have a lot of drinks."

They both did. Kate drank brandy and B.J. drank Jameson, both of them sitting on the floor in the living room, their heads back on the seat of the couch, waiting for John to show up with the latest news.

"I should be doing something," Kate said, staring straight up at the ceiling.

"You should be sitting here getting pleasantly drunk. Now, shut up and do it."

She shook her head. "You don't understand."

"We keep having this conversation."

"I'm losing control," she said. "Everybody's taking it away from me again: you, John, the news, the hospital. And whoever it is who is doing this. I've got to get it over, Beej. I need some resolution, or I'm going to fly apart at the seams."

She wasn't telling him a thing. He wished he knew how to comfort her. He wished he could hold her together with his own hands. But he'd spent too long keeping his distance. He'd thought he was safer that way. He celebrated the idea that only the most stupid bastard on earth could believe such a thing with another great slug of Jameson.

That was when Kate decided sitting was too easy. She lurched to her feet and began to pace, her eyes suspiciously bright. "I don't know what to do anymore. I close my eyes and expect to have Tim haunt me. But he's too damn polite. It's my sisters who are haunting me, and that doesn't make sense."

"Your sisters?" B.J. asked, not moving. "Not your mother?"

Kate laughed as she lifted the brandy bottle for another dose. "My mother doesn't haunt me."

"You're sure? You're sure this isn't because you feel guilty that you couldn't save her?"

That got Kate to turn toward him. B.J. thought he'd never seen those sharp eyes so bleak.

"Guilty?" she retorted, and then smiled, a terrible smile of self-loathing. "No, I never felt guilty. I felt relieved. I was glad she'd finally gotten it over with, and we could get on with our lives. Shows you how much a fourteen-year-old knows."

Goddamn it, he hated this. Hated knowing he had nothing in his bag of tricks to help her.

He did the best he could. He got to his feet, walked over to where she was standing with her arms wrapped around as if to hold herself together, and put his own arms around hers. Pulled her close. Held her until he could feel her relax against him. Then he lifted her face so he could see her. He couldn't offer any words, but he could offer solace.

She was shaking. So was he. She was just too pale, her eyes too big, her forehead too tight.

"Have you been eating?" he demanded, stroking her cheek.

She laughed. "That's the most endearing damn thing I've ever heard you say."

He grinned back and felt better. "I don't want you passing out again when I kiss you."

Her eyes widened even farther, and B.J. thought he saw the ghosts dim for just a minute. "I do not pass out," she insisted.

He just nodded. "Good."

And then the phone rang.

"Ignore it," she said.

He did. He kissed her instead, pulling her cap off so he could weave his hands into the short curls that had begun to hide the scar, inhaling the last traces of the perfume she'd put on that morning, forgetting the phone completely.

The phone didn't forget them. It kept on ringing until finally even B.J. had to pay attention to it. It still took him six more rings after he'd lifted his head to pull himself back into control.

"Don't go away," he commanded, stealing one last kiss that tasted like brandy.

"Don't think I can."

He laughed for the first time in days, which made John mad when he finally answered the phone.

"Well, maybe you havin' a good ol' time, my man," he snapped, with uncharacteristic surliness, "but I am hip deep in alligators."

"I was busy," was all B.J. would say. He was still watching Kate, thinking this was the damndest twist his life had ever taken. Of all times to feel like things were beginning to look better.

Kate had wandered over to the dining room table where she was picking through a small pile of envelopes. B.J. ran a quick hand through his hair, pushing it back from his suddenly slick forehead, as he did his best to concentrate on John's voice instead of Kate's body.

"You keep dat girl dere," John said simply. "We got some work to do I don' want her interferin' wid."

He had B.J.'s attention. "What's up?"

"I'll let you know soon as I know, but we maybe have a big break for ourselves here."

"You know who it is?"

He shouldn't have said it. Kate whipped around so fast she almost fell over. B.J. just waved her off again.

"Maybe. Maybe not. Do me a favor. Katie got dat chart?"

"Yeah."

"Good. Have her go over it one more time. And ask her if she sure she don' know somebody collects beads."

"You've got an idea about it?"

"I'll talk to you soon."

And then B.J. was left to explain it to Kate. But when he turned to do that, she wasn't paying attention. She was focused on her table, her drink forgotten. She'd reached out to stroke one of the envelopes with her index finger, as if rediscovering an old keepsake in her trunk.

"Kate?"

"My mail," she said absently.

B.J. walked over. "I know. I saw it. John wants you to go back over the chart one more time to see if anything occurs to you. He'll be here in a while to talk to you—"

She looked up at him, and the brief contentment had gone. "My mail," she repeated, as if he hadn't heard her.

He looked down at it, but it didn't look any different from when he'd walked past to get their drinks. "What about it?"

She shook her head. "I didn't bring it in, B.J."

That was when he finally saw what she'd been stroking. Another envelope, the address typed, with no stamp, no cancellation.

"Oh, shit."

Neither of them picked it up. They just watched it, as if they'd never seen anything like it before.

"Does John think he knows who it is?" she asked.

It wouldn't do any good to lie now. "Yeah. Are you sure you don't know anybody who wears beads?"

She looked up at him. "No." She turned her attention back to the envelope. "I don't think so. I think it's somebody I don't know. Somebody I've never met."

"Kate . . ."

"No one I know would do this," she insisted.

"Why don't we look at the chart anyway?"

She shook her head and picked up the envelope. "I think I want to know what Florence has to say."

B.J. was going to stop her. They should leave the message intact for John, just like the last one, even though there hadn't been any kind of evidence on it, no prints, no fibers, no identifying marks. It was good forensics to preserve evidence. But right now B.J. was more worried about preserving Kate's sanity. So he let her open it. He didn't even lean over for a look. And when the doorbell rang, he went to answer it, ready to head John off before he interfered.

The note was the same, folded so haphazardly that the envelope didn't lie flat. Kate pulled it out to find letters pasted over each other, gaps where there had never been gaps. Someone else, Mary had said. Another of Kate's friends warning her to stay away until the murderer had done her work.

Well, hadn't she? Florence had walked straight to the top, from Attila to Warner to Fleischer to Gunn. Who else was she going to kill, Saint Simon himself? Just set fire to the hospital and hope the right people got out?

DON'T INTERFERE. YOUR CONSCIENCE ISN'T CLEAN EITHER. JUST ASK MOLLY.

"No," Kate whispered bleakly. "Oh, no."

"Kate?"

She couldn't look away. No one knew. Not B.J., not Jules, not even Aunt Mamie. No one knew that Kate carried all the blame, kept it buried so deep that nothing could ever pry it loose. Nothing.

And yet, someone did know, and it was all changed again.

Kate finally felt a hand on her arm and looked up to find Jules glaring at her from six inches away. Behind her, B.J. had just closed the door behind Sticks.

"Are you taking care of her?" Jules demanded of B.J. without looking away.

Kate shoved the new fear away and tried to smile. Tried to react at all.

"I'm just . . . tired," she managed, refolding the note as carefully as she could with hands that shook even worse than before.

"Yeah, you look like it," Jules retorted.

B.J. made it back around to insert himself between the guests and the latest letter. Kate couldn't even look up at him.

"Actually," she said, dragging up her courage from where it was cowering somewhere near her knees, "I'm glad you're both here. I still need to go over some things with you."

"What things?"

She faced her friend with every ounce of determination she could muster. "I need you to finally tell me what happened the night of the Rashad boy. I think it's more important than we thought."

Jules and Sticks exchanged glances. Sticks started playing with one of her earrings, which usually meant she had nothing to say. Jules set her hands on her hips and checked with B.J. before answering. "You have the chart, Kate. What else is there?"

"There's the murderer," she said, ignoring the note. "I think all this has something to do with what happened to that baby. And I think it was my fault."

My fault, my fault. It seemed it was a litany she'd chanted her whole life. If she'd done something different, her father would have stayed. If she'd been a better daughter, her mother wouldn't have been so nuts. If she'd fought a better fight, she could have protected the girls. If she'd forgotten her old ghosts and gone after the murderer sooner, Tim wouldn't be dead.

"What did I do, Jules?"

It wasn't B.J. whom Kate expected to react. B.J. did, though, shoving past Jules to take hold of her by the arms. "I'm getting a little tired of this," he threatened.

Kate didn't know how to answer him. He didn't understand. Maybe he never would. "Something set this off. Something I did. Something maybe I don't want to deal with."

"Just like before?" he demanded. "Just like always?"

"Yes," she finally admitted, looking him right in the eye. "Just like always. Only this time I can't deal with it because I don't know what happened. Even reading the chart over and over again, I don't know what it was I did that night that might have set off a killer."

He let go of her, but Kate knew he wasn't appeased.

"I told you before," Jules said. "Nothing happened that night you should be ashamed of."

"Is that what I should tell my defense attorney?"

"Should John be here for this?" B.J. asked.

"No!" Jules and Kate retorted simultaneously.

The strength of Jules's objection sent Kate's stomach skidding. "You might as well tell me," she said. "I'm going to find out sooner or later."

"Nothing went on," Jules insisted, too strongly.

B.J. made a point of handing Kate her brandy. "Might as well sit down," he said to them all. "Sounds like it's gonna be a long evening."

Jules never looked away from her friend. "That's okay. I don't have much to say."

"Weiss said I kept that little boy too long. So does the chart. Why?"

Kate had almost forgotten Sticks, standing there just inside the door like the school truant waiting to see the principal. "You might as well tell her," the girl said.

"It was a busy night," Jules insisted. "Nobody else really saw what went on."

Kate shouldered past Jules to face Sticks. "Will you tell me? You were there."

Sticks looked over at Jules, her fingers in her hair making the feathers dance at her ears. The feathers she always wore, attached to the hoops with bright little beads. Kate suddenly couldn't take her eyes off them.

"Jules is right," was all Sticks said, although it sounded more like a challenge than an offer of support. "It wasn't your fault."

Kate backed up and faced them all. "What?" she demanded. "What wasn't my fault?"

It was Jules's turn to move. She flanked Kate and headed for the couch. Around the couch as if she were pacing the work lane. Revving up her memory with movement, like all people who think on their feet.

"I'm not lying, Kate. It was too busy to know for sure. Hell, we even had Mary Polyester in with the family, because none of us could do time in there. You can just imagine what good she did."

"What good did I do?" Kate demanded, terrified.

Jules skidded to a stop right in front of her. "You did everything you could for that baby. You went toe to toe with everyone from Phyl to Weiss to Warner to Fleischer. Shit, Kate, you were fired, did you know that? We didn't tell you because we figured you didn't need to know. They were going to toss your ass out for trying to get that kid good treatment."

"Why? There isn't anything on the chart to suggest why I waited. What was it? Was there something there, or was I just pissed off because Fleischer wouldn't accept an uninsured kid?"

"You were sure that kid was cooking a bad head injury, all right? You said your instincts were telling you that even though he looked all right, that kid was too sick to transfer. You were terrified he was going to crump on the way into the city, so you did everything you could to make sure he was in a good facility when he did go bad."

"But he didn't."

Jules couldn't quite look her in the eye anymore. "Not while he was there."

Kate was having trouble breathing again. Maybe Billy had gone bad after all. Maybe she'd been right. But the only people who might have told her for sure were dead. She turned to B.J., even knowing how little he could help.

"You did the post on him," she said.

But he shook his head. "I wish I could give you something definite, pogue. The damage was too extensive. I don't know whether it was pre-crash or post-crash."

Kate never heard the doorbell this time. She didn't notice B.J. leave her. Her eyes were turned inward, searching for a memory that wasn't there.

Finally she couldn't do any more than shake her head. "So now all we have to do is find the person on that night who was most affected by what happened, and we'll have our murderer."

"We already have."

Kate turned from the window to find John and Mary standing just inside the door. John had a card in his hand. Mary was frowning over at Kate as if she wanted to apologize.

"What are you talking about?" Kate asked, and remembered the beads. Turned stunned eyes to Sticks, who looked, if possible, even paler.

But John didn't turn to Sticks. "Jules," he said with sincere sorrow, "we'd like you to come down to de station wid us, please."

✦ Chapter 18 ✦

"JULES?" KATE DEMANDED of John. "What the hell are you talking about?"

Jules, for once, didn't seem able to say anything for herself.

Over in her corner, Sticks forgot to be quiet. "Goddamn it, Kate, who else you gonna turn in, me? Mary Polyester?" Her face was suddenly flushed, her young eyes hard with accusation.

"Shut up, Sticks," Jules snapped.

"You wan' me to read you your rights?" John asked Jules.

"It was just a few faxes," Kate protested. "She didn't mean anything. You know that."

John turned those sad brown eyes on her, and Kate knew she didn't want to hear what he was going to say. "I'm sorry, Katie girl."

"But we agreed it couldn't have been her. She was too big for anybody to think it was me."

"She was," he answered, pulling a plastic bag out of his coat pocket. "But not her frien' Davy."

And there it was, Kate's missing cap, the chartreuse one with the big RN in purple letters.

Kate looked over at Jules, who was staring at the thing as if it had grown eight legs and danced.

"Where'd you get that?" the big woman demanded.

"Your locker. De hospital let us look after we foun' out you were in poor Mr. Gunn's office today. You went in wid him when he brought in his gin and tonics, girl. An' you came back later. Everybody up dere notice you. And den we got to t'inkin'. Maybe it didn't need to be a girl poor Bose saw dat night. Maybe it was a man dressed to look like one. Maybe a man helpin' you."

"Wait a minute," Kate protested. "Are you saying she's the killer or the person sending me the warnings?"

"I'm sayin' I t'ink maybe she's both."

"But that's stupid," Kate retorted. "Why would she suddenly do something so dumb when she's been so smart before? We agreed it had to be somebody nobody'd think twice about being up in Gunn's office. Like Suzie. Ask her, for God's sake."

"Suzie don' make nice pretty moccasins wit' beads on dem. Does she, Jules?"

"That's what I was doing there, John," she said. "He bought a pair of moccasins from me. I swear it."

"Gunn wanted moccasins?" Kate instinctively demanded.

But John was waving everybody off with his Miranda card. "You listen to dis before you talk to me. And I t'ink it better if we do dis someplace else. Katie don' look too good."

"Fuck Katie," Sticks retorted, tears in her big eyes. "Who says *she* didn't do it and plant the goddamn cap?"

"Shut up!" Jules yelled.

"She's not going anywhere," Kate said without thinking. "This is ridiculous. You're convicting her on what was in her locker? Anybody can get in her locker. For God's sake, they got in my apartment. Again. They dropped off my mail when they brought in the newest love note, damn it. And who says that was her bead? Look at Sticks's earrings. There are probably a lot of other people I haven't even thought of yet who have beads."

"New love note?" Mary asked B.J.

"You talk 'bout dat later, little girl," John warned. "After de rest of us are gone."

"Why?" Kate demanded. "The whole hospital knows about 'em. Jules sure as hell must. Isn't she the one who's supposed to be sending them?"

"Sending what?" Jules asked, her attention swinging back and forth between John and Kate. "What notes?"

"Those damn letters from Florence," Kate said, gaze locked on John. "The ones he thinks you've been sending me to warn me off."

"You got another one?"

John was beginning to look dangerous now. "Katie, don't. You're hurtin' worse dan you're helpin'. Now, let's go."

Jules turned panic-stricken eyes on Kate. "Do you know a lawyer?"

"Of course. . . ."

Steve. Tim's brother. Tim, who was one of the victims Jules was being arrested for murdering.

"Don't ask her," Sticks pleaded, hand on Jules's arm. "She's coverin' her ass on this one, damn it."

Jules shook her off like a small dog. "Go on, Sticks. Get on back to work before I hurt you."

"But Kate—"

"But Kate nothing. Grow up for once and pay attention. She's not any happier about this than you are."

John took the other arm in a grip that wouldn't be shaken. "Jules, I wan' you outa here before de media fin' out. Please. An' you," he said with enough force to make Sticks flinch. "Not a word about notes. I'll hear."

Jules finally nodded. John lifted his Miranda card. Kate fought the urge to throw herself at him, as if it could make a difference.

"We'll get somebody down there," B.J. said for her. He was there, his arm around Kate's shoulder. He sounded as bad as she felt.

"Can I have the latest note?" Mary asked, blocking Sticks's way out. The girl glared at the FBI agent with the same venom she'd reserved for Kate. Mary didn't seem to notice. "I'd like to talk to you a second before you go," she said simply. Sticks headed for the window so she could watch Jules leave.

Mary looked at the note and frowned. Shook her head. "Another copycat," she concluded, standing in the doorway as John and Jules disappeared down the stairs.

"A copycat with the key to my apartment," Kate retorted. "Which, I might add, Jules doesn't have."

"At least you don't think so."

B.J. held on to Kate again, this time more tightly, as if expecting argument. Kate couldn't even manage that anymore. She just wanted to be gone. To be quiet and relieved of everyone's expectations.

"Molly," Mary mused, then looked up. "Kate?"

Kate just shook her head. "My sister," she said. "It's . . . a long story. B.J., you didn't . . . ?"

But Kate already knew even B.J. didn't know this. B.J. would never have told anyone something that could hurt Kate this badly, no matter what the cause.

B.J. shook his head anyway. "Who knows about your sisters?" he asked.

"Nobody knows," she said, truthfully, because no one did. "No one."

"You got a look at the chart," Mary said to Kate. "Anything in it help?"

"Help what?" Kate demanded. "Jules? I don't know. Just how upset was she that night, Sticks? You were there. Did she take sides with me on that little boy?"

Sticks stood on one foot, rubbing her ankle with the other, suddenly looking like the little girl she really was. "Don't expect any help outa me," she said.

"I'm asking you to help Jules," Kate retorted, too upset to be angry.

Sticks tried a little more glaring before she

finally gave in. "Jules was telling the truth. It was so busy she didn't know what was going on until she saw Mrs. Warner piling your stuff on the floor outside your locker. The only people who were really upset were the ones involved with that kid." She darted a look around at all of them before returning to Kate. "Especially you. I've never seen you so pissed. You said you wished somebody would have the guts to do something about all the assholes who keep us from doing our jobs."

"And somebody took me seriously."

"Thomas à Becket syndrome," Mary muttered. "We were right, Kate. It all hinges on that night, after all."

Kate hardly heard her. "Jesus Christ, Sticks. You never told anybody about this, did you?"

"So I could do what, protect Mr. Gunn?"

"So you could protect Tim."

"Who was there when she said it?" Mary asked.

Sticks shuffled a little more, gave another half-hearted shrug. "I don't know. It was so busy, and things happened so fast. I do remember Phyl had just told Kate that Mrs. Warner wouldn't let her have a helicopter. And that Phyl would personally fire her if she tried to go over her head one more time."

Kate was rubbing at her face. "There has to be something we've missed."

"Maybe not," Mary suggested quietly.

Kate dropped her hands and glared. "Jules didn't do it," she insisted.

"You just don't want to believe any of your friends would be involved in something like this," the agent responded. "But one of them is, Kate. One of them is."

"Can I go now?" Sticks asked. "I need to get back to work."

Mary moved aside and Sticks made for the door, pausing only long enough to give Kate one last look. Kate saw the struggle in her, the need to blame, the fierce loyalty and frustration. Kate couldn't fault her a bit, and that hurt almost worse than seeing Jules being led out the door.

Kate tried to sit back down. It didn't work. She felt the walls closing in, and there didn't seem to be any way of stopping them. Something was wrong and she knew it. She just couldn't say what. Something felt cold and sinister in a way that it hadn't before. Calculated. Evil. Different from the beginning, with those polite little notes and people dropping over so quickly they'd have to have chased down their own near-death experiences.

She took a deep breath and tried to consider it all logically. She couldn't. She knew too much now about that night and still too little. She knew Jules couldn't be the culprit. She knew whatever was wrong lay just beneath the surface like a bad itch. She knew she couldn't sit still.

"Maybe if I call them all," she said to herself, rubbing her hands together to ward off the numbness of exhaustion. "Maybe if I step up the threats, she'll come forward. I haven't done enough. I haven't—"

"Step up what threats?"

Kate looked up to see Sticks gone, the door closed, and Mary and B.J. standing head to head, their attention now on her. It was B.J. who'd heard her, evidently.

"Maybe you could go over the chart for me, Beej," she said, lurching back to her feet. "See something I missed. Something that would point in the right direction. I could give her information she wouldn't think I had."

B.J.'s features were tight and unhappy. "Step up what threats?" he asked again, stepping away from Mary.

Kate batted his hand away as she bent for her bag, for the records inside that held all the clues. "You didn't give me enough time. It would have worked, I know it. I could have convinced Florence that I was the only one who knew what was going on and she'd have had to come for me. Come for me here."

This time B.J. wasn't going to be waved aside. He grabbed her by both arms and yanked her away from the bag just as Kate was pulling out the folder. Contents flew everywhere, scissors and tourniquets and the chart, which hit the floor and spread. Kate dove for it again without success.

By the time B.J. got her to face him, his expression was thunderous. "What have you been doing?" he demanded.

"I'm trying to find the real killer," she snapped, struggling to get loose.

"Are you crazy? Just what did you think was going to happen?"

"I'm going to force her out of hiding, because the only way I'll stop is if she kills me. And the only way she'll know what I've told anybody else is to meet me face to face."

"You were just going to invite her over here for another hanging party?"

"Yes!"

Kate glared at him, furious. Terrified. "Don't you understand? It's the only way we're going to know. It's the only way my friends are going to be safe." It was the only way she was going to discover what other people had found out.

He actually shook her, as if he could work the obsession loose. "Goddamn it, Kate—"

"But it doesn't make any difference now," Mary insisted.

"Of course it does," B.J. retorted. "Jules is no more the murderer than I am. Kate's setting herself up to be the next target."

"But I'll know," Kate protested. "I'll be able to protect myself, because she's going to have to explain herself before she acts. She has to get my approval—"

There it was again, the snag that had been bothering her. The notes had asked for understanding. The murders had been some odd kind of offering. All the murders but one.

Kate turned on Mary with a vengeance.

"You can't possibly believe Jules really did it," she accused.

That shut both Mary and B.J. up in a second.

Mary recovered first. "It's not just the beads, or the faxes. One of the typewriters used on the notes was from the emergency department. Her time cards match. And she fits the profile. Adult child of an alcoholic, needing approval, seeking control over her environment, neat, meticulous, thorough."

"Shit, Mary, so am I. So is three-fourths of the staff over there. But Jules wouldn't kill Tim. You know it. I know it. That's what it keeps coming back to. No matter how you try and stretch the psychological profile you've put together, it falls apart. Tim just doesn't fit the picture. You'd know that if you'd ever worked with him."

Control. Kate could feel it seeping back in, just a little. Funny how even a taste of it was like a stimulant. They all needed it in different ways. Kate desperately needed tidiness, predictability, structure. As long as someone told her where and when to come to work, what was expected of her, and where to find the right tools, she could accomplish damn near anything. Mary thought their killer was seeking control through the murders. Maybe she was. Maybe they all were, with whatever way they handled the entire matter.

"I can't believe I didn't think of it before," she said. "It's been there all along."

"It couldn't be that you'd been a little preoccupied," B.J. drawled, from where he was moving to pick up the mess she'd just made.

"What's everybody else's excuse?" she retorted.

"What was there all along?" Mary asked.

"Tim," Kate said. "Tim. He's a puzzle piece that just doesn't fit. I mean, shit. If you think Jules would kill him, think again. She'd rather hang her husband than Tim. And as for anybody else doing it, if she's murdering to get my approval, why would she commit the one act that would guarantee she'd lose it?"

"Even if Tim was gay?"

"That has nothing to do with it! He was a good man. He was my friend. He was everything the killer was trying to protect in medicine, not what she was trying to get rid of."

Mary should have looked more chagrined. At least more belligerent. Seeing her reaction, Kate realized that Mary had agreed with her before she'd ever opened her argument.

"Then tell me what you think," the agent suggested, deliberately sitting herself down.

It took Kate a minute to change gears. To cool down enough to think. Then she followed Mary to the couch. Finished her forgotten brandy. Pulled her rattled brain cells into order to cull some sense from the whole thing.

"These murders weren't a taunt," she said finally, thinking of the lettering of the first notes as she leaned forward, elbows on knees, words deliberate and slow, as if that alone could create order. "They were a gift. An apology, almost. At least the first three were. Each of those people came into contact with me on the night of the accident. Each could be seen hurting me in some way, Fleischer and Warner by arguing about Billy Rashad and Attila by the rough care she gave me."

"That's what you found in the chart?" Mary asked.

Kate nodded, her eyes unfocused, her memory on what she'd read instead of what she remembered. She didn't even realize that Carver had leaped onto the couch to curl up alongside her. She didn't see that B.J. had bent back down to retrieve the copied chart that lay in a fan on the floor.

"What about Mr. Gunn?" Mary asked, leaning forward.

Kate shook her head. "I argued with Fleischer, Weiss, Phyl, and Warner. If anybody was next, it should have been Weiss or Phyl. Why would Gunn have been killed?"

"Maybe Jules knew she was running out of time and wanted to go straight to the top."

Kate shook her head. "I didn't have any contact with Mr. Gunn."

"Maybe you overlooked something in the chart. Maybe Gunn was called."

Kate shook her head. "No. It never got higher than Warner."

She was fighting a losing battle to keep her attention focused on the problem. There was so much to consider, suddenly, and she was already so very tired. She didn't want to try anymore. She didn't want to have to be responsible, and she was.

"Maybe that's why she used strychnine this time," she mused, absently scratching Carver's ears.

Out of the corner of her eye, she saw that B.J.

had retrieved all the papers and was paging through them. Good. Maybe he could come up with a different spin on revenge and logic.

"Kate?"

When Carver heard the tone of B.J.'s voice, he bolted. Kate damn near followed right behind, especially when she realized that B.J.'s attention was still focused on the reassembled chart in his hand.

Oh, God, she immediately thought. He's found something.

But instead of reading from the chart, he pulled something out of it: a plain white carefully folded note.

"How long have you had this?" he asked.

Kate stared at the letter in his hand and then at the page beneath. The last page of notes reporting the fact that no transport was immediately available and that Lindbergh would be transporting Billy Rashad. The culmination of everything. The last entry was that the parents had been apprised.

"I haven't," she said, dread snaking down her back. "I spent all afternoon looking at that page, and I didn't see any note."

B.J. looked down at her. "Then I think we'd better call John."

Mary grabbed another pair of gloves from her purse and took the paper. "No envelope," she said. "Otherwise it's identical."

Kate made it to her feet as Mary unfolded the note. Kate supposed she shouldn't have been surprised. She'd certainly seen that kind of plain white paper before with magazine letters that marched across the page in absolute precision and a fold so sharp it could have caused paper cuts.

"Jesus," she whispered with a sick shake of her head. "Doesn't this chickie have anything else to do with her time?"

BLESSED ARE THOSE WHO SEEK JUSTICE, FOR THEY SHALL BE CALLED CHILDREN OF GOD. I DEDICATED MYSELF TO DO GOD'S WORK FOR YOU, KATE. FOR ALL OF US. HOW CAN YOU SAY I DIDN'T.

There was something there, something Kate knew she should see. She could feel it in the same place that said the rest of what was going on was wrong.

"Oh, my God." Mary yanked the note close, holding it up, holding it away. "That's it."

Kate and B.J. looked too. "What?"

Mary's eyes suddenly held an unholy light. "What's been bothering me about these damn notes. What didn't fit!"

She held it for them to see.

"*This* is the way they're supposed to look! Folded so carefully you could use them for a T square. Absolutely precise. Don't you see?"

"I see," B.J. agreed. "What was wrong with the other ones?"

"The letters were all perfectly aligned. You remember? But all the notes except the first one were folded so badly they barely fit in the envelopes. Sloppy. It didn't make sense."

Kate looked carefully at the note. "But this does?"

Mary was frowning again. "You're right. Why change now? Why not look like this all along?"

They didn't get their answer. Two things happened simultaneously to prevent further discussion. The doorbell rang, and the front window shattered.

✦ *Chapter 19* ✦

B.J. REACTED FIRST.

"Down!" he yelled, slamming into Kate even before Mary had her gun drawn.

Kate hit the floor with a thud and a *whoosh,* just about the time she heard the crack of a rifle somewhere outside. She wanted to curse. She wanted to scream or demand answers or yell. She couldn't so much as breathe, especially with B.J. on top of her.

She did see Mary crouch into position, her gun in one hand, the door knob in the other. She saw the agent yank the door open. She saw the poor guy from maintenance damn near wet his pants when he saw Mary's pistol barrel in his face.

"Jesus!" he yelled, hands up, tools down. "I'm only supposed to change the lock! I got no money, lady!"

Mary straightened carefully. B.J. climbed to his feet and edged around to the corner of the window so he could peek out. Not that it was going to do him much good. Even with all the lights in

the world on, there were just too many damn
bushes planted along the drive to hide behind.
Kate would have told him that if she'd had the
breath to do it.

"I'm sorry," Mary apologized to the poor distraught workman as she lifted her gun out of the
way. "Did you see anything outside?"

"Are you nuts?" he demanded, shaking worse
than Kate. Then he saw Kate lying on the floor, her
chest heaving ineffectively, her eyes wide with the
effort to get a breath. "Hey, Kate. What happened?"

All Kate could think of to say was that whoever
fired the rifle hadn't been a bad shot. He'd nailed
one of Matisse's bright birds right through the
chest feathers. She wondered if he could hit something that moved.

That made her want to giggle. The sight of
B.J. and Mary remembering they'd left her on the
floor made her want to giggle even more. The two
of them hurried her way, one more flustered than
the other.

"Are you okay?" B.J. demanded gruffly, as if it
was her fault he'd been more interested in the
source than the destination of the bullet.

She couldn't quite answer him. He gave her a
hand to yank her up, but she couldn't quite do
that either. Her body had evidently decided it had
had one shock too many and was refusing to
work at all.

When she didn't answer, his face immediately
crumbled into uncharacteristic distress. "Kate,
damn it, talk to me!"

He was down on his haunches, pulling her up

to him as if he were gathering broken parts, checking her with a doctor's hands. Kate wanted to laugh.

"She had the wind knocked out of her," Mary offered.

B.J. didn't bother with the opinion of a mere law officer. So Kate supplied her own.

The pressure system in her chest must have finally righted itself, because this time when she tried to haul in a breath, air rushed in. She choked with the unexpected pleasure of it.

"That's it, O'Brien," she managed on a rasp. "Next time I'm on top. You're too damn heavy."

"You're shaking," B.J. accused three hours later as he downed his second straight shot of Jameson in almost as many minutes.

Kate wished she could laugh. "I have a right to be." She wasn't far behind with the brandy. "I think you broke a couple new ribs when you threw me down."

He yanked the rubber band out of his hair and dragged a hand through it. It was still damp with sweat. "Old instincts die hard, pogue. I'm sorry."

Kate waved off the apology. She was sore, her nerves were shot to hell, and her butt was momentarily in one of B.J.'s chairs. She should have been settling down a little. But even with the stereo and TV both droning in the background to ward off the silence of a Brentwood night, she couldn't quite manage to close her eyes. Even ten miles away from St. Simon's, with the brightest lights coming from the high school track field and the neighbors walking their dogs in the late spring night, Kate couldn't overcome a sense of desperation, the feeling that it was all getting past her. Like a good ER nurse, she specialized in delayed reaction, and she was having a beaut.

"It wasn't Sticks," she insisted again.

"Probably not. They're talking to her anyway."

"Fine. That ought to raise my stock with her." Kate rubbed her chest and then rubbed at the burning in her eyes. "It's got to stop, Beej. I just can't take much more."

"I know, pogue. I know."

She shook her head. "No, you don't. You know just what you can survive. I don't."

"You're more of a survivor than I am."

The phone rang. B.J. ignored it. The news crews had showed up on the tail of the first police cruiser to answer the shooting call and hadn't left them alone since. Even Aunt Mamie had gotten through to Kate before she left the apartment. Not only was her aunt not amused by all the notoriety, she was furious at Kate for asking whether she'd talked to anyone about the twins. Mary Anne Henderson did not tell tales out of turn. Kate had been forced to sweat through another round with her aunt with the evidence crew not ten feet away.

"Who could have told Florence?" Kate asked again. "How could she have known?"

"About your sister?"

Kate looked up, surprised she'd spoken out

loud. "Aunt Mamie said she never mentioned a word about them to anyone. How could Florence have known?"

"You didn't tell anybody?"

"Just you. And you didn't tell anybody."

B.J. just shook his head. Climbing from the chair when the Cream CD ended, he popped in some Stones. Kate took another slug of brandy and watched him.

"It might be a good idea to try and find your sisters," he warned, his back still to her as the side started with driving drums and guitars. "Before the press does."

It was Kate who came off her chair this time. Panic drove her across to the window and back again. "No," she said with every last ounce of control. "I can't."

"Why not?"

She shook her head. "I just can't."

"Then how 'bout some sleep? You really look like you could use it."

Kate almost slammed into him as she turned for another circuit of the room. The brandy was making her warm. It was not making her sleepy. "You really know how to make a girl feel good, O'Brien," she accused halfheartedly.

B.J. simply stood in her way to keep her in place.

Kate damn near bolted over backward to get away.

"Want me to tuck you in?" he asked.

She came much too close to saying yes, and not because she needed sleep. She saw B.J. react even before she answered, two porcupines testing each other's quills. She wanted to laugh and run at the same time. And then B.J.'s beeper went off.

The tension broke like a soap bubble. "I'm on call," he apologized.

"You'd better call in," she said at the same time.

They laughed and backed to safe corners. B.J. headed for the phone in the old tile kitchen, and Kate sat on the couch and very slowly and deliberately drained the last of the brandy in her glass. Then she settled her head against the back of the couch and closed her eyes.

It was autumn. It was always autumn, where the leaves curled into crisp little gloves and the sky looked empty. Where street sounds echoed against brick and asphalt. Where ghosts roamed, and sorrow was a physical thing.

Of course it would be autumn. Autumn was the bad time. Her father had disappeared in the autumn. Halloween, when the girls had waited for him to come home from work so he could take them around to the other houses on Tamm Avenue. When the three of them had sat on the green sofa in the living room, stiff-legged and silent in their too-small ballerina dresses, until their mother had finally locked the front door and sent them to bed. There hadn't been any Halloweens after that.

She walked up the steps to that house again, where the leaves skittered across her feet and the door creaked in sympathy. She looked up, just like always, slowing, suffocating. Afraid. She saw the shadow through the screen and stopped, mesmerized by the sway. Terrified by the silence.

But this time, finally, she opened the door. This time she saw who it was. She saw her and knew why she'd never finished the dream before.

Kate bolted upright and struggled for sanity. For a minute she didn't know where she was. She remembered sitting on B.J.'s couch with the lights on and the stereo pounding away. Now she was somewhere silent and dark and terrifying.

The den. She could see the window now. She could hear the faint sounds of suburbia. B.J. must have gotten her into bed on the foldout couch.

Then she heard it again, a harsh cry of terror, and she knew what had startled her awake. It never occurred to her to stay in the den where it was safe.

"Go back to bed," B.J. ordered as Kate reached his bedroom doorway.

The bathroom light betrayed his secret. Kate could see him sweating and shaking and trying to escape the tangle of bedclothes. He was breathing even faster than she was, the respirations of a runner. Kate thought how she stood away from her dreams and observed. B.J. seemed to drown in his.

She never bothered with turning on a light. "I couldn't sleep either," she said, heading on in to help.

B.J. leveled a look at her that should have frozen her on the spot. For some reason, this was one threat Kate had no problem facing. "I have dreams about people hanging," she said, picking up one of the pillows that had landed over by his pile of well-thumbed science-fiction books. "I bet yours are far more interesting."

B.J. sighed and climbed out of bed, his movements just a little off-balance with the effects of shedding sleep. He wore only his gym shorts, and his skin gleamed with fresh sweat.

"It's nothing," he insisted. "I told you. Some things are just harder to forget than others."

Kate nodded. "Uh huh."

"Jules will be released in the morning," he said, straightening up bedclothes without making eye contact.

Kate didn't know what to do with her sudden distress. His hands were shaking; she'd never seen that with B.J. She retrieved another pillow as if it were the most normal thing in the world. "Good."

B.J. nodded, as stiff and uncertain as she. "There isn't any more information on the guy who put the potshot through your window. I talked to the office."

"I know."

"Damn it, Kate, stop looking at me like that."

Kate didn't know whether to laugh or cry. Another level of fear, of involvement, of everything she'd been avoiding all these years. Damn him, damn him, damn him for complicating this so much. Damn him for making her come over here where he really lived.

Because suddenly it wasn't enough anymore that she hurt, that she was terrified and confused and guilty. One lousy nightmare and she was hurting more for B.J. than she was for herself. And damned if that wasn't what dropped the last barrier.

"So if I fell in love with you," she said in a very small voice, past the acid in her chest, "would this happen very often?"

That brought him to a sudden and thorough halt. It finally got him to look at her. And she finally knew just what B.J. had kept locked behind all that legendary control all those years.

"This isn't the time to be making jokes," he warned.

Kate couldn't so much as smile. "Trust me. I'm very short on jokes lately. In fact, I think this is the scariest thing I've ever done in my life. Do you want a drink, maybe?"

He at least had the grace to smile. "My head hurts from the last round."

She nodded abruptly, the admission making her awkward. "Mine too."

All Kate could think of was that this was the very worst time to ask him to make love to her. It wouldn't ease either of their nightmares. It wouldn't do a damn thing but complicate their lives beyond redemption. But at the moment, Kate didn't really care.

"You're shaking," B.J. accused gently.

Kate's nod was jerky. She felt fresh tears of frustration burn the back of her throat. "Help me out here, pogue," she pleaded, suddenly gawky and afraid.

He took a step forward. Halted. Took a breath as if girding himself for battle of some kind. "This is gonna change everything, you know."

"I know."

It did.

It might have been the greatest mistake either of them had ever made. But it didn't feel like a mistake. It felt simply like the punctuation in the conversation they'd been having for a very long time. They fit together easily, even in those well-wrung sheets, and there in the small hours of night when pretense disappears, B.J. was as passionate and fierce and tender as Kate had always known he would be. And Kate, who had spent too many years barricading herself against getting involved, laughed with the unexpected pleasure of abandon.

They never quite fell back to sleep. Some barriers were just too strong to overcome all at once. So they lay there waiting for the sun to come up and pretended that nothing had changed.

"So, why did you marry Michael?" B.J. asked, chewing on an unlit cigarette.

A little preoccupied by the pleasant lethargy she'd all but given up forever, Kate shrugged. "Because I thought he was safer than you, I guess."

"Was he?"

"Sure. He never found out any of my secrets. But then, he never talked to me either."

B.J. didn't move from where he had one arm curled around Kate and the other curled around that third pillow he seemed to need. "Asshole."

"Why'd you go to Philadelphia?"

"Same reason."

Kate nodded. Grinned. "Asshole."

It was when they were getting ready for work that Kate noticed B.J. rubbing his temples.

"Rubber band too tight?"

B.J. just scowled as he kept an eye on the morning news while stuffing his regulation monogrammed shirt and silk tie in his carryall for those quick-change moments at the office where he kept his one and only suit. "Remind me never to drink with you again. I never feel like this the morning after a bottle of Dr Pepper."

"Too much activity," she retorted. When he reacted with rare discomfort, she added in a deadpan voice, "At the apartment, when you were throwing people all over the room."

He went back to packing. "I saved your miserable hide."

"Yes," she admitted, with just the right hint of subtext. "You did."

That didn't make him any happier. She shut up completely. Kate knew perfectly well what the words "too soon" meant.

" . . . a suspect is in custody. Police won't comment, but a source close to the case states that it is another nurse from Saint Simon's, not, as previously thought, Kate Manion. . . ."

That was all it took to kick-start the pressure right back into high gear. "Well, at least my name's off the front page," Kate mused blackly as she turned to the TV. "Maybe now I can get to the door without being force-fed a mike."

The screen showed the stock shot of the hospital's west facade, St. Simon statue and all, where the reporter stood looking appropriately studious. " . . . In a surprise development, hospital officials now admit there might have been some turmoil under Leo Gunn's direction."

That got not only Kate's attention but B.J.'s. And there on the screen was one of the Administration guys who'd harassed Kate, Brooks Brothers suit and all. "As anyone who has been a patient here throughout this time knows, our staff has maintained the highest standards of care. No patient has ever been, or will ever be, at risk. We feel we owe it to our staff to institute new policies that we hope will help reaffirm our commitment not only to our patients but to our employees."

"Who is that?" B.J. demanded.

"I don't know. They all look alike to me. Either Mr. Fellows or the lawyer. Curly, Burly, something like that."

"Mighty strong words."

Kate could only nod. "Mighty. I wonder if he means it. . . . Oh, why'd they bother Polyester?"

Sister Ann Francis appeared, smiling and nodding as if she were handing out rosaries. Spokeswoman for the order that had left her behind like the last whale in a mighty lonely ocean.

"It is so very difficult to fulfill the tenets of Sister Maria Goretti in this day and age," she admitted, hands fidgeting, eyes decorously down.

"We struggle against apathy and avarice and disdain. It is a good thing to have help in doing this."

"At least they didn't interview Edna," B.J. retorted evenly. "They would have heard about conditions in the Crimea."

Kate was losing interest. She had to get her stuff together to get home.

"Other reactions from staff range from caution to fear. And, on occasion, empathy."

"I understand the frustration." A female voice spoke up. "Sometimes I think the sense of commitment to others is gone from medicine, and if that's what you've dedicated your life to, as most of us have, well . . ."

Kate's head came up. Her stomach plummeted.

B.J. wasn't paying attention. He'd already gone back to getting ready for the day, stuffing Clannad tapes in with his Hendrix. Kate looked at him, looked at the screen where Mary Polyester's vaguely passive face had been replaced by the somber features of Lisa Beller. Then Lisa, just as quickly, was replaced by the reporter, who discussed the economic impact of a serial killer in a hospital and the concerns of the community.

And all Kate could hear were Lisa's words.

It was just like before, one little stimulus setting off a cascade of reactions. This time, memories: " . . . we have dedicated ourselves . . . dedicated . . ."

Suddenly Kate knew. She remembered. As simple as that. As stunning.

Not all of it. Not the full picture of what had gone on that night. Not what she'd given away, but what she'd been given: the support, the understanding, the promise.

" . . . when we've dedicated ourselves . . ."

Suddenly, Kate knew what she should have been able to see in the heartfelt words of those notes. She knew what it was she was being told. And by whom.

She couldn't move. She couldn't think. She didn't want to think. Not like that. It didn't make any sense. Jules would make more sense. At least Jules was a decisive person. Jules could go out there and get things done.

But Jules had never once said anything that reminded Kate of the pleas in those notes. And listening to Lisa Beller, she realized why.

All she'd wanted had been resolution. A name to indict, a face to challenge. An answer.

This wasn't the answer she wanted. Because her first reaction had been right. She did recognize herself in the murderer's eyes, and that made less sense than anything that had gone before.

B.J. went in to shave. Kate stood at the window and stared out at the street where neat little lawns sported rows of tulips and daffodils, and the trees were coming to life. Tidy little brick and stone homes on tidy green lawns with tidy middle-class cars. Such a calm well-ordered world should have made her feel better. All she could think of was that there were suddenly more questions than ever before, and she was not going to like the answers.

She had to get back to the apartment and get her bag. Then she had to get to the telephone.

She thought she'd felt guilty before. God, that was just a warm-up for what she was about to do.

"B.J.?"

"Yeah."

"Did you tell me the truth about Tim? Or were you sparing me?"

There was a small pause, and then he appeared at the door, shaving cream smeared across his chin. "What are you talking about?"

She had to ask. She didn't want to. Every time she thought about it, she thought about Tim. She saw that terrible shadow again and wanted to vomit.

Even so, nothing else would make sense unless she asked. "Did he struggle? Was he bound or gagged?"

B.J. seemed to need to consider that for a moment. Finally, though, he shook his head. "No, pogue, he wasn't. There weren't any contusions but that one in the occipital area, no defense injuries of any kind. No ligature marks anywhere . . . anywhere else."

"Then it really doesn't make any sense," she said.

"What doesn't?"

"How could a woman weighing only a hundred fifty pounds or so get him to hang himself without a struggle?"

"It's one of the first questions on John's list, okay?"

She nodded, not feeling any more settled. "Okay."

She had her answer. She still didn't think it made any sense.

Or maybe she hoped it didn't. So she turned back to the window and let B.J. return to his shaving.

"I don't suppose I could sit in on Gunn's autopsy," she asked, as she watched one of the neighbors kissing his wife good-bye in the driveway.

"Conflict of interest," B.J. said from the bathroom. "I'll call you if I find anything, though."

Kate tried to generate enthusiasm for what she was about to do. She was going to get her answers. Closure. Understanding.

She didn't want it anymore. She'd been right. The answer this time was going to be worse than the question, and Kate would end up cast as the Judas for coming up with it.

She should tell B.J. At least warn him what she was going to do. She couldn't. Not until she was sure. Not until she had the chance to face Florence alone and ask why.

Florence. Kate couldn't stop thinking of her that way. It didn't matter. The name wasn't so terribly inappropriate after all.

B.J. was wiping his face with a towel when he walked out, his hair brushed and tied back, his jeans and T-shirt spotless, his features still tight with discomfort.

"Did you take anything for it?" Kate asked, knowing better.

"Dr Pepper."

He bent over to pick up his bag and stumbled. Righted himself even before Kate could reach him. It was then she noticed that his face had lost some color.

"Beej?"

He waved her off, closed his eyes for a minute. "I told you. I can't keep up with you."

"You've had Jameson before."

"Not as much as I had yesterday. You scared the hell out of me."

There had never been a problem of space with them before. Suddenly there was. Kate wanted to hold on to him, and he was keeping her away. They'd changed everything after all.

"Are you sure?" she demanded.

For that she got a patented O'Brien glare. "I know what hung over feels like, Kate. Now, shut up and stop looking at me like a mother."

Kate hauled in a deep breath. "I've already lost Tim. I can't lose you too, you idiot."

That got his attention. He stopped, scowled, gave in to the kind of sheepish smile no one at the hospital had ever been witness to. Then he opened his arms to her. She took him up on it and hid there as long as she could. She didn't know whether to feel better or worse that his heart rate was fast. She did know she liked the proprietary feel of his arms around her.

"Are you tied up all day?" she asked.

"Gunn and a homeboy with bad timing. Other than that it's paperwork."

She nodded against him. "Good. I may need you to come over."

That quickly, he was B.J. again. "Why?"

Kate backed away and gave him her best buck-up smile. "Because I think I may have something, and I don't want to force anything without backup. All right?"

"You may have something? What? Why aren't you calling John?"

It was Kate's turn to scowl. "Shut up, pogue. I'm not going to do anything stupid, I promise."

Just how stupid was walking back into work? she wondered as she did just that about an hour later.

"Anybody heard from Jules yet?" she asked, as she walked down the hall, scrubs and lab coat back on, nursing bag in hand.

Three people ignored her and a fourth asked who she had in mind to frame next.

"I thought you were going to come in at eleven," Phyl said without preamble, when she came upon Kate by the soda machines ten minutes later.

"Couldn't sleep."

Shoving change into a slot, Phyl just shrugged.

Kate noticed her friend the cop sitting in his usual chair beneath the television and wondered whether the police thought she was stupid. If they really thought Jules was their man, why leave a tail on her? What was there to protect her from? Nothing anymore, she thought, and turned to follow her supervisor back toward the nurses' lounge.

"Phyl," she said, juggling her bag and the soda for the door. "Can I ask you about the Rashad boy?"

Phyl went very still. "I'm not sure I'm supposed to talk to you about that," she said. "Since it's in litigation."

"It's not about the suit," Kate said. God, she hated this. She hated trying to dance around the situation without giving herself away. Because once she did, she would never be forgiven. So she opened the door and hoped Phyl would join her inside. "It's about the murders. I think I'm not getting the message because there's something about that night I can't remember."

At least she had Phyl's attention. The supervisor followed Kate in and closed the door behind her. "Have you talked to a lawyer yet?"

"Yes, I did. We both decided I should only handle one disaster at a time, and right now the answer to this question is it. Can you tell me about that night?"

Phyl shook her head. "Not much. It was a zoo, and you didn't help."

"Anything stand out?"

"Yeah. You disappearing for twenty minutes. That stood out just fine."

Another surprise. Another little tidbit nobody'd thought to share with her.

"I disappeared?" she demanded. "Where?"

Phyl scowled at her. "You don't know?"

"I still don't remember anything. As far as I'm concerned, I went directly from lunch to ICU." Not totally true, but true enough.

"I don't know where you took off to. You were in with the family for a minute; then you weren't anyplace. I looked, Sticks looked, Jules looked. Even Mrs. Warner looked. Finally you just came strolling back with Edna."

"Edna?"

"She was acting nursing supervisor that night. She came down to help and spent most of the time trying to keep Weiss from climbing down your throat. She went in with you to talk to the family a couple of times."

"You didn't think Billy was bad either?"

For a second Phyl just stood there. Then she sighed. "I think you'd been getting burned out for a while, Kate. That night was just the straw that broke everybody's back."

So it was time for honesty. Finally. Kate leaned against the conference table and faced her boss. "The hospital doesn't plan to keep me around, does it?"

"Do you want to stay?"

Kate took a few minutes to sample the soda she'd taken such pains to get, considering it rather than her panic. Where else would she go? she wondered. What else would she do? What friends would have her?

"You'd have to fight for it," Phyl said.

And that was where it would ultimately rest, because Kate finally admitted to herself that she just wasn't sure she *could* fight for it anymore.

"Somebody heard you say you never wanted me to go over your head again," she said instead, her attention on the can in her hand. "What did they mean?"

"They meant you tried to talk past everybody from Edna to Fleischer to change our minds. I even had Sister Ann Francis whining at me."

Kate did look up then. "Would it have been so awful?"

"This hospital does its share of charity," Phyl defended instinctively. Rotely. The automatic reaction of a woman caught in the middle, more afraid of the layer above than the one beneath. "We simply can't help everyone. We'd be broke in a month."

"Oh? Is that how we managed to snag Central Medical?"

Phyl actually paled. "How'd you know about that?"

"The grapevine. It's true then? We've bought out Central's two hospitals?"

"No one can know that," Phyl insisted. "Especially right now with the negative press from the murders."

Kate offered what might have been the last challenge of her career. "Why? They afraid the staff won't be as excited as Administration is? I'm sure they'll gladly exchange frozen wages for a real conglomerate."

"There you go again," Phyl accused. "What makes you so self-righteous? This is the nineties, Kate. A hospital has to survive in the business world, or we can't do any good for anyone."

"Makes sense. Too bad Mr. Gunn didn't live to enjoy the fruits of his labors. He would have been the most powerful hospital CEO in town."

"That's not what he wanted."

"No," Kate agreed. "He wanted to be the most powerful hospital CEO in the Midwest."

Kate knew it was time to leave before she got more than she'd bargained for. She'd almost made it through the door when Phyl stopped her.

"Tell me something," she said in a tone of

authority she rarely used. "Who do you think is doing it?"

Kate looked up to see Phyl watching her. She was standing so still, Kate wasn't sure she was breathing. Kate shrugged. "You were pretty upset that night," she said. "Weren't you?"

Phyl didn't answer right away. She didn't move either, like a handler eyeing an unpredictable snake. "Furious."

Kate nodded. "Sticks said the only people really upset that night were the ones directly involved in the case. I figure one of us got so upset she took off after some of the culprits."

Kate managed to get out the door before Phyl said anything else.

"You're going to talk to me," she threatened Sticks a little later.

"Or what?" Sticks retorted as Kate helped her clean a room after a trauma. "You're going to turn me in?"

"I'm trying to keep Jules out," Kate insisted.

"So I guess that means the next candidate for the rack is Doctor Beller," Sticks snapped, clanking instruments together like dissonant handbells. "Or maybe Parker. Or me."

"You were there."

That at least got Sticks's attention.

"Phyl said I disappeared for a while," Kate said before Sticks could escape. "Do you know where?"

"No." She turned away. Slammed a chest-tube tray on the counter and shook open another trash bag for the debris left on the floor. "But when you came back you'd been crying."

Kate found herself standing in the center of a bloody, littered room, staring at Sticks as if she'd lost her mind. Crying. She couldn't remember the last time she'd cried at work. She couldn't understand why she would have done it this time. Hell, she might have fought for her patients, but she didn't get personally involved. That was a sure path to suicide. She patted and soothed and protected. She held and healed and conversed. She did not take her patients or their problems home.

What could have brought her to tears that night?

"And Edna didn't say anything about where she'd found me?"

Sticks just glared at her. "Edna didn't kill anybody."

"Please, Sticks."

"No. She just said everybody should have left you alone. All right? You happy?"

No. She wasn't. But there were only two more people she could talk to who might have her answers. Three, actually. Mrs. Rashad. But Mrs. Rashad wasn't killing anybody in this hospital. One of the other two women was.

"You're doing what?"

"You heard me," B.J. heard her say. "I've been talking to people all day, and I'm convinced that this twenty-minute gap on the night of the accident is the key."

B.J. settled his aching head into his hands and tried to concentrate. "So you're inviting her over to discuss it."

At first, he just heard static. Then Kate's voice, suddenly young and unsure. "I think I might have said something then about the girls. I need to know what it is."

"Not alone with a serial killer you don't. I told you. We have the results on Gunn and it was strychnine. Lots of strychnine. Don't be an idiot, Kate."

"That's why I'm calling you," she insisted. "B.J., I have to know. I have to find out what I told her. Why she's doing this for me. . . . Please, Beej."

B.J. had made it through more close calls in his life than he wanted to count. He'd been afraid. He'd been so close to a man with a gun who wanted him dead, he'd been able to smell him. Could still smell the sharp stink of his sweat every night when he woke screaming. But he couldn't ever remember fear like this.

Damn her. What did she think she was doing? Didn't she realize he couldn't survive this again? It had been bad enough when he'd been blindsided that night by the call from the ER to tell him she was hurt. When he'd shown up to find her shaved and swathed and intubated, damn near as close to dead as didn't matter, so that all he could do was hold her hand and curse. He could still see her slack, silent features every time he closed his eyes. He could call up the terror of knowing she might simply not wake up. He couldn't do it again. Goddamn it, she couldn't ask him to help her.

He couldn't stop her, either.

He looked down at his hand where it was resting on the pile of paperwork still spread across his desk. It was shaking. His T-shirt was soaked with sweat, and he wanted to puke in the worst way. His eyes hurt like hell and his stomach hurt worse.

He'd just put it all down to a hangover until it wouldn't go away. Which meant he'd either picked up a bad case of flu or somebody'd been doctoring his coffee too.

And now Kate was asking him to help her develop the same symptoms. And he was going to do it.

With conditions.

"Wait until I get there," he demanded, wondering if he could get somebody to drive him over. He'd ask John, except John was already there somewhere. Besides, John wouldn't let Kate face her demons in the privacy of the apartment. "You hear me?"

"B.J.? Are you all right?"

He closed his eyes and thought of what a hypocrite he was for yelling at other people for wasting their lives when he'd wasted his for so long. No matter what, he wasn't going to do it again. Whatever happened after this, he wasn't letting Kate out of his sight as long as the two of them lived.

"I'm fine. I'll be there in twenty minutes. Don't do anything until I get there. And for God's sake, don't drink or eat anything."

"Don't worry," she answered, already sounding stronger. "I won't. I have one more person to talk to before I face her. You'll be here in plenty of time."

He hung up and then called Mandy in. She arrived no more than three minutes later, looking curious. When she saw B.J., the curiosity crumbled into concern.

"B.J., my God. Are you okay?"

B.J. wiped the sweat from his forehead with a shaking hand and struggled out of his lab coat. "I need you to do something."

"You need to go home and get under the covers."

"Run a tox screen on me, Mandy."

That finally brought the toxicologist to a full stop. She took another, more considered look at her boss. "What are you talking about?" she demanded.

B.J. tried his best to glare. He had a feeling he didn't look very intimidating at the moment. "I'm talking about a simple blood and urine sample. Now do it. And call the results to Kate's as soon as you get them."

"Kate's? Are you crazy?"

He actually smiled. "Yeah. I think I am."

Kate couldn't hold still. She stood and she sat and she paced. The stereo was on and the Matisse print was back on the wall with a Band-Aid over the violated bird, but the view out front had been boarded up until a new window could be found, and Carver had decamped to another doctor's apartment until the danger was over.

Her invitations had been accepted. She was going to get her answers today. Soon.

She couldn't do this. It was enough to be responsible for her father and her mother and her sisters. She'd spent her life carrying that backpack around with her. She didn't want to find out she was the catalyst for this one too.

She didn't want to know that Tim would still be alive if it hadn't been for her interfering, or her not interfering soon enough, or her not understanding what was going on.

She didn't want to bear the collective traumas of all the suspects who had been prodded and poked and accused on the way to the truth. She didn't want to hurt anyone else.

"I talked to Mrs. Rashad," she said, her chest tight with dreadful anticipation. "She said that you and I left the quiet room together and didn't come back."

"Yes, that's right."

Kate tried once again to sit. She tried to hold still long enough to get the answers she so badly needed. "I need to know and I can't remember," she admitted softly, instinctively trusting this woman with her gentle eyes and sincere heart. "Did I talk about my sisters?"

She didn't get her answer. The abrupt knock on the door startled both of them. Kate had been expecting B.J., but not this soon. She jumped to her feet to forestall the answer she wanted, the answer she wasn't sure she was ready for just yet.

She wanted B.J. here for this. For the confrontation when it came. She wanted his help.

More, she wanted his vindication. Only B.J. could be trusted with what she'd evidently given away the night of Billy Rashad's death. Only B.J. would keep it safe for her.

She pulled open the door and forgot everything.

"Jesus! Oh, Jesus, Beej, what's wrong?"

Without even thinking, she grabbed onto him. Held him up where he swayed in her doorway, ashen and sweating, his mouth open to breathe, his hand clutching that stupid bottle of Dr Pepper to his chest.

He was cyanotic and wheezing. His body moved in fits and starts and his pupils were pinpoints, but his eyes stayed focused on Kate. She saw the chagrin in them. "Fuck me for . . . stupid . . . I didn't listen . . . to my own . . . advice."

Kate caught him as he faltered and got him across the threshold. Instinctively she reacted with the yell any medical personnel left in the apartment would recognize and respond to. "O-o-Oh, shit! Help!"

"Not in my ear," B.J. gasped, struggling to get to the couch to sit. "It hurts . . . everything hurts."

Kate turned just enough to include her other guest. "Call for help," she barked before she even thought about it.

Instincts honed over almost forty years had the passive little woman picking up the phone. Kate turned to B.J., pried the bottle from his grasp, tried to get him up to breathe better. Heard the call to 911 and the next one to the ER, heard the door slam upstairs and knew help was coming.

It wasn't soon enough.

"B.J.?" she shrilled, seeing his eyes begin to roll. "Stay with me, damn it!"

He grabbed onto her arm as if physically trying to hold on. Kate spun around, desperate.

"What is it?" she screamed at the frightened woman by her phone. "What did you give him?"

But Sister Ann Francis, the ex-pharmacologist who had the run of St. Simon's, who was so innocuous that no one could remember just where she'd been seen, couldn't seem to drag her attention away from B.J. to answer, because just then he began to convulse.

✦ Chapter 20 ✦

IT WAS MARTIN Weiss who heard her, Weiss in his bike shorts and muscle shirt, who careened into the apartment as Kate pulled B.J. off the couch and onto the rug.

"What the fuck is going on?" he demanded, shoving furniture out of the way.

Kate was overturning her nursing bag, scrabbling for the airway she always kept there. Everything fell out: books, scissors, trauma cards, pen lights, syringes, tourniquets, lint-covered taped tongue depressor. Rosary.

Brown plastic rosary with the oddly carved little beads Sister Mary Polyester had pressed on her that day in her hospital room.

"What did you do to him?" she screamed at the stunned woman as she wedged the tongue blade between B.J.'s clamped teeth and struggled to get the airway in. He was in a full grand mal seizure, and Kate was on autopilot.

"To him? Why would I ever—"

"You're the one poisoning people!" Kate screamed. "I saw you in the unit!"

"Well, of course. But I'm sure I didn't do anything to this nice man."

"What do you have?" Weiss demanded, down on his knees beside Kate as she tried in vain to hold B.J.'s arms still, as if that alone could stop the seizures.

"Headache, constricted pupils, diaphoresis, nausea . . . he said he hurt . . . everywhere. . . ."

"Oh, dear," Sister said behind them.

Kate heard the ambulance. She heard shouts and the stuttering rumble of a rolling cart and knew the ER crew was beating the paramedics to the scene. She'd never felt so helpless in her life. B.J. was dying and she didn't have anything to help. She who could do anything in the ER suddenly realized how useless she was without her equipment and rule books.

"It's—uh, does his breath smell like garlic?" Sister asked, joining them on the floor.

"This isn't arsenic," Weiss informed her.

"No, dear. TEPP. An anticholinergic insecticide."

Martin leaned close. Sniffed and nodded. "Bingo."

"Well, do something!" Kate shrilled.

Weiss raised the calmest eyes she'd ever seen on him. "As soon as I can get some atropine and Valium in here."

"But he's the wrong person," Polyester insisted yet again. "I wouldn't ever hurt this nice young man."

That nice young man had a pulse so thready and irregular Kate was sure the team wouldn't arrive in time. His eyes were rolled back, and his body flailed uselessly on the carpet.

"They're coming," Polyester crooned, patting Kate on the shoulder, "and then we can talk about your Molly."

Kate swung on her, hand up to strike. "Shut up," she snarled, stopping just in time. "Just shut up."

Lisa and Parker slammed through the front door, wheezing under the weight of the code equipment, and Sister Ann Francis sat back down in her chair and shut up.

"Kate, I wouldn't lie to you. He's going to be all right."

Kate nodded. She didn't move.

"You have to go home, honey."

Honey. Now it was honey. Kate shook her head at the nurse and held on to B.J.'s hand and wondered if this was what he'd felt when he'd visited her in the ICU, helpless and frustrated and afraid. He was slackened and silent, with tubes and lines and machines attached everywhere until she had trouble finding the person beneath. She held on to his hand as if that alone would connect him to the humanity the units kept away, all the while threatening him that he'd better damn well not be having another goddamn near-death experience at her expense.

She cried and she prayed and she held on to the little brown rosary Sister Mary Polyester had given her as a talisman against death. The talisman that had been the physical link between Sister and a string of murders already becoming known as the Sister Merry Murders.

Kate would think about that in a while. She'd think about what she still had to say to the little nun, who had turned around after poisoning B.J. and saved his life.

It had been Polyester who'd kept her composure when the room filled with police and paramedics and doctors and doctors' wives. Polyester who'd calmly given Weiss the pertinent information as he stayed one step ahead of the deadly seizures and arrhythmias the poison produced. It was Sister who'd suggested that B.J. must have been ingesting small portions over a sustained period to have been able to cope so long.

That had been twelve hours ago. Kate hadn't slept and she hadn't changed and she hadn't paid any attention to the ambivalence of the staff who understood her terror and yet shunned her for handing Mary Polyester over to the police.

She wasn't going to get her resolution after all. After they'd swept B.J. up onto the cart and run him out the door, John had read Sister Ann Francis her rights and guided her out behind. Kate hadn't seen any of it. She'd stayed with B.J. She'd fended off well-meaning co-workers when they'd tried to get her to back out of the treatment room while they intubated him, and screamed at the less well-meaning when they'd tried to keep her from helping out. She'd battled her own demons as she'd seen him stripped and mauled and invaded, just like all the trauma patients she'd ever cared for, his singular mind and body nothing but meat for the knackers.

And there beside her had been her most unlikely champion. Weiss again. Suddenly sensible, sharp Martin Weiss, who had kept the interlopers away and let Kate help as she could. Who damn near single-handedly pulled B.J. through with nothing more than the lightning-quick speed of his decision-making skills. Martin Weiss, whom Kate had written off as lost, pulling a rabbit out of his hat just when she'd needed it and then turning his considerable wrath on anyone who tried to keep Kate away.

He must have made an impression, because nobody had yelled at her for at least six hours.

So she sat in the only place where she felt she could make a difference, knowing she'd never get the chance to face Sister Ann Francis so she could demand explanations, knowing this time wasn't going to be any different from any other time. The person responsible would simply disappear and leave Kate holding the bag, the system that should have prevented any of it silent and unhearing.

"What the hell are you doing back up here?"

Kate barely heard the voice. She recognized it, though: Hetty Everson. Hetty, who had taken such good care of her, who hated visitors more than body lice, who had been so angry about Tim.

"I told his mom I'd stay with him while she got some rest," Kate said without turning away.

Mrs. O'Brien was in the hospital somewhere. With her bad heart, though, she simply couldn't suffer with her son through this. Her family shielded her down in the cafeteria or the courtyard while Kate held watch. Kate was perfectly comfortable with the arrangement. She didn't want to have to face the grief in that lovely woman's eyes.

So here she sat, watching the terrifying stillness in B.J.'s face while the world went merrily on
around her.

"Seems awfully soon to be this upset about
somebody else," one of the wags in the background said, as if they'd been the first one to think
of it. "Just how long has Tim been dead after all?"

Kate didn't care. Hetty turned on them with a
vengeance. "Shut up, you asshole. Didn't you ever
figure it out? Tim was gay. Now leave her alone."

Kate managed to look up at that. "Nobody
knows," she said instinctively.

Hetty huffed as she pulled her stethoscope
from around her neck and started her patient evaluation. "Of course they do. We just didn't want to
believe it. Have you had anything to eat?"

Kate didn't bother to answer.

Hetty went right ahead with her work. "This
stupid son of a bitch should have been dead. Did
you see what his cholinesterase level was? I've
never read it in negative digits before."

They had him on Dilantin and phenobarbital
drips for the seizures, a dopamine drip for his
blood pressure, a bretylium drip for the dysrhyth-
mias, a regular dose of steroids and atropine and
Tagamet for everything else. Circling IVACs, they
called it. An addendum to Murphy's Law that
claimed the chances of a patient's survival were
inversely related to the number of automated IV
infusers hung over a bed. And B.J. was over the
magic number of four. Hetty checked them all,
checked the monitors and Swan and the ART line
and the respirator that just clicked and sighed

along without interruption. High-tech medicine at
its finest. Terrorism at its most terrifying.

Then it sank in that Hetty was out of place.
Kate craned her neck for a glance. "What are you
doing here? You don't work MICU."

Hetty's smile was almost piratical. "Everybody
else is scared to death of your friend over there.
So since I survived him during your recent tour in
surgical, I volunteered. I am being tolerated."

Kate almost managed to give a smile back,
because she knew just who had the bigger attitude problem among the units. "Fuck 'em," she
said anyway.

Hetty laughed. "Up the rebels."

Wrong answer. It almost made Kate cry all
over again.

"What can I do to help, Hetty?"

Hetty never hesitated. "Go home and get
some sleep."

Kate shook her head. "I feel so goddamn useless. At least let me feel useless here where I
know what's going on."

Hetty lifted B.J.'s head to replace the tape on
his tube. Kate shut her eyes.

"Notice any spontaneous movement?" Hetty
asked.

"His hands, I think."

Kate could hear the snip and slash of tape
being prepared.

"Won't be long," Hetty said. "We're tapering all
his doses to see how he tolerates it. You know the
FBI's looking for you. I think Edna was holding
them off in the ER."

"She tried. It didn't work."

Kate heard that voice, too, and refused to react. She opened her eyes to see Mary Cherry settle herself against the far wall out of Hetty's way. "He looks better," she offered, the way lay people did in intensive-care units.

"He looks dead," Kate and Hetty replied simultaneously, because, of course, he did. Then both of them laughed, because Mary looked so discomfited by their honesty. Oddly enough, it was the first time Kate had felt better since opening her apartment door to find B.J. standing there the evening before.

Mary must not have gotten home since then, either. She was rumpled and disheveled and rubbing at eyes that for once weren't made up. She kept her place and her silence as Hetty finished her work. Kate tried to ignore her, even though she knew it wasn't going to do her any good.

And then, too soon for Kate's tastes, Hetty left to take care of her other patients. And, just as Kate knew she would, Mary got down to business.

"I need to ask you a favor, Kate."

Kate didn't bother to make eye contact. "I think I've already done you a favor," she said.

Periodically she'd squeeze B.J.'s hand, hoping to feel a response. She didn't really expect it, not with the load of sedatives they had in him. Even so, she desperately needed that proof of all the optimism around here. He really did still look dead. He had since his seizures finally stopped for good about five hours earlier.

If Kate had been waiting for an apology from Mary, she was going to be disappointed. Mary wasn't the type. Which was probably why Kate liked her, no matter what she looked like.

"Sister Ann wants to talk to you."

"That's nice."

"She won't talk to us until she does."

Kate couldn't even summon the energy for a sigh. "I don't really care, Mary."

"Really? You don't want to know how she managed to kill Tim?"

"I don't even want to know how she managed to damn near kill B.J."

"She says she didn't."

Kate nodded. "I heard. If she didn't try to kill B.J., how'd she know about the insecticide?"

"She says she mixed it up for Doctor Weiss."

That one wormed its way through the fog. So Polyester had been meaning to kill Weiss after all, just as Kate had thought. Weiss, who had worked himself into an exhausted sweat trying to keep B.J. from dying.

Ever since Attila had first died, Kate had been waiting for a reaction to what was going on: grief, regret, anything. Funny that it should finally happen with Weiss. Weiss, who had personally fileted several layers of skin from Kate's professional hide. Weiss, who could be such an ass, such a pompous, self-serving jerk.

Weiss, who had held her when she'd finally broken down in the ER when B.J. wouldn't stop seizing.

"Son of a bitch," she said, surprised at her

own outrage at the thought of losing Martin Weiss. "I'm really glad she didn't make it."

"Well, she almost murdered B.J.," Mary said. "Aren't you interested in seeing that she takes responsibility?"

Kate got her attention around to find that Mary wasn't exactly the objective professional she'd thought. There were tears in the agent's eyes as she considered the husk on the bed.

"Did she say anything at all?" Kate asked.

"Nothing but that she'd meant for Weiss to be next." Mary never bothered to look away. "I did think it was interesting that she'd mixed poison for Weiss and ended up putting it in B.J.'s Dr Pepper."

Kate held on harder. "I always told him that shit was bad for him. He should have stuck to the hard stuff."

"That's what he thought it was in."

Now Kate knew she didn't want to hear more. She tried hard to focus on the agent just as the sun topped the parking garage and shot a beam of light to highlight her very blond hair. Blond hair like Tim's. Perfect, beautiful, damn near white. Kate wanted to cry.

But Mary wasn't as compassionate as Tim. She turned her attention back to Kate and let her have it. "He had one of the toxicologists test him before he left the office. Told her he thought it was in the Jameson at his house. And then he went to see you."

"I'll go when B.J. wakes up," Kate said, ignoring the agent again.

Mary sighed and shifted position against the

wall. "We really need to get this thing going, Kate."

"Tough shit."

"I thought it was what you wanted."

So did she, Kate thought, as she watched the sun gild the machinery that crouched by B.J.'s bed. So did she.

She'd thought she'd wanted a lot of things. The last few weeks had only proven her wrong.

"How hard is it to ride a horse, Mary?" she asked, concentrating on the hand she held, with its long spatulate fingers and callused palm. A hand she'd never seen still until now. A hand that had so much strength and grace, and she'd taken it all for granted for too long.

Out of the corner of her eye, she saw Hetty had walked back in the door. She and Mary exchanged glances. Hetty must have shrugged, because Mary did too.

"Easier than trauma nursing, I imagine."

Kate laughed. Then she nodded. "In that case, I think it's about time I learned how to saddle up."

Kate wasn't exactly sure what she'd been expecting to feel when she finally sat down across the table from the person who had singularly rearranged her life. She'd spent some time fantasizing about the feeling of vindication, of vengeance, of understanding. When she pulled the hard-backed chair away from the Formica table and slid into it, she felt nothing but numbness.

It was now midafternoon, and the day was

turning out to be as grim and depressing as Kate's dreams. In the Serious Money medical intensive-care unit, B.J. was off the respirator, extubated, and beginning to live up to his reputation among unit nurses. Kate had left him threatening bodily harm on the next person who came near him with a sharpened object of any kind. Here at the inter-rogation room at the county detective bureau, Kate sat at a battered table and sipped her coffee and wondered just how soundproof the room could be with its worn old walls.

The cop who walked Sister Ann in did so with the air of a man who'd had a few knuckles slapped. He stayed a respectful couple of paces from the little woman in her white polyester dress and veil and left once she'd been seated. Kate didn't bother to get up.

"How is he?" Polyester asked, real concern in her eyes as she settled into her chair across from Kate. "I've been praying for him ever since I got here."

Kate was much too battered to give her any grief. "He's doing fine. They think he'll be out of the unit tomorrow sometime."

The little nun beamed, nodded her head with satisfaction, and clasped her hands before her on the table. To their left was the mirror, the one behind which Mary and the Little Dick were sit-ting. John had somehow made himself inconspicuous in the corner with a tape player and note pad. Sister had evidently instructed her attorney to get a drink of water down the hall, like a good boy.

"I'm so sorry," she said. "I tried to think how I

could have made such a mistake, but I can't. I never meant to hurt Doctor O'Brien. Never."

Kate couldn't quite come up with any gratitude. "You wanted to talk to me, Sister?"

Mary Polyester leaned forward. "I didn't realize that you didn't understand, Mary Kathleen."

"Kate."

She smiled, fluttered. "I'm sorry. Of course. You told me."

It was Kate's turn to lean forward. "What exactly did I tell you?" she asked.

The little woman patted her hand. "You really don't remember. I feel so foolish. I wanted so badly for you to understand."

"Understand what?"

"What I did, of course. Why. I wanted you to know that not everyone is guilty of aggravated neglect. Not everyone wished to punish you for trying to save that little boy—for trying to save your sisters."

Kate closed her eyes and did her best to pretend it was B.J. sitting there alongside them instead of John. "I told you about them that night?"

"Yes, dear. You did. I think it was to help me understand just how much that little boy meant to you. But I kept my promise. The only person I told was Father, and that was in confession, so of course he can't possibly tell anyone else. After all, he had to know too."

"Know? You confessed the murders?"

"Every Thursday since Frances, right in the chapel at Saint Simon's. I may be doing God's work, but I know I displease him a little too."

"And you did kill Attila and the rest?"

For the first time since she'd known her, Kate saw real anger in the little nun's eyes. "You think you're the only one who despairs? You think no one else fights for those little lost souls? Something had to be done, Kate. Someone had to begin to put an end to the conspiracy of harm in medicine."

"But why them?"

For a minute the nun backed away, sought her own counsel. "Frances was an accident," she admitted. "An impulse. I was so angry at the way she treated you, especially after you'd sacrificed so much for that little boy. After you'd entrusted me with the truth about what you'd been through." She took Kate's hand before Kate could back away. "You were in such pain that night. It was as if we were all tearing you apart. I couldn't abide it."

Kate heard the words, but somehow they didn't sink in. She should have at least felt rage, maybe frustration. She felt impatient, as if she were still waiting for something, when there was nothing left to wait for.

She had her answers. She had her confrontation. She should have at least felt relief.

And then the little nun smiled and gave Kate another pat. "I did it for Molly, really. To give her some peace."

Please, Kate thought. No more. No more answers. She didn't want to know, after all. She didn't want the face of her tormentor to have sweet eyes and a serious heart. She wanted monsters, and she couldn't find them.

"But how could you send me that note?" she demanded.

"I only asked you to understand."

"You blamed me."

Polyester pulled away, stricken. "I would never do that. I don't chastise the martyrs. You dedicated yourself to others. So did I. I was just trying to help."

"Yeah, I know."

Kate tried again. Tried for something solid.

"But why hurt Tim?" she asked. "Why B.J.? How could you do that to them?"

"Tim?" Suddenly the lights were off again. Polyester reached into her pocket and pulled out a worn lacy handkerchief to wring in her blue-veined little hands. "You mean that lovely Doctor Peterson? No, dear. I wouldn't hurt Tim. That must be a mistake too. I'm sure that wasn't supposed to be him at all."

"You hanged him!" Kate insisted, catching those fleeing hands and making her pay attention. "Right in my apartment. You did it because you knew what it would do to me!"

The nun was shaking her head, backing away. "No, oh, no, that's not right. Are you sure you don't mean that nasty Dr. Arnstein? Now, he would make sense."

"And B.J."

"No, dear. That terrible Doctor Weiss. I told Father how vile Doctor Weiss had been, how he was just another problem. There were others. Oh, yes, there were. Odd how once I started the list it kept getting longer and longer."

"Long enough to include Mr. Gunn?"

The little woman nodded, her stiff gray hair not moving around the veil. "I did not like that man, Kate. I did not. He didn't care for the people under his control. Not his staff, not his patients. It could not go on. Now, I realized strychnine wasn't at all Christian, which was why I was going to use digoxin instead. It would be better, don't you think?"

Kate let go of the nun's hands. She wanted out. She wanted some sleep. She wanted to know what it would be like to take a horse up over the high plateaus of New Mexico and not smell one more gomer the rest of her life. She wanted to find someplace free of judgment and contention, and then she just wanted to lie down. She wanted closure, and she was never going to get it.

"You do understand, don't you?" Mary Polyester begged. "Please tell me you do."

For the first time since she'd known her, Kate paid close attention to the little nun she'd over-looked all these years. She had wanted to find something reprehensible. What she discovered instead was another victim. Someone who had been stripped of her worth and left to wander her own hospital like a vague, uncomfortable ghost without purpose or direction. An innocent, trained to virtue and deserted by the church and order and career to which she had devoted herself. All Sister Mary Polyester had wanted to do was the right thing. Kate understood so well she actually found a smile for her.

"Yes, Sister," she admitted. "I really do understand."

Sister Ann Francis smiled back as if she'd just seen her own redemption. "Up the rebels," she offered, making it sound oddly like the beginning of a psalm.

Kate nodded. "Up the rebels."

And then she got the hell out of there.

"You did fine, little girl," John assured her with a big hug back out in the hallway.

The Little Dick was glowing with good humor. "A slam dunk with clusters," he said. "Maybe I should be Catholic. They seem to really get off on this confession shit."

Kate glared at them both. "The rosary was a match?"

"Absolutely, completely, an' definitely," John assured her. "Dose were her little brown beads we foun' on de carpets. But don' you worry. Your little Sister won' be hurt any. Dey probably put her in a nice little sanitarium someplace so she can talk to God like she wants."

Kate nodded absently. "Their order has a nice one in Texas, from what I hear."

She'd heard it from Sister Ann herself, who'd managed to strong-arm a drunk right to the floor. Who'd gotten a round of applause from the whole staff for it and then blushed like a curtsying deb.

"How did she hang Tim?" she asked anyway.

Little Dick laughed. "You don't know as much about crazy people as you thought."

"But he didn't struggle," she insisted.

"He had a shitload of barbiturates in him and a pop on the head."

Kate shook her head again. "So you think she sweet-talked him into standing on her stool with a noose around his neck and a glass of downers in his hands? Or did she just throw him over her shoulder and ease him into place?"

"Dat's somet'in' we gonna find out," John promised. "Okay? Now, you go home and take it easy. It's all over, little girl."

Then why didn't the little girl feel like it was all over? Kate wondered. She didn't bother sharing congratulations. She just turned for the door.

"And Katie," John added from behind her, "t'ank you. You are a real sport."

"Oh, yeah," Kate agreed miserably as she headed on down the hall. "A real sport."

The press met her at the front door of the detectives' bureau. Kate was suddenly the heroine of the piece, the single person in the county, where the police and FBI had had one of the biggest investigations of recent memory going, to finger the Angel of Death. Everybody wanted to know how Kate had figured it out. Kate offered a few four-letter words and hid in Mary's car.

"You really should get some sleep," Mary suggested as they pulled up in the emergency garage at St. Simon's twenty minutes later.

It had been the first words out of either of them since they'd pulled away from the pack of minicams back in Clayton.

Kate could barely get her head off the back of

the seat. She kept her eyes instead on the Lindbergh ambulance that had pulled in just ahead of them. "I know." But she kept thinking of trying to sleep in that apartment where the litter still lay all across the living room floor from the struggle to save B.J.'s life. Where Tim's shadow still swayed in her sleep. She had nowhere else to go, but she still didn't want to go there.

Mary shut off the engine. It still took Kate a minute to say anything.

"Did you ever figure out why the notes didn't match up?"

"My next order of business," Mary told her.

Kate just stared ahead as the paramedics unloaded their rig. They had what looked like an LOL in NAD. Little old lady in no active distress. Perfectly coiffed and decked out in her best housecoat, jowls dusty with powder, hands clasped as if offering thanksgiving. A lonely old thing who probably just needed somebody to tell her troubles to. Kate found herself resenting the poor thing for taking up their time.

She'd been right in the unit. She couldn't go back.

She had nowhere else to go.

So, as always, she opened the door of the car to go inside. "There's still something missing," she said simply.

Mary looked over. "Missing?"

Kate nodded, considered the pristine sweep of the white-walled hospital as it lifted into the clearing afternoon sky. It was an imposing build-

ing, a testament to health and healing and compassion with its white-on-white expanse, its carefully
planted grounds, its meticulously tended ad
campaigns.

It was a farce, and everyone who worked in
that building knew it. What it was was cutthroat
profiteering and any number of sleight-of-hand
tricks. It was bad smells and bad luck and bad
health. And that was what was wrong.

"The evil," she said. "Something about all this
was cold and calculating and evil, and that little
nun saying her rosary back in the interrogation
room simply didn't have it in her."

"That's for us to figure out," Mary said.
"You've done enough. It's time to take care of
yourself. Okay?"

Too late, Kate thought, opening the door the
rest of the way and pulling herself out to go
inside. "Okay," she said instead.

"It's finally over," the little blonde from public
relations said from the television screen in B.J.'s
room two days later. "We wish we could say we
knew why Sister Ann had her breakdown. We certainly wish there had been something we could
have done to prevent it, to understand it. To help
her before it came to this. On behalf of Mr.
Fellows and the entire staff of Saint Simon's, I'd
like to say, however, that we are behind her. We
would also, of course, like to express our deepest
regrets and condolences to the families and
friends of her victims. . . ."

"Bullshit and more bullshit," Jules pronounced from the doorway.

Kate looked up from where she had taken over the easy chair in B.J.'s room to greet her friend on her first day back after what Jules preferred to call her "unfortunate incarceration."

"Nice to know your recent bout of bad luck hasn't changed your basic good attitude," Kate offered, wishing she had a little more enthusiasm for her friend.

"Where is the man of the hour?" Jules asked.

"Down getting CAT-scanned."

Jules allowed the first sign of worry to creep in. "They don't think—"

"Nope. But why pass up a good chance to gig his insurance a little?"

That produced a big smile. "Nice to see your attitude hasn't soured, either. How's the staff been treating you?"

"Like Hitler, thanks."

"Ah, screw 'em. One good shift and it'll all be back to normal. Here, I got something for you. Made it myself."

Kate did her best not to cringe. She was afraid she was going to see something fur, and after what she'd found on her table, she never wanted to see fur again as long as she lived.

It wasn't. What Jules pulled out was a pair of buttery-soft leather moccasins with beads of every color sewn over the top.

"Mementos." Jules beamed.

Kate scowled, teary. "Whore dog."

"Slut puppy." She reached into her nursing

bag and brought out another, larger pair. "Here. I made a pair for your friend. Matching. Isn't that cute?"

That made Kate want to cry all over again. She hated this. She should have been feeling so much better. She accepted the moccasins anyway and settled both pairs on her lap.

"These aren't the ones you made for Mr. Gunn, are they?" Kate demanded.

Jules snorted. "Hey, a girl has to make a living. Just ask Suzie—who has asked for a transfer to urology, by the way."

Kate laughed. "Urology?"

"The ER is too stressful."

"Hallelujah."

Jules settled onto the unmade bed, her eye half on the TV, half on Kate, who didn't realize she was stroking the soft leather of the shoes in her lap.

"You're really serious about this shit," Jules marveled softly.

Kate looked up to see true wonder in her friend's eyes. "What do you mean?"

Jules just motioned to the unmade bed.

Kate fidgeted with the moccasins. "Yeah," she admitted. "I guess I am."

Jules nodded. "About time. I mean, I loved Tim. You know that. But you two just weren't right for each other."

At least that could make Kate smile. "Yeah. I know."

Jules didn't pull anything else out of her bag. Instead, she pulled Kate to her feet. "Come on. He won't need his hand held for an hour or so. You're going to eat lunch."

Kate's reaction was automatic. "I'm not hungry."

"I don't care. Mrs. O'Brien made it a point to come down and beg me to take care of you, and I'm not going to disappoint somebody that cute and small—she's not really his mother, is she?"

Kate scowled. "No. He rents her on weekends from her real family. Don't be an idiot."

"She's still too cute to disappoint. Now, come on."

If Kate had been feeling better, she would have made a stronger show of protesting. As it was, she allowed herself to be pushed out the door and down the hall.

She was tired. For some reason she'd expected some kind of relief. She should have known better. Almost in punctuation, a couple of staff turned her way from the elevators. One look at Kate and they damn near turned to stone. Behind them, the floor secretary caught sight of her and waved hello. The PR department insisted that the hospital was getting back to normal. Kate didn't see any signs of it. If anything, the arguments were getting bigger, the divisions greater.

Jules was not one to let the obvious go unnoticed. "So," she said, punching the elevator button. "How does it feel to be the star?"

Kate leaned against the wall by the elevator and sighed. She'd been thinking about this one a lot. As a matter of fact, it had kept her awake.

It had been forty-eight hours, and Kate was still plagued by that feeling of waiting. She'd finally gotten back into the apartment with its new picture window and locks and spent four hours cleaning up the living room from the last time she'd been there. She'd tried to feed herself from the unopened cans and bottles the police had let her keep after checking for possible poison, and tried harder to relax, cranking up Queen on the stereo and stretching out on the couch with a newly uncorked bottle of cabernet sauvignon Tim had never had the chance to try. She'd still been there the next morning, her eyes still open, the bottle half finished, waiting.

Everyone else was celebrating either the end of the case or the identity of the veiled avenger. Kate listened and watched and wondered what was wrong.

"It doesn't fit," she finally said.

The doors opened and the little drama reenacted itself as a gaggle of employees stepped off the elevator rather than be on with Kate. By now Kate was too tired to care. Jules guided her onto the elevator and let the doors shut. "What?"

"It's like there's been this tune going on in my head, ya know? We'll call it the Song of the Serial Killer. And when Mary Polyester was caught, I thought it would stop. But only the high voice stopped. I keep hearing a real funny harmony, kind of like the low drone on a bagpipe after the playing's stopped."

Jules shook her head. "You're not making any sense at all. She confessed. They have evidence placing her at the scenes."

Kate nodded. "I know. I was there, remember?

But nobody's ever really given me a really good reason for her killing Tim."

"She didn't want you to help the investigation."

"She wanted me to understand everything she did. Why ask me to look closer and ignore what was going on at the same time? Why set it up so deliberately to shadow the worst moments of my life if she thought she was helping me out?"

Jules had her answer even before Kate finished. "She got one wrong. She misread your cues. Who knows? I mean, hell, Kate, she's never really been wired to code, ya know?"

Kate flushed with quick frustration. She understood the reaction. Every person who had donated to the original defense fund had echoed it. Polyester was the folk hero now. Polyester was the Florence Fucking Nightingale they'd all manufactured. Righter of wrongs, defender of the working stiff, avenger of the mistreated. The money in the defense account had been rerouted to her, even though the Little Sisters of Good Grace had promised full support of their wayward and confused member. The Fax Fairies had sent wanted posters with a bandolier-strapped, machine-gun-toting nun promising that she'd be back, and the Pig Nurses had given her an official cap in absentia. They had needed her, and she had fulfilled their darkest fantasies.

It wouldn't be the same if there was more to it than that. They wouldn't be quite so vindicated. Their cause, somehow, wouldn't be as just. And Kate, who was resented for turning in the hero, would be even more resented for unmasking her.

So Kate kept her suspicions to herself, which left her sleepless and restless and afraid to walk in the apartment where Tim still seemed to wait to remind her of something.

"The funny thing is," Jules admitted, "I miss her. She may have been a commissioned officer in the space cadets, but she was always around when you needed a little hand-holding."

Kate just nodded. She'd heard this part too. Never speak ill of the dead or the recently indicted.

"I mean, I had to run interference in the cry room this morning. We had a DOA from out in the boonies, and of course the entire goddamn township shows up for the wailing services, and I don't even have Polyester to be a warm body. I felt like the only can of mace in a roomful of mad dogs. And, of course, you know what it's been like to get anybody from social services down there lately, so we didn't even get one of those, much less a friggin' priest like the guy's wife kept begging for. Shit, I almost dressed Parker in a cassock and pushed him in with a Bible, just to shut 'em all up."

Kate had only been paying marginal attention as she watched the floor lights blink toward ground level and waited for Jules to finish canonizing Polyester. Suddenly, though, what the big nurse was saying sank in.

The elevator doors opened onto the teeming lobby. Jules stepped off. Kate couldn't move.

"Oh, my God," she whispered, not seeing the people staring at her.

She was trying hard to remember everything

she'd heard. Wanting so very badly to be sure about this before she put herself squarely back on the shit list again. Almost as terrified that she was right as terrified that she was wrong.

But she was right. She knew it. She felt it strike that low harmonic instinct like a perfect fifth. "I should have remembered."

Jules leaned in to nudge Kate in the right direction. "Remembered what?"

Kate followed her out, not even aware that half a dozen people were glaring at her. It couldn't be right. It was too simple. Somebody should have picked it up.

Reaching the foyer, she started searching, her heart suddenly racing. A phone. She needed a phone.

"Kate?" Jules insisted, following right on her heels. "What the hell's the matter with you?"

But Kate didn't answer. She'd reached the information desk that held, among other things, a phone and a hospital directory. She checked, blinking a couple of times to read the number. She was so damn tired she couldn't even see anymore. She wasn't so tired she couldn't be afraid.

"Pastoral care, may I help you?"

Kate held her breath. Closed her eyes. Asked the question that might change everything or consign her once and for all to the wasteland of wondering. "Hi, I have a question. I heard that you'd recently been able to get a priest to do confessions. Is that right?"

On the other end of the line, the voice hesitated.

"Uh, no. I'm sorry. Is there some way I can help?"

"You're sure?" Kate asked. "I could swear somebody said they were seeing a priest every Thursday morning for confession here."

"No, I'm sorry. We haven't had a full-time priest for three years. A local parish priest says mass on Sundays and holy days. Although our chaplains aren't Catholic priests, they do offer spiritual support. May I refer you to one of them?"

Kate automatically shook her head. "No. Thank you, though. You've been a great help."

She hung up the phone, feeling worse. Light-headed with the knowledge. Damn near clammy, as her mind stuttered to life amid the myriad questions that followed.

"What was that all about?" Jules demanded.

"What that was all about," Kate said, focusing on her friend, "is I want to know how the hell Polyester could have been confessing her sins in the Saint Simon's chapel like clockwork every damn Thursday when we haven't had a priest here for three goddamn years."

It took Jules a second. People shoved past them, some none too kindly, but Kate and Jules remained there, stuck in place in the middle of the tile floor by the information desk.

Jules shrugged. "Easy. She imagined him."

Kate shook her head. "But what if she didn't? What if she was laying out all her plans every Thursday like she said?"

"What are you saying?"

"I'm saying it suddenly occurs to me that

maybe Mary Cherry was right all along. Maybe the reason it looked like there were two people involved in this damn thing is because there were. And we only have one of them."

✦ *Chapter 21* ✦

"SLOW DOWN. I'M still a sick man."

Kate did her best to rein in her anxiety. "It's what Tim's been trying to tell me all along," she insisted, knowing how little sense she was making. "We only have part of the picture."

Still trussed up with IVs and attired in a unit gown, B.J. rubbed his face and sighed. "You're telling me. What the hell are you babbling about?"

Kate took a breath, paced a little to try and order her thoughts. "Mary Polyester. She's been absolutely honest all along, and we're not listening to her."

B.J. gave up and closed his eyes. "I know you're going to tell me all about it."

"Nobody'll listen to me, Beej. Everybody's so thrilled to have an answer, they're not using common sense. Why would she be happy to admit to three murders and not more? Why would she be so insistent that she didn't kill Tim, when one of her notes was pinned to his chest?"

"You're asking me?" he demanded. "You know perfectly well I don't get involved in that shit. I do bodies. Period."

"Well, I don't. I've been thinking about this, Beej. It makes sense."

"Nothing makes sense," he assured her. "I can't even think in complete sentences yet. Why don't you talk to John?"

"There was a little girl murdered last night. They've all moved on to that. I can't even get him to answer the phone."

"Mary over at the FBI?"

"They say she's not available. I think that means she's in Albuquerque roping cows with her ex-husband. And nobody'll let me talk to Polyester without permission."

That brought him straight up. "No," he told her, his eyes hard. "You are not going to go off half cocked and play Nancy Drew."

"Why?" she retorted. "Do you think I could be right?"

"No," he answered. "I think you could piss off Mother Teresa when you try, and right now I'm not in a position to run interference."

For just a moment they glared at each other. Then they grinned in a weird kind of relief. Things were getting back to normal.

"Just listen," she begged. "Just tell me if I'm that far off the mark. If I am, I'll shut up."

"No, you won't."

"All right, I won't. But I know I'm right."

B.J. slumped back against the pillow. "In that case, theorize away."

Kate paced again, sought out the sunset beyond the highway, then the door to the hallway, where staff meandered by at an odd, almost ataxic pace.

"It's the feeling I've been getting all along that the murders don't fit the same pattern. Sometimes I've felt the murders are impulsive, almost apologetic. Attila, Warner, Fleischer. Polite, ya know? Just like Mary said. But other times I'd get this cold feeling, like there was someone watching. Someone who was hiding behind the black curtain pulling the puppet strings. Someone who was taking advantage of Sister's frustration and desperation for other goals."

"What goals?"

"I don't know. But Polyester herself said she'd changed her mind about the strychnine. She was going to use digoxin instead. But Gunn got strychnine. Gunn got it big time and died in agony."

B.J. couldn't seem to help a grin. "Kind of."

"And Tim—"

"It's always going to come down to that, isn't it?"

She stopped and faced him. Faced herself and her ghosts. "It doesn't matter whether Tim died painlessly or not. His death was cruel. His death was deliberate and well planned to create a particular effect. To send one message. To me."

"To remind you of your mother."

"More," she admitted, and turned away. "To remind me of Molly."

Behind her, B.J. rustled uncomfortably. "Your sister?"

Kate looked for the sun again, but it was gone. "I've been lying to Aunt Mamie, Beej. My sisters aren't on the coast. They aren't fine."

"Molly?"

Kate took a deep breath, closed her eyes, and offered up the last of her secrets. "Molly's dead. She killed herself five years ago, just like Mom. I've never told anybody."

"Come here."

She turned. "What?"

His movements were impatient. "Come here."

She did, where he could hold her as she talked. Kate didn't know whether that hurt worse or less. It hurt better, though.

"You told Polyester that night, didn't you?"

"I must have. I think maybe I was trying to get her to understand just how frustrated I was about that little boy. I mean, it was just like with the girls, ya know? Nobody listened to me. Nobody. I tried to get somebody to understand about my dad. I tried to get them to take the girls from my mom, and then from my Aunt Mamie, because I knew what it was doing to them. I pleaded, Beej. I told them I'd stay with Aunt Mamie, but I wanted the twins safely away."

"And the girls blamed you for trying to get rid of them."

Kate turned, all the old evils spilling free once and for all. "Wouldn't you?"

B.J. held on tight to her hand. "Yeah, probably. If I didn't know any better. What about your other sister, Mary Ellen?"

Kate didn't know whether to laugh or cry. She never did with Mary Ellen. "She finally did escape. She's living in a cloister in Minnesota where she never has to see me again."

"Then she made it okay."

"No. But at least she's safe. But what I'm saying is that Polyester really hurt for Molly. I could tell when I talked to her in the interrogation room. And if that was true, why would she send a note about her?"

"I thought she didn't. I thought somebody from the hospital did."

"Exactly. Except the only person she told was the priest she confessed to every Thursday ever since she killed Attila."

"Priest."

Kate nodded.

"But there isn't a priest at Saint Simon's anymore."

Kate rewarded him with a tight smile. "Now you see why I'm beginning to think there's something else going on here?"

If she'd thought B.J. would be excited by her news, she was sorely disappointed. For a moment he thought about it, his forehead puckered, his hand tapping a tattoo on the bed rail. Kate waited, knowing his synapses were still a little fried. She knew he'd catch up with her. She knew he'd give her the great aha! so they could get to the point where Kate really could get closure.

Instead he shook his head. "Shit, pogue. I have to get you someplace safe."

Kate all but pulled B.J. right out of the bed when she jumped to her feet. "Don't you dare start this again," she demanded.

"What are you talking about?"

"Get me someplace safe." She glared at him, appalled. "Don't be an idiot. Get yourself someplace safe. I've never been the target."

"Who says that hasn't changed?"

"B.J.," she pleaded. "This isn't a game. I have to know."

"Pogue—"

"Don't pogue me," she retorted. "Help me. Nobody else will listen, and if they don't, whoever this guy is will get away with it."

"No, he won't," B.J. assured her. "I still have to sign off on Gunn. I won't until I'm satisfied, all right?"

Kate almost broke down on the spot. "All right. Now, what do we do next?"

"We find out who had the most to gain from Sister Ann's little crime spree."

Kate tried again to get hold of John. She tried Mary. She even tried Little Dick, but he wasn't interested in the phantom priest theory, since it would just generate more work on his part.

She had her best luck getting in to see Sister Ann Francis, who by now was hand-holding without bond in the county jail. It took most of the afternoon and evening, but she secured permission from Polyester's lawyer, another silky-smooth carnivore with an agenda. After spending another night with nothing but a half-finished wine bottle and a cat, she got in to visit first thing in the morning.

Trying to get used to the sight of Polyester in drab prison dress instead of habit was tough. It was like suddenly seeing your favorite old auntie in jeans. Nevertheless, Kate knew she couldn't waste any time. She asked the little woman specifically about the priest, whom Polyester had never seen except behind the screen. She asked about the murders, to be told once again that Sister had no desire to hurt that nice Tim or that nice Dr. O'Brien, and oh, my heavens, it really was strychnine Mr. Gunn died of?

"What about those notes?" Kate asked the little nun through the Plexiglas barrier. "Did you really send those to me?"

Polyester frowned a little, as if Kate hadn't been paying attention. "Why yes, dear. Of course I did."

"Which typewriters did you use?"

"Typewriters? I didn't use typewriters. I used magazines. The old ones in the admitting waiting room. Only ones over a year old, you know. They should have been thrown out anyway."

Kate shook her head, impatient now. "No, Sister. I mean on the envelopes."

"Envelopes? I didn't use envelopes, dear. Why would I? After that first note on your bed when you were still a patient, I simply taped them to the inside of your locker. After all, you were at the hospital so much, and I couldn't remember exactly which apartment you were in."

Kate did her best not to jump at the barrier that separated them. "Then you were never in Tim's and my apartment."

"Well, I was never invited."

"You never sent me a note that said Molly was my fault."

Polyester smiled again, and Kate was reminded of all those grade-school teachers who had reacted to her inappropriate behavior. "Now, why would I do that after I went to all the trouble to tell you I understood?"

Kate just nodded, not yet equipped for more. "Why the cut-out letters and all?" she asked. "I mean, if you wanted me to know anyway. What difference would it have made?"

"Well, I knew you wouldn't tell the police unless it was necessary. Besides, isn't that the way it's done?"

Of course. Kate wished her own logic system were so simple.

"And you discussed everything with the priest."

"Why yes, dear. A confession is only good if it is a full and sincere confession. I told Father all my plans. All my reasons. Everything. Otherwise I wouldn't ever be forgiven. I already told the police that, though. In fact, I told them about the digitalis I'd been collecting to give that terrible Doctor Babbit. You know, the one who swears at her patients while they're under anesthetic and throws instruments at the nurses? I'm afraid she's been mistreating some of her patients. I mean, since I'm doing it anyway. . . ."

By the time Kate walked back out into the lobby, she was jittery with exhaustion. She had more questions than answers, but at least they were pointing in a certain direction. She'd also found herself promising to visit Sister again in the future. Now that she knew what she should have realized all along, that she'd been right about Polyester not being able to kill Tim, she felt sorry for the little woman. After all, wasn't she back in the same old rut? Her idealism taken advantage of by someone for his own gain?

Maybe Polyester should have been the patron saint of the hospital after all.

Kate made it back to work in time to drop off her information with B.J., who was still waiting for somebody from Homicide to call him, and to get onto the hall to clock in before eleven so she wouldn't be docked another day's pay.

She'd stopped by the apartment to change, only to find herself straightening up the rooms yet again, and she sat down to have something to eat, only to find herself making a list of people who could have had access and motive for killing the two people Polyester didn't.

It came down to either Gunn or Tim, the two people Polyester swore she had nothing to do with. Tim or Gunn who might have incited murder above and beyond the delusional needs of a burned-out idealist. So Kate made up a list of anyone who might want either of them dead. Tim's was too short and Gunn's was too long. She dropped both off with B.J. and headed down for work without saying a word to anybody about what she was up to.

Kate was putting her nursing bag down alongside the row of other bags in the lounge when Phyl popped her head in the door. "Can I see you in my office?" she asked.

Kate sighed, slipped her lab coat on over the fresh scrubs she'd changed into. Phyl backed out even before Kate's answer, as if she needed to settle herself behind her own walls before facing Kate.

Kate felt as if she were walking blindfolded over old bogs. The world was treacherous out there, only she couldn't see where. So she took a moment to compose herself by reading the notices on the bulletin board before going. There had been a time when it had been full of parties and ball games and baby announcements. Now, besides the usual health department updates on things like hepatitis and AIDS and the anticipated rise in suicide rates with the good weather, there was a notice that mandatory meetings were being held to teach the staff how to present a more pleasant attitude toward their clients. Below this was an in-house memo that as of this date, overtime would not be paid unless previously approved by the administrator on call. And, as of almost the same date, laughter would no longer be tolerated on the halls, since this presented a negative image to clients and their families who sought serious medical care at this facility.

Kate's stomach did all her protesting. Maybe if she could eat something she'd feel better. But she was tried. She was frustrated at having to watch everyone for undetected motives. She was afraid, because it wasn't all over, after all.

"It's over," Phyl said, five minutes later.

A very popular theme in the last few days. Kate decided it bore questioning anyway. "What's over?"

Phyl waved her hand over the stack of paper-work in front of her, as if trying to make it disappear. She smiled. "Your problems with the hospital bill. The workmen's compensation board has reconsidered and decided that you should be given full compensation because of the fact that you were transferring a patient to another facility."

Another smile, bigger, begging reaction. Kate felt even more nauseated than before.

"No fifteen-thousand-dollar bill?" she asked.

Phyl shook her head. "Completely covered."

Kate could see that Phyl was truly relieved and expected Kate to be, too. For some reason, Kate felt more hemmed in than ever. She heard that damned dissonant chord, because this was simply not the way the hospital worked.

"And the lawsuit?" she asked.

"The hospital hasn't said anything official, but between you and me, I believe they're going to settle. I think you might share the information with your insurance company and your lawyer."

Kate couldn't do much more than nod.

It was over. She was being rewarded or bought off or both. She hated herself, because she was going to accept. But not without questions.

"Who made the final decision?" she asked.

"I don't know," Phyl said. "I just got word from Jane Mangelsdorf this morning." Jane Mangelsdorf, the vice president over nursing. A link in the never-ending chain upward. "She said the decision had been reached sometime yesterday."

Another nod. "Uh huh."

Kate simply couldn't offer any more than that.

Jane Mangelsdorf. Bland, almost faceless, now that she'd changed her nursing shoes for Papagallos. Someone aspiring to step up to the next rung on the ladder, not, Kate thought, to control the whole thing. She did her best to fit Jane's face on the suspect she'd been trying to form. She couldn't seem to do it.

"And one other thing," Phyl said. "You're being recommended for a special commendation. For helping the way you did."

Kate had to get out of that office before she lost whatever acid she'd built up in her stomach all over Phyl's much-too-neat desk. "Recommend away," she said, getting to her feet, "but I'm turning it down."

She didn't go back to the lounge, at least not right away. The air was a little cleaner outside, where all she had to inhale was exhaust fumes, so she leaned against the beautiful white brick and she shook.

She'd just been set free of this place. Beholden to no one now that her medical bills were paid up, now that she had a hold over Administration. Over Phyl. Over everyone. That shouldn't have made her so sick.

It did, because it had the terrible feel of manipulation to it.

She'd been right. There was something dark and ugly and evil here, and she'd recognized it in a gesture that should have been generous.

She heard the commotion the minute she walked back through the automatic doors. Three doors away from Phyl's office, there was a crowd spilling out of the nurses' lounge, all eyes intent on what was going on inside. Kate headed for the action.

It was the TV news. The same KSTL reporter was doing a stand-up in front of the postmodern gray of Central Medical East.

"Are they kidding?" one of the techs was demanding, incensed.

"Guess not," Dr. Mendoza retorted. "Well, at least we know our frozen wages went to a worthy cause."

He had several pens thrown at him and one half-eaten orange.

". . . In making the announcement of the merger between Central and Saint Simon's today, the new CEO of Central Medical Centers Incorporated named Robert Fellows as new president of Saint Simon's. Mr. Fellows has been acting administrator since the death of Leo Gunn. Mr. Fellows promises . . ."

And there they were, the Brooks Brothers. Fellows and the lawyer; what was his name? Both of them shaking hands and smiling as if they'd just hit the gold spike on the first intercontinental railroad. And there, standing just beyond the periphery of the camera lights, someone else. Someone Kate recognized.

"So, we aren't Saint Simon's anymore?" somebody asked.

"I think we're Mr. Simon's."

"Central Simon's."

"Simon Says."

"This Simon says we've been screwed again."

"Well, at least now we've been screwed by the biggest hospital conglomerate in the bistate area."

"Who's that guy?" Kate asked, pointing to the vague, smiling face at the edge of the action.

Everybody looked.

"Who?" Mendoza asked. "The thin guy with the dark hair?"

The thin guy who had been sitting in the waiting room all those nights. Whom Kate had seen at the periphery of her vision and assumed was watching her for the police. Protecting her from the people who had been terrorizing the hospital.

"Yeah," she said. "Him."

Ramirez nodded. "I'm not sure. Doesn't he have something to do with the new security team?"

"Yeah," somebody else said. "Name's Thompson, I think. I saw him around here the other day. Somebody said he'd been looking around. Sizing things up, I guess."

Kate stood there awhile longer watching the crowd, watching the report, watching the sharks' smiles, and thinking of how, as badly as she was seeing right now, that blur of a Young Turk with his dark hair could almost pass for a tall young woman with short hair in a baseball cap, given the right lighting.

She thought she was crazy.

But Mr. Gunn wasn't supposed to have been on Sister Ann's list. At least not yet. And certainly not with strychnine.

She had to talk to B.J.

She had to protect B.J., because if she was

right, he was in the most dangerous hospital in the city, and not just because it had bad hiring practices.

She was getting onto the elevator for the fourth floor to do just that when she heard her named called. In the mood she was in, she almost ignored it.

"Kate, hey, wait up! I need to talk to you!"

Kate turned to find Mary Cherry behind her, bouquet in one hand, Vuitton briefcase in the other. She was in full-dress suit, hair wrapped and sprayed, any remnants of the Wild West missing. In the time it took for her to realize who was after her, Kate went from one of the unhappiest women to one of the most relieved.

She held the door just long enough for the agent to join her in the otherwise empty elevator. "I thought you were spending quality time with the little dogies."

Mary followed along, beaming like a kid with a good report card. "Not me. I was working. Did I hear you went to visit Sister Ann this morning? I thought I told you I'd take care of it from here."

"I thought you guys were happy with the single bullet theory. It just so happens Sister Ann wasn't the only one involved in sending me those notes after all. Wanna hear about it?"

"I already know about it. The report came back this morning. I thought we'd discuss it with you and B.J."

The elevator reached the second floor, where it opened for the four people waiting there. Kate smiled, hit the CLOSE button, and kept them off.

"Medical emergency," she said with a tight smile as the doors closed on their thunderous faces.

"Bitch," was the answer.

For the first time in a long while, she didn't mind. "So you agree that Polyester couldn't have killed Tim?"

"I agreed all along. John and I thought we'd let you sit this one out, though. Since it seems you can't, why don't you guys help me figure out who did?"

Kate's smile was truly satisfied. "I already know."

"What do you mean, now we can leave it to the professionals?" Kate demanded, outraged. Her heart was pounding again, filling her chest with the enormity of her anger. Her head hurt and her stomach was threatening.

B.J. didn't look much happier. "I mean you've done enough. You've put yourself in too much danger as it is."

"Oh, yeah," she retorted, only having to eye the IV he still sported to make her point. "You're right. Tim's dead, you're still barfing up every third meal, and I've just had all my bills paid and my job secured into the twenty-second century. I'm in horrible danger."

B.J. went red in the face. "You know what I mean."

"No," she insisted, on her feet, finger out at both B.J. and Mary, where they sat trying to take her out of the action again. "I don't. What I know is, I'm the one who figured out that Polyester was being used. I'm the one who figured out that it had to be somebody powerful enough to pay me off, to have access to the keys to the lockers and the staff apartment building, and to get hold of any number of drugs and equipment without anybody's asking. I'm the one who figured out just how this guy operated. Damn it, Beej, I've had to pay all the penalties. At least give me the answers, too."

"Not at that price."

"I'm waiting to hear from John now," Mary offered as quietly as she could, in her corner. "I think the police should probably handle it from here."

"And do what? What evidence do they have that could get them a search warrant, much less an indictment? You think the prosecuting attorney's going to go after somebody this big with only my say-so?"

"I think it's a possibility. Nobody wants Sister Ann to pay for crimes she didn't commit."

"Nobody cares. She's already admitted to three murders. What's a couple more? After all, like John said, she's not really going to pay. They're going to put her away where she can do penance in peace, and this son of a bitch is going to get away scot-free with murdering Tim."

Even pale and wasted and exhausted, B.J. could still be the most intimidating person Kate had ever known. At any other time, the fury in his eyes would have sent her running. But this time, she had nowhere to run. She had to know. She had to find justice for every person in that hospital who had found their idealism pimped on the open market for money. She wanted to accomplish what Polyester had set out to do. She wanted to bring down at least one manipulator.

"I got a rise out of him the last time," she insisted. "I can do it again. I can get him to tell me everything, I know it. Please."

They shook their heads in unison. "No."

They left her with no choices at all.

For the position, the office was subdued. Unlike Gunn's with its chrome and slate and lithographs, this one bore no personal stamp at all. A couple of framed pictures of kids and dogs and a pretty, vacuous-looking blond woman in natural fibers. A lot of files and a bookcase filled with important tomes. Walls empty of everything except an aerial shot of St. Simon's and another of St. Louis from the arch. Kate sat in one of the simple brown-leather chairs and waited, her hands clammy, her heart pounding, her stomach ready to empty itself for the third time in fifteen minutes.

She felt like hell. She wanted to go home. Now that she'd actually done it, she decided she'd been an idiot after all. Outside the window the sun was teetering at the edge of the highway, and the rest of the administrative offices were closed and empty. She'd made the appointment knowing that perfectly well.

Tough to get a confession with a secretary popping in every five minutes or so.

She might not have done it if Mary hadn't managed to unearth that one piece of crucial information that afternoon. If Kate hadn't finally known just what the stakes were. But she did, and she knew she could finally put a face to her monster.

So she sat very still and willed her body to behave. She listened to the distant hum of the hospital and waited for her monster to appear. She heard the soft tread of expensive shoes on the carpet outside and knew that, whatever happened, this time it would be over.

"I'm sorry I'm late," he apologized in a quiet, smooth voice as he walked into the room.

Kate never turned to acknowledge him. "That's all right."

Her chest tightened and stumbled. Her heart wasn't just racing anymore, it was tripping over itself.

"Actually," he said, closing the door, "I'm glad you called me for this appointment."

Kate finally turned to acknowledge him. Just in time to see him engage the lock.

Then he turned back to her and smiled, and she knew her challenge had worked.

"I thought you would be. Congratulations on your new appointment, Mr. Wurly."

✦ Chapter 22 ✦

WURLY. HIS NAME was Wurly. Kate would remember that now. She'd remember that he did look different from Fellows. His hair was neater. His eyes were brown, and his ears were tipped out at the top like an elf's. His smile was absolutely cold and self-satisfied.

He eased himself down behind his desk and shot his cuff so he could check his watch. Nodded. "Sorry I couldn't make it before now," he said. "I've had so much to do. It's quite a change in workload to be CEO of a network of hospitals."

Kate curled her fingers around the arms of her chair to keep from wiping sweaty palms against her pants. She shouldn't have fortified herself with so much wine before showing up here. It was making her sick all over again. "That's okay. Your secretary let me in before she left. Your new title is quite a coup," she acknowledged.

He smiled. "Thank you. I thought so. I'm really looking forward to making the Central Medical Centers into state-of-the-art institutions."

"It really means that much to you?"

"I think you know that answer, Ms. Manion."

"But why? This is medicine, not banking. Not . . . government or multinational investment."

"It's the only real growth industry in this town. Think about what the future is, with the population steadily aging and more and more resources being diverted to health care. With the chairmanship of CMC, I can gain my place on boards of all the really important organizations in town: the MAC, the Veiled Prophet Committee, the Regional Commerce and Growth Association."

The real old-boy network. The real power in the St. Louis area. The biggest fish in not much more than a medium-sized pond.

Kate found herself nodding. If it had been anything else, she would have understood. If this had been a book she'd been reading, Wurly's motives would be perfectly acceptable. But his greed was compounded here. He fed on the helplessness of others. Layers and layers of helplessness, and people she knew, so that in the end his big plans ended up seeming a bit of a disappointment. All that effort for something really just mid-level. The story of her life, she supposed. Her monsters were never as big as she'd thought.

"I imagine it's an even greater thrill when you know that, if he hadn't died, Mr. Gunn would have gotten the chairmanship and you would have been back to real estate deals."

For a second, Wurly simply watched her, the smile absent. "Your sources are quite good. Not many people know that."

"They will if you and I don't come to some understanding."

Another small silence. A waiting, as if the questions waiting to be asked presented themselves in some certain order.

"And Doctor O'Brien?"

She shook her head, praying she could hold it together. "He doesn't know anything. He still thinks Mary Polyester did it."

Another pause. A nod. "How did you realize?"

Well, Kate thought. At least there wasn't going to be any feigning. Cards right out on the table.

"Molly," she said simply. "I've never told anyone in the world except for Polyester. Who only told her priest."

Wurly smiled again. "The mark of a good administrator is his ability to take advantage of opportunity. I couldn't believe it when I walked past the chapel that morning and heard that crazy old woman babbling to herself about killing that nurse. Talk about a sign from God."

Kate felt colder, emptier. Passion she understood, rage and frustration and desperation. This man was coloring his crimes with indifference. A simple means to an end.

"Why are you talking to me?" she asked. "Are you that willing to pay my price?"

Her question brought him back from his glow of self-congratulation. "I won't have to. You'll be dead."

Kate laughed. "How? You gonna coax me up on a chair and talk me into hanging myself?"

"No. I'm going to wait about another twenty

minutes. I've been watching you today, you know. You haven't been feeling well."

Suddenly Kate understood B.J.'s chagrin when he'd fallen into her arms at her doorstep. "What?"

"You finished half a bottle of wine last night. You're so predictable, really. Thompson told me it was that simple. I'm going to have to give him a raise."

"Thompson told you?"

An eyebrow lifted. "You don't think I'd do any of this myself? I'm a lawyer, Kate, not a murderer. Thompson, on the other hand, is very handy with things like poison and needles."

"But I thought—"

"That I did everything? Hardly. I'm renowned for my delegating skills. Sister Ann took care of all the hard work, and the rest simply fell to Thompson. He was a security guard over at Central, which is handy. He does know how to look like he belongs places, you know?"

"And I bet he handles weapons pretty well, too."

"Oh, you mean the gunshot? No, actually I have no idea who did that."

Kate struggled to control herself long enough to find out the rest, the most important. "Wait, wait, wait." She shook her head, trying to clear it. "What did he give me?"

"Oh, that. Quinidine and digoxin. A personal favorite of Sister Ann's, I might add. I figure with the amount we put in those bottles—not to mention the fact that if you acted true to form you went home before facing me and downed at least another glass of wine—your heart should just give out."

Kate's heart threatened to do that on the spot. Well, fuck me too, she thought with desperate silliness. All that work to change the locks, and they'd forgotten that the bosses always had the master key. "You're nuts," she said instead, terrified she wasn't going to have the time for her answers. "How do you know I haven't gone to the police yet?"

But Wurly didn't appear particularly nuts. He seemed quiet and calm and methodical. Just the kind of person who might have gotten past the precautions the police had taken for her. The kind of man who would have organized something right to the last brown bead. She couldn't believe it. She almost puked on the spot.

"Because I've been talking to Dick Trainor, and he can't keep his mouth shut about anything if he thinks he'll get something out of it. It's nothing personal, Kate. Really. But you've outlived your usefulness. I figure that when they find the wine and the needle puncture in the corks and caps of your liquor bottles where the medication was injected, the police will realize that Sister Ann Francis left behind a little time bomb for you. You just happened to be sitting in my office when the medicine reached maximum performance, or whatever, and sent you into cardiac standstill."

"My usefulness?" Kate asked, the adrenaline that washed her pushing up the half-life clock a little. "Wait. You never wanted me involved in the first place."

"On the contrary. I spent an inordinate amount of time assuring just that. The police weren't having any luck at the hospital. I needed somebody inside who wanted to help. Somebody who would have the brains and the tenacity to fly in the face of popular feeling and finger that little nun. And you do have a certain reputation."

It was getting harder to think, harder to remember that she needed him to keep talking. "Wait. But why?"

"Several reasons. First, to catch Sister, of course. After all, if we let this go on too long, business would really suffer. Second, to create a certain amount of disharmony that would accelerate staff attrition. And finally, to get you out of our hair, especially with this Rashad thing ready to catch fire."

"But you had to know I wouldn't stop with Polyester."

He nodded. "I knew. Which was why it was all so carefully planned. My timing had to be damn near perfect. You know I took a psych minor in pre-law? Amazing stuff. As for you, I needed a way to get your full and undivided attention. When Sister Ann Francis told her 'priest' what she learned about your sisters, I knew I had it. I couldn't just threaten you, for you to get motivated; I had to threaten your friends. And it worked."

Kate's vision swam. Her chest hurt like hell. But she wasn't sure whether that was medication or rage. Grief. "You mean Tim . . ."

Wurly lifted his hands. "I told you. It was

nothing personal. But you were taking too long, and I had to make an impression fast enough to get Gunn out of the way and the nun blamed for it. As it was, I almost lost Central twice. They were just a little fussy about all the administrators dying. Of course, between your fingering that nun and my getting Fellows to promise big changes, we got a better deal than we'd hoped. They really did need us more than we needed them, after all, no matter who was dropping dead."

Kate didn't even hear him anymore. Tim. Her sweet, caring, considerate Tim nothing more than a red flag. She wanted to kill Wurly on the spot. "You son of a bitch. You goddamn, stinking . . ." Tears pushed up and dimmed her vision entirely. "He was the best goddamn surgeon to hit this hospital in twenty years, and you hanged him?"

A shrug. "He was gay. How long did he have before he contracted something anyway?"

Kate found herself on her feet. She saw it now, the monster, the twisted, dark thing lurking in the depths of this whole nightmare. It lived in a perfectly normal middle-class male—a mid-level bureaucrat with deadly ambition. It had killed Tim for no reason, and that was the worst crime of all.

"Besides," he said. "He didn't suffer. We couldn't chance any noise, so he was out from the barbiturates when Thompson lifted him up. The blow on the head was just for insurance."

Kate's ears were ringing. Her heart was slamming uncertainly against her ribs. Her knees were melting. But she couldn't take her eyes off the man seated so calmly behind his desk. "I'll see you dead!" she hissed. Knowing it was over. Knowing it was time.

He checked his watch again. "Not before I see you dead. I figure I'll wait just about ten minutes after you arrest. That way the code team won't be able to get you back, and I can be sufficiently distraught over the whole thing."

He didn't seem to understand why Kate smiled, tears streaming down her face, her respirations ragged, her limbs shaking. "You mean you're not going to do CPR on me?" she asked, knowing it wasn't supposed to happen this way. Not caring anymore.

Wurly blinked. "What?"

"CPR," she insisted. "You're not going to do CPR?"

He tried to smile, but something was missing. "Why would I?"

When Kate laughed, he got to his feet. When she began to pull her scrub top from her pants, he stopped dead in his tracks. "Why, so you can see this," she said, and showed him the wire John and Mary had taped to her chest. "Ollie-ollie-oxen-free!"

The quiet, colorless little monster suddenly roared with fury. Kate saw him leap the desk even as she sank to her knees. She heard the thunder of footsteps down the carpeted hallway and knew it had worked. It had all worked, and if she could manage to get over the embarrassment of being poisoned after B.J. had warned her and the police had protected her, everything would be all right. She kept thinking that as the door splintered in on its hinges and people poured in to find her lying on her side on the rug.

"Up the rebels!" Kate intoned.

"Up the rebels!" the room thundered in answer.

Kate was back in a wheelchair, the IV still in, her energy level hovering somewhere around her knees, her full Pig Nurse on Parade color guard uniform on. Alongside her sat Jules and Sticks and Lisa Beller and Parker and about a hundred others, ready to celebrate Tim's Irish wake. Back at McGurk's to lift their glasses to him and to Polyester and to Kate and B.J., who had brought down William Wurly. The noise was incredible, the beer flowing like water. Completely ignoring her nurse's threats as Kate had been swept out the door of her room, Kate partook of her own.

Up on stage, the band of the week was poised to play: Paddy O'Brien, bespectacled genius of the concertina; Martin Hayes, baby-faced fiddler and poet; Pat Broaders, bearded, earringed, and wry on his bazooki and pipes. And along with them, the freshly sprung wizard of the uileann pipes himself, Dr. Brian Joseph O'Brien. Gathered here to pay the kind of final tribute that would have had Tim wincing.

B.J. lifted an eyebrow. Kate nodded. It was time.

Bending to his fiddle, Martin kicked off the festivities. For Tim, Kate had chosen a simple rendition of Erik Satie's *Variations on a Theme*. The

house fell quiet to the sweet poetry of the violin.
Glasses were raised. People smiled. Kate thought
of Tim, who had once spent an entire night studying a difficult case to the sounds of the piece. She
smiled, too, and lifted her own beer with an
unsteady hand.

B.J. followed Satie with the slow, moving Irish
lament "Carrickfergus" on his pipes. Kate let the
tears come. The rest of the people followed suit.

And then, just like an Irish version of a New
Orleans funeral, the rest of the band, poised like a
tableau for that last hovering note, swept into a jig
called "Jerry's Beaver Hat" and the place exploded.

"He would have hated it," Jules assured Kate
with tears streaming down her face.

Kate laughed with delight. "I know. But you
can't have a good Irish wake to Handel."

"O'Brien looks pretty good, considering."

Kate nodded, sipped at the bitter stout in her
glass. "Yup. He does."

"He ever forgive you for that stunt you
pulled?"

"You mean holding them off till the last
minute?" she asked. "He'll never forgive me for
that. Ask me if I care. I couldn't let them all come
barging in until I had all the answers."

"But you don't. You still don't know who shot
at you."

"Superfluous. I might have shot at me too, if I
hadn't known any better."

She'd ended up with a lot of enemies from all
this. A lot of friends. A new share of secrets the
powers that be would never know. Harve Pfieffer

wouldn't find out that Jules had begun to look elsewhere for her affection, and no one would discover that in a moment of desperation six years earlier Lisa Beller had helped her sister die. Like Kate had said. All superfluous.

"You sure I can't change your mind?"

Kate looked over to where Jules sat, her own Pig Nurse cap missing, since it had been officially awarded to Edna until a new one could be made. Even Mary had one on, which just made the snout and black stripe look like a fashion statement. "About B.J.?"

But Jules wasn't laughing. "About quitting."

Kate shook her head, drank some more. "It's an LOA, remember? Approved by the estimable Mr. Fellows himself."

The same Mr. Fellows who had surprised the community at large by turning down the offer of corporate CEO in favor of staying at the hospital he swore he still loved. Fellows who had personally paid for the defense counsel for Sister Ann Francis, who would be spending a lot of time at her dear little institution in Texas.

Jules was not appeased. "But you're not coming back."

Kate finally had no choice but to face her friend. "I don't know," she admitted. "B.J. wants to show me Philadelphia, and Mary wants to show us Albuquerque. Personally, I just want to meet Junior. He's going to teach me how to rope calves." Taking a long, cold pull of her drink, she gave in to the rest. "I also have an appointment to keep in Minnesota."

Time, finally, to put all her ghosts to rest. She'd already called Mamie and told her to take that other five thousand dollars and stuff it up her ass. Then she'd spent an hour with Steve, who'd accepted Carver and the keys to the rest of Tim's possessions, and who had delivered her in return the news that after hearing the truth about what had happened the night of the accident, the Rashad family had dropped their suit against Kate. The hospital and all others involved would settle, and the matter would be over.

She was free and clear, for the first time in her life. She had opportunities and a slightly used forensic pathologist who seemed to want to see the world with her, and a sudden taste for it.

She would be leaving her dearest friends. She would be running just as she had the chance finally to convince Martin Weiss to get in and get treatment, just when the position of head nurse was coming up, since Phyl was being bumped up into the slot Edna had vacated by being too senior.

But Kate had had her own epiphany during her latest stint in the hospital. Maybe she wouldn't ever have a near-death experience to sort things out, but she'd twice come too close to ignore what it meant. It left her with the understanding that the rest of the world could get along fine without her interference. Martin was a big boy. The hospital would go on. Her friends would find some other loudmouth to fill the vacuum she left. She had to find out if she was really as brave as B.J. insisted.

"Hey, pogue!" he yelled as the jigs gave way

to reels. "What about taking six months in Ireland while I really learn to play this thing?"

"Up the rebels!" Kate intoned.

"Up the rebels!" the rest of the room answered.

"Hey, Kate!" Sticks yelled, bare inches from her left ear. "You never told us. What does pogue mean?"

Kate grinned. "Not what we thought it did when we first started using it."

"Well, what does it mean?"

"It means 'kiss,'" she said.

"Aw," Jules cooed. "Isn't that sweet?"

"What did you think it meant?" somebody asked.

Kate and B.J. exchanged glances. Kate laughed. "Asshole," she said.

The floor was never completely dark. Even at three in the morning, there were lights on out in the hallway that bled into the room; there was the spectral green and red glow from the bank of monitors that kept track of the patient in bed.

Kate never really slept in the hospital, and this time wasn't any different. Even though she was pleasantly buzzed from the evening she'd stolen down at McGurk's, she couldn't quite relax. She listened to the way the monitor still stuttered as it recorded the rhythm of her heart and wondered at everything that had happened.

Outside the hall was empty. It was somebody's birthday and everybody was in the lounge dishing up cake, the monitor alarms turned up so they could be heard. Kate didn't mind so much. She was kind of enjoying the unusual quiet in the place for once.

Then she heard the soft pad of footsteps. The hiss of a door being opened by a stealthy hand. She opened her eyes and saw a shadow detach itself from the surrounding darkness and realized that it was making its way for her.

Her heart reacted first, slamming uncertainly against her chest wall. Her lungs seemed to collapse with instinctive terror. She was alone, tied down to monitors and IVs. She was half drunk, which effectively took care of any balance she might have had left after the overdose of cardiac medication got through with her.

She was completely vulnerable.

She'd felt it before, that trepidation about people who had control over her when she couldn't control herself. But before she'd only been frustrated and angry. She hadn't been afraid.

Tonight she was afraid. Because the truth was, it wasn't just that any person could touch you or expose you. They could harm you.

It must feel like this to every patient in this hospital, she thought. Each anxious, uncomfortable soul who saw strangers walk with impunity through their doorway. Each disabled, controlled, constricted person who depended so completely on the hope that others who approached did so only with goodwill.

Hospitals, Kate realized with dreadful understanding, were terrifying, dangerous places to be.

She turned a little in the bed so she could better see who was coming her way. She heard the rasp of anxious breathing and smelled Aramis cologne. She saw a wide, boxy hand reach out toward the side of her blankets, where both she and he knew he'd find exposed skin, and she recognized him.

Arnstein.

Arnstein the asshole. Arnstein the pig, who had ridden to the OR suite atop her chest with his hand in her aorta. Arnstein, who would have thought nothing of taking advantage of her. Who had, Kate was suddenly sure, taken advantage of other people made totally dependent by disease and therapy. Other women, who might not have been able to fight.

Arnstein, who was about to do the same thing to her.

Well, she thought with a certain amount of fatalism. There is one last thing I can do for this hospital before I go.

She waited for him to get close enough. Steeled herself against the first contact of those seeking fingers. Saw the flicker of color as he bent and his tie fell clear of his lab coat.

And then, without a sound, she simply reached for it.

And yanked. Hard.

She pulled his face right down to hers, close enough that she could see the whites of his eyes reflect the green from her own monitors. She heard the high-pitched little squeal of surprise he gave off as he froze. And then she smiled.

"I killed once," she warned. "I can do it again."

He didn't drop dead. He just ran like hell, which made Kate smile. A much better way to end things, she decided, and finally fell off to sleep.

EVERY CROOKED NANNY
by Kathy Hogan Trocheck

In this high-caliber debut, Trocheck introduces Julia Callahan Garrity, a former cop who now runs a cleaning service in Atlanta. Sue Grafton calls this novel "dust-busting entertainment," and *The Drood Review* picked it as a 1992 Editor's Choice selection.

LOOD SUGAR
Jim DeFilippi

he tradition of the movie BODY HEAT, this gripping suspense el has just the right touch of sex and a spectacularly twisty end- Long Island detective Joe LaLuna thinks he knows what to ect when he's sent to interview the widow of a murder victim. ther routine investigation. What he gets is the shock of his life. widow is none other than his childhood sweetheart, and now, must defend her innocence despite the contrary evidence.

HarperPaperbacks *By Mail*

A ROARING FIRE, A CUP OF TEA, AND A GOOD MYSTERY...

AH, SWEET MYSTERY
by Celestine Sibley

A lot of people hated Garney Wilcox. Just about the only person who had anything good to say about the ornery re estate developer was the woman whose land was making him rich—his mama. But when Garney is found dead, it is his mama, Miss Willie, who confesses to the murder. able to believe that her sweet neighbor could be capable such a crime, Kate Mulcay, local newspaper columnist c sleuth, sets out to clear Miss Willie's name without beco ing a murder victim herself.

PRIVATE LIES by Carol Cail

When small town reporter Maxey Burnell's boss is killed in a fiery explosion, she's determined to pull her best investigative skills and dig for some real answers. What she finds is a whole lot of trouble, and a very handsome detective with whom she'd like to spend the rest of her life—if she has one left to live.

SOMETHING'S COOKING
by Joanne Pence

For sassy food columnist Angelina Amalfi, life's a banquet—until the man who's been contributing unusual recipes for her column is found dead. Not one to whimp in fear, Angelina insists on helping the tall, dark and han some police inspector who's assigned to the case. What lows is a spicy smorgasbord filled with danger and romance that's sure to whet your appetite.